D1206557

Books by
Antonya Nelson

The Expendables

In the Land of Men

Family Terrorists

Talking in Bed

Talking
in Bed

· · · · · · · · · · · ·

Antonya Nelson

Scribner Paperback Fiction
PUBLISHED BY SIMON & SCHUSTER

SCRIBNER PAPERBACK FICTION
Simon & Schuster Inc.
Rockefeller Center
1230 Avenue of the Americas
New York, NY 10020

First Scribner Paperback Fiction edition 1998
Published by arrangement with Houghton Mifflin Company
SCRIBNER PAPERBACK FICTION *and design are trademarks
of Simon & Schuster Inc.*

Designed by Melodie Wertelet
Manufactured in the United States of America

1 3 5 7 9 10 8 6 4 2

Library of Congress Cataloging-in-Publication Data
Nelson, Antonya.
Talking in bed / Antonya Nelson. — 1st Scribner
Paperback Fiction ed.
p.   cm.
1. Man-woman relationships—Illinois—Chicago—Fiction.
2. Women—Illinois—Chicago—Psychology—Fiction.
3. Married people—Illinois—Chicago—Fiction. I. Title.
[PS3564.E428T35   1998]
813'.54—dc21   97-39945
CIP

ISBN 0-684-83800-1

For Robert
and Jade and Noah

Talking in bed ought to be easiest,
Lying together there goes back so far,
An emblem of two people being honest.

Yet more and more time passes silently.
Outside, the wind's incomplete unrest
Builds and disperses clouds about the sky,

And dark towns heap up on the horizon.
None of this cares for us. Nothing shows why
At this unique distance from isolation

It becomes still more difficult to find
Words at once true and kind,
Or not untrue and not unkind.

— "Talking in Bed," PHILIP LARKIN

I
. . . .

One

· · · · · · · · · · · · ·

THEY MET at a hospital nurses' station, a smooth, flesh-toned, bent elbow of a desk separating two hushed corridors, an axis around which wheeled all the facets of living.

Their fathers were dying. While at one end of the desk Paddy Limbach, wearing a cowboy hat, was commanding an Oriental woman in whites to come immediately, with morphine, to his father's room, which was down the south wing, Evan Cole stood at the other end of the desk, smugly taking it all in behind his thick eyeglasses. He was attempting to get drugs for his father, too. The difference was that Ev wanted his father to die as quickly as possible — he'd been languishing for years — whereas Paddy was desperate to keep his alive. The other difference was that Ev knew the Oriental woman was a doctor. He knew the man's badgering her was pure presumption and ignorance.

Ev thought, *Sexist, xenophobe, asshole, cowpoke, tough guy.* He made a sneering curled-lip expression. But Dr. Ono wouldn't hold it against the man; she was secure enough, majestic enough, to extend automatic forgiveness — akin to pity — to the dope, the hayseed whose father would not live through the night. Ev could only wonder, and only mockingly, at a man whose feelings about his father were so uncomplicated. Ev himself had indulged fantasies of murdering his father. *Patricide,* he'd whispered, tasting the specificity of the English language, marveling. His wife, Rachel, had grown alarmed at the exquisite detail Ev could provide — the pillow, the closed

3

door. "You've imagined it too thoroughly," she had said. "You're frightening me."

"Who would ever in a million years order an autopsy?" Ev had demanded as Rachel made a show of covering her ears. "No one, that's who. We should order an autopsy *now,* while he's living, and find out why he's *not* dead. That's the real mystery."

"It's an enigma," she had agreed, unbuttoning her blouse for bed, kicking off her shoes, and nudging down her jeans zipper — always three or four things at once, Rachel. "But do you think you'll be given conjugal rights in prison?" she had asked him, pulling off her panties and spinning them on her finger. "Please don't suffocate your father."

Ev left Paddy at the desk and returned to his father's bedside, where he sat and stared in a way he could only describe as dispassionately. When had he last looked with passion at this person? His father might live another month, but no more. That he had survived the last fifteen years was shocking: he'd suffered so many strokes that Ev imagined his brain and bloodstream as a veritable fireworks display.

His father's stubborn survival — "He's unkillable," Rachel had claimed, "the first immortal!" — had made Ev alternately sloppy and cautious about his own life. Some days he believed genetics would keep him invincible. He certainly *looked* like his father, in physique and complexion and features; wouldn't that suggest a similar physiological disposition? But other days he believed poetic justice would prevail. He'd spent his life opposing his father, becoming contrary at every turn as a matter of principle. Why wouldn't this contrariness in the end tell some nasty ironic joke?

He could convince himself that he'd be struck dead in a car accident driving home from the hospital, that his father would live to hear the news of his death by four-car pileup and respond with a satisfied grunt.

That grunt! Those rolling eyes!

Before him on the bed, his father's face was yellow. His whiskers were yellow, his fingers were yellow. The long nails, thick and opaque like bear claws, were also yellow, and appeared to be more substantial than the flesh from which they erupted. There was no way not to imagine them continuing in their ugly stubborn growth, the body feeding on and excreting from itself into eternity. Did everyone picture death the way Ev did — the decomposing corpse in its dark box, the slow encroachment of nature, the tactless tread of living feet far above?

"How is he?" a nurse asked Ev. She had entered tentatively, as if Ev and his father might be involved in a final moment of bedside tenderness, and Ev pretended to be startled so that she would apologize.

"I'm sorry," she said. "How is he?"

"He's unkillable," Ev said flatly. In life he sometimes found himself required to shock people. Women such as this, polite and timid, he frequently saw as his most significant targets. Their meekness was dishonest, as if a demurely averted gaze and a capacity to blush might hide the fact that, on a daily basis and with indisputable competence, they wiped the foul naked buttocks of dying strangers.

But she smiled pityingly at him, focused on his father, her patient. Perhaps she had not recognized the word *unkillable*. Perhaps she took that to be a grieved and mangled pronunciation of his father's illness; Ev had a tendency to snarl and mutter and be misunderstood. As she stood calmly beside the bed, squat and firm like a pincushion in her whites, measuring pulse, touching the bottom eyelids to reveal the surprising deep pink beneath, she ignored Ev. He was not her concern. He was a miscreant child proceeding through familiar stages of grief. And Ev felt too tired to prove himself otherwise, grateful for her composure. He could always respect a professional.

"I'm Amy," she told Ev as she ran her hands beneath his father's sinewy yellow neck, tilting the head back.

"Night shift," Ev said. "I don't suppose you call it graveyard duty in a hospital?"

"No, you don't," she agreed.

"Lousy hours."

"Oh, it's not bad, once you adjust for sleeping during daylight. In the night, it's peaceful. Hardly any visitors."

"Except annoyances like me," Ev said.

"No, I didn't mean that." She spoke without missing a beat in her evaluation of his father, pulling down the thin hospital blanket to lay a stethoscope on his skeletal chest. "He's a tough bird," she said.

"Unkillable," Ev repeated. "Immortal."

When Amy pulled back the covers to check lower reflexes, Ev's father suddenly got an erection, the lump unmistakable beneath the thin gown, rising in a slow, regal manner. Ev looked away, then back, too fascinated to ignore it.

"How's that for reflex?" he asked Amy.

She shared a smile with him; small lines spread from her eyes and mouth. She was older than he'd thought originally, and instantly more interesting to him. She'd seen plenty of boners, had probably been propositioned and insulted by a hundred horny old men, had cleaned up their semen and saliva and blood, had seen all life forces exert themselves, bloom, and fade. Ev fought the temptation to slap at his father's hideous hard-on, now the staff of a tent erected in the middle of his bed. It was ludicrous and pathetic, undeniable.

Fortunately, there was a yell from down the south hall; Ev and the nurse both started for the door and passed through it at the same moment, shoulder to shoulder.

They found Paddy Limbach throwing a fit at that amazing nurses' desk, Dr. Ono beside him, gazing in a pained way at the floor. Paddy's father had been whisked away to the ICU only a few minutes earlier, his rolling bed flying through the halls, then disappeared as if in the wake of a startling blast, as if an unexpected train had come suddenly roaring through. He hadn't made it. He'd died despite everything, there one minute, gone the next, forever. Paddy, a large blustery blond who obviously did not have to explain himself very often, was trying to articulate his considerable rage, his impotence. His hands opened and closed in front of him as if he were squeezing teats, and his expression flipped like a light switch from horror to fury, off and on, off and on.

"You said the surgery was a success, you said he had good prospects, you said his signs were strong, you said —" Here he broke off to sputter, a man unaccustomed to crying. He had no idea how to do it. Instead, he gave a magnificent blow with his booted foot to the base of the nurses' station, a rattling impact that yielded him the seeming satisfaction of his own injury. "Oh my hell!" he cried. "Oh my frigging hell!"

Ev almost smiled, then thought perhaps the women were waiting for him, as the only available man, to do something. He said, "Hey, now."

Dr. Ono, though a conscientious doctor, was not big on bedside manner. This had always been perfectly fine with Ev; he mistrusted the jolly golf-playing fat doctors who'd previously dealt with his father. Dr. Ono never smelled of bay rum or spearmint. She did not leave town for extended vacations on yachts. She did not tell distasteful jokes. And she did not know how to offer comfort to an unpredictable former athlete. The blond looked like the sort of male grown from farmland — *strapping*, Ev thought, like a big healthy bull pawing at the ground, preparing for the charge.

Like Zach, Ev thought. Instantly his younger son's face flashed to mind — the slow crooked smile, a goofy expression, as if a tooth were permanently missing, as if Zach knew your secret foolishness and could summon it forth. Zach was the good-natured husky one, a slightly dense boy who ordinarily suffered the nasty jibes of his intellectual older brother with an astonishing patience — resignation, Ev thought, admirable resignation — but who also occasionally exploded, his temper being of the volcanic variety. Brawny and Brainy, Rachel called them, her two boys.

But Paddy Limbach seemed to have exhausted his fury. Defeated, he simply wept, which was maybe worse. "Oh my hell, oh my hell," he moaned, wiping a bedraggled blue bandanna across his face. Ev turned back to his father's room. Women, after all — kind Amy and awkward Dr. Ono, the candy stripers who watched fascinated from the sidelines — could better handle this sort of grieving. Ev would gladly have offered up his own father's life for Paddy Limbach's father's; obviously the man required a paternal presence. He was not done with it, while Ev felt decidedly over done.

Under the cold fluorescent light of Ev's father's private room, the erection had wilted away and the yellow hands with their thick talons covered the smooth place where it had stood, an illusory gesture of modesty. Ev's sons often slept with their hands over their penises in this precise manner, protective. Rachel had pulled back the older's, Marcus's, sheets to show Ev the wet-dream stains, blossom-shaped gradations of yellow splashed together like an old-fashioned map of Europe. Rachel had wanted to know how normal this ejaculation business was; how much would be too much?

"How much did *you* play with yourself?" he'd asked her.

"Constantly," Rachel said. "I was a maniac."

Ev shrugged. "He inherited it from you."

"Girls don't leave stains," she said. "Nobody had to clean my sheets."

In his pleasure at considering his son's sexual life and his wife's serious but unnecessary concern, Ev took a moment to realize that the blanket before him, the cover over his father, had ceased its rising and falling. He stared transfixed at the chest, the area bracketed by his father's yellow arms, waiting for its faithful swelling, for whatever tenacious purchase the body had on this world to assert itself once more. His father had finally died; Ev felt relief well inside himself like warm water, a flooding sensation of happiness. The misery, his own and his family's, his father's too, had ended.

Seconds passed, and then others, and then, just as Ev was beginning to go dizzy under the spell of his own held breath, of the warmth inside, of the pure reprieve he'd been granted, his father's breathing resumed. Ev watched, incredulous, horrified, enraged, as the old man reignited, as the bellows of his lungs drew in again, ambushing Ev with their ability to perform against all odds. Ev watched his breathing father so long and so hard that his peripheral vision began to burn away, the center to turn plum-colored, blurred.

And then he simply watched himself reach down and hold the old man's nose with his fingers, rest the convenient palm over the open mouth. His other hand he braced against his father's chest, as if pushing him into a too-small space, something like a coffin. Over his shoulder, he watched the doorway, waiting for witnesses. He did not watch his father's face, the yellowed eyes, cow brown in the center, which would be open now, revealing understanding, however briefly, of who was responsible. Ev held firm against his father's struggle, which was not as fierce as his own. His desire for his father's death was larger than his father's for life, and in this discrepancy resided Ev's slim faith in his behavior. He was prepared to exert more force if necessary, but it was not necessary, and soon there was no struggle at all.

He released his father, shuddering as if chilled, as if the warmth had drained away, wiping his palms on his pants. Then he rubbed sweat from his forehead, pushing it up into his hair, his hand still heated from his father's face. His own face was more than damp; his glasses slid down his sweaty nose. His heart banged. And then he reached to smooth his father's hair over his head, alarmed at how similar their two heads felt, his father's hair just slightly sparser and coarser, his skin just slightly drier. This gesture was one he would recall over and over in future months, one that would imprint itself more fully than the preceding one of suffocation.

What a strange coincidence, he and Paddy Limbach would agree later, when they were friends, that their fathers had died at the same time.

"Papa," Evan said, the word like two popped bubbles, leftovers from childhood. Finally he had let his father go. He had made his father leave him.

• • •

Paddy Limbach sat on the edge of the bench alongside the bank of telephones in front of the nurses' station, where he'd kicked a foot-size ragged break in the tongue-and-groove paneling. Peach-colored lights shone on the desktop in perfect cones, giving the place the feel of October, harvest twilight, though it was eleven-thirty on a hot summer's night outdoors. Could that dusky, autumnal light be intentional? Part of the gently guided drift toward death?

Paddy leaned over his spread feet with his elbows on his knees, his face in his hands, his hat shielding him from observation. He had no idea how to proceed, no idea who to call first nor what to say. The females waited: his mother, his aunt, his wife, his little daughter, all of them at home praying for Peepaw. Who was he to tell them their prayers had failed?

His hair was gritty and his hands smelled of fish. Up under each fingernail was an arc of slate-colored fish matter, stinking, possessing an odor Paddy immediately associated not with fishing, which is where he'd acquired it, but with sex, which he hadn't had in weeks. He sniffed his fingers, his hat creating a kind of trapped airspace, and forced the smell to conjure a cold lake and pointed trees. Twenty-four hours ago, he and his father had been camping in Wisconsin. Paddy supposed he was in shock, unable to raise his nose from his own fingers, unable to remove himself from the nurses' station.

The man who looked like a Marx brother returned now, wiping his face as if smelling *his* fingers. "My father has died," he told the nurse typing at the computer terminal behind the desk. She made an O with her mouth. "Just to let you know," he went on, as if it were a joke. "Down there, room 14D. He went peacefully, for the record, and quite uncharacteristically."

Quite uncharacteristically, Paddy repeated to himself, wondering if the man was crazy.

Quite uncharacteristically, Ev repeated to himself, wondering if the cowboy thought he was an asshole. He supposed he should be troubled by his own calm, but it was not his habit to manufacture emotions to suit conventional wisdom. He was a criminal according to the letter of the law, but as far as the spirit of the law went, he wanted to believe himself some sort of an angel of mercy. Now he would have to wait and see if that was the proper name.

As the nurse radioed for assistance, Ev sat down beside Paddy, who'd rested his head against the wall behind him, his cowboy hat at his feet. Ev, suddenly generous, said, "Sorry about your father. Mine just died, too."

"They're 0 for 2 here," Paddy said, trying on a joke. It felt dangerous. The men shook hands, Paddy mishearing Ev's name and calling him Ed.

Paddy was waiting for a death certificate from Dr. Ono and some change for the five-dollar bill he'd given a candy striper. He had to phone his girls, the thought of which made him tremble; he didn't like to be the bearer of bad news. Two days ago, he and his father had gone camping. Then last night there'd been seizing chest pain and a frenzied drive to Beloit, Wisconsin, and then a screaming ambulance ride down to Chicago. Paddy had had to phone his mother three separate times in the last twenty-four hours, on each occasion listening to her fearful breathing. She'd never been comfortable with the telephone; Paddy supposed he'd inherited his own uneasiness from her. She picked the nearest hospital to her son's home in Oak Park and then put herself on a train from Normal. When his father had stabilized, Paddy's mother and aunt and wife and daughter had all gone home in the car, which also smelled of fish. They believed the worst had passed, and now Paddy would be responsible for more bad news. Was it any wonder he was putting it off?

As he told Ev these things, Ev realized how few calls he would have to make: the friends of his father who'd outlived him; Rachel, who would cry, despite her resentment and revulsion concerning her father-in-law; and his sons — Marcus, who'd learned to play chess and bridge from the old man, and Zach, who'd simply tolerated his grandfather's belittling remarks. "Hey pudgy," Ev's father had always said to poor Zach, "you get enough to eat?" Always in a tone that was intended to be understood as teasing, lighthearted, but that was transparently hostile. Even though Ev hated these jibes, he often felt tempted to make them himself, to indulge the same antagonism, the little niggardly desire to feel superior. That was the true aggravation between him and his father: they shared a superiority complex.

His brother Gerry he would have to wait to hear from; there would be nowhere to call to locate him.

No one would be sorry; no one would mourn his father's passing, Ev least of all. At night, his dreams had been teaching him how he would react when the old man finally died. His father would die in these dreams, and Ev's reaction in each and every instance was relief, pure relief. Although there'd been one dream, recollected now for the first time, which made Ev jerk and blink, wherein his father had pulled Ev along with him, through a door, over the edge of the universe, into the unknown, away. His father had never wanted to go

anywhere alone; death was no exception. And Ev, naturally, understood himself to be the only possible escort.

"I hate the phone," Paddy muttered beside Ev.

The simple act of lifting a phone receiver and punching familiar
numbers seemed impossible for both men at the time. They'd placed
themselves before that remarkable nurses' desk — so serene and un-
blemished, pink Formica flecked with gray like spilled pepper — and
were staring at ordinary objects without registering their identities or
uses. They watched the station as if watching television. The hospital
drama: Dr. Ono had gone home; Dr. Kneister, one of the golfing good
old boys, had come on duty wearing tartan pants and matching cap.

Paddy rotated his big blond hairy wrist to study the compasslike
clock strapped there, a waterproof, indestructible model designed
for people who climbed cliffs and overturned kayaks. "Thirty hours
ago, Dad and I were fishing on Sugar River," he announced. "Having
our dinner beside the fire, shooting the breeze."

"I'm sorry about your father," Ev told him, recovering composure. "You seem completely unprepared."

"Who could be prepared? This is the first I ever heard about a
heart problem."

"I know this is going to sound cold, but you're lucky not to
have to watch him deteriorate. My father has been dying for years
and years. *Had,*" Ev corrected himself. "Had been dying. Now he's
dead." These words meant almost nothing to Ev. He felt instantly
giddy with meaninglessness, acting his part in the hospital story, the
bereft mourner, the grieving actor. He was processing his role, trying
to behave the way he would behave if his father had died naturally.
So far, guilt had not made much of an appearance. Nor had fear. He
felt that dreamy relief.

Dr. Kneister bustled over to give his generic condolences: he was
damned sorry to hear about their losses, damned sorry.

"I'm relieved," Ev told the doctor. "I'm happy. I've been waiting
for years for him to die."

"Oh, hell yes, your dad was in some bad shape, I know how you
must feel."

Ev recalled Dr. Ono's quiet look at the hall floor and her own small shoes, the way she seemed incapable of manufacturing this ghastly patter. Dr. Kneister spoke too loudly, as if certain he could offend no one in the range of his considerable voice, and had a tendency both to stand too close and to spray. On his hip, he wore a holster and a telephone.

"I would have smothered him with a pillow years ago," Ev went on, gloriously indiscreet, "except my wife kept telling me someone would find out."

Dr. Kneister snapped his mouth shut. Paddy moved his hair out of his eyes to get a better look at Ev. His expression was hurt, as if Ev had disappointed him. It was an odd, shaming glance, and Ev's certainty about his own indifference faltered for a second. A little plume of regret came wafting toward him.

Dr. Kneister rested his hand on his phone, as if it might protect him, and decided to ignore Ev. He said to Paddy, "How old was your dad, son?"

"Fifty-four," Paddy answered promptly. Ev could not immediately remember his own father's age. Seventy-two? Seventy-three? Had he been born in 1918 or '19? "Just fifty-four," Paddy repeated. "I thought he was middle-aged, you know, only half done with the thing."

Dr. Kneister gave him a clap on the shoulder, one meaty-pawed mammal to another — "Brings you right up to mortality, doesn't it, son? I know, I know" — and left them at the nurses' station, where the women came and went softly, eyes fixed on the middle distance in disinterest, a state of mind they must have had to cultivate in order to work with continuous death. They murmured to one another in passing. Amy had been flipping papers over the wide metal rings on a clipboard during the exchange among the men, her red hair shining like gold under the peachy light. On the exposed nape of her neck were the inevitable freckles of a redhead. Her round buxom chest and the small mound of tummy beneath her uniform soothed Ev. She could manage men like Dr. Kneister and Ev, each difficult in his own way, and she could manage Paddy, the grieving jock, the cowlicked cornpone. It was she who delivered their death certificates to them, like report cards to grade-schoolers, she who took instructions on what to do with the bodies, she who dispensed the personal effects of their fathers, in two white plastic bags soft and bulky as trash.

She could have patted their bottoms and sent them on their way.

There was nothing to do now but leave.

"You need a lift?" Ev asked Paddy as they followed the exit signs through the winding halls of St. Michael's, their bags in their hands. Ev offered because he was not yet ready to be alone, not quite yet. His deed required some fraternity for just a little longer.

The hospital was old, perpetually under renovation, so that they passed through ancient clattering hallways with dangling metal-cased bulbs into hushed low-ceilinged ones lit by recessed fluorescents into ones curiously half and half, with rolls of industrial carpet parked alongside the doorways like sentries, stepladders laid near the walls between rooms, the heady odor of glue in the air. Ev had suggested that his father spend his final days at Northwestern Hospital, but his father had insisted on St. Mike's: the neighborhood institution, the place where Ev had been born, where his mother had died. It was small and hopeless, like the public schools Ev had attended, functional brick structures built optimistically in the 1920s, overloaded and underfunded ten short years later.

Paddy accepted Ev's insistent offer of a ride home. "I guess so," he said, as if he might agree to anything anybody offered him at this moment, as if he needed a new parent. Ev kept an eye on him as they charged through the corridors. Paddy was like Ev in his quick gait, and together they seemed to be trying to stay ahead of each other; they were practically running when they approached the big glass doors. They burst into the humid evening.

Ev instantly felt a sweat break on his forehead and chest, and the moist air seemed a forgiving cushion, the doors a gateway to the enormous forgiving world. His pace increased again; he felt curiously nimble. Metaphors filled his mind: he had set down a heavy load, left a great weight behind, the monkey had leapt off his back, from round his neck the millstone had been removed.

Literally he'd killed his father, but metaphorically his father had been trying to kill him. He let this supposition float around his mind, trying to decide if he could take solace in it.

The parking garage was catalogued by numbers, letters, and directionals. Ev had parked in 3F West, a confusing trek from the exit, down two flights and all the way through South. He spotted his Saab beside a dripping concrete post and suddenly grabbed Paddy's arm, pointing. "That woman's stealing my car!" he said.

Paddy lifted his eyes from the oil-spattered deck he'd been watching — his downward gaze had caused him to run directly into a fire lane sign — and said, "What?," focusing on Ev's words as if they were a single tree in a vast forest.

The woman had stopped poking at the keyhole of Ev's car and shuffled around to the car beside it, feeling her way like a blind person. By the time Paddy and Ev reached Ev's car she was yet another one over.

"Excuse me!" Ev demanded over the car tops. "Should I report you inside?"

The woman turned. Her face beneath her hat was wide and pale, her mouth caving in on itself, her expression caught. The lights in the parking garage were green, and thousands of bugs fuzzed around them like aureoles. The woman's skin looked unhealthy in this light, but no doubt Ev's did, too. Paddy, beside him, said "Wait" and reached for Ev to shush him, his large hand warm and solid on Ev's forearm.

"I've lost my car," the woman said.

"Uh-huh," said Ev. No longer interested in her, he was reaching for his door, shaking loose Paddy's grip, his own keys in his hand. She could be crazy — she was dressed in a hodgepodge of colors, a man's suit jacket and a canvas fishing hat — but was probably harmless, checking for change in unlocked cars. And who was he to judge someone's nefarious nighttime business? Ev slid into his seat and reached for the passenger door lock.

It was her hat that made Paddy look at her more closely, made him understand she was in shock — a cotton fishing hat just like his father's, just like the one jammed into his effects bag.

"Let me help you," Paddy said, moving toward her without taking his eyes off her, squeezing in between the bumpers and hoods, his own hat in his hand — the polite gesture of a boy before a woman —

then placed on a car hood as he reached her and produced his blue bandanna, still damp from his own tears. She began crying, holding the dangling ring of keys in front of her for explanation.

She said, sobbing, "I borrowed my *neigh*bor's car to come here with my daughter. I have no *idea* what kind it is. I can't remember a *thing* about it."

"Where's your daughter?" Paddy asked, taking the keys from her and fumbling with them.

"Oh," she said, her crying too violent to permit her to speak. "Inside," she finally said, covering her face with her hands.

Paddy turned to Ev, holding up a big key that opened an automobile, and told him they had to find a Toyota. "Her daughter's sick inside there."

"She's got a fever of a hundred and six," the woman said, recovering some control. "*No* one knows what's wrong — it's been hours."

"She borrowed a car to come here," Paddy explained to Ev, who'd reluctantly joined them. Paddy had straightened up, grown confident in this new wrinkle. His own crippling sorrow he had put on the back burner; the woman's need was more dramatic, distracting.

"It was like my father was the one who really led her to that Corolla," he told Ev excitedly after they'd helped the woman on her way. Down four lines of parked cars they'd gone, G, H, I, and J, as a trio, trying each Toyota until they found the little white one she'd been looking for. "It was my father," Paddy insisted later, "like an angel of mercy."

An angel of mercy, Ev noted; precisely the way he would have liked to think of himself. They'd shaken the woman's hand goodnight and wished her good luck, Paddy's eyes welling with bothersome tears like those he'd had such trouble shedding earlier.

The men returned to Ev's car afterward, Ev silent, brooding. Did Paddy understand his embarrassment at being suspicious of the woman? Thinking she was first a thief, then a bag lady? Had Ev been suspicious of her because he'd committed his own crime, never mind that he could justify and qualify it? For an instant, Evan pictured himself in a courtroom, actually having to defend what he'd done, asking Rachel and the boys to corroborate his story.

Paddy folded himself inside Ev's small car almost happily, as if proud to have come through the episode looking better than his companion. He inhabited the world without guilt. Ev sighed, sorry for himself and his big guilt.

"Never ridden in one of these," Paddy commented, checking around his seat. "My dad always bought American. Kind of like an egg, isn't it?"

"Kind of. Where are you from?" Ev asked as they circled the ramp down.

"Normal," Paddy replied. "Just outside the city limits."

"Just outside Normal," Ev mused. "I've always thought Normal was the funniest-named place in Illinois."

"Huh," said his passenger. "I don't guess you ever heard of Goofy Ridge."

"I guess not."

A storm was moving in over the lake, reflecting the city's lights from the east. Behind him, clouds hid the Sears Tower and Hancock building goal posts. Ev assumed there were whitecaps on Lake Michigan tonight. He took solace in the presence of Lake Michigan even when he could not see it; it made him feel singularly melancholy and isolated, even in a city peopled with millions of strains of melancholy more severe than his. He knew this — as a psychologist, he listened all day to the various themes of ubiquitous isolation — and yet the lake still offered the absolute promise of uniqueness.

Paddy said, "Twenty-four hours ago I was casting line up in Wisconsin with my dad." He looked at his cumbersome clock. "Well, actually we were asleep."

"Change," Ev said, "by definition means quick." He snapped his fingers, felt again his father's face beneath his hand, the still warm forehead.

"At least it wasn't my daughter," Paddy said, staring out the window at the passing storefronts. "I have a little four-year-old girl."

"I have boys," Ev said. "Nine and twelve." Zach and Marcus, asleep in their beds, mouths slack. Rachel sitting in her stuffed chair reading a book, drinking wine. They were a comfort, pinned there in Ev's mind, safe, alive.

By the time they got to Paddy's bungalow in Oak Park, it was after one. Ev had not spoken with Rachel since dinner; these days it was understood that Ev's appearances at home would be sandwiched between work and hospital. A creature of habit, Ev had almost enjoyed the regularity of his time the last few weeks, the predictability of traffic, the instant familiarity of the hospital, the pleasingly lonely drives home down empty streets. He had begun seeking radio phone-in shows, excited and repulsed by the tone of the advice dispensed. Why were all the hosts so angry? The callers so timid and cowed? These forays into average America always stunned Ev; his own insulated life — his family, his practice — allowed him a safe distance from such encounters. They would charm him for a while, then appall and depress him.

He'd arrive home exhausted, yet lie in bed beside Rachel wakeful, with ridiculous images scrolling inside his eyelids. He seemed to have been having dreams while awake, and they weren't unpleasant. Best of all was his magical ability to put into them whatever he wanted: flights around Europe, unusual sex partners, his lost childhood self.

Again he recalled that frightening dream of his father pulling him through the door of death, a tall door, a black-and-white, film-noirish dream, the long bright beam of death's light.

Now his father had died. The routine was over. Ev had hastened the inexorable future and there were arrangements to make (he'd told Nurse Amy to have his father cremated) and debts to settle. People who might genuinely mourn the old man's passing would soon come to Ev expecting cathartic reciprocity. A new era was on its way.

Beside him, Paddy Limbach said, "Man, my mother's going to take this like a ton of bricks."

"Mine, thank God, is already dead." He told Paddy that his father had killed her, had driven the life out of her, had made living miserable and dying a salvation. He found he liked Paddy, who listened attentively, although Ev did not typically like his type.

Too rugged, too entrenched in the league of the dumb and fit, the ones Rachel called body Nazis. But his pain had shown on his face. There'd been that ridiculous kick, and then that shaming, hurt glance. Paddy had understood the woman in the parking lot, the one Ev had missed completely, and, maybe predominantly, he represented the antithesis of Ev's relationship with his father. Here was genuine grief, completely unlike the vague anxiety that Ev felt creeping toward him, an anxiety that had everything to do with getting caught and nothing to do, as far as Ev could tell, with having pushed forward the end of his father's life.

"Thanks for the ride," Paddy said, swinging open the car door. "Hey, you seen my hat?"

"You left it on the hood of a car, back at the garage."

"Shoot."

"And your bandanna, too," Ev told him. "With the woman."

"I'm always losing my hankies, but I don't usually forget my hat." Paddy looked toward his house, the place thoroughly ablaze except for a softly lighted room on the far side: his daughter's night-lighted room, no doubt. "Lot of sad girls inside there," he said. His instinct was to shut the car door, stay in Ev's passenger seat, avoid his home, suspend the moment. "All praying my dad'll be O.K. I feel like I let them down." Going fishing had been Paddy's idea, and if they hadn't been so far from help, maybe his father's heart wouldn't have had to work so hard in damaged condition. No one was going to blame Paddy except Paddy himself, but just looking at those female faces was going to make him want to die.

"I'm sorry about your loss," Ev said — the one time in his life he'd uttered the words, the one time he could imagine meaning it.

"Oh yeah. Ditto," Paddy told him. He shook his hair from his eyes and nodded to Ev, then climbed clumsily from the car and walked up the steps with his hands jammed in his pockets. He rehearsed his entrance: *I have some terrible news,* he whispered. *Peepaw has died.*

Ev listened to his engine idling, the Saab's chirpy thrum, the sound of a machine eager to go places pretty fast. Where he wanted to go was a bar, and what he wanted to drink there was scotch. He hadn't had scotch for eight years, and his sudden desire for it made his heart grow alert and begin thudding. Ev had not had scotch or any other alcohol, hard or fruity, neither for social nor for ritual reasons, in eight years. All of his bad habits he'd been paring away over the years, beginning with smoking, when he was in college, and progressing through all the others, sugar and salt, red meat and dairy, then white meat and fat, always preserving alcohol as an indulgence, until he excised it, too. If he was going to be honest, he would have to let it go. He loved it best, so clearly it would harm him worst.

"Why are all the good things bad?" his poor son Zach had once wailed, saddened by the withholding of his glorious Halloween loot.

It was only after Ev had driven away, speeding with his racing heart toward a neighborhood bar called the Elms, that he noticed the effects bag left on the floorboard, white, glinting under passing streetlights. He pulled over, switched on the dome light, and peeked in the sack to make sure it was Paddy's and not his own. There was the soft fishing hat, folded away to one side, brown with a tidemark of sweat along the rim. Checked shirt, blue jeans, dock shoes, jockeys, wristwatch, pocket knife, key ring, wallet. Utterly dull. Opening the wallet was an invasion of privacy, though the other perusal had been justified. Inside were the usual series of cards and ID: Visa, Diner's, NRA, AARP; a driver's license from Normal showing a red-faced blond not very different from the son, a meat-eating, beer-swilling good old guy, smiling, gap between the front teeth; photographs of Paddy and a woman who must be his wife, big teased head of hair, bright red lips. Little girl in Paddy's arms. And then there was the photo of the deceased's wife, a black-and-white picture taken a good thirty years earlier, one of those studio portraits wherein the subject seems to be rapturously viewing heaven. This woman was one of the earth's kind sorts. She had a tender uncertain smile, eyes sloped by apostrophe-like curves on either side, and a tiny dimple in the center of her chin. She looked as if she were sentimental in life, a woman who cried easily and often. Yes, she would take her husband's death like a ton of bricks.

He spun a wide U-turn on Chicago Ave., the Saab just as eager to go this way as that, back to Paddy's house. The lights still burned; even the Limbachs' doorbell was lit — little orange button — but Ev didn't ring it. He pulled open the screen door and set the effects bag between it and the wood door. He heard voices, Paddy's and one other — his wife's, Ev supposed — the two of them murmuring together. At first he thought he was overhearing their intimacies, the inflections of sex, the up and down, bad air and good air being exchanged as they pressed on each other's lungs, the happy gasps and sighs. So rarely did a person actually interrupt sex, Ev couldn't believe that was what he was hearing. Then the noise suddenly clarified, as if he had located an elusive radio station: prayer. It was words, but not known ones, a sort of *hey-nonny-nonny,* the solemn nonsense of an auctioneer. He shivered, aware that overhearing sex would have been less abashing to him. An unfamiliar litany but with the familiar supplicating rhythm, begging, beseeching, bad air and good.

He listened for only a few seconds, then gently closed the screen door. From the yard, he glanced at the soft pink glow in the far window; apparently the little girl was spared the liturgy. The annoying metallic racket of cicadas surrounded him, insisting on a sense of the average and incessant.

His desire for a drink had died; he'd been rescued from his bad habit.

It was only when he was finally perfectly alone with his father's death — just him and his own bag of effects, driving in his closed egg toward home — that Ev felt the single fragment of remorse, like a burst of snow in his chest: he would never see his father again.

Two

· · · · · · · · · · · ·

RACHEL COLE was wakened that night by her husband's hot naked body curling around her. Bored, she'd drunk too much wine and now felt woozy, cotton-mouthed, and eye-achy. Her hand lay pocketed between her thighs, reminding her that she'd had an idea about masturbating before she had simply plopped into sleep. The digital clock read 2:22 — orderly time, as usual. Ev said, "He died."

She was immediately awake, riveted, un-hung-over, eyes wide. Excited. Her husband's erection bobbed around her backside, his coarse springy hair causing its usual tickling friction. He was excited, too. She rolled over to hold him. "You O.K.?" she asked.

"I'm good," he said. "Suffering some nonspecific weirdness, otherwise fine. I almost went to a bar — it's just a weird old night. Let's fuck."

Rachel turned over his words while they had sex. Although she hadn't thought he needed to quit drinking when he did, it still bothered her that he might be tempted now to start up again. He seemed to know himself best, to predict his own lapses, to execute punishment. He was hard on himself, critical and exacting, but perhaps his diligence had kept him from falling into the kind of decline his brother had fallen into. Even after fifteen years, Rachel did not feel qualified to pronounce with any kind of certainty on her husband's dormant character.

He could not come, although they tried for a long while, the clock's little green slashes clicking and contorting along — horizontal, vertical, Rachel compliant beneath him, active on top of him, adaptable in between. Still, nothing happened for him. Finally Ev flopped exhausted beside her, kissed Rachel's neck, then climbed out of bed. "Go to sleep," he told her, but, not surprisingly, she found herself unable to do so, her drunkenness fuzzing up once more to muddle and woo her unsuccessfully.

Rachel was not sorry to see the last of her father-in-law. He had on the one hand enraged her and on the other terrified her. The rage came from his meanness; that was easy enough to explain. But the terror was less simple, since it came from his being related to her husband, from the physical resemblance Ev bore to him: the long scaly feet, the disarming squint of his left eye when he concentrated, the mesmerizing vein in his temple. Rachel hadn't known her father-in-law long before he became ill; her entire marriage to Ev had taken place in the shadow of the old man's alleged former personality, gone for good. So wasn't it possible that Ev's progress through this world would mirror his father's? That he would turn from moodily complex to witlessly malicious? Rachel could stare at Ev, the man she loved, blur her eyes in the way one does to generalize impressions, and see her father-in-law. The signs of Ev's aging — graying, sagging, slowing — troubled her.

Her father-in-law's latest hospitalization had lasted two weeks, but before that he had been living with her and Ev and the boys, staying in the pantrylike space beyond the kitchen at the far end of the apartment, a cozy little nook Rachel had intended to use as a kind of private office for herself, a place to take phone calls, a tax writeoff. She'd enjoyed the bright white walls, the nearly seamless job she herself had done of the sheetrocking and taping, with indentations like thumbprints where she'd pounded in nails. It had taken her months to finish the room; it had still held the optimistic odor of newness when, at the last second, her father-in-law had been evicted from his nursing home. The coincidental timing made Rachel feel tricked, as if all along she'd been preparing a place for him rather than for herself.

His caretakers at the home were sick of his behavior; they

couldn't be paid enough to endure him any longer. Who could? Rachel wondered. Only family was ever expected to tolerate such conduct, to take you in when what you deserved — and sometimes needed — was to be tossed out. The home had called Ev, and Ev had no one to whom he could pass the buck. That was Ev's fate in the world: being responsible. His only living relative, his brother Gerry, who literally had no home, couldn't be reached. Rachel had been forced to imagine sad, woolly Gerry, wandering around downtown from heat grate to heat grate in his coats and hats. Many winters past, he had lived on the roof of their very own building.

"I'm tempted to let my father try to make it on the streets," Ev had told her, perhaps also thinking of Gerry, or of how he would like to question what everyone assumed was self-evident, dispute what was perceived as indisputable: namely, that family had to open the door when you knocked. This was on the night the nursing home staff called. He'd been given thirty days to get the old man out. Two different caretakers told Ev stories: his father was peeing in drawers and trash cans, smoking in no-smoking lounges, making harassing phone calls (Rachel herself could attest to those; she had listened and seethed as her father-in-law swore about her husband), upbraiding his black roommate, announcing obscene intentions to the women nurses, and spitting whenever the urge came over him — on the floor of his room, on the wheels of his chair, on the perennial towel-bib that, tucked into his ratty shirt, covered his chest. In the past, it had been his scathing words alone he wouldn't control; now, more literal bile spewed forth.

"If I simply didn't respond," Ev went on, "what could they do? They'd have to either keep him or throw him out on his ass."

"I'd like to see them try," Rachel said, picturing her father-in-law with his heavy wooden cane, swinging at orderlies from his wheelchair as they shoved him through halls.

But despite the subject matter, Rachel enjoyed that conversation with Ev. They sat at their kitchen table, Rachel with a glass of wine, Ev with hot tea. She liked to talk to Ev in the kitchen, at night, after the boys were asleep. She liked to stare over his head at their cabinets full of pretty pottery and china; she liked the look of their appliances after the dishes had been done, in the warm haze of what Ev called her evening toddy. Although he did not drink, he liked her to. Her husband liked to feel he was openminded and accommodating, a big strong umbrella under which others' weaknesses were sheltered. Superior to them, evolved beyond them.

Rachel was pleased with the kitchen's black windows, the way everything in the world was shut away from her and Ev, as if they sat in a lighted box, alone. These conversations occurred late, after the time when one of the boys would rouse himself to demand a parent's steady presence beside him, after Ev's crazy client Dr. Head's nightly call. Dr. Head phoned every evening to review the day with Evan, always after the boys were in bed: a brief conversation to calm him, to permit him to sleep, a kind of prayer-and-absolution combo. From Rachel's occasional exchange of pleasantries with Dr. Head — he never failed to ask a few polite questions of her — she would never have guessed his paranoid delusions. He would extend his cordial greetings; she would pass the phone to Ev. Then Dr. Head would notify Ev that his downstairs neighbors planned to murder him in his sleep. Or that the newspaper had buried in its articles a code designed exclusively for the discerning readership, one that would tell them where to meet on the day of apocalypse. For the duration of her marriage, Rachel had never gotten familiar with more of Dr. Head than his educated voice and impeccable manners. Often Ev argued with him, but they always ended their calls civilly, ritualistically agreeing to disagree. Dr. Head had a notion that the planet would die when he did; he'd once been convinced that Dutch elm disease would include him as it made its way up his neighborhood street. At night he phoned to put himself, and the world, to bed.

And after that, there was nothing in the apartment but Rachel and Ev, their reflections cast back at them from the dark glass, their range of topics shared, their understanding rich. Whatever Rachel said, her husband would comprehend. She had no need for carefulness or for taxing explanation, hesitation or premeditation. They were comfortable together. Had she anticipated such a state of comfort when she'd imagined marriage? Such contentedness with the mundane? Not likely.

But, too, she assumed that her former self would never have conceived of this — a brooding, picky, forty-five-year-old man in a modest kitchen wearing slipper socks — as a fantasy life. Yet she was happy. Or, more exactly, she was not unhappy. She had done what Ev called leveling off, something his manic-depressive clients were encouraged to do, too, those bipolars. They were made to stop that up-and-down stuff, that globe-trotting, to settle for a moderate middle ground. The secret, Rachel deduced, was finding it satisfactory, was naming it lucky or blessed instead of dull.

Of his father, Ev said, "With our luck, he'd come live on the roof, like Gerry."

"Our own gargoyle," Rachel said. "Pissing over the sides, making a mess like the pigeons. The neighbors would bring back their plastic owls and fake snakes and rifles. Only this time I wouldn't complain."

Ev hesitated in finding this funny. Although his feelings about his father seemed kindred to Rachel's (she had learned from him how to hate the man, after all), he did not like to see them so blatantly laid before him. It was a slender little line that Rachel mostly understood, but sometimes she got careless and stepped over. This time, however, Ev relinquished a snort. He was disinclined toward real laughter; a snort was as close as he got. It had once been Rachel's secret goal to make him actually break down and guffaw, become helpless with laughter, but she'd given that up. Apparently his father had driven giddy hilarity out of Ev's character.

"He'd be bad for business," Rachel went on. "Imagine if your clients discovered that your father *and* your brother were street people."

"To hell with what my clients think."

"Uh-huh," she said, well aware of his desire to believe he did not care what people thought. She knew better, and she knew he knew she knew better. A flare of marital love went up inside her; the elaborate, convoluted, knotty way they knew each other still delighted her, made her feel toward Ev as she did toward their sons, full of an irrepressible, absolute affection, not sexual but deeply fond.

And not always not sexual, Rachel reminded herself. There were times, rare and poignant, when sex with Ev was dramatic and heart-stopping — it was heady and holistic, like loving a long, sad novel, feeling wrung out and nobly wounded when it ended. Something like that. Good novels and married sex were related that way; Rachel filed this away as a topic to broach some other time with Ev, a kernel of smartness to give him like a gift at an unexpected moment.

"I certainly hope you've inherited his endurance," Rachel told Ev, for the hundredth time. It was the sole silver lining she could unearth. That and the fact that Ev's saintly mother had died early in his father's progress toward Bastard Incarnate.

Ev said, "I'm afraid he's going to have to come live with us."

"Ugh," Rachel said. When they were first married, she had sworn to succeed with Ev's father where others had failed. She would be the one to bring him out of his grim stinginess; she would delight him with flattery, listen to his stories without judging their contents. She would flirt with him. She would charm him in the way only a skillful young woman could. This was Rachel's intention, to prove herself superior to any others who might have tried before with Ev's father. Her faith in her own femininity carried her for months, an arrogance derived from her happiness in having found Ev, from her smug youthfulness. She could not envision a greater happiness; she wanted to spread it around like a big pollinating insect fluttering from person to person, infecting them with her own copious magnanimity.

But Ev's father hadn't wanted to be converted. He didn't want to be seduced by his daughter-in-law. He didn't want to be mesmerized into revealing his lighthearted and kind self. Instead, he wanted her to sit in subdued silence while he berated his son. He wanted her to deliver another generation of boys before him so that he could inflict his venom upon them. He was a snake, and Rachel had later had to explain to her sons when they came to her in tears after Grandpa had rapped their shoulder blades with his cane that he was a big grumpy bully, like the ones they'd heard about in stories, whose path they should avoid. He seemed set on defying the modern notion that people could not be evil, only misunderstood.

Rachel put her feet up in Ev's lap. He spread his thighs to make room, laying a hand on her bare toes. "Cold feet," he said.

"Warm heart," she answered. They looked at each other with shabby, tired smiles. "He can stay in my pantry," she offered. She had learned to act when she felt generous; otherwise, she might never be generous. It wasn't often she regretted generosity. Even if its recipient was ungrateful, she could later rationalize one of her own less than generous acts. Who was keeping tabs, she could not say.

Ev and Rachel got up from the kitchen table to investigate the little room for future use as a bedroom. "No carpet," Rachel said, already cataloguing its virtues. "One can clean up linoleum more easily than carpet."

"One can," Ev agreed.

"Room for a bed here," Rachel said, standing beneath the window, whose sash she'd just painted that afternoon, using a spongy trim brush and a paint called periwinkle, her favorite color.

"A twin bed," Ev said.

"Of nails," Rachel added. "At least with a rubber sheet, am I right? He must wet the bed?"

"I suppose."

"What besides a bed? He's got his wheelchair, so no need for a chair."

"A dresser."

"He'll pee in the drawers. You said they said he peed in drawers."

"True. Maybe just a coat rack for his clothes."

"It's hard to believe he'd pee on his own clothes. Maybe it was his roommate's clothes. He never did like that black guy, what was his name?"

"Maurice. A television would be useful, almost essential."

"Cable." Her father-in-law liked to fire through the channels, grunting in disgust: all his worst expectations, confirmed again. Nothing was on, but he wanted to complain about it anyway; Rachel entertained the thought of her father-in-law answering one of Dr.

Head's nightly calls, not comforting him as Ev did by providing evidence of the randomness of fate (randomness being as close as Ev would come to optimism), but attesting to the world's malevolent designs. "Of course the newspaper editors want you to die," he would say. "You're a filthy schmuck, you deserve to die."

Rachel sighed. Her little room, which had had its birth in hopes of a chintz loveseat and an antique bookcase, desk and chair, flowered lampshades, old photographs, was turning into a cell: single bed, TV bolted to the ceiling. Her father-in-law would smoke in here and the paint would turn mustard yellow. Everything he touched turned mustard yellow; he had a sort of anti-Midas knack. Up to now, the room had held a huge broken freezer and a lot of shelves full of tools and boxes and castoff appliances. It hadn't seemed like a room at all, more like a closet, a dark place to store things you couldn't make decisions about. There'd been a real sense of joy and discovery in opening it up, cleaning it out, covering its dinginess with white and blue paint. The window, a coal chute that Rachel punched larger and glassed in when she began remodeling, gave a view of the slate roof over the elevator shaft, a quaint mottling of green and gray stone where rainwater ran as if over a streambed. Sun struck in four bright patches on the new floor every afternoon around two. Rachel had begun feeling she'd moved somewhere new, started a slightly different, better life. Now her father-in-law was coming.

And this fact suggested a different, harder life. But sometimes harder was better, too. Character building, soul enriching, heart expanding. She could not deny her very familiar, foolish urge to shake things up just for novelty's sake. She and Ev and the boys would most likely rally round the old man's presence. And it would be O.K. unless it went on too long, unless he stayed with them for years and years, unless his influence began to feel influential.

"When do you think he'll finally die?" she asked Ev then, standing in the blank, vaguely noxious-smelling new room. Small as it was, it gave the impression of echo.

"I don't know," Ev told her. "He's been dying so long now, it's as if he's already gone."

"If he moves here, he might come between us."

Ev studied her. It had always bothered her when he did this, narrowing that left eye at her, thinking about her words. She was not careful when she spoke around him, and on rare occasions she regretted that.

"We could try him in another home," Ev said finally, crossing his arms over his chest.

"We're running out of ones that don't know him," Rachel answered, although the old man had only been in two others before the current place.

"Blackballed by the rest homes."

"Ev," she said, "if your father could have seen himself the way he is now, back when he was sane and human, do you think he would want you to . . ." She stopped. What was she saying, anyway?

"Kill him?" Ev finished for her. "You've already convinced me that that wouldn't be a good idea. All I can say is that if it were me, if I saw myself becoming that monster, then I would want myself gone, offed. The thing is, I can't know what his truth is. What's his world like, anyway? We might seem like sadists to him, bigger assholes than he seems to us."

"No way," Rachel said.

"But we can't know. We could all be headed in the same direction."

She didn't want her own worst-case scenario voiced by Ev; she wanted him to think it impossible that he would become like his father. She stuck her hand between her husband's crossed arms and pulled free one of his hands, then pressed herself against him. If she wanted to make love with him, then he could not resemble his father — that was her logic. They kissed; then came the single moan Ev always began sex with, as if sex's power gave him an ache even in anticipation. That night, on the floor of Rachel's pantry, they made love, Rachel's buttocks cold on the linoleum, her jean skirt bunched at her waist, her own slipper socks still on her feet. Her husband, though smallish, was solid and heavy, like a paperweight. His density made her shoulder blades hurt. In the middle of things, Rachel wanted to talk again.

"He'll need a babysitter, just like the boys," she told Ev, who had begun a quick series of thrusts, darting in and out of her in a way that reminded Rachel of hummingbirds.

"True," Ev said, slowing his pace. He didn't mind stopping to chat.

Rachel reached between her body and his and held his testicles, running a finger up the crease, winding his springy hairs around her knuckles. "I like you hard," she said.

"I like you soft," he answered. He rested on his hands, staring down at her. The vein at his temple throbbed crazily in this position; gravity pulled his flesh toward her.

"Your face is very red. Don't have a heart attack," she warned him as he started slowly moving in and out again. "You feel . . . good," she added.

In truth, it frightened her to feel his heart against her chest. His was an active heart, loud when he came, pounding on her rib cage as if hammering its way out of his. "Wait, wait," she said, pushing his chest up.

"What?" he asked, smiling. Making love made him happy. It was the one time Rachel could see his childishness, the boy that got trampled on and left, for the most part, behind. She cherished that look in his face, the open revelation.

"Why wait?" he asked, his lips at her hairline.

"You ever think about your parents while we're fucking?"

"I try not to do that."

"Sometimes I can't help it. I think about my mother. I wonder if she ever let herself enjoy sex, or if it seemed like too much work — getting ready, cleaning up after, all that technical, houseworky part of it."

Ev said, "Maybe you'd prefer thinking she didn't enjoy sex?"

"Oh, please!" Rachel pushed his shoulders up. "No analysis, please. I can have fun without it, thanks."

"If you're sure . . ."

"Positive. You still like me?" she asked. "Even though I'm kind of old?"

"Not that old."

"Not as old as you," she agreed. He'd begun moving again, this conversation having happened many times before. "You still like my breasts?"

"You have amazing breasts, very nice breasts." He pushed up her shirt and sucked one happily.

"Maybe it would bother you if I were on top and you could see all my extra skin hanging around?"

"I like you," he said. "You're beautiful."

"But not like I used to be."

"Better. I love you better." His desire for her, for release, for pure pleasure, was transparent in the instant he came. And her own satisfaction — the thrill, the melancholy, the urge to cry — followed. Their sex had metamorphosed to this point. How did they know how to care for each other? How did Ev know to stop his pumping precisely now, to push his pelvis against hers, to wait while she oscillated two or three times, then to move again? His understanding of her physical preferences was like masturbation, as if she were responding to her own hunger. In the beginning, years earlier, sex had not been like this, had been not tacit but clumsy. In that clumsiness was delicious fire and tumult, but there was a power in this sex, this accomplished, timeworn thing between them, that Rachel had not expected, had not even tried to explain to herself. There used to be simple but substantial passion. Now the passion had slid away, leaving in its void this thorough knowledge of each other, a giant black universe Rachel continued to navigate, by intuition and other ill-defined resources. Everything they were and knew and had created between them existed here, a great voluminous invention, entirely invisible, inexplicable, exclusively theirs. She reeled while they made love, then forgot it later. Sometimes she mentioned it to Ev just before they fell asleep, and he would briefly hold her, wiping away her tears.

Rachel felt she would cry, her achievement now in sex not joy but fullness — all the emotions at once, simple Dr. Seuss emotions, sad, mad, glad. She ran her fingernails over Ev's sweating back. He'd fallen like a dead weight against her; he was exhausted. Their birth-control method was withdrawal, so he'd left on her tummy what they'd named, between them and only them, white mud. He would sleep that night like something dead.

But she would lie awake later, just as she was this night, the night of her father-in-law's passing, sailing on the murky current of her marriage, her sex life with Evan, following its long and uncharted course. A few weeks ago, on the floor just off the kitchen, she had pressed her thumbs into the solid muscle of Ev's buttocks. She had pulled the teardrop of flesh at his earlobe between her teeth and given it a nip. She had bitten his shoulder and studied the mark. She had traced the scary bolt of lightning at his temple that was just exactly, just precisely, like his father's.

Three

. . . .

PADDY MIGHT have forgotten Evan Cole altogether. His widowed mother, his own wife and daughter — they were enough to occupy him in the coming months. The grief of women made his own, by contrast, stoic and dignified. There was to be no more weeping from him. His father's death reverberated through their lives relentlessly: it had come too fast, a severing rather than a gentle easing away. Paddy could not get over the urge to call his father up and ask his advice. And since he couldn't call, his decisions felt faulty. Everyone had faith in him suddenly. They turned to him, and he could neither refuse nor consult. There was a farm to dismantle, animals to feed and then sell, Paddy's senile great-aunt in Normal, who couldn't reconcile herself to her nephew's startling absence during visitors' Sunday.

But Paddy felt fraudulent as he handled it all, like somebody pretending to be a grownup man. *Hey,* he wanted to say, *I'm not really this competent — are you sure you want to trust me?* He imagined his father staring down at him from some unnamed height, smiling pityingly, knowing that Paddy wasn't ready, but what could he do? Paddy would construct elaborate conversations with his father, composed of real and extrapolated knowledge of him, then suddenly realize that there was nothing to support it, that his father was simply gone, a whoosh of wind.

He remembered, months after meeting Ev, that Ev had said he

was a psychologist. Things kept happening that seemed remotely related to Paddy's father's death: his mother took up smoking; his great-aunt began wandering in traffic outside her nursing home; Paddy's four-year-old became convinced she could fly and jumped from the top of the piano, thus breaking her arm. Suddenly his females seemed to have death wishes of their own.

He drove his daughter to the hospital wondering what part of her mind had short-circuited. She *looked* normal, but something must certainly have gone wrong inside, something he, Paddy, should have been able to anticipate and prevent.

Confused, Paddy searched for Ev in the telephone book and called one E. Cole, Psychiatrist, in order to discover that Ev was "the other Cole," *psychologist*. Paddy had never been clear on the difference. He phoned one morning in March, eight months after the deaths of their fathers, just to say hi. Ev returned the call promptly at 10:52, after what his secretary called his session. He remembered Paddy but didn't seem to feel particularly friendly. Paddy had the sense Ev was waiting for him to prove himself worthy.

Paddy said, "Everything's pretty bad since my dad died."

Ev breathed noisily into the phone, like a pervert. In the background Paddy heard nothing. He pictured Ev's office as a black-and-white, windowless cell, a room in which to judge a person's sanity. Ev said, "You're what, thirty?"

"Thirty-four."

"Uh-huh. I'm forty-six. Now I think of my own death every day, don't you? I have my father's ashes here and I still can't decide what the hell to do with them. I never could figure out what to do with him."

Relieved, Paddy wanted to confess everything. Something about Ev, even over the telephone, inspired him to talk — maybe it was Ev's tangible impatience, that hovering irritation that made Paddy feel as if his problems were probably going to be revealed as trite. He remembered the sick joke Ev had made at the hospital about suffocating his father; such a person commanded Paddy's respect, the way his professors had, years earlier, at the University of Illinois. He'd often wanted to phone them up, ask them just to keep talking to him, fill him in about the truly significant concerns. From them, he learned that there was another way to look at the world, a way that opened it up like the 3-D glasses they used to hand out at movies; he wanted in on the trick. Now that Ev had mentioned it, he knew he would contemplate his own death every day, too.

"What can I do for you?" Ev asked.

Paddy said, "Well, this will sound kind of dumb . . ."

"Nonsense," said Ev impatiently.

"My daughter thinks she can fly. I mean, she just jumped off a piano and expected to go. I started to think she was, well, disturbed." Because his wife had been so shaken by Melanie's jump, by the sickening cartoonish angle of her broken arm, Paddy had had to become the firmly convinced member of the partnership, the man. To her, all the way to the emergency room, he had said Melanie was a typical four-year-old. To Ev, he admitted his deep fear that his daughter was — he dropped the euphemism — insane.

"Back at old St. Mike's, eh?"

Paddy paused, the setting of his father's death visited upon him. The place had not seemed like the same place when he'd gone there with Melanie and Didi. He hadn't given it even a glancing consideration. Of course, the season had changed, and the ER was in an entirely other part of the hospital, but his own state of mind was the largest variable, and it had been different, no denying it.

"What is it I can do for you?" Ev repeated into Paddy's ear. "You want me to see your daughter for an evaluation? I don't take children as clients, by and large, but I can recommend one of my partners here who's —"

"No," Paddy said. "Oh my heck, no, I was just thinking about getting together for coffee or something, maybe bring Mel along to meet you, or . . ." He did not like the silence that greeted him. People generally filled silences for him. He only learned this about himself as he listened and Ev did not accommodate him. At last there was a faint crabby sigh from the other end.

"O.K.," Ev said. "But let's don't just sit. Let's walk around somewhere with her."

Paddy suggested the first place that occurred to him, a place with animals, whose presence never hurt.

The three of them, Paddy and Melanie and Ev, were to meet at the Shedd Aquarium the following Saturday. For some reason, Paddy felt critical of the little girl's clothing after her mother dressed her that day. He removed her silver princess skirt — as she shrieked — and put her in jeans and a panda bear sweatshirt, easing her broken arm into the tight sleeve. In order to get her to cheer up, he promised to buy her something at the aquarium gift shop. Her casual and unfeminine outfit made her seem more presentable to his new friend, the psychologist.

During the episode of the clothing, Paddy's wife stood watching from the doorway, saying, when Melanie appealed to her, "Daddy wants you in pants, baby. I don't know why," using a sticky voice Paddy particularly disliked, one that was intended to glide over Melanie and adhere to him. "Have fun," she added, her tone suggesting he'd already ruined the possibility of doing so.

Paddy had not told Didi that he was taking Melanie to be unofficially checked by a shrink (maybe *that* was the difference: you didn't call psychologists "shrinks.") No need to have an argument; no need to upset her. Already she had her suspicions about his suddenly wanting to make an excursion alone with their daughter.

To Melanie, alone in the car, he said, "Daddy's friend Dr. Cole will be coming along with us, won't that be fun?" Or maybe psychologists weren't doctors. He then amended it to "Daddy's friend Ev, a nice man I met at the hospital when Peepaw died. Remember when Peepaw died, and I came home late from the hospital? It was Ev who gave me a ride, wasn't that nice of him?" Paddy loved talking to her in the car, chattering at her, his hostage audience.

"Does he have some children?" she asked.

"He has two sons."

"What are their names?"

"I don't know. You can ask him that." They stopped at a red light. When Paddy inspected his passenger, she was rubbing her cast, a habit she'd quickly fallen into. A big ugly smudge had formed where her dirty hand had been at work.

"Whattaya waiting for?" she asked him. "The pole to turn green, too?" She then laughed uproariously. Her favorite car line, learned from her Peepaw.

At the Shedd, Ev was waiting on the steps, stretched in the pale spring sunshine, eyeglasses blazing in the light. He was smaller than Paddy remembered, also fiercer and more frightening looking. Though the hair on his head was still mostly black, his eyebrows sprouted on his forehead like steel wool.

Beside him, an old fellow in a seedy brown suit had set up a booth for taking photographs. Melanie made a beeline for his display. He swept his hand over the variety of things onto which he could apply his photos: T-shirts, pins, calendars, coffee mugs. Most people passed by his booth into the museum without seeming to see him. Melanie studied the mugs. "We could get one of these for Mama," she called to Paddy. When looking for gifts for her mother, the two of them had often fallen back on coffee mugs, although Didi, who was Mormon, didn't drink coffee.

Paddy looked at Ev, but Ev didn't appear to be in any hurry. His long legs extended before him, he scowled in the bright light, and Paddy noticed a vein at his temple, a throbbing zigzag that made him seem angry. The man in the suit had begun selling the mug idea to Melanie, telling her she sure was a sweet pretty girl, asking if he could put his John Hancock on her cast. Paddy felt bad about the disaster he'd manufactured earlier concerning her clothes, and agreed. "Sure. Let's get Mama a cup."

The photographer sat Mel on the top step and asked her to smile. She shook her head. "Mama likes me just like this," she told him. Paddy grinned, looking again at Ev to see if he'd heard this healthy self-report. He hadn't, was staring up into the branches of an overhanging tree. When the man had completed his photo, and while he was waiting for it to finish making in his machine, he tried to scoop Mel up in his arms, nuzzle her neck. Melanie screamed, clawing for her father. She came into Paddy's arms like a monkey and he held her as she cried, comforting her, trying to persuade her the guy was friendly rather than menacing.

"I'm a grandpa, myself," the photographer said defensively.

"I've got lots of grandbabies, I love them all. Love children, wouldn't make one cry to save my soul." He continued to pat Melanie's back as she clung to Paddy, clubbing him with her small cast. She screamed and screamed, lurching away from his touch, clinging so that Paddy nearly fell over backward. Maybe she was going insane, Paddy thought. Maybe a complete breakdown was about to happen.

It was then that Ev, standing to join them, focused on her. "Keep your hands off," he told the man sternly. "And your John Hancock, too."

Paddy, who'd been raised to treat his elders politely, was stunned.

"I wouldn't make a child cry to save my soul!" the man was repeating as Ev led them away, Paddy's thirty cents change neglected.

"He was mean," Melanie explained a few minutes later.

"Probably," Ev agreed. Paddy had been about to scold Melanie, to remind her to give people the benefit of the doubt. He had a basically charitable vision of the world, one it had never occurred to him to question.

"You think?" he asked Ev, genuinely surprised.

"Sycophantic sleazebag," Ev said.

Paddy laughed nervously; he didn't know what *sycophantic* meant, but it sounded as if it ought to be funny. Ev smiled with half his mouth, a sly expression.

The aquarium was crowded yet peaceful, everyone moving through the dusky light from tank to tank, room to room. And there the fish were, ignoring the people, going along with their lives without caring who watched. Paddy breathed easier among animals, even cold-blooded slimy ones like fish. It was probably a good thing that Didi was allergic to most pets; otherwise, they might have a whole brood of them, a regular urban farm.

Melanie held the coffee cup with the scowling picture of herself on its side, thumping it against her leg. On her other arm was the cast, glowing green in the murky illumination. Paddy was glad she seemed to like Ev, who'd begun giving the fish dialogue. "Move, fat thing," he said for the slinking stingray. "Shut your mouth, will you?" he made the neons say to the grouper. "Turn out the lights, boys," the grouper mouthed back. Soon Melanie thrust her new cup at Paddy and took Ev's hand.

Ev was startled by the child's hand in his; he'd forgotten the specific comfort of a small child's hand. Melanie's was tiny inside his, a reminder suddenly of the power of his grip. He held on lightly, aware that he could crush her fingers, thinking of his hand, this same hand, over his father's mouth and nostrils, his father's hands rising, motioning, then ceasing.

Paddy ambled behind them, unhurriedly reading the placards beside the tanks, standing for long periods of time just studying the fish, engrossed in an aspect of their existence that Ev did not believe he himself grasped. At home, his sentimental son Zach approved of Ev's vegetarianism, believing that his father loved animals. But Ev had no particular thought for them; he was interested in his own health. Fish did not move him; they seemed an embodiment of meaninglessness, caught in their small tanks, circling as they waited for food — affectless metaphors in a godless universe.

"I need to go potty," Melanie suddenly announced, dropping Ev's hand to clutch her crotch. Ev smiled as Paddy looked confused.

For his part, Paddy couldn't think what to do: send her alone to the ladies' room? Give her to a friendly-looking woman for safekeeping in there? Or take her to the men's?

Ev said, "I'd take her to the men's if I were you, and let her use the stall."

"Good idea," Paddy said, leading her hopping away. While standing crushed against the inside door of the tiny toilet cubicle, waiting for her to finish, Paddy reflected on his past adventures with his daughter. Hadn't she ever had to pee before when her mother wasn't around? He couldn't think of a single time. Of course, she'd been potty trained late, and he didn't often take her places without Didi. Still.

She concentrated on her task, her face squeezed in the breathlessness of expulsion, red. Looking down at her, Paddy was saddened by the wad of hair stuck to the grubby ceramic, by the soiled toilet paper on the floor all around her. The tile was sticky and the metal walls were lousy with graffiti — he was glad Melanie didn't yet know how to read; he hoped the crude pictures weren't inciting her imagination in some damaging way. He envisioned her in other public bathrooms, her future in them, at gas stations in the middle of the night, in restaurants on dates, in loud bars as she sat, drunk and reeling. Perhaps she'd flee to one to smoke, as Paddy had done in school, or perhaps to cry over some worthless boy who'd broken her heart. It occurred to Paddy that the next man to see his little girl sit on a toilet would probably be her husband. He hoped she would marry the kind of guy who wouldn't make a big deal out of bathroom sharing. He hoped Melanie would be the kind of woman who joined her husband in the bathroom without making a fuss, an intimacy her mother tolerated but did not feel particularly comfortable with. One of Paddy's most striking childhood memories was of his parents both disappearing into the bathroom near bedtime, getting ready together, shuffling about in their scuffs and bed clothes, the single flush of the toilet. He had loved that knowledge he had of them, and that they had of each other. He hadn't thought of it in many, many years, and his eyes filled suddenly, this image of his father sabotaging him, his own adulthood making him sad.

"Wipe me," his daughter ordered, leaning forward off the seat and revealing her pink puckered bottom hole. Paddy knelt with the coarse tissue provided by the dispenser. Outside the stall, he heard two teenagers talking as they used the urinal, and he waited until they'd left before opening the door.

"Wash hands," Mel reminded him. He hurried her through this as a group of boys came yelling in.

Ev was circling the coral reef tank, watching the diver get ready for the feeding session. He lifted Melanie up to see the woman fall backward into the tank, the turtles and fish lazily floating away from her.

"I want to be a underwater lady," she told Paddy from Ev's shoulders.

"Girls can be whatever they want," Paddy replied loftily, "just like boys." He thought this was a good response.

Melanie said, "Girls can't be daddies."

Ev said, "Or brothers." They both gave Paddy the same challenging look. "Or uncles," Ev continued.

"Or bad guys," Melanie said. "Can they?" she asked Ev, leaning down to watch his face.

"Girls are not bad guys," he agreed.

"And girls can wear anything," Melanie went on, "but boys can only wear pants."

"So true," said Ev. "I wish I were a girl."

"Poor boys," Melanie said.

In the gift shop, Melanie asked Ev what he would get if he were getting something. "I'd buy that big killer whale and sleep with it at night," Ev said. "I'd make it watch for bad guys for me."

The killer whale had pink gums and white teeth, a kind of snarl. "Isn't he cute?" Melanie crowed.

They purchased it. Outside, the photographer was packing his cart up, the spring wind flapping his banners and shirts. His expression when he saw Ev was full of hatred. Paddy turned his face away, embarrassed to seem to condone his friend's rudeness.

"Fucking pedophile," Ev muttered. Paddy again felt thrilled, scandalized. Also curious; was *pedophile* related to *podiatry*?

Ev had ridden the train down to the aquarium but accepted Paddy's offer of a ride. "Good God," he said in the parking lot before Paddy's Bronco, jumping back as if receiving an electric shock.

"All-terrain vehicle," Paddy said. "Better for potholes."

"Need a ladder?" Ev asked Melanie as he hoisted her up. "Maybe an elevator?"

They rumbled out of the lot. "What a view," Ev said. "You can see right into the laps of the other drivers. What a frightening prospect."

They were quiet a while. Melanie fell almost instantly asleep in the back seat. Ev turned to check on her, then said, "How would you feel if some complete stranger jerked you off your feet and put his mouth on your neck?" He meant the photographer, the event that had started the day, and he meant it from Melanie's point of view.

"I wouldn't like it," Paddy guessed.

"No shit."

And she wouldn't have liked going to the bathroom with a stranger, either. Paddy felt a precarious and tender pride in himself, and looked in the rearview mirror at his daughter, at the way she listed sideways in sleep and resembled her baby pictures, with her hair stuck to her chubby cheek. Watching her sleep often made him ashamed of himself, as if he would never be good enough to be her father. He now wished that he'd let her wear her princess clothes, and that it had been he instead of Ev who'd bawled out the photographer, but he was nonetheless glad he'd taken her to the men's room.

"She seems O.K. to me," Ev was saying, "but that's only an informal guess." Paddy was bewildered for a moment, having forgotten entirely his excuse for inviting Ev along. They had reached Ev's building on Fullerton, and he pulled over before it, his right wheels up on the curb to allow traffic to continue past him. Ev went on. "She's smart, she has a healthy mistrust of assholes and a good curiosity about the world."

"She wasn't afraid of you," Paddy said. He'd watched carefully the way Ev handled her, the way he stooped to listen to her, the way he did not try to read every single sign to her. As a father, Paddy often felt obliged to narrate and impart knowledge endlessly, loading Melanie up with data he himself didn't know, couldn't hold on to. An appetite for learning things was not enough; he wanted to fill her full. She would embody his reverence for education. This, he supposed, was the result of his not having finished college.

"She doesn't consider me an asshole," Ev said, opening the door. "Say, don't you think you could just charge on up the stairs in this thing?"

Paddy gunned the engine, grinning. "Thanks," he said, truly grateful. "Thanks for coming with us."

"My pleasure," Ev said, unbuckling his seat belt. He'd climbed out and was about to close the door when he leaned back in. "Did you get that sack I left at your house last summer? Your dad's stuff?"

"Oh yeah. Thanks for that, too. I was a mess that night."

"Actually," Ev said, frowning, "you seemed pretty sane. I admired how you kept your head with that woman."

"What woman?" Paddy summoned the faces of nurses, visitors, the Oriental woman who turned out to be a doctor — Dr. Ono, Dr. Oh No. He couldn't think of anybody. Behind him, another big vehicle honked. Paddy waved, as was his habit, left over from his young life, when honking at fellow drivers had been a way of saying hello.

"That crazy woman in the parking lot. The one I thought was trying to steal my car. Remember?"

In an instant, she inhabited Paddy's mind, with her funny hat like his father's. "Oh yeah. Her. I wonder what happened to her daughter?"

"I don't know. But I have to say, I really did admire how you knew she was in trouble. I didn't see it, myself. I learned something from you." He was squinting at Paddy with one eye in a way that made Paddy uncomfortable. Exhaust fumes were filling the car; the truck honked again. "Sometime I want you to come meet my family," Ev said. "My wife and sons. My youngest is only a few years older than Melanie. You guys could come for dinner. You want to, sometime?"

"Sure," Paddy said. "Why not?"

"Good. That's good." Ev held his palm out as if to show Paddy his life line and then pressed the door quietly shut. Melanie, deeply asleep, clutching her killer whale with her good hand, did not stir.

Four

. . . .

ON WEDNESDAY Ev saw only women. He and Rachel called it Seven Brides Day; at breakfast, Rachel would sniff around his collar and make comments if he'd used aftershave.

Long ago Ev had acquiesced to his gloomy, guilt-ridden conscience and made it his policy to reserve roughly a third of his client hours for indigents, people in the same straits as his brother Gerry. Try as he might, he could not rescue Gerry; he hoped to have better luck with his clients, not his own sibling but the siblings of others. He would have to have faith that Gerry would meet with similar generosity. And was it generosity? Because Ev knew that his actions, though they *looked* kind, did not *feel* kind. He was pantomiming kindness, method acting mercy.

The dilemmas of the impoverished were not, in general, as tantalizing as those of the middle class. They seemed more physical, meatier and less cerebral. The poor were typically caught up in a conundrum of bureaucracy and bad luck, often topped, like a cherry, by violence, becoming victims or perpetrators of it. Ev had been known to babysit a feverish child while her mother went on a job interview, to hold the door against a brutal husband who'd come gunning for his wife. Once he'd installed a wheelchair ramp to a double-wide trailer in the dead of winter, when no one else would. His partners considered this the purview of their lesser comrades, the social workers, but Ev adamantly refused to find it demeaning.

And although these services were useful, it was true they weren't exactly tapping his expertise. The poor did not have as much idle time as the middle class to worry over parental favoritism, over marital peccadilloes, over general philosophical angst. Of course, the poor did not concern themselves with the care of their corgis, either. Their problems did not usually involve the question of *whether* or *how* to be; they involved more immediate issues, like custody and rehabilitation and recovery. He could appreciate this, the fact that they did not seem to be whining. But they also had a curiously fierce hold on their problems, an especially difficult time in abandoning them, which made his work harder. He did not like to be bored by them as they pursued the same stubborn path week in and week out; it occurred to him that his boredom had to do with their simple bullheaded dishonesty. They were not often interested in arriving at the truth — the truth was too frightening, too abstract. They were not interested, and not skilled in the imaginative pyrotechnics it might require to get there. If a man beat his wife, she did not possess the luxury of contemplating her own complicity; first, she simply had to get out of the range of his angry fist.

And then return, tearful, loyal to an innocent and fundamental lie: he needed her, she him.

Yet Ev's favorite client was one who could not really afford his services. This was Luellen Palmer, assistant to a fashion photographer. Today, during the ten-minute break before Luellen's hour, the time he usually spent making himself a cup of tea or glancing over last week's notes, he sat perfectly still at his little desk in the corner, pinching the inner flesh of his elbow. Why couldn't he feel this? He pinched his forearm, which hurt, then moved back to the place inside his elbow, the soft fold. No pain, no matter how hard he pinched. In fact, when he released the spot, a bit of his skin came away beneath his thumbnail. Horrifying. "I'm numb," he told himself out loud, then snorted. He quickly dialed his home phone. When Rachel answered, he said, "Do me a favor."

"O.K."

"Roll up your sleeve and pinch the fold of your elbow."

"What?"

"Inside your arm, the other side of your elbow, the anti-elbow. Pinch it for me."

"Yeah, and what?"

"Are you doing it?"

"Sure."

"And can you feel it?"

"Of course I can feel it. I'm pinching my arm. What is your story, Ev?"

"I can't feel it." He was doing it again, phone tucked between ear and shoulder, pinching the other arm with all his might. "It's weird, but I've done both sides now, and I can't feel a thing. My skin appears to be completely insensitive here. Why would that be?"

"It's your big brain," Rachel said. "Sapping your feelings. Most unyusular."

Evan smiled. Until Zach was seven, he'd completely jumbled the pronunciation of many words. Ev missed the *hambgubers* and *hostipals* and things that happened *sunnedly* or that *goed* instead of *went*. It was difficult to remember the boys as toddlers, difficult to reconcile their apparently grownup characteristics with their former naive selves. Ev missed their naiveté; he thought of Paddy Limbach's daughter, her little hand in his as they wandered around the Shedd. Maybe he and Rachel should have another baby. Maybe his father's death had made room for another family member, the way Ev's mother's death had made way for his two sons.

And maybe his numbness had to do with the circumstances of his father's death, his questionable expediting role. Perhaps he'd turned himself into a man without feelings. It wasn't his big brain but his tiny heart that explained the lapse.

Rachel said, "You've discovered a new evolutionary trick. You're being selected for something."

"Such as what? Intravenous feedings?"

"Show me when you get home," she said. "Show me where you don't hurt, and I'll fix it."

"Stop my crying or you'll give me something to cry about?" he asked. And wasn't he whining, anyway, just like his most irksome clients, dishonest and dull?

"You O.K.?" Rachel asked.

"Just numb."

Why, he wondered, did he not want to tell her what really bothered him, the other places he'd found where he was also numb? Ev had begun wondering about the deepening malaise he seemed to be suffering. He was unwilling simply to attach it to his father's death, disappointed to think of it as standard male midlife crisis. Some days he didn't have sufficient energy to stand up straight; he just slumped through those days. His life had been a persistent inquiry into the nature of humans, into their various motives and rationales, their checks and balances, their quirks and quarks. He thought he'd even felt suicidal before, but probably only as melodramatic entertainment for himself, thrilling himself with the possibility while understanding his true inability to follow through. Since having children, he'd no longer considered that an option. Now he felt more seriously frightened of the prospect, unable to hold his sons' bereft faces before him as adequate deterrent. He knew himself to be depressed. Shades of paranoia and apathy were afflicting him, lethargy and distraction, regret and anxiety, periods of time that genuinely disappeared without his knowing where.

He'd been out walking just yesterday and suddenly discovered himself literally miles from his office — say, three — late for his next appointment, going through a neighborhood he shouldn't have been anywhere near. How had he wandered so far? Thinking and, more alarming, not thinking. It was the not-thinking that worried him, the lapse of consciousness — as if he'd taken a nap on his feet, to wake way down on Wabash, transported deep into the South Side. He'd come to with a squawk, reversed himself like a soldier, located the defaced street sign, and then hastened north until he could hail a taxi. He felt like a befuddled old man, exclaiming to his indifferent driver over the startling terrain.

The last thing he'd had consciousness of was the word *bound*. Two of its meanings, he'd realized, were opposite: to progress and to be restrained. His legs had trekked forward while his mind went spiraling around an etymological corkscrew.

Shouldn't a man wonder, after such an event, if he was qualified to oversee the mental health of others, even those whom society has deemed economically unfit and therefore expendable? Maybe all he should ever do was build wheelchair ramps and babysit preschoolers.

Less disturbing was his current new habit of testing his emotional state, asking himself in many different daily situations how he felt. Angry? Happy? Contented? He found himself annoyed not only by the heightened consciousness this imposed on each and every moment of his day — as if he were his own biographer, narrating his life in order to find its point — but by the fact that most often he answered himself with *Nothing*. *The man walked aimlessly,* he told himself. *The man felt blank.* As if sedated. As if that scrim of significance that had previously sheltered him had been lifted, leaving him flat, without affect. As if the backdrop to his drama had disappeared. He'd wakened down in a neighborhood that had always scared him, one that he'd prohibited his sons from even thinking about entering, but, disallowing his anxiety about how he'd gotten there, he discovered himself not very concerned about actually standing there. His fear of getting shot or mugged or even heckled had evaporated.

The man was asking for it, he thought.

"I don't care," Marcus had repeated like a mantra between the ages of three and four, to which Rachel had always responded: "You know what happens to boys who don't care? A lion eats them."

Ev envisioned the open mouth, the big cat's ring of teeth like a sparkling ivory cage. Did the man care?

Was it the fact of his father's death that left the man without meaning? Had he needed the example of his father's unhappiness to see the scale of his own happiness? Had his life been a sort of taunt directed at his father? Or was he imagining his own death, the point at which his sons would be glad to see the man go, would gladly press a pillow over his face? The probability profoundly depressed him. He felt the cycle of the generations, how his own place in the great turning wheel had been nudged that much closer to oblivion. His living was not giving him much pleasure — nor much pain, it had to be granted — and aside from the grief his demise would cause his sons and wife, he had little to keep him from simply lying in the street and letting something large and diesel-powered crush him, put him out of his not-misery.

Was it his father's dark cruelty that had kept Ev a kind person? Had he lost his barometer? Had calibration so surprisingly left his life? And why didn't he want to tell Rachel about it? What preposterous self was he indulging, safeguarding?

Thus Ev entertained himself between clients all day this late spring Wednesday. Outside it thundered; the electricity kept trying to snuff itself. Lights flickered; the signal buzzer sounded erroneously and halfheartedly, like a misfiring synapse. His office was as familiar to him as his home; it held plenty of amenities for making him comfortable, for padding his behind, for soothing his senses, for bathing him in restful light. He had a stereo and a hotpot, a Persian rug and an ashtray. He took little naps on his sofa. He'd once offered to let Gerry live here, at least stay here on the coldest Chicago nights. But Gerry preferred being outside, preferred camping out on the floors of friends' homes or on roofs or in parks. And to be realistic, Gerry could never have figured out the office alarm system.

Luellen was Ev's last client today. Her problems weren't new, but the peculiar slant on them interested Ev. She hated her father — nothing fresh in that, something decidedly stale, in fact, in that — but hated him because he *hadn't* abused her. He had molested the other three daughters in the family — prepubescent intercourse — but not her. Why didn't he do it to her? This was her unanswerable question. She wasn't the oldest, she wasn't the youngest, but she was, probably, the least attractive of the children. When she'd begun to trust Ev, she'd brought in a photograph of herself with her siblings. The other daughters were blondes, big-toothed tan girls. Luellen was simply less pretty, a brown-haired girl whose ears stuck out. She most resembled the father, in the photo, and it was her ironic human quandary to feel competitive for abuse.

But her likableness as a client had more to do with her intelligence and quickness, her ardent honesty, than with her unusual spin on her family molestation drama. For example, she had noticed right away when Ev brought in the metal box containing his father's ashes — the only one of his clients who ever commented on its presence. The ashes had been placed discreetly on a bookshelf behind where his clients generally sat, but Luellen had enough curiosity about settings to be always aware of the one she inhabited.

"New box," she'd said.

"Ashes," Ev had answered, coming the nearest to intimacy he would ever achieve with her or any of his clients.

"Your father?"

He nodded. She had begun therapy only a few months before Ev's father had died. Her own father had died recently, too, which may also have explained his liking her, feeling comfortable with her. Ev imagined a club, the Dead Fathers, he and Luellen and Paddy Limbach as three of its charter members. Also, Luellen had the unusual distinction of being someone whose dislike of her father surpassed Ev's. Her darkness was bigger, her father's darkness was bigger, and together they had the charm of subsuming Ev's and *his* father's.

"Did I tell you what I did with *my* father's ashes?" she had asked, sitting down and tilting her head at its familiar confidential angle.

"No."

"My sisters and I each got a portion of them, just like in some dumb fairy tale. The first daughter took hers to the lake, on a sailboat, and scattered them to the wind. The second daughter keeps hers in a safe-deposit box. The third daughter buried them in her back yard and planted a tree — which died, by the way. But the fourth daughter took hers into the mortuary bathroom, poured them in the toilet, pissed on them, then flushed." Her eyebrows jumped in the way they did to punctuate statements. "You could do that."

Ev nodded. "I could."

"But you wouldn't?"

"Probably not." In truth, he could imagine doing it if his anger hadn't already been served by his suffocating his father, if the itch hadn't already been scratched. He didn't find Luellen's gesture that of somebody lacking sense or reason, just that of somebody seeking justice. Long ago he'd understood that the crux of his business, the slogan he would have to live by, would be *It's not fair.*

But Ev was not the kind of therapist who described his own experiences as a way of eliciting client trust or confidence. He did not want to bring more than his intelligence and sensitivity into the relationship. His clients frequently sickened him with their weakness, their victimization, their victimizing, their boring deceptions. He didn't like imagining the enormous normal-looking infrastructure that kept all the grossness hidden. Their secrets occasionally disgusted him, and he didn't want to touch them, or their problems. He didn't want to be so constantly steeped in suicidal or homicidal thinking. He was tired of the sameness of their complaints, the fundamentally flawed basis of his relationship with them. He was a make-believe friend, a paid listener, a bottomless pit, a pet, a basically blind confessional. It disturbed him that his clients might feel genuinely absolved; after all, he was praised for *not* judging the scrupulousness of their morals. They were safe with him, like harbored criminals; he did not report their corruption, merely took it from them, gave it shelter and them relief.

A *real* secret, though, must not be spoken, must never be confessed. Must worm its way around inside a person until it meant something. A person could tolerate more secrecy, he thought. A society could benefit from some repression.

He tormented himself on this subject for a minute or two, then welcomed Luellen, who always liked to begin her time with anecdotes from her job. She worked in a photo studio as a lowly set designer, which meant she painted props, moved scenery, sometimes posed as a stand-in for what she jeeringly called the talent. She always had a funny story to entertain him with before they launched into the familiar but abiding enigma of her family. Perhaps this was intended to make her feel less like a client and more like a friend, or perhaps it was merely a part of her character, her desire to please him, as if there ought to be something in their sessions for him. Ev liked to hear about other people's jobs — and maybe she'd figured that out about him. He liked to pretend, even to himself, that his clients' jobs had something to do with their problems. And some-times they did. Luellen, for example, had wanted to be a photographer. But she'd ended up as an underling, running errands, taking 'roids, sometimes being in modest ways creative. Luellen would oblige Ev's interest in her work; she was very sane at work, very talented and appreciated, something that cheered Ev. Her personal life, however, away from the photo studio, both saddened and repelled him. She slept with a lot of men. She had a kind of death-wish sexuality, picking up strangers, allowing them into her home, then not using condoms. It was a practice she kept trying to quit — "Yes, I remember *Mr. Goodbar*," she'd told him early on, "that old chestnut" — treating herself to just one picked-up man a week, or occasionally agreeing to go out with the same guy more than once, forcing herself to suffer through the motions of standard dating practices.

At first Ev thought her father must have molested her, too. Then he thought the man had probably not abused any of the children. Now he believed Luellen: her father had chosen to have sex with her sisters and not to have sex with Luellen. The father always determines the sex, Ev thought idly as he listened to Luellen, from the X and Y chromosomes right on through to adult preferences and perversions. And what constituted a perversion? he asked himself. It was a question he would never successfully answer. Mightn't the human animal instinctively mate with many? Mightn't Luellen's sex drive be perfectly normal, albeit out of keeping with contemporary prudence and paranoia?

But so much interfered with what was natural or animal. The oversize human brain, for example. The more you could disengage it, the better. Ev himself had never managed to feel comfortable making love in any house where his father slept. It had made his and Rachel's sex life awkward during the months the old man had lived with them, right before dying. Before even considering fucking his wife, Ev had had to tiptoe through his own apartment, an adult man, and listen for the harsh but steady breathing — "Darth Vader," Rachel had nicknamed it — that signified his father's deep sleep. Utterly humiliating. But not unusual, Ev knew. Many of his clients complained of feeling uncomfortable about having sex in the same house as their parents. That was one of the many confessions he'd heard that he could have empathized with. But he didn't — not to the client, not even privately. He might pretend to empathize in order to impress Rachel or friends, practice his miming altruism. But though his clients' troubles resembled his own, he did not consider himself among them, he was not *of* them, the messed-up humans. He was above them. That was his largest problem, he knew, the fact that he could not see himself as an ordinary man among others. That was his legacy; he considered it his father's curse, the narcissistic confidence in his own specialness, his superiority complex. It was not as imperiling as Luellen's father's curse on her, but Ev knew it had as lasting an impact.

Today Luellen told Ev about an errant generator that had rolled down a hill during an outdoor shoot, the driver who'd tried to stand behind it and gotten run over, which broke his leg and collarbone. She had a talent for storytelling, and instead of tragic, the event was rendered comic. Ev appreciated it. She dressed neither too casually nor too formally for her sessions, so that she appeared to have a healthy relationship with him, her therapist. She did not flirt with him; she did not offer titillating stories of her sexual escapades, though presumably she could have. She was only a few years younger than Ev, so that their frames of reference in the world were identical: they remembered all of the same national assassinations and vanishings; they hummed the same songs. They shared a cynical, passive, left-wing ideology. They both disdained smiling and sentimentality. They scowled at people. They deprecated themselves as a kind of competitive sport. Ev *liked* Luellen; if she hadn't been his client, he could imagine inviting her to meet Rachel. But even then, even in his own home in the role of friend, he would have felt slightly superior to her, capable of understanding just a shred more of her neuroses than she ever would of his.

His business encouraged this, he thought.

Luellen's mother and oldest sister were coming to visit her. Neither of them believed that Luellen's father had passed her over. The other three sisters had such clear memories — evoked only through therapy within the last few years — that the mother was convinced Luellen, too, would begin to recall. But what Luellen recollected was her father inviting one or another of her sisters to go places with him, to restaurants or movies or even into his study. She could not remember ever having been touched by her father in any context. He had not liked her. She was unattractive. Now she picked up strangers and endangered herself as often as possible, amassing a whole fleet of men who found her worthy. It was a simple equation. Ev understood her, and he didn't mind covering precisely the same ground with her week after week, because she was telling the truth, she was diving for the source of herself, never mind the danger down there. Ev operated on the premise that she was better than she'd been a year ago (he made a mental note to check his file on her, ascertain that she had actually improved).

He did not like to keep clients for much more than a year. He liked to feel that they left his office slightly better after their time with him, slightly more objective about their problems, clear on what they were responsible for and what they weren't. Mostly this happened, with a few exceptions; Dr. Head had remained a client, though only over the telephone, for more than fifteen years. Ev felt his usefulness for Luellen was about to expire. He would soon suggest closure; she would agree, because she was smart enough to know that if he recommended it, even if she didn't feel ready to quit, it would be best if she did.

"I've been working on figuring out exactly how I feel every second of the day," Luellen was saying.

Ev perked up; this was what he'd been doing. *The man felt kinship with his client.* "And?"

"Well, in the morning I have a lot of willpower, but in the evening I'm a disaster."

Ev sighed, recognizing his own tendency to lose enthusiasm during the day. Perhaps he would start canceling his afternoon sessions, going home and taking a nap with Rachel. He remembered to ask Luellen if the nights she had class were better.

"Well, until class is over, they are. Then I stop at Friendly's. And I don't think avoiding the bar is the best idea, although I know that's what you recommended."

"I asked you if *you* would recommend it to yourself."

"Right, well, I don't. I recommend to myself that I just *straighten up,* for God's sake, and stop fucking strangers. Stop feeling like I have to." She sighed pleasantly. Her frustration with the gap between what she knew and what she felt was large but familiar to her. She had a partner to call when she was feeling especially bad, another woman obsessed with sex. This woman was in deeper trouble than Luellen; she was a woman with two children she'd sexually abused, though she was now trying to stop. It was good for Luellen to have a partner in worse straits, good for her to feel *not that bad.* Like Ev's father, whose badness kept Ev's in perspective, Luellen's partner could be counted on to offend more gloriously.

Luellen said, "Isn't that what you'd like to tell all of us, your fucked-up clients — *straighten up?* When Meredith calls me, that's what I want to say. *Just don't do it.* What could be so difficult? And she could say to me, *Physician, heal thyself,* or something like that. We talk and talk and talk, and then we go out and do and do and do, as if the two things weren't related."

"It's very human."

"Like that's a good reason?"

"No." Ev nodded; she was smart, and she made him feel less bland. If she was lucky, Luellen would survive. And perhaps something about the men she chose illustrated her own self-protectiveness in operation. Perhaps they were nice men, or at least healthy and with some moral sense intact. But he doubted it. Luellen had told him she was afraid of being tested for AIDS.

"It's funny, but I'm realizing how angry I am at my mother all of a sudden. This visit makes me furious. I don't want to see her. I don't want to hear her tell me how bad she feels about our past. I'd like to have been born without her. Why can't I just live like I never knew them, either parent?"

"Same problem as before — head and heart in opposition. But simply naming the discrepancy is useful, don't you think?"

"What discrepancy?"

"Between what you want intellectually and what you feel emotionally."

"Intellectually, I'm fine. Emotionally, I suck. And I'm a big coward, too, because I won't just tell her how miserable she makes me, she and my sisters, all chatting long-distance on the phone about how I still haven't broken through, haven't unrepressed. They probably think you're a lousy therapist."

Ev agreed. They probably did. He wouldn't have exactly denied it, today.

"But," she continued, "you should be grateful not to deal with my sisters or mother."

He shared with Luellen a big skepticism about the literature her mother and sisters continued to send her, bestselling books that simplified matters to the point of pablum, that encouraged wallowing in victimization, the whining manuals of crybabies. Ev didn't want to talk about Luellen's sisters or mother; it was unfortunate she was at the mercy of clods, but why dedicate time to them? He had conflicting feelings about family, similar to his outlook on organized religion: had it done more harm than good, historically speaking? Had blind faith more sustained lives or crushed them? Was coping with bad family a test of character or an unnecessary expenditure of energy? In Luellen's case, Ev couldn't help thinking reconciliation with the family was a nearly hopeless prospect. There were too many of them; they seemed allied unfairly against her. He didn't want to talk about them today.

He said instead, "Tell me about the last man you picked up. Describe him to me."

Luellen cleared her throat. "Well, actually, it's kind of interesting, because he's also in the modeling biz, though I've never worked with him except this last catalogue cover. I picked him up at the bar near the studio, and he told me he knew who I was, that he'd seen me at the shoot."

"Did you worry about meeting him again at your job?"

"Sure, that's a problem, and I did think of it before we went to my place, but I hadn't seen him before, so why should I see him in the future? Anyway, the sex was only so-so, and I've been avoiding being anywhere near where he might be at the studio. So I'm a big chicken." She sat for a moment; Ev let silence fall. Luellen said quietly, "He was a premature ejaculator."

"Did you like him?"

"No," she said. "I can't like anyone who isn't a shit. And he wasn't a shit, and I didn't like him. And I can make fun of his eager dick, too. You know, sometimes I'm feeling worse instead of better about my problems. I'm starting to sound kind of hard-ass, don't you think?"

"No, I don't think. You wouldn't be here if you didn't want to beat this." Ev stared at her suddenly with a frightening clarity: he could see her as a child, an average little girl — not unlike little Melanie Limbach — with three pretty sisters. The conflict would have started so simply, with small remarks about her looks, about her being the brain rather than the beauty, or perhaps they said *beast*. It all took on hideous proportions, grew like some cancerous cell in the psyche, came to inhabit her at the expense of nearly everything else. A small seed, growing to devour everything else inside her. The fact that she survived at all overwhelmed him for a moment. How did anyone do it? He had an impulse to rush to his own sons, lock the doors, and hold them close.

Luellen had begun crying. "I'm so tired of thinking about this stuff," she said. "I wish I could just stop thinking about it and start thinking about other things."

"What things?"

"I don't know. What do you think about? What does a normal person think about?"

"I think about the exact same things you do," Ev told her. "I think about my father. I blame him and forgive him and blame him and forgive him. I get tired of my problems. I fall asleep hoping I'll have an interesting dream. I look forward to sleep, then can't actually fall asleep. Like that." Ev put his hand to his forehead and swept it over his hair, feeling as he did so his father's head, the surprising way his father's head, in the hospital immediately following death, had felt just like his own. Now he had a curious dislocation when he felt his own head, as if he were touching both his father and himself simultaneously. Every time it gave him a small shock.

"I think about words," he added. "I was thinking about an oxymoron this morning — *casual sex.*" He stopped. Maybe Luellen wouldn't think of this as an oxymoron at all. "And *recover,* which seems to mean two opposite things — to find, and also to cover again." *Nuclear* and *unclear,* he might have continued, just two funny words.

"Uh-huh," Luellen said, uninterested. It was so rare to find someone fascinated by your fascination. That was one thing Evan had always appreciated about Rachel; she pretty cheerfully tried to follow along.

"You like your kids?" Luellen suddenly asked. "I mean, you think having kids is a good idea?"

Evan sighed. This can of worms was a troublesome one, especially in cases of abuse. There were only three kinds of parent to be: good, bad, or good and bad.

"For some people," he said. "It's true children can be thorough distracters from problems. Better than other addictions. They're kind of friendly addictions."

"I was thinking I ought to get pregnant. My sister the anorexic got over her anorexia by getting pregnant. You know, hatched her own higher being. I was thinking I might stop fucking around, stop drinking, all my dirty little habits. Maybe it'd help me get over my dad."

"It might."

"Of course, I'm probably not even fertile anymore, forty-two years old. My uterus probably looks like a saggy saddlebag. But will you do me a favor and think about that? Will you think a lot about my having a baby? So we can talk about it next time? I can tell you're about to cut me off, so I want to have just a few more conversations about what to do next, O.K.?"

"I won't cut you off," Evan assured her.

"Yeah, yeah, yeah." She stood abruptly; Ev joined her and walked her out to the waiting area. Clarissa, the office receptionist, had gone home. His partners, Lydia and Jean, had also left. Downstairs, the hairdressers would be sweeping up the clipped curls, the foyer would smell of mousse and shampoo and ammonia. Outside it was growing dark; a spring wind sent eddies of loose trash down the street; cold rain waited in the air. Luellen felt like a friend today. Ev was tempted to tell her she'd be a good mother, because she probably would be. And it would help her to hear it, he knew, in dealing with her own mother, who was coming tomorrow. But she was addicted to a dangerous lifestyle and had sex nearly every night with strangers; he wouldn't accept responsibility for her becoming suddenly pregnant, on the chance that his praise might be understood as advice.

"Take care," he told her at the door.

"Oh, boy, am I bad at that," she said, laughing caustically. "I take almost everything but."

Five

. . . .

ALTHOUGH RACHEL had agreed eagerly to entertaining Ev's new friends the Limbachs, she regretted that eagerness on the day of the dinner party. She had a habit of dishonest enthusiasm, of leaping into things without looking at them carefully. What made her believe she would feel anything but exhausted at the prospect of meal-making and sociable chitchat? Her sons were unpredictably rude, and sometimes the healthful food she and Ev cooked turned out badly, organic sludge. Besides, her house wasn't clean and she needed to lose eight pounds.

But Ev had been despondent lately, silent and frowning, irritable and silent. He was distracted and unhappy; she asked him one night if he was having an affair. He looked at her with such scornful disappointment that she was embarrassed. Her husband liked to think of her as someone above petty assumptions. "Not every problem is grounded in infidelity," he told her with disgust. "Not everything has to do with you."

"I know," she said, relieved, yet also more deeply frightened. Her initial worry had been that he had fallen in love with someone else — one of his many women clients, somebody whose psychological snafu had become irresistibly infatuating — and though there had been times in their marriage when this wouldn't have particularly hurt her, times when she herself had thought she might want to have a reason to leave, now was not one of them. The death of his overbearing father had created an intimate space, a susceptible pocket in Ev that she'd been certain she could expand into and fill: that dopey optimism again. They could become more and more of each other, interlinked like those twisted DNA ladders, molecular, inseparable. Their long marriage had its ebbs and flows; before, they'd seemed to inhabit those fluctuations simultaneously, floating apart, gravitating back. Now Ev was straying off, creating a wholeness through some other source while Rachel felt vaguely untethered. She did not want to go chasing after him, to flounder at his heels. She supposed she should be grateful it was not another woman. But what?

So perhaps he needed new friends. And she would accommodate him. Somehow during the day of the dinner party her hostess confidence came back to her. She hoped Paddy Limbach was charming, because she liked to flirt. She hoped that she herself was more interesting and jollier than Paddy's wife, because she liked to have Ev be reminded of how lucky he was to have married her. And she hoped that Ev would not fall into a sulk during the evening and begin to argue over things that did not deserve argument. He had mostly liberal views that occasionally lapsed into stubborn defenses of the apparently indefensible. Because his father had held a nasty and unfounded antagonism toward blacks, for example, Ev had developed a blanket endorsement of all blacks: they were never guilty, in his book. It was a flaw in his otherwise reasonable consideration of things. It was also something she could never tease him about. Tonight she would miss his drinking personality, the one he'd given up nearly nine years ago, because alcohol had softened him and made him silly and affable. Rachel could remember trusting alcohol to bring out his true character, and in truth he was a goodhearted, sweet-natured man.

In the late afternoon, she changed out of her sweats and into a calf-length black dress with a fat belt. She checked the time — four o'clock; she never drank before four — and then opened a bottle of chardonnay and poured herself a big sturdy tumbler of it. The bread dough was rising, the gamehens were marinating — stewing in their own juices, she thought — the salad greens were denuded, tossed, and drying on a pile of paper towels. Little pansy blossoms had been included in this bag of greens, something her sons would find funny. Piñon nuts had left their urinelike odor in the room when she'd roasted them, so she opened the kitchen window wide and switched on the ceiling fan. Her skin instantly broke into goose bumps; outside it was humid and brisk, weather like a fever: one moment you were sweating, the next suffering chills. So far, it was a sopping, blustery June. The lightning storms in the evening gave everything a familiar yellow childhood tint — tornado weather.

Rachel liked being alone in their apartment. She liked especially the fact that her little office space was now hers, precisely the way she'd imagined it, complete with a phone extension. She thought she could move into it and live for a while, as if it were a bomb shelter. Whereas the rest of the apartment was scantily furnished — Ev's preference was to live in a museum, a big empty space — this room was full of flowers and photographs and useless throw pillows. It reminded her of her childhood bedroom, of her college dorm room. Only in it did she realize how compromised her adult taste had become, how overwhelmed by Ev's. *His* taste hadn't shifted in the sixteen years she'd been married to him; his nature was to winnow away, to cull excess, to reduce everything to its barest essence, its functional minimum. He'd carried that aesthetic into every aspect of his life: food, clothing, conversation, friendship. He was a bone-skinny man with few possessions, little in the way of manners; Rachel pictured herself for a moment as the wife of Jack Sprat, the wife who ate the fat, who collected little useless bottles and dried flowers, whose address book listed people from more than twenty years in her past, the maniac collector compensating for a spouse's asceticism. One side of her room's door was painted the inconspicuous white of the kitchen; its other side, out of view and facing her room, was a sweet periwinkle blue. She kept it closed, the way Ev did in his study, at the other end of the apartment.

Ev arrived home early to help out, and swatted her on the behind as he passed. Rachel was searing the birds; she loved the tender white the pieces turned, like succulent baby skin. Meanwhile, Ev straightened up, throwing away mail and papers. He cleaned house impatiently, because although he insisted on tidiness, he did not think the activity in the least bit gratifying or worthy as a way to spend time. On this point they agreed, Rachel and Ev. The place looked bedraggled, dusty, and tub-ringed. Ev went through with a damp sponge and then with the vacuum, leaving the air filled with unsettled dust. Perhaps it would float around long enough to leave the surfaces clean for the evening.

"What do these people do?" Rachel asked Ev as he passed through the kitchen with a sack of trash.

"Don't know," he said, clattering down the three outside steps to the trash chute on the landing. Returning through, he added, "You're going to think he's a hayseed."

"Really?" She laughed.

"Really," Ev replied, not laughing. "A country bumpkin in a *Hee Haw* hat."

An hour later, she was tempted to laugh again when Ev's new friend handed her a bouquet of daisies and a six-pack of wine coolers. Bringing wine coolers instead of wine for dinner was the kind of thing Rachel and Ev's other friends might do as a joke, but she saw that Didi and Paddy Limbach were perfectly sincere in their intention of drinking the things, straight from the fruity bottles. Rachel was obliged to join them in sipping at one, a peach-flavored fizzy soda-pop–like drink that didn't carry any kind of punch at all, as far as she could tell. Its taste reminded her of high school, the depressing period of her life when she drank only in order to get drunk, and only things like this, alcohol disguised as Kool-Aid, the worst kind of drink in the world — and accompanied by the worst kind of memories.

"Inauspicious," she told herself in the kitchen, pouring the pink liquid down the drain, washing it guiltily away; from Ev she had learned to hate waste, even to this small degree, and though sometimes she wished for a big chowhound to eat scraps, she considered the wine cooler unfit even for a dog.

Armed with a healthy coffee cupful of stout cabernet, she rejoined the group. Paddy and Didi had brought their little daughter, a scrawny child who clung to her mother's legs and whimpered unintelligibly. Rachel squatted in front of her and asked if she'd like to see Zach's computer games.

"Uh-uh," the child said. Her mother shuffled over to the couch, pulling the girl behind her, and sat.

"Melanie, Mrs. Cole would like you to go play with a computer, wouldn't you like that?"

"She can call me Rachel," Rachel said. "I can't stand being called Mrs. Cole." Then she wondered how she would introduce her sons, who were late home from chess club and soccer practice, to the Limbachs. Was she supposed to say Mrs. and Mr.? Rachel felt slightly displaced, as if returned to her own childhood for a second, to that time before she'd learned the rules.

When Ev held out his hand, Melanie took it, surprising both Rachel and the girl's mother. "Come with me," he said. "We'll find toys." They disappeared down the hall to Zach's room, leaving Rachel with the child's parents.

"Your apartment is beautiful," Didi said cheerfully, sending her gaze on a cursory rove of the room. "Did you just move in?"

"No, we've lived here sixteen years." Rachel tried to see what made the place seem incomplete. The room was arranged like a gallery: walls of paintings with a coffee table in the center, chairs arranged around the table. Track lighting ran around the ceiling and beams of light shone on paintings. The coffee table was a kidney-shaped piece of glass mounted on a brushed steel sculpture. A naked young woman supported herself in a backbend with her feet and one hand, while the other hand rose up through the glass, palm open. Ev's father had once used her hand as an ashtray; there was still a silver smudge between her fingers where his cigarette had burned. He had a talent for finding the thing that enraged people the most; Rachel had pushed him angrily to his room afterward, banging his wheels along the way, tempted to stop short and dump him on the floor. He seemed always to be provoking her, wanting to see her furious, wanting everyone to reveal the very worst of their characters.

Rachel loved this coffee table; it was her favorite piece of furniture in the world. The girl's tense stomach muscles made her sad. She hoped Didi and Paddy weren't going to say anything about the table. There wasn't anything they could say that would make Rachel happy. If they'd loved it, they would have said so immediately, overtaken by its beauty and poignance. But of course they found it disturbing, and now they would have to remark on it, find some halting, compulsory piece of stupidity to utter.

Paddy knocked on the glass with his knuckles and said, "Somebody you know make this?" As if the table were a piñata or a globular lump of clay.

"No," Rachel said. She wondered what his reaction would be if she told him it had cost over four thousand dollars.

"Sixteen years!" Didi exclaimed. "The last place I lived for sixteen years was my parents' farm. Can you imagine living in the same apartment sixteen years?"

"Yes," Rachel said. "I can."

"You own?" Didi asked.

"Yes."

Rachel and Didi were nodding at each other, smiling insincerely, and Paddy was staring at Rachel as her head bobbed, his mouth suggesting a smirk. Why was he smirking? He was handsome in a way Rachel did not trust. His type, the jockish boys who always traveled in boys' groups — football teams, fraternities, Marine platoons, golf foursomes, paramilitary organizations — had always made her suspicious. They were too big for normal furniture; their knees got in the way; they wore their uniform du jour. And what was with that flap of blond hair he kept pushing out of his eyes? Why was his type always so cheery and cocky? What did they discuss when they were alone in their locker rooms and bunkers, wrapped in their towels, urinating in tandem? What did their sneering brainless chivalry hide?

He put his large hand on the sculpture's arm, dwarfing the woman, making her seem suddenly, to Rachel, younger. He looked at Rachel and smiled innocently. Probably he had received everything easily in life; handsomeness had a way of working like that. "Pretty," he said, of the girl.

His daughter and Ev returned with armfuls of old stuffed animals, ones Zach had begun to pretend not to need. Melanie said to Ev, "Make them talk." This was his sole child's trick, giving the speechless speech, and Rachel wondered how Melanie already seemed to know it. Although Didi patted her lap for the child to come sit with her, Melanie followed Ev's lead and sat cross-legged on the floor beside him, ratty animals dumped around them.

"Is that a real lady?" Melanie asked, pointing at the coffee table, and Rachel pictured a young model dipped in molten metal, frozen as if she'd fallen holding a tray of hors d'oeuvres in her hand. After Ev explained the art of metalwork, there was an extended silence.

Paddy smiled once more at Rachel. "Evan and I met at the hospital," he announced.

"Yes," she agreed, nodding.

"On a fishing trip, my father suddenly had a heart attack."

"No one could have expected it," Didi added. "So tragic. Peepaw wasn't even sixty yet."

"Peepaw," the little girl said sadly, without looking up.

"I haven't been fishing since," Paddy said. "I miss it."

"I went fishing once with my father," Rachel offered. "A hook flew right into my eyelid, like destiny."

He hissed with horror, the hand he'd laid on the sculpture involuntarily flying to his own eye. "Ouch."

"Yes." She nodded again. The hook had actually lodged itself in her hair, not in her eyelid. But she liked a more dramatic anecdote.

On the floor, Melanie arranged a semicircle of animals, all of them listing sideways. Ev had relaxed his gaze on the middle distance, absorbing rather than participating in the conversation, an irritating practice of his derived, Rachel supposed, from his day job. Rachel found herself still nodding, like someone with a quivering neurological illness, sipping at her wine, wondering what sort of music Didi liked to listen to while she drank her wine coolers. She felt suddenly self-conscious about there being no music on, about being barefooted, about the toenails emerging from Didi's white sandals, all painted a pearly peach, the same color as Didi's blouse and hair ribbon and pants buttons and damned drink, angry for absolutely no good reason that these strangers were in her home. She had enough friends. She should have told Ev that last week, when he'd said he wanted to get to know Paddy better. Making friends irritated her. It was so much work getting to the interesting parts of people, like peeling an artichoke.

"Ev didn't tell me what you do?" Rachel asked them.

Didi leaped to answer this. "Paddy here owns his own business, roofing. Right now he's working over in Naperville, you know that new subdivision around the Amestra plant?"

"No," Rachel said, finally able to work her head in a direction other than up and down.

"Oh, where the geese are? All those geese they had to spend so much money to root out of there? They were on the front page of the *Tribune* last Sunday?"

"Had to spend an arm and a leg," Paddy said. "Called it a wetlands instead of a darned swamp and charged the company to get those birds moved."

"Wetlands habitat," Didi scoffed.

"What'd they do with the geese?" Rachel asked.

Paddy smiled at her once more. "I worried about that myself. But they transported them right down the road to the fountain at the Plytel plant. Geese are ornery," he added.

"Ornery," Rachel repeated.

"They've got the ugliest tongues," he said, "like a man's fingers." He wiggled his thick pointer to illustrate.

"And I stay home with Melanie," Didi continued. "I might work at a day care this fall, when she starts kindergarten. Do you work?"

"I used to be a public defender," Rachel said. "But not anymore. I consult on occasion, some semesters I teach over at Circle, and I'm trying to decide whether to set up a private practice."

"As what?"

Rachel blinked. "Well, as a lawyer."

Didi nodded. "Oh, a *lawyer.*"

"Guess we won't tell any lawyer jokes," Paddy said, chuckling. Rachel hated chuckling; it reminded her of people who thought they had a sense of humor, the ones who had to practice how to find things funny.

"Go ahead," she said. "I love jokes." She did, in fact, love jokes. She would tolerate an evening with anyone who could make her laugh.

"I don't know any lawyer jokes," Paddy admitted.

"How about some other kind of joke?" Rachel asked, enjoying his discomfort. "Do you know any shrink jokes?"

"All I know are knock-knock jokes." Didi laughed, then added, "Knock knock." When Rachel was slow to supply the next line, she did it herself, "Who's there? Mindy."

"Mindy who?" Melanie said from the floor.

"Mindy oven — lemme out!"

Evan and Melanie toppled all the animals over, as if they'd laughed themselves supine.

"Knock knock," Melanie said.

"Who's there?" Rachel said quickly.

"Not you," the child whined, pointing at Ev. "Him."

"Who's there?" Ev said. Rachel abruptly stood.

"May I help you with supper?" Didi said, rising from her perch on the couch.

"Sure," Rachel said.

"Who's there?" Ev repeated.

"Oh, a little old lady."

"You can come, too," Rachel told Paddy, since he was poised on the couch as if trying to decide where he belonged. He followed gratefully.

In the kitchen, the Limbachs stood awkwardly together while Rachel pulled food from the refrigerator.

"I smell bread!" Didi exclaimed happily. "Do you have one of those machines?"

"Machines?" *Oh, a little old lady who?* Rachel thought. A yodeling joke.

Didi said, "A breadmaker?"

"No," Rachel said, working at keeping the disdain from her voice.

"Those machines are great. My mother has one. She makes bread every day, just throws in the mix, comes back in four and a half hours, bread's done. She's gained ten pounds since Christmas, which is when she got it, on sale."

"You could slice mushrooms for me," Rachel said, handing Didi the cardboard carton and a small knife. To Paddy she gave two red onions. He looked surprised to see them in his beefy hands.

Didi said, "I don't remember the last time Paddy helped out in the kitchen. His method of cooking goes like this: apply heat."

Ignoring her, Rachel said, of the onions, "You need to remove the skin." She enjoyed listening to him snuffle as he chopped.

He said, "You hear about the farmer who's so dumb he thought you spelled farm E-I-E-I-O?"

Her sons arrived home just in time. They'd met up on the bus, Zach thoroughly mud-smeared and Marcus carrying his chessboard, which folded and fastened like a briefcase. He was a perfect replica of his father, down to the frameless glasses that reflected surfaces and hid his eyes. It had apparently bothered him to sit next to Zach on the bus. They came through the back door arguing about humiliation, Zach's single line being "But I'm your *brother.*" He was ten; his feelings showed on his soft face.

Marcus said, "You didn't have to take up a whole other seat with your bag. That old man could have sat there."

"Say hi," Rachel directed.

Zach dropped everything — soccer ball, dirty backpack, worn textbooks — in the middle of the floor and said hello to Didi and Paddy, who introduced themselves as Mrs. and Mr. Limbach. "Why are you crying?" he asked Paddy.

"Onions," Rachel explained. "Move this stuff, and clean up. You're late. Marcus, say hello."

"Hello," Marcus said sullenly, sliding through the crowded room with his black case, heading for his bedroom. It would not occur to him to come to dinner without clean hands; he worried too much about germs. Perhaps he would be a surgeon, Rachel always thought. Or perhaps just uselessly obsessive, like most everyone else on the planet.

"That was Marcus," she told their guests.

"Mom," Zach said, reaching around her to grab a cherry tomato. "Mom, Marcus called me illiterate."

"And?"

He shrugged. "Just thought you'd like to know." He popped the tomato, spilling seeds down his chin.

"You stink, son. Go clean up."

Zach left his things where they'd fallen and thumped down the hall to his room.

Rachel decided not to apologize for her boys. Instead, she took the mushrooms and onions from her guests to drop them into their places and then declared the meal finished. She asked Didi to help her move it to the table. She directed Paddy to retrieve Ev and the little girl.

The three children sat on a long bench on one side of the table, facing Didi and Paddy. Ev and Rachel took head and foot. Bowls circulated. The Limbach child refused everything.

"Try a little," her mother wheedled.

"I don't like chicken," she complained. "I don't like these green things, either, or these toadstools."

"Mushrooms," Paddy corrected her. "Try one. Mommy cut them. And this isn't chicken, it's Cornish gamehens. From Cornland."

Rachel watched Marcus roll his eyes.

"How about some bread?" Rachel said, handing down a slice, thinking that Paddy seemed hatched from Cornland.

"It's brown bread," said Melanie. "It has raisins."

"Seeds," Marcus corrected her, leaning around his younger brother to address the girl. "Caraway seeds, not raisins. Bite one — it tastes like licorice."

"Black licorice," Zach added.

Melanie pouted as if she would cry.

Didi said, "It's very good bread. Mrs. Cole worked hard to make it for us."

Rachel, embarrassed by this, stood, asking Melanie what she *would* like.

"Macaroni and cheese," the child said, in a tone of voice daring Rachel to satisfy her.

"Sniveling thing," Rachel muttered in the kitchen. Fortunately, she found a frozen box of macaroni and cheese in the back of the freezer, its expiration date unreadable for all the hoarfrost. While it was microwaving, she poured herself another glass of wine, happy to be alone.

When she got back to the table, Melanie stared at the bowl. "It's the wrong kind," she whispered to her mother.

"Try it," Paddy repeated. Maybe this was his parenting technique, to be always the chorus.

Rachel's boys were eating in their usual way, Zach with a full plate he would slowly proceed through, Marcus with tiny servings he would rush to finish, his arms near the plate as if fending off someone else's fork. Zach frequently stayed at the table eating from the serving bowls, grazing, after everyone else had moved on.

Paddy and Didi seemed as confused by the little hens and mushrooms and piñons as Melanie did.

"Good gravy," Paddy commented of the sauce.

"Thank you," Rachel said.

"He sounds like a superhero," Marcus said. " 'Good gravy.' Like Superman, isn't it?"

Ev gave him a glance, in response to which Marcus ducked, as if struck. There wasn't anything in the world Marcus would rather avoid than displeasing his father. He behaved in his father's presence like a whipped dog. Rachel hated this about their relationship, perhaps because Marcus did not grant her anywhere near the same power over him.

Rachel had had enough wine by now to feel less upset with the evening. She liked her own cooking, even if her guests didn't, even if Ev wouldn't eat meat, and she knew her working part of the entertaining was done. The bread, a rye with caraway, was particularly good.

Melanie, under duress, had taken a large bite of macaroni and cheese. She said something with it in her mouth, and her mother asked her to wait until her mouth was empty. Instead of swallowing, Melanie removed the food and held it cupped in her hand. "I said, 'It's yucky,'" she said.

Zach, beside her, laughed long and loud. Like Rachel, he enjoyed being amused.

Ev stood, dropping his napkin on the table, and hurried to the kitchen. Rachel waited with everyone else, uncomfortable with his unpredictable impatience. But he returned in a moment with a box of crackers and a jar of peanut butter. "Here, Mel," he told her kindly, kneeling beside her to open the jar.

"I don't want to sit by her," Melanie told Ev, meaning Rachel. "I want to sit by you."

The Limbachs cried out as a team, "Melanie!"

Dinner proceeded in this way, with little or nothing besides Melanie's comfort and preferences being addressed. Rachel had never in her life felt so hostile toward a child. Even Ev, who generally did not coddle, seemed set on making the girl comfortable.

During dessert (whole wheat and carob brownies that Melanie optimistically bit into, then spit out, crying over the nuts), Rachel discovered that Didi was a Mormon. "A little bit Jack Mormon," she admitted, meaning the wine coolers earlier. "But no thanks to the coffee."

"A Jill Mormon," Zach said, grinning at his cleverness. He wasn't generally very quick about such things. "Because she's a girl," he explained.

"We know," said his brother. "We just didn't find it humorous."

"A Mormon?" Rachel said. "I don't think I've ever met a Mormon."

"Well, I'm not really of the church any longer."

"Huh."

"I'm not Mormon," Paddy said. He pulled at his shirt collar. "No long johns, and only one woman." He laughed.

Ev joined the conversation by mentioning that Rachel wasn't

Catholic anymore and he wasn't Jewish anymore. "None of us are who we used to be," he said, a line that Rachel decided to remember for later, for review.

"Oh, you're a Jew," Didi said, attaching herself to a topic. "Well, I guess I'd guessed that, the hair and the nose and being a shrink and all."

Rachel watched Ev. His reaction was only a mild pained smile, and Rachel's interest in the disastrous dinner now focused exclusively on her husband. What was it about Paddy Limbach that Ev found compelling? When she looked at Paddy to study him, she discovered him already looking at her, which was oddly disarming. He smiled yet again; perhaps someone had once told him that his teeth were his finest asset, that he should show them as often as possible.

"I've heard that Mormon women only have two career opportunities outside the home," Marcus said, for the first time interested in the conversation. "Nurse or teacher, the helping jobs. Is that right?"

Didi said, "I'm going to teach in a day care. My sisters don't work at all, they take care of their kids."

"How many sisters?" Marcus persisted. "How many kids?"

"Eight, and, let me see . . ." She rolled her gaze upward to count all her nephews and nieces. "Thirty-two kids — thirty-three counting Mel here."

"Oh my god!" Marcus said. "Can you believe that, Dad? And that guy, that Brigham Young, he got to the Great Salt Lake and said, 'This is the place,' right? He thought it was the ocean?"

"The ocean?" Zach said. "He thought a lake was the ocean? Kind of lame, huh?"

Rachel laughed. "I always thought Mormon men must have got together and said, 'Hm, maybe if we tell the women God wants them to stay home and breed, they'll believe us. We'll just have us some harems, and go hang out together in the temple.' "

Didi had laid down her silverware. Her face was red. Rachel realized that she'd gone too far and felt humiliated by her rudeness. Didi said, "Well, polygamy has been frowned on for some time now," then stared at her plate, at her untouched hen and mushrooms. The stems of sage seemed to be giving her problems. Ev hadn't cleared her place when he had the others, and now there was hardly room for her dessert plate.

"Frowned on?" Rachel said.

Paddy pretended to be chewing his brownie, overmasticating to avoid filling the gap. *A pall fell,* Rachel thought, dreamily imagining the conversation she might have later with her ironic friend Zoë.

Finally Ev said to Marcus, "Give us some imitations, son."

Marcus shook his head, tucking a slim brownie into his mouth.

"Marcus does impressions," Ev explained. "He's very talented. Show them George Bush, son."

"Do Arnie," Zach encouraged with his mouth full.

Marcus did not really require much prodding, especially from his father.

"O.K., here's George Bush," he said, swallowing, then tilting his head sideways and pulling his lower teeth in, flattening the air before him with his slender hands. "Now, folks, let's be reasonable here about this economy thing," he whined, shaking his head, smiling hollowly, letting the light from the overhead chandelier catch the surface of his eyeglasses. Ev applauded. Rachel smiled. Paddy and Didi sat, bewildered. Marcus launched into others without pause, moving from Sylvester Stallone to Barbara Walters to Larry King to William F. Buckley. He did a savage British accent that Rachel was quite proud of. Their guests, watching him and frowning as if he might be insulting them in another language, did not appear to appreciate Marcus's talents. Didi didn't seem to recognize any of the impressions; her openmouthed, quizzical expression remained unchanged through them all. She was revealed as not having a clue as to who the secretary of state was or why Marcus's imitation of Jim Lehrer's phony ingenuous lower lip was so perfect.

Rachel laughed until tears came to her eyes. The evening was ludicrous. She retrieved the liqueur tray from the buffet and poured herself a stiff brandy, then passed the clinking bottles around the table. No one else had any, and once more she sort of wished Ev would take up his old habit. After dinner, he used to enjoy sipping port. The effect of having a Mormon in the house was to make Rachel feel guilty about drinking, a response she supposed Mormons intended, and guiltiness made her want accomplices.

Marcus finished his repertoire and excused himself. Zach invited Melanie to play Nintendo, but Melanie was hanging on her mother.

"Maybe it's time for bed?" Didi said plaintively to Paddy. They made their goodbye noises — the gratitude and apologies, the compliments on the food they hadn't enjoyed, the apartment they'd found confusing, the company that had offended them, the promise to return the hospitality — then hurried away to the elevator. Didi's small bottom was the last thing Rachel saw before closing the door.

"If she's a Mormon, why doesn't she have a dozen children, like all the rest of them?" she asked Ev as they cleared the debris of the evening.

"You're just mad because you put your foot in your mouth," he said.

She followed him through the swinging door into the kitchen. "Fuck you. I'm serious, how was I supposed to know? What kind of intelligent human in the final hours of the twentieth century is a Mormon?"

Marcus, who'd appeared from his room and begun helping as a way of eavesdropping, said, "Who says she's intelligent?" as he entered with a load of sticky dessert plates.

His father spun at the sink, fork in one hand, dirty platter in the other. "You don't *ever* get to talk about our friends that way, you understand? *Ever.*"

Marcus deposited the plates without looking up, the tops of his ears turning red.

"You understand?" Ev demanded.

"Yes." He fled down the hall.

Rachel felt bad for her son, who cared so violently what his parents — in particular his father — thought of him, although it was usually Rachel who had to censor his tongue.

"You're the one who encourages him to be critical," Rachel told Ev. "You're the one who usually thinks it's funny. He always talks about our friends this way." She did not add that most of their friends were not such easy targets.

Ev didn't answer; his back at the sink was a tense and forbidding thing. His anger made Rachel furious, as if she ought to step carefully around it like a child. It made her want to taunt him.

After rinsing and stacking plates, he called the boys to finish the dishes. He stuck his hands in his pockets and disappeared down the hall toward his study. Marcus, in his absence, took a huge bite of leftover meat, then pulled the messy wad from his mouth to say, "Yucky! I hate everything but mac and cheese, and not *your* mac and cheese, only a special kind of mac and cheese, princess mac and cheese!" Zach giggled, and Rachel, though she ought to have done otherwise, joined them. "Oh, I just *knew* you were a Jew," Marcus went on, "with that *nose,* or do you call it a *schnoz?*" In his regular voice, he said, "She was dumb. Are they really your friends?"

"Yeah, Mom, who are they?"

"Mr. Limbach's father died at the same time your grandfather did. That's how your dad met Paddy. Mr. Limbach."

"So what?" Marcus said.

"Ask your father," she answered. "And don't forget to wipe down the countertops. I don't want to encourage the rodents."

Rachel left the boys in the kitchen. She went to Ev's study door and listened to his silence. On the other side of the closed door was nothing but an easy chair and books and a stereo and old jazz albums, which he listened to with headphones, by himself. When the boys were young, before he'd given up all his bad habits, he'd gotten high in there, also by himself. He had a capacity for privacy that Rachel could not understand. This room probably replicated his childhood bedroom and his adolescent dorm room, the way Rachel's did hers — a comforting womb, a place to sulk or weep. He was a mysterious man, even after sixteen years. Rachel liked his mysteriousness. Liking it, she would have to accept Paddy Limbach as part of its continuing evolution. She touched the door with her fingertips, as if she might discover it to be hot.

Later, Rachel listened from bed as Ev received his nightly call from Dr. Head. He adopted a particular tone for this phone call every evening, a smooth, patient voice, fully accepting and forgiving, dispensing a lulling benediction to a troubled old man. "No doubt," Ev said to Dr. Head, "but that needn't bother you."

"What?" Rachel asked him when he came to bed. When he didn't answer, she repeated herself, stubbornly pretending it was an average evening.

"The post office," Ev told her, pulling off his socks. "They're withholding his letters so that his family can't reach him."

"His family doesn't use phones? *He* certainly uses the phone."

Ev didn't respond; he continued undressing slowly, throwing items across the room into the hamper.

"Don't be angry," Rachel said. "Please don't be angry with me."

"I'm not angry with you," Ev said. "It was just an awkward evening. It was my fault." He stretched out naked on the bed and tossed the pillow onto the floor. His chest hair had turned gray lately, to match his eyebrows, but his pubic hair retained its black shine. "Did you find Paddy attractive?"

"No," Rachel said without hesitating, pushing away the image of Paddy's smile. "He's so typically handsome, like an L. L. Bean guy, like an L. L. *Bean* — so empty in the eyes, so looking-into-space-with-a-vacuous-expression."

"You think he's vacant?"

"Like a legume. Like a trout."

"No sexual tension whatsoever?"

"None. How about you, with Didi?"

"Kind of Didi-like, isn't she?"

"Very." Rachel sighed, relieved they agreed about Didi, and switched off the lamp. In the dark, she moved closer to Ev's naked heat. "Why do you like them?"

"I don't know that I do like her, but Paddy interests me. There's something about him I'm drawn to. You didn't think he was sexy?"

"No. I just didn't find him attractive, to me not interesting. *You* find him sexy?"

"No, I don't find him sexy." He was silent a moment. "I find him simple. I find him kind."

"An idiot savant," Rachel said.

"Possibly."

They frequently revealed their attraction to other people. It was one of the things that kept them interested in each other, guessing predilections and tastes, talking about desires. It would never be more explicit than that: sexual tension. Flirting. Rachel had once spent a lot of time having crushes — on her boys' pediatrician, Dr. Nixon, and on a former college boyfriend who'd dropped her unfairly long ago, a man she saw frequently still and who she liked to think was sorry he hadn't recognized her worth. So she knew she did not feel sexual tension with Paddy Limbach. With him, she had felt somehow defensive, as if she would have to explain herself very slowly, as well as a kind of mean desire to provoke him, to make him display something besides cheerfulness.

No, the interesting thing was that Ev liked the man. Usually their feelings about people were nearly identical, their impressions so highly tuned to each other's that they would lie in bed after an evening's social assembly in a kind of celebratory shakedown of the various offenders. About people they enjoyed, they said very little. About people who incensed, they could go on and on. They might have scolded Marcus in the kitchen for questioning Didi Limbach's intelligence — they weren't trying to create monstrously rude children, after all — and later laughed at the boy's flawless aim in targeting her.

Not tonight. This was a letdown for Rachel. Ev lay quietly on his side of the bed, hands crossed behind his head, feet crossed at the ankles, radiating heat. Eventually he pushed back even the sheet, despite the chilly air. It was raining again; the blinds clicked against the windowsills, letting in damp bursts of breeze. Rachel, wrapped in a cocoon of bedclothes, curled on her side away from him, wishing she had something lightweight — a trashy mystery novel — to read, so that the little nodule of disagreement between her and Ev wouldn't keep her awake. Inside him, something was changing, and as far as Rachel could tell, it was a change going on without a concurrent, symbiotic one in her.

Six

· · · · · · · · · · · · ·

EVAN HAD A THEORY that all people had secret lives, ones
that went on simultaneously with their public lives. These secret lives
involved blatant betrayals — having affairs, robbing homes, hurting
children — or they involved squinting offenses, things one might
catalogue under the heading Bad Habits: smoking cigarettes, reading
pornography, shopping compulsively.

For many years, Evan had known of his own secret life without
considering that Rachel, too, had one. His included having a hidden
bank account, one that he kept for his brother. He had added to this
the fact that he had hastened his father's death, something he had no
plans of confessing to another human. Alongside these secrets sat
another, his correspondence with a woman he'd met six years earlier
at an APA conference. They were friends, and Rachel would have
understood that, but they were also more than friends, and it was
that part that Evan himself didn't fully understand. He saw her only
once a year, when they met in large anonymous hotels and sat together at the inevitable hotel bar. He'd never slept with Joni, did not
plan to. She would have slept with him, if he'd wanted to, but she
seemed content to keep things less messy.

Oddly, Joni was very little like Rachel. Evan had assumed he
preferred a type of woman, someone with large breasts and a sense
of humor, someone who liked throwing parties and having children,
someone with a stable presence, a wry clearheadedness tempered by
a dollop of sentimentality, a longsighted patience that Ev supposed

one might call wisdom. Joni came nowhere near that description —
a description based on his wife, Rachel.

Joni was small to the point of boyishness, her face crinkled
brown with fine lines by the sun, and she claimed never to have
needed a bra in her life. She rarely smiled, did not particularly like
people (in fact, enjoyed frightening them with her unkind wit), and
had had herself "fixed" when twenty-two. She was two years older
than Evan and never wore colors, only black, like a little widow.
She had dark hair cropped to the pumpkin shape of her head. No
one would have called her pretty, but most people would have said
"striking." She was striking, and precisely the person under whom
Ev would have chosen to go to therapy. Whenever they convened
with their fellow therapists, he realized this anew. He would choose
a woman and it would be Joni. Her expression eschewed bullshit.
Her demeanor said, "Get to the point." She was the embodiment of
the whole idea of "literally." It was possible that she literally had no
secret life. Or maybe her whole life was a private one, rendering the
notion of two lives completely meaningless, something Ev envied.

Or thought he envied. Maybe he loved his secret life the way
people love their own guilt. Maybe he hoarded it as if it were proof
of his uniqueness.

Or, Ev thought as he sat typing Joni a letter, maybe he bestowed
on her the qualities he admired, ones he could not seem to adopt for
himself. He had described his numbness to her in his last letter — his
boredom, his ennui. He liked the word *ennui* and had digressed for a
parenthetical moment. Joni, he thought, was his reader. She read his
letters without assuming he needed fixing. She was interested without being implicated. She looked at him, and maybe all humans, as if
he were simply another natural phenomenon, not necessarily a benevolent one — in fact, most assuredly not a benign presence. But
she had the great ability to scorn most of humanity. Evan felt like her
apprentice in that way.

Or maybe he was making up her character. Perhaps she was a
mere mortal woman, not so different from Rachel after all. Some
part of him understood this, some barely acknowledged part, and it
was that part that did not permit him to sleep with her. Everything

would shatter into a million meaningless pieces if they slept together — all the expectation and tension, all the forbidden longing that was so central to Ev's private existence.

Unlike his clients, Ev had no desire to confess his secret life. Instead, he retreated to it as if it were a closet in his heart, a lightless little room containing his life, a core of confidences like a box of chocolates he squirreled away, sharing the bittersweet morsels only with himself.

He did not assume that Rachel's private soul needed the protection his seemed to, although he knew she must have secret impulses. She drank too much, but she did not hide that fact. Evan assumed she talked about him with her friend Zoë, and probably with others, but he knew she thought of their family life as blessed in some way, above the average sinking tendency toward disaster. She had to fight her own smug urge to brag about it. Their children liked them, they liked their children. They liked each other. And though Ev kept in mind the narcissism such an arrangement was supposed to breed, he also felt that Rachel protected his sanity; he had a feeling that Joni could make him crazy.

Joni's letters arrived from New Mexico in recycled envelopes, former addresses and cancellations covered over; Joni thought stationery ostentatious, phony. She shared with Ev a hatred of waste. She wrote on a computer someone had willed her, an ancient model she attached to a printer whose daisy wheel had lost both H and R. Like most people, she'd fashioned a life for herself that accommodated her habits and desires, that was in most ways healthy and in a few ways not, that included a paying practice and a small house in Santa Fe, that included a friendship with Ev.

In July, a year after his father's death, Joni did not answer one of his letters. Typically, she wrote back to him within a day of receiving his correspondence. She did not play games, letting time pass or being sticky about taking turns. There'd been a season when she'd written to him too frequently for him possibly to keep up with — nor did he have that much to say to her. But he had been there to listen, and she'd written without caring that he answered only every fifth or sixth letter.

For a while, Evan assumed that Joni was away, or that the letter had gotten lost, but then it came back to him unopened, with a red notice over her P.O. box number reading DECEASED. Supposing that the tangle of former addresses and postage on the recycled envelope had confused some postal employee, he did not fret as he phoned her office in Santa Fe.

Her practice was a cooperative one, and he reached, finally, one of her partners. From the way the secretary handled the call, he knew Joni had died — people gave themselves away so subtly, in the barest of inflections, in the most minute mistiming — but he waited until the partner came on the line.

"A letter was returned to me," Ev said, the first time he'd mentioned his letter-writing aloud to anyone except Joni herself.

"I'm sorry you had to find out that way," the man answered. Evan pictured him bearded, wearing those hideous sandals he imagined everyone in Santa Fe wore. "She had a hiking accident, up in Colorado."

"What happened?"

"She fell. She was at about eleven thousand feet and it was still a little icy — this was last month. Apparently she slid, tumbled down some slide rock, and then free-fell. It was quick. I'm sorry, I thought her friends had all been contacted."

What friends? Ev wanted to ask. He thought of himself as her only one, though of course that was laughable. "Who was she hiking with?" he asked suddenly. He could sense the man's need to get off the phone, the busyness at the other end — all the crazy Santa Feans with their crystals and purebred hairless cats — but he wasn't willing yet to give up this last contact with Joni.

"She was alone," the partner said. "All by herself where she shouldn't have been by herself. If you want, I can send you the article about the accident."

Evan gave him his office address and hung up. He sat with his elbows on his blotter, his hands useless by his temples. The last time he had seen her had been in March, in New York, the two of them at a piano bar debating whether the player wore a wig or not. She had toasted Ev's abstinence with her own double Glenlivet neat, followed by a glass of icewater. She liked very simple silver rings, one on every finger, including her thumbs, a couple on her toes. She wore no bra; her hair conformed to the roundness of her head; she had a mole on her earlobe like a raisin, a faint mustache of downy hair on her lip, a thin band of white skin across her nose, a way of smiling and blinking her dark eyes that alluded to sex without promising a thing. He summoned this image as if to hold on to it; it was the last one, and he needed it. She'd been seductive because Ev wouldn't permit himself to achieve her. And now she was gone. How could he mourn her? There wasn't a soul to tell, no one who would quite understand; the closet in his heart was suddenly a deep well and no place to seek solace. He felt death's big blankness once more, the same feeling he'd experienced for a brief second when his father died, the lightness, the sense of being less attached to the world — and of having brought it on himself.

He had failed her, he thought, panicking. He had done or not done, said or failed to say, felt or refused to feel *something,* some crucial thing. It was familiar, this spacious sense of responsibility, of fatal failure. A man without feelings, the numb man, cannot be expected to feel for others. Sensitivity appeared to have drained from him. Ev quickly took inventory of his other relationships, of people who might be faltering because he'd forgotten to properly care.

And then the image of Paddy Limbach appeared, his lumbering manner like an anchor. Ev remembered the curious comfort Paddy had produced in him the night of his father's death. It wasn't exactly that Paddy had been disappointing in other circumstances, it was just that he had been a particular help in the face of death. Paddy's grief was so pure, Evan thought, it was as if he suffered enough for two people. Or maybe Ev was constructing Paddy's character to suit his own needs? No matter. He resorted to his first instinct, which was to tell Paddy.

• • •

"I never liked those things," Paddy said of Ev's cigar, which bobbed between Ev's lips. "But my father used to enjoy one now and again.

You get those gummy leaves? On your tongue?" They reminded him of eating dirt, picking grass from his teeth. The stench of the smoke always gave him a headache. But he sort of liked knowing that Ev had a vice, that Ev wasn't as holy about health as he'd seemed to be, and that Ev didn't want him to tell his wife about it. He was pleased to think of them as friends, buddies with secrets.

"It's an acquired taste," Ev said, blowing out smoke. "I haven't smoked one of these in a long time." He held the cigar the way a pirate held a spyglass, spying land, and seemed complete with his new prop, his resemblance to Groucho Marx nearly perfect, an uncanny likeness.

The bar was midway between Ev's office and Paddy's, a sports hangout with four television sets tuned to twenty-four-hour coverage of events ranging from basketball tournaments to bass fishing. Paddy had watched the fishing show with his father just to make jokes with him about the fishermen's methods. Paddy's father had taken pride in being a fly fisherman, tying his own flies, working quietly up tributaries on foot, throwing back most of what he caught. There was an art to it not everyone understood; there was a mysticism, a meditative quality, that Paddy could not hope to discuss with his fishing friends. It was this subject that he wished to broach today with Ev, as he sensed that Ev might be sympathetic to it as a conversational topic. Plus he wanted to talk about his father with someone who hadn't known him. He wanted a clean, deep response today.

"I had some bad news earlier," Ev said. "A friend of mine died, sometime last month, and I didn't find out until today."

"Oh, drag," Paddy offered. "A close friend?"

"Very close. A woman I've known for six years."

Paddy frowned. Although he liked the cigar secret, he didn't want to discover that Evan had affairs. He'd thought of Ev's and Rachel's marriage as something to aspire toward; he'd been having serious doubts about his marriage to Didi after seeing Ev's life as a model. At dinner, he'd caught them exchanging glances, Ev raising his eyebrows, Rachel grinning brattily, turning her head away as if Ev had signaled something suggestive. So he didn't want to see the flaws in the idol. That was on one hand. On the other, he was thrilled to obtain Ev's confidence. Having someone confide in you was like receiving an undeserved gift: it was a mark of affection, of esteem.

"Six years," Paddy finally said, realizing it was his turn to talk.

"Yes. Six years."

Well, Ev wasn't going to make it easy to be his confessor, that was clear. He held up his drink — straight scotch — and then drank it in three swallows, something Paddy saw in movies but rarely in life. He said, "Want another?" and Ev nodded, which also reminded him of cinema.

With the second drink — scotch again, icewater chaser — came Ev's story. He'd met a woman who sounded like a dyke to Paddy, but she was someone Ev had grown very attached to, even though he only saw her once a year and they didn't sleep together. Paddy was impressed with Ev's ability to charm her. Women like her — Ph.D.'s with muscles, women who did not play girls' games — intimidated Paddy. They did not seem to need men. He wondered if there was a similarly independent category of men, the type who didn't need women. Even homosexual men seemed by and large fascinated by the culture of women, or, more specifically, the culture of teenage girls. Were there men out there who thoroughly had no use for women? Probably not. That was women's great advantage, Paddy discovered; men were expendable to them.

Ev was still talking, but Paddy had lost the thread. He listened to catch hold again.

". . . a suicide? I'm very afraid she killed herself up there, and I should have known to intercede, there should have been something I could do. Will you read this and tell me what you think?" He was pulling an envelope from his coat pocket.

Paddy took the paper, anxious about what he would say. Either her typewriter or her typing was of poor quality — letters were missing. The words concerned some article she'd read about depression. Then she went on about a rattlesnake she'd killed, or thought she'd killed, which had come back to life.

"I've heard about ducks and other wildlife doing the same,"

Paddy said to Ev, who scowled. "Here," Paddy said, shaking the letter. "This stuff about the snake."

"Right. Go on."

"Just nothing, I think it's interesting that it came back to life." The woman — Joni, he saw her signature at the bottom; she was one of those people who don't believe in capital letters — had jabbed a shovel blade at the snake's neck but had apparently only stunned it. She'd put it in the refrigerator in a plastic bag and then found it moving its head when she opened the door the next morning. *Then I used the axe,* she wrote Ev. *Then I learned the head has to be removed before you can be sure a rattler's dead.* Paddy wondered if that line was supposed to have larger meaning, either by Joni's estimation or by Ev's. He himself simply thought it wise to ascertain a wild animal's death before putting it in your refrigerator.

The remainder of the letter concerned an upcoming trip, and the last line was *I am extra in your life, Ev, I know that, but you are extraordinary in mine.* Nice line. Paddy liked that sentiment. He thought she had a way with words.

"My question is," Ev said, refolding the letter and slipping it back where it'd come from, "should I have known something from that letter? Should I have done something?"

"You're thinking she took her own life?" Paddy was stalling, asking questions to keep from making statements.

Ev slowly closed his eyes, then opened them. "Precisely," he said.

"I don't see how you could have told from that letter that she was all that sad. She talks about that depressing article, but that's her business, right? And the snake, well, she made it sound like an outdoor adventure, not a — what's the word? — an omen. I don't know, the very last line, maybe that's the ticket."

"That 'extraordinary' thing? That?" When Paddy nodded, Ev went on. "I thought the same thing. Maybe I should have heard a cry for help."

The line had seemed poetical and possibly portentous, but Paddy suddenly realized that his role here was to convince Ev he was not responsible for Joni's death, even if he was. So what if he was?

What good would it do him to take the blame now? Paddy revised his image of the woman; she was not a dyke but in love with Evan, who was married and unavailable, who was tempted by her but saintly. She'd killed herself because she realized the hopelessness of the relationship. She'd sent Ev a letter to terrorize him, to make him guilty. A manipulator, a menace from the grave.

Paddy said, "You're not responsible." But then he thought his interpretation could be a lie. The truth could be that Evan had been leading her on for six years, promising to extricate himself from his marriage, meet her in the West, and marry her. Perhaps they'd been sleeping together all these years; perhaps Ev had used her. She'd killed herself out of despair, for him. "There's nothing you could have done," Paddy went on, thinking that perhaps Ev should have left his wife, gone to New Mexico, saved the woman. "How could you possibly keep her from killing herself? That's like thinking you could keep me from having a car accident on the way home, knock wood." He knocked the tabletop with his knuckles, hoping he hadn't jinxed himself, vaguely curious as to how much wood the Formica-covered surface had in it.

Ev was nodding thoughtfully, his cigar riding on his thin lower lip. Paddy reached for some more helpful phrases. "You did your best," he said. "You did all you could. You have your own life to look out for." It seemed to Paddy that the more of these things he uttered, the more of them came rushing forward. Maybe this was all it took to be a psychologist? A stock of soothing responses. Didi told him he wasn't a good listener, but he felt like he'd done quite well in figuring out Ev's problem and pretty well in answering it. "If you'd gone out there, then your wife would have been upset. Out of the frying pan, into the fire." He almost told Ev he couldn't have his cake and eat it too, but he realized just in time that the gist of that one was off.

Now Ev said, "I can't believe she's dead. I can't believe I'm not going to see her again. I feel as if I played some part in her death. I really do."

And Paddy, for an instant, understood. He understood that Ev *wasn't* uttering the first thing that popped into his head, that he was saying exactly what he felt. He remembered Ev's declaration last year, at the hospital, that he would have killed his own father; he remembered his rudeness to the photographer at the Shedd. It was both exhilarating and exhausting to be with someone like Ev, someone who didn't seem to lie, not even to be polite, not even to himself. This made Paddy wonder how honest he, Paddy, was being with himself. What lies was he telling himself? How deluded was he?

"You couldn't have saved her," Paddy said, this time meaning exactly what he said. "She had a choice, and she made it. And if she was thinking about you, well, she decided to hurt you. That's her hurting you, not you hurting her." Paddy was proud of this. He'd given himself goose bumps.

But Ev just sighed. That vein in his temple was standing out, and his curly hair was pressed flat on one side. He needed a shave, and his face signaled impatience, boredom. His cigar had gone out and his glass was empty.

"You want another?" Paddy asked, and Ev shook his head. The intimacy between them was fading rapidly.

Ev stood up to motion for the check, and Paddy jumped up to pull his wallet from his back pocket. But Ev waved away Paddy's offer of a five-dollar bill. "No, no, good God, no, I'll get it."

They emerged from the cool dimness of the bar into bright cloudiness. Paddy followed as Ev started walking south, both of them moving fast. To avoid looking a panhandler in the eyes, Paddy gazed upward. A flock of small black birds floated high above the street, swirling together on an air current, rising swiftly between the buildings. This sight calmed Paddy, as visions of animals nearly always did.

Evan, also looking up, pointed at the birds. "Look at that."

"Can't tell what kind they are," Paddy said, squinting at the brilliant haze.

"No, not birds," Evan said. "Charred stuff. There must have been a fire — this is debris." He knelt to pick up a burned paper. "Chinese restaurant. See the menu?"

Paddy studied the piece of paper — the crinkled plastic lamination, prices still legible, $5.95, $6.95 — then the sky. The flock was gone; now there were just bits of ash floating downward, right in front of him. He'd imagined the birds, seen them as if they were swooping far above the buildings, an optical illusion, the dissipation of which left him feeling oppressed by the city, as if it had won, as if the atmosphere had squeezed him, as if Ev had laughed at him.

"I liked them better as birds," Paddy said glumly.

Ev smiled at him and clapped him on the shoulder. "That's what I like about you."

They shook hands, then Ev stepped off the curb and thrust his fist in the air; a taxi swerved expertly beside him. "See you soon," he called, and disappeared downtown.

Paddy turned around and ambled distractedly north, passing the beggar again without seeing him, heading toward his office, though it was more than three miles and as usual the sky threatened some form of precipitation, either hail or rain.

Didi had said of Paddy's friendship with Ev, "Friends don't make you feel stupid. Friends accept you for who you are." All the way to his business, along the busy streets, Paddy replayed the conversation in the bar, the way Ev had nodded, then seemed to dismiss him, then disabused him of his vision of birds, then grasped his shoulder. He was as unreadable as a woman, Paddy decided. Then he frowned, wondering if his affection for Ev had any effeminate undertone to it. Maybe Ev was a homosexual emerging from the closet, attracted to Paddy, who had, he admitted, often been described as good-looking.

He watched himself in store windows for a hundred yards, his long legs and his blond hair. That dopey expression on his face he had worked at to change, but he couldn't help it, and maybe other people didn't concentrate so much on it. He'd heard it took fewer muscles to smile than to frown, which probably explained his incessant grin: laziness. He practiced keeping his mouth closed.

For over an hour Paddy walked, making plans to return to college — nothing vo-tech, something impractical like Italian art — to call up Ev and ask him how he was doing in a few days, to think of a thoughtful problem to lay at Ev's feet, one that he might actually need help with, like the one with Melanie a few months ago. He walked, not realizing until he'd pulled the glass door behind him at

90

Limbach Roofing that he was soaking wet, that water was dripping from his forelock onto his flushed face. Jim, the flashing guy, was waiting and laughed at him when he shook off, saying, "Say, boy, you'd think you were born yesterday or something, going off without your umbrella."

. . .

Evan considered the taxi ride back to his office an indulgence; he should have taken the bus. He was thinking of his secret life once more, of two deaths sitting in his conscience like an ethics test. There was a sinking ship and a confusing mob of passengers: who would he save? The old man he'd clearly sacrificed; the woman he'd have wanted to save, but how? And did he flatter himself with this sense of control? Wasn't he on the ship as well, the one going down?

He deeply regretted having drunk the scotch; he'd regretted it before he asked for the drinks. He'd drunk them in order to feel regret. He'd confided in Paddy in order to feel regret, too. He'd lost Joni, but he'd gained the confidence of Paddy. Or, more accurately, he'd handed over the confidence. Paddy was a questionable vessel for its storage, Evan thought, but the mere fact of sharing it, of opening the door to his private heart and giving Paddy a peek inside, brought on a heady dizziness that Ev associated with losing control: a not entirely unpleasant sensation, a guilty joy like alcohol singing in his system. He'd sent part of himself — a vulnerable part, like a robin's egg, like a lit candle — with Paddy to the regions of the blue-collar class, to the purely imaginary roofing business that Evan had constructed in his mind for Paddy to toil at, and later to the tastelessly decorated bungalow in Oak Park, perhaps even to the dumbbell Didi.

"Dee, dee, duh-dee," he said aloud as the cab jerked to a stop outside his building. He sincerely hoped Paddy would not say anything about Joni to Didi. Ev could not bear to have Joni's name, that fragile egg, that flickering flame, uttered anywhere near Didi Limbach.

He waved to the hairdressers at the Clip Joint and rode upstairs. In his office he sat at his desk and laid his dizzy head on his green blotter, which smelled of grade school. He'd thrown away all Joni's letters but the one he'd shown Paddy, one that he now covered with the letter he'd written to her, the smudged returned envelope. Two pieces of correspondence lying together, his words and hers. All his other letters to her he'd erased from his computer as soon as he'd written them. There was nothing left to show he'd known her but these envelopes, their two names pressed together here the way a child might press together Ken and Barbie dolls, a chaste burlesque of sex. Their names also sat near each other on the APA mailing list; her address, in her square, no-capital-letters handwriting, was on one of Ev's Rolodex cards. He understood suddenly the desire to pilgrimage to hallowed sites, the penitent's urge to occupy the space where his savior had last stood; these words before him were so incomplete, so flimsy. He felt the vast stretch of the plains separating him from where Joni had once been, vaster now in her absence, an emptiness without end, inhabited by unknown species, pitiless animals without names. She'd been there once like a goal, like an emblem of the future, a touchstone, a secret and a promise. As if she were the place he intended to someday go.

He pulled open a desk drawer and retrieved pain reliever, preparing for a headache. The container was a prescription bottle of Rachel's, and seeing her name — Cole, Rachel Eliz — made him summon her image for the first time that day. He had not been tempted to phone her, was not planning to tell her about Joni, alive or dead. In fact — he took his emotional temperature — he felt an odd anger at Rachel, at her healthiness, at her love of laughter, at her being alive right now in their apartment, sitting in her sloppy little room off the kitchen, that phony floral shrine to femininity, unaware of her husband's unhappiness. She indulged herself, he thought angrily. Then he turned his anger over in his mind — pandered to it, knowing that he would not bestow it on Rachel; studied it, wondering what it meant. The longer his anger circled, wearing itself out, the less potency it had. Soon he was merely confused, curious about the strength of his love for his wife, the dissatisfaction that characterized him. Did he love her, or was it merely habit that made him return to her night after night? Did he take her for granted? Was he simply afraid of being alone, like his father? Was his relationship with Rachel becoming one of those endurance tests, the marriage marathon, the fifty-year hurdle?

Was his secret life looming larger than his other one? Was he going to have other drinks, now that he'd had these? Was he going to turn Joni into a missed opportunity, into tragedy, into longing?

His anger, his frustration, reignited and flared up, but he recognized its source now. Would he take out his rage at Joni Breyer on Rachel? Was it Joni, off in unknown New Mexico with the cold-blooded lizards, who'd safeguarded his love, who'd made him choose every year, who'd kept him married?

After his last session — a disaster, a distracted parody of psychological methods, with a wintergreen Life Saver clicking around in his mouth to hide the odor of scotch — he picked up his phone and dialed Paddy Limbach at work. "I think I'm going to move out," he told him, sure of his words only as they emerged from his mouth, only as he saw the ease with which he constructed a plan. He needed to be alone; it was all he could think, all he could want. If he was breaking — bottoming, crashing, flying or falling apart — he wanted the asylum of solitude. "Can I borrow your truck?"

There was a long silence on Paddy's end. In that silence, Ev felt his leverage in their friendship slide; he felt himself allow it to slide, the way he had allowed himself to discuss Joni this afternoon. He had let Paddy in on his weaknesses, let him touch the soft, creaturely spot. He had asked Paddy for a favor. He was going with a flow that included Paddy Limbach.

"You want some help?" Paddy finally asked. "I got access to a dolly."

Seven

· · · · · · · · · · · · ·

"MOVE YOUR FAT BUTT," Marcus told his big little
brother Zach.

They shoved and rolled and heaved and half carried their father's cumbersome futon from his study to the front door of the
condominium, knocking against paintings, wroggling the rugs, then
flopped it through the hall to the elevator, clipping light fixtures,
barely avoiding the belled glass of the fire alarm. There they had to
punch and kick it inside while the doors bumped against it every few
seconds, like a mouth gumming the ungainly stuffed thing. They
were sweating on the way down the sixteen floors, Zach riding on
top of the bundle, Marcus pinned between it and the metal doors.
Marcus said, *"Now* will you consider using deodorant?"

Neither of them had moved enough furniture to know that the
futon was one of the most difficult pieces to manage. Marcus assumed that he was not strong or clever enough, that he'd failed —
as he often failed in endeavors — to discover the secret of easy trans-
portation; Zach, by contrast, assumed all activities such as this,
grownup work, were simply backbreaking, another adult fact to
assimilate in his cheery trudging way.

Marcus, who was too old to cry, had been doing so all week.
Zach, who wouldn't have minded crying, did not feel the urge.

"Move your fat butt," Marcus repeated tiredly when the doors
opened on the ground floor. The older brother was accustomed to
blaming the younger unjustly for their shared problems, and the

younger was accustomed to accepting it. He rolled off and they began the disgorging into the lobby.

Outside, beyond the glass vestibule doors, double-parked, sat their father's friend's Bronco with the emergency lights flashing. "Of course it's a black car," said Marcus sourly.

"I like black cars." Zach gave up and let loose his grip on the hefty futon. It fell, free at last, into its full thudding sprawl. "What's wrong with black cars?"

"*Heat,*" hissed his brother. "Pick up your end, idiot."

"Why are you crying?" asked Zach as they bumbled through the foyer doors and into the muggy daylight.

"I'm not. Can you believe he left it locked? He's such a moron." Marcus pronounced *moron* the way their father did; Zach liked to say *maroon,* like their mother. Although it was usually Marcus who took the wily route in evaluating situations, Zach sometimes displayed his own scheming personality, the one that today made him not altogether unhappy about his parents' separation. He imagined his mother would allow the boys privileges that their father did not. He thought he might get to spend the night in her warm bed now and then, for example. And he liked his father's apartment over by Wrigley Field; he'd been told he could ride the el there from school on occasion, and he liked to envision himself marching up the three flights of stairs to his father's new front door.

"Marcus," he said now, once more dropping the awkward bulk of futon, "we're going to have to carry this up all those stairs at Dad's!"

"No duh, dipshit."

"Whew," said Zach, shaking his head.

"It's so stupid," Marcus declared, tears in his eyes.

But unlike Marcus, Zach did not want to cry over his parents' separation. He knew they would return to each other. He asked himself, plopping on the crudely folded futon, what made him sure they would unseparate, what made him think there wouldn't be a divorce and some custody arrangements in the offing. (For a moment he digressed, trying to decide which parent he would choose to live with if they divorced. His mother's inclinations were like his: lazy.

Food and television and driving instead of walking. But his father could be very funny and frequently took the boys places children weren't supposed to go, like R-rated movies and pool halls. Marcus would definitely choose their father, and that alone could push Zach into his mother's camp . . .)

"We cannot just sit here," Marcus was saying. "Move. Your. Fat. Butt."

"Where are we going to go?" Zach answered, rolling off the bulk. They'd dropped the futon on the sidewalk and now a parade of ants was mostly circumnavigating it, though a few had strayed onto the brilliant white canvas surface. Zach watched as they meandered along. His brother snuffled, and Zach resisted the temptation to remind him of what their father had said about letting tears come out, about how dangerous it was to hold back crying when you felt like crying. He claimed you could get a sickness from letting sadness stay inside. Zach imagined his grandfather sneering at this theory, naming the tears of boys baby behavior. In the year since his grandfather's death, Zach had not once missed him; had, in fact, been quite delighted to celebrate his tenth birthday without the old man's vulturelike presence at the festive dining room table. His grandfather had put out his cigarettes in his piece of cake.

Marcus threw himself onto the futon beside Zach and said "Ow," rubbing his elbow and pretending to have hurt himself. This was so he could gracefully explain his crying. Zach knew all about it. He would have liked to tell his brother he didn't think any less of him for crying. He really didn't, but Marcus had a suspicious nature and wouldn't have believed him. In fact, Marcus would most likely have tried to hurt Zach for suggesting such a pathetic deception. They waited quietly in the heat.

Soon Paddy Limbach, their father's baffling new best friend, emerged from the building behind them with a load of books.

"Keys," Marcus said to him with disgust.

"Right," said Paddy. "Good job with the futron, boys."

"Fu*ton*," said Marcus, rising from the mattress. "Fu*ton*, not fu*tron*."

"You hurt yourself, son?" asked Paddy, lifting his mirrored sunglasses to peer into Marcus's teary eyes.

"No, I did not hurt myself," exclaimed Marcus, spinning away from Paddy. "Just my elbow," he muttered. Zach shrugged when Paddy looked to him.

"Well, let's load this honey up." Paddy unlocked his Bronco. "Whooee, she's hot," he said.

"Whooee," echoed Marcus unkindly. "Move your —"

"Fat butt," Zach finished for him. "I know, I'm moving it."

. . .

Rachel spent moving day at her friend Zoë's house. Zoë lived in Evanston and had a yard, unlike Rachel, who felt the need for a big sky full of fresh air, even though it was blistering hot and nasty with mosquitoes. All up and down Zoë's suburban block the window units hummed.

"I can't stay in the sun anymore," Zoë declared, leaving Rachel on the parched piece of grass, banging the aluminum screen door when she went inside, her own air-conditioner compressor hissing in the back window. She shared a two-flat she could afford only because it was located down the incline from the train tracks; above her odd-shaped yard the commuter line clattered by, an overwhelming noise made worse by the shrill whistle its conductor liked to pull in residential areas.

Rachel wore a straw hat and an old maternity dress; in the reflection in the kitchen window she looked middle-aged, like her own mother, shapeless and swaybacked. She held the garden hose like a whip, her free hand slapping the irksome mosquitoes, which were attracted to the water. It felt good to pour water into the ground; she'd been doing it for a long time. Zoë had baked popovers and made iced coffee, but Rachel felt restless in the house. Outside, they'd sat on the stoop for a while, but even that hadn't been quite right. She'd volunteered to kill dandelions but ended up with the hose in her hand, the cool water pulsing through. Beneath her feet, the neglected grass had grown squishy.

"Don't overreact," her husband had warned her five nights earlier, "but I'm feeling the need to be alone for a while. Really alone, living alone." He wore the look of bad news, of having reached the end of his rope.

Rachel was paying bills, swearing at the children's solar calculator as she held it under a light bulb. "Living alone?" she'd said. "What does that mean, living alone?"

"An apartment, another place, just for a while. I know you've noticed I'm not happy." He'd sat down delicately across the table from her, as if either he or the chair were newly fragile, and removed his glasses, which had the effect of making him seem vulnerable and frank, when in fact it allowed him to lose a clear focus on the person to whom he was speaking. In other words, it was cowardly, not forthright, for him to take off his glasses.

"Why aren't you happy, Ev? What does that mean, you're not happy? Put your glasses back on, so we can talk." Rachel's shock had made her continue drawing with her pen on the checkbook, a loop all over the page designed to record entries. "Goddamnit," she declared, seeing the mess. She was impatient with Ev's ennui; she wanted to tell him to snap out of it.

"Goddamnit," she repeated on Zoë's pathetic lawn. She pressed her thumb over the hose end and let a big iridescent arc land on the sunflowers, which were grotesquely huge, like something from the *Wizard of Oz* set, their blooms larger than a human face. Rachel aimed the spray right at their noses until they bent.

"You guys don't deserve my anger," Ev had said.

"Oh, please," Rachel had responded. "You think we deserve your desertion?" For the rest of the night they had done nothing but talk and cry, argue and weep. In the morning Rachel's face looked bee-stung; Ev left for the office without shaving, simply dipping his head in a sinkful of water and shaking like a dog. They'd embraced in the tired, resigned manner of people who've survived an emergency, whose emotions have been so thoroughly wrenched there seems to be nothing left to feel — big bland potatoes. It occurred to Rachel that it was this state that Ev had been trying to describe to her all night.

In this mode — tired, tubers — they had survived the week. Perhaps this explained Rachel's urge for sunlight.

She was startled to feel someone tapping her. Zoë handed her a sweating can of orange soda. "You like this stuff, right?" Rachel did indeed like orange soda. And Zoë knew she couldn't keep it stocked at home, as Ev didn't want the boys drinking it. Rachel was grateful for Zoë, grateful to have a place to run to where orange soda sat in the fridge awaiting her, grateful for a friend whose particular dramatic pitch was neither too high nor too low, whose own eccentricities dovetailed nicely with her own.

"I should have married you," she said. "You wouldn't abandon us."

"I wouldn't abandon you or Zach, but that Marcus . . ." Zoë raised her eyebrows. In fact, she didn't particularly like either one of the boys, but her skepticism was supposed to be a joke, so Rachel pretended it was. "Ev'll be back," Zoë said. "This is a midlife crisis. It isn't even a crisis, it's just a minor situation, a little pickle." Zoë had never been married herself. All of her relationships with men ended after less than a year, a fact that made her slightly limited in being helpful to Rachel concerning Ev and her long marriage. Zoë had never considered a man her best friend; she had the charming ability to see men as incomplete and mostly interchangeable beings, like household appliances. Her own solution to breakup was to go looking for the replacement.

Rachel could have called her married friends, possibly her brother, but she could not bear the thought of the spreading news of Ev's departure, the way the speculation would run, the way she and her life would become the subject of analysis, all of it erroneously facile. Or, maybe worse, all of it excruciatingly insightful. Everyone enjoyed other people's troubles.

"And you know who called me this morning?" Rachel said, outraged afresh at the leak she *did* know existed.

"Who?"

"Didi Limbach."

"Do I know her?"

Rachel explained. Didi had invited Rachel to *her* home, but

Rachel had of course declined. "Can you imagine?" she asked Zoë as she flipped water over the dry birdbath. "I'd rather help haul Ev's junk in the heat than talk to that woman."

"She was being neighborly," said Zoë wryly.

"She was gloating. Either gloating or nosy."

"Oh, nobody gloats or noses the way we do," Zoë said. "I think you're projecting."

Rachel smiled. It was true, and she was relieved to be standing in Zoë's yard admitting it. Together, they were as immature as teenagers — and Rachel had always felt she deserved such a friendship, that she'd been denied the small-minded intimacy of those years while she'd been deep into her tragic, sophisticated, peerless phase. The other girls had been busy scratching and hissing, and she'd missed all the catty pettiness.

Zoë was Rachel's friend from law school, forty-two years old and still single, no longer the beauty she'd been but now something more exotic. She'd grown into a different personality as her body aged, her hair becoming aggressively gray and frizzy, her hips heedlessly wide, her jolly sexiness candid and amiable. Rachel frequently yearned for her friend's life, the serene little flat like a harem of scarves, the artfully arranged satin clutter of Zoë's possessions, the address book teeming with international entries, the leftover income that Zoë used to travel the world. Zoë had made herself a promise to see as many countries as possible; so far, she'd been to thirty-five of them, occasionally during wars or plagues, droughts or floods, tromping intrepidly through her wayfaring life. She brought back currency and stamps and flags, wall hangings and garments and ceramics, slides and sunburns and strange rashes, frightening tales of parasites and hitchhiking and ancient two-seater aircraft and titillating one-night stands. Rachel's friendship with her seemed based in part on their vicarious use of each other's lives. Neither truly envied the other, but rather, each *pretended* to envy the unlived life. In this way, each shored up faith in her own path, Zoë in her wide global fraternity, Rachel in her deep domestic union.

For a second, Rachel wondered if her life was falling apart, if now she would inhabit neither a comforting family nor an intriguing solo existence but the disappointing hybrid, the life of the martyred single parent, the harried, single-minded frump. Soon Zoë would lose interest and abandon her, too.

The hose drained on her own foot. She had the potential to become pathetic.

"There's nothing to do but let time pass," Zoë counseled. "Nothing will make it pass more quickly, although I could recommend some videos, if you like, all with Arnold Schwarzenegger."

"Ugh."

Zoë's obnoxious cat sneaked through the privet hedge. Had Rachel been alone, she would have soaked him with the hose; usually *he* was soaking something of *hers,* purse or coat. "What's that on William?" she asked of the white tape he sported today midway down his thick orange tail.

"An infection burst. Want to hear about it?"

Rachel admitted that she didn't; Zoë watched her cat and absently asked Rachel, for the fourth or fifth time, why Ev was moving out. It was so simple, Rachel thought, to be a good friend: you just had to ask the same question all day long, like a refrain. Ask it, and then just shut up and listen.

"He's going crazy," she said, trying on a new answer, glad to leave the petulant William and his wound and Zoë's wasted maternal concern about it behind. Rachel found herself selfishly eager to discuss her husband — a *real* problem — and to reveal something besides the imperturbability everyone seemed to expect of her. Her sons had looked at her with identical open-eyed blank expressions when Ev had told them he was moving out, as if it were up to Rachel to supply the appropriate response. "He'll be back," she'd said to them, so that they could look mollified. To Zoë, she said, "He wants to be alone, he says — he says he's having a kind of breakdown."

"Has he seen anybody?"

Rachel scoffed. The last time Ev had been in therapy had been during his doctoral research, since his mistrust of and disdain for his therapist peers, coupled with his arrogance, ruled out counseling. "He doesn't think anyone can help him. He doesn't talk to anyone about his problems." Rachel wondered if this was true. "Except maybe this goof he's started hanging around with, this guy he met when his dad died, the husband of the woman who called this morning."

"And he's not having an affair?"

"No." Rachel paused. Honestly, it was hard to imagine anyone being tuned specifically enough to Ev's personality to tolerate him. He was picky and cynical, his sense of humor black, his aesthetic monastic. Surely only Rachel herself could live with him, especially now, all these formative years into his disposition.

"Do *you* think he's having an affair?" she demanded of Zoë, who, because she had them herself, might know something Rachel didn't.

Zoë made her gestures of retreat, the shrug and the wagging hands, as if to erase what had gone before. "Surely not," she said, taking the empty orange soda can from Rachel and throwing it in the direction of the alley. "Surely not."

"But in another way, it might be easier to understand if another woman *was* involved — then I'd know what the quandary was, what I was up against, how old she was and what she looked like. I could go on a diet or something. It's this *angst* I can't get a handle on, this melancholy. He's so listless."

"Like poor William's tail," said Zoë. "He's got no feeling in the back half, it just hangs around like a rag, poor thing." William was skirting the yard, warily attempting to reach the back door without getting wet.

"Could you water the zinnias again?" Zoë pointed and Rachel pivoted, still thinking of Evan, of finding him asleep in Marcus's room the week before, lying curled on the wood floor as if avoiding Rachel and their marriage bed. In his hand he'd held his eyeglasses by the fragile stem. Marcus was curled in the bed above him in precisely the same pose. Could she be angry at someone so obviously needy? She wondered if Paddy Limbach had recommended that Ev leave her.

"This friend," she told Zoë, "that country bumpkin, that lunk, that Paddy Limbach, Laddy Pimbach, the roofer."

"The roofer?"

"Yes, the roofer. The tarrer," said Rachel. "A roller, a shingler, an asphalter. The ass fault."

"Well, maybe he talks to the roofer goof," said Zoë.

"Maybe he does."

Ev had said, "I have to feel like I'm choosing my life." To which Rachel had responded, "Now you're a fucking greeting card? If I love you, I'm supposed to set you free and see if you come flying back? Well, to hell with that, Evan, to hell with that."

She'd left the bills and the solar calculator by then. Instead, she trailed Ev as he wandered around the apartment, moving into rooms and striking stances, then leaving them as if to block the scene more successfully. It was four in the morning and theirs were the only lights still lit in the building. Rachel was aware of their neighbors on all sides, up, down, south, and north, and kept her voice low. What confused her was the response she was entitled to; if he didn't let her know his reasons, how could she know how to feel?

To Zoë, Rachel said, "Sometimes talking with Ev is not unlike being on acid."

"Oh, acid," Zoë said nostalgically.

"No, not in a good way, in a bad way, when everything turns itself inside out and isn't what it is. When each mundane comment signifies something enormous, when everything is a microcosm, or a symbol for another thing. Do you know what I mean? I'm sure you don't." Zoë rarely said much when she was around Evan; she studied him, she claimed to like him, but she had little to say to him.

"You guys always seemed mated for life," she said. "Like cranes or wolves. I can't imagine either of you with anyone else."

"That's flattering," Rachel said. It did flatter her, though it also made her feel dull, reliable, and without sufficient imagination. "Really, you can't see him leaving me?"

Zoë shook her head. "And *you* certainly don't have flings," she said. "You just fall in love. I can have flings, but you'd just get hurt. You'd *think* you were having a fling, it might *look* like a fling, someone *else* would call it a fling, but all of a sudden you'd be in love. That's just who you are."

"A stick-in-the-mud, a wife."

"It's not such a bad thing." Of course, Zoë didn't believe this. She believed it was a terribly unsatisfactory thing. She herself thrived on flings, on relationships coming and going like comets, like fashions, like annuals. But Rachel liked her own solid perennial affections. She was fond of herself in regard to love, in which she fell rarely and like an anvil.

"Come to Turkey with me," Zoë offered cheerfully, without any hope of Rachel's agreeing. "It's almost the off-season. We'll buy fat pants and eat baklava."

"I'm allergic to pistachios and I don't have a passport," said Rachel. "I don't even know how to get one. I'm afraid of flying, afraid of leaving the boys, afraid of foreigners, afraid of public restrooms — those women's toilets? with the extra spout? One stupid phobia after another. I can't go to Turkey. International travel is like flings: I don't do it."

"Oh, a phobia of flings," Zoë said. "Isn't that interesting?"

"Yes. You know, sometimes I think it's just fear that keeps Ev and me from having affairs, not loyalty but fear. I think you're brave to sleep with so many men, to go after your passions, to honor them. Even the ones who are married."

Zoë laughed. She knew Rachel didn't really believe this, but it was something she'd become proud of in herself, despite suffering some modicum of guilt over her affairs. "Yes, that's what I think as we're humping away — 'Aren't I a brave girl? So brave and honorable? Won't Rachel be proud?' He'll be back," Zoë added suddenly, when she saw the wet gloss on her friend's eyes. She reached past the pouring hose to put her hand on Rachel's. Zoë's fingers were wide, freckled, and tapered, ending with smooth bullets of chocolate-colored nail. They were comforting, friendly hands. "He hasn't gone for good," she said.

"I know," Rachel answered, deciding not to cry. Even though she was angry with Evan, she felt she'd betrayed him, discussing his problems.

At one point in the long night, she had persuaded him to come lie down with her, in their bed, in the dark. Talking there comforted her usually. On occasion they'd lain awake for hours, after sex or before, chatting, playing. On other nights one of them would wake, possessed by the dreaded nighttime anxieties — insufficient money, mortal illness, a harmed child — and the other would reach out to reassure. Rachel had felt as if they were in the middle of such an attack, and said so.

"But what if all that reassuring is bullshit?" Evan said. "What if you discover not that your nighttime fears were exaggerated and melodramatic, but that your daytime sunniness was the lie?"

Rachel had stared up at the ceiling, seeing not it but the blurring colors on her own retinas. She felt as if she'd been turned inside out, becoming exposed and helpless.

With Zoë, in the yard, she changed the subject, hopping back to William's tail, which had been, it turned out, slammed accidentally in a storm window.

"After a bird," Zoë said. "Stupid thing. I can't stay out here," she added, patting her broad fair face and its various precancers. "I'll watch you from the window."

"You don't have to watch me from the window." Rachel aimed the hose at the upstairs tenants' rusty swing set and sun-faded plastic playhouse, soaking everything. "I'm fine," she added after Zoë disappeared inside. Cars roared by and mosquitoes whined. Rachel took the opportunity to shoot William with the hose. "Fucking cat," she said venomously.

"Are you thinking of killing yourself?" she'd asked Ev as colorless daylight returned. The elevator began humming as their neighbors left for work.

"I have," he said, "and I'm not going to do it, but mostly because I don't want to hurt you or the boys. That's the truth — I just can't see it as an option." They sat huddled on opposite ends of the couch, staring bleary-eyed at the coffee table, the woman with her hand pushed up through the glass. All night long she'd held her muscles tight; Rachel ached as if she herself were in an eternal backbend.

"You're scaring me," she told him, but he was also depressing her, wearing her out with the weight of being who he was. She recalled that her LSD trips had all come to this point as well: a desire to be done, to have the siege over. In the end, she was not unhappy to send him off to work, to fall into bed and rest.

Now as she flung another arc of water toward the privet and William, the flow simply stopped. Rachel studied the nozzle like a cartoon character waiting for the inevitable prank. Zoë had turned the water off, and crossed the tiny mulchy yard demanding to know if Rachel had finished grieving.

"I'm not grieving," Rachel said, presenting her dry face for Zoë's inspection. "Fuck him. Let him find himself, then he can come look for me."

"Of course you're grieving," Zoë said. "What do you think all this watering has been about, anyway? You've been crying on my lawn all day. Enough already. The place is flooded." Zoë lifted her feet in the squish of her swampy yard, moved close to Rachel, and placed a peck on her forehead. "He'll be back," she promised.

• • •

Alone in the condo with the last load of Ev's papers pulling his arms — had Ev actually *written* all these pages? — Paddy stood for a full minute ogling the Coles' coffee table. He'd been having dreams about this table. He'd had some hard-ons over this piece of furniture — the woman with her hand reaching from one side of the glass through to the other side, the bracing way she held her balance, her silver thigh and stomach muscles like a straining animal's, her riveted facial expression that reminded him of athletes in a seamless moment of perfect play. He wished Ev were taking the table with him to Wrigley Field; he'd like a chance to help carry it to the elevator, load it in his Bronco, embrace it in his arms, and learn the mythic woman's weight.

II
. . . .

Eight

· · · · · · · · · · · · · ·

GERRY COLE had once been described as a wastrel, connoting for his brother Evan, who'd been eighteen at the time, the image of a wandering minstrel wasting away in a carefree, drug-induced, utterly contrived euphoria, someone skipping along playing a brainless tune on a flute. Although Evan was only three years older than his brother, it often felt to him that he and Gerry belonged in separate generations, Ev with his parents' and Gerry with the one that followed, the one famous for never having learned restraint or responsibility, its males reputed to feel no particular desire to grow up.

"It's all or nothing with Gerry," Evan had liked to say, mock mature, pretending to have a grudging admiration when in fact Gerry's life revolted him, infuriated him. Gerry, who'd been earmarked from birth as the doctor in the family, could not even finish the vocational school training that would have made him a simple lab technician. He'd been arrested for drug thefts; he'd had his driver's license and his voter's registration revoked; his blood was so polluted he could no longer be a donor — and the only reason he'd ever donated was for the money. He had only two sorts of friends, those he stole from and those who stole from him. *Wastrel,* Ev would think, recalling their father's face as he uttered the word, the contempt in his eyes, the consummate dismissal: he did not love his younger son.

It became Ev's adolescent reckoning that he would have to be twice the son to make up for Gerry, to tip his side of the scale so solidly that Gerry's offenses wouldn't particularly register — an attitude in part protective of his brother, in part malicious toward him; the percentage of each, Ev did not know. He wished to disassociate himself, too, to join the ranks of the adult members of the household: the three grownups who would despair of Gerry's ever making much of himself.

But it was their mother who'd kept them a family, their mother who'd forgiven each and every one of them each and every weakness. Until her death, Gerry had remained at home, on the top floor of the duplex they'd grown up in on Diversey. His mother called him shy and goodhearted, a late bloomer; a few weeks after her funeral, Gerry's father called him a freeloading junkie and sent him away.

That Ev would always be responsible for his brother was taken for granted by everyone — first his mother, who had died comforted by Ev's steadiness, and then his father, who wouldn't again mention his younger son's name. Ev's duty to Gerry was held up by Rachel as an object lesson for their sons, whose inclinations showed every sign of leaning the same diametrically opposed ways his and his brother's did.

Here was his problem, he thought: he had reconstructed his early life — two parents, two brothers, his sons born three years apart, the younger one vaguely slothful, banking on forgiveness and luck, the older driven and humorless. Evan didn't want to be his father, yet he'd made a life that looked just like his father's. His father had died, and Ev had taken his place, cheerless and angry and unpleasant to be around.

He'd also sought the opposite of his brother Gerry his whole life; doing so prevented him from becoming a wastrel himself. Perhaps he had Gerry to thank for that. But of course he resented it. Evan knew all about his own feelings, but his intelligence didn't change them. "Intellectually, I'm fine," he heard his client Luellen saying. "Emotionally, I suck." He was furious with Gerry. He wanted to hit him when he saw the bulky, woodsmanlike shape of him lumbering along like a harmless, tourist-fed bear.

Evan moved away from Rachel in July; in October, Gerry appeared at Ev's office, his weather-worn face grinning shyly up when

Talking in Bed

Ev stepped out. Gerry sidled closer, automatically sliding his hands into his pockets. "Wallpaper," he said mysteriously, meaning that Ev had redecorated since Gerry had last seen the office. Ev stuffed his hands in his own pockets, as if the two of them might butt heads instead of shake. Gerry's appearances were seasonal; now it was autumn, and this visit was his announcement of it. They'd met most recently at the bank, in the summer, where Ev had withdrawn five hundred dollars for him. Gerry had asked for it in small bills: tens, fives, ones. He owed people, he said. He shrugged affably, still smiling, as if his debts came simply as the natural consequence of his character: he could not help them, any more than he could help the dimple in his left cheek, the recession of his hair, the vague limp when he ambled.

When they were young, Evan had lit Gerry's first cigarette and poured his first drink; later, he'd fed him his first psychedelic mushroom, razored his first line of cocaine. "All or nothing," he'd said as Gerry slid out of a chair at a college party Ev had taken him to. Gerry slumped onto the floor in a pasty puddle, face drained and nearly green: an almost overdose. Whatever moderating force exerted itself over Evan's life was completely absent in Gerry's. When Ev quit drinking, he understood that part of his doing so was yet another firm proof of the difference between him and his brother. That he'd taken it up again bothered him for the same reason: he was one step closer to Gerry. The proximity made him queasy.

"Come on in," Evan told him now, noting that despite Gerry's apparent lapses, he still managed to show up between clients, ten minutes before the hour, when Ev was free. "How much?" he asked when the door had closed between them and the waiting room.

But Gerry would not get to the point quickly. In the ten minutes Ev could spare him today, he would fashion a loose weave of topics, ranging from the political (what did Ev make of the upcoming presidential election?) to the seemingly intimate (a rash on Gerry's chest, itchy and red) to the ridiculous (had Ev noticed how closely an eggplant resembled a sweat gland?). These topics were pursued in a juggling and systematic method, one broached, then dropped, the next rotated in. That Ev had grown accustomed to his brother's style was beside the point; it had lost its charm for him, although others still seemed to find Gerry endearingly eccentric — "unique," Ev had heard one of them lovingly declare him. His own son Zach displayed what Ev considered a dangerous devotion to his miscreant uncle.

When Ev had reached Gerry to notify him of their father's death, Gerry had had a kind of seizure, grabbing at his heart, rotating on his feet, setting one heel like the point of a drawing compass while the other spun wildly around. The purely physical response shook Ev; his own had been so cerebral. This was the last time his brother had been to Ev and Rachel's apartment, more than a year ago.

Gerry found it difficult to sit down, ever, and now wandered around Ev's office, picking up things, turning them over, studiously avoiding the box of their father's ashes, as if he might begin an uncontrollable spinning once more. The clothes Ev bought him — *Rachel* bought him, Ev corrected himself, Rachel in her thoughtful way finding practical clothing for her homeless brother-in-law, hiking boots and fishing vests and woolen shirts, traction for the snow, plenty of pockets, warm and waterproof, thoughtful of her, genius — became instantly worn out and filthy. Or he gave them away, blithely trading them for a meal or a high or a lay. "I'm a generous guy," Gerry would say when asked where his wool sweater had gotten to. "Or maybe just a chump." Between the two, Ev thought, lay a very fine line, one he himself would never be likely to overstep.

At the bookcase, Gerry turned to waggle a wrist. A heavy bracelet jingled. "Got myself some dog tags," he said, muffling the end of his sentence in his sparse beard as if embarrassed. *As if, but not genuinely embarrassed,* Ev thought unkindly, then scolded himself. If Gerry were his patient, he'd have offered to hang up his coat, to make him a cup of tea, to listen without annoyance to his fragmented bits of friendly conversation, to insist, for God's sake, that he sit down and take a load off. He would be able to extend all this magnanimity if Gerry's hopelessness didn't seem so creepily to include him. He would be able to inhale his brother's body odor without recoiling if he didn't fear exuding the same odor himself.

"And?" Ev said, resting his rear end impatiently on his desktop, crossing his feet at the ankles, his arms over his chest, defensive and demanding — a posture he assumed against his will. His brother made him hate himself.

"Read it." Gerry fluttered his hand once more, forcing Evan to step forward, hold the metal disk, make contact with Gerry's weathered, dirty hand. Gerry's ring finger ended above the second knuckle, the result of a childhood bicycle accident, thirty-five years in the past. Evan had carried him home from beneath the el tracks, where it had happened, leaving behind their bikes, allowing his brother's blood to soak down his neck and shirt, steadfastly not caring when he returned to find both bikes stolen, knowing that his virtuous behavior would earn him another one, one purchased immediately; his mother would make sure to replace his first, because he was older, because he'd traded on his own noble behavior in thinking of his injured brother, the flapping fingertip, the shock. As soon as he'd lifted Gerry in his arms, he'd imagined his new bicycle, imagined his mother's pleasure in his selflessness. He waited several hours to return to the tracks, banking on larceny. Did he hate Gerry because Gerry seemed to know that he was not truly merciful? Or was he miscalculating, assigning Gerry the role of idiot savant when in fact he was merely a benign drug addict with a faltering neurochemistry?

The bracelet was for identification; it listed Ev's name, address, and phone number. It was literally a dog tag: *My name is Gerry,* read one side, and on the reverse *I belong to.*

"Used to have a wallet, then I lost it. Can't stand things around my neck," Gerry said, tugging at nonexistent neckwear. "Never have been able to. You think I should have this rash looked at?" He was opening his jacket and shirt once more, making a path through the layers for himself to peer into. "How about another hundred fifty or so? Hundred fifty O.K.? Maybe just forty-five, one forty-five?" He was speaking into his chest, the patch of acne that had cropped up. Asking for money appeared to embarrass him, but it also appeared to amuse him, being a kind of taunt, a demand that Evan would never deny.

Gerry's body odor would linger, although Ev had a functioning window he could open after Gerry left. He had dropped his brother's wrist and now plunged his hand into his back pocket, was counting out cash without thinking about anything but opening the window, perhaps purchasing a small fan to circulate air better, about his next client, a woman whose two children and husband had died in a car accident, who couldn't overcome her grief, who was paralyzed now with a barrage of fresh phobias and worst-case scenarios.

"Oh yeah, great," said Gerry, taking the cash without touching Evan's hand, which was precisely the way Evan wanted him to take it. "Oh yeah, this is the ticket, this fits the bill. You gonna vote? I was thinking of not voting this year, what the hell, make a statement, it never helps, but you can never tell. I like Bill's wife, I'm thinking of becoming Gerry Rodham Cole myself, what do you think?" He was buttoning his shirt, zipping his jacket, stuffing money in his pockets, pulling on a hat — not the thermal one Rachel had taken the time to order from a catalogue for him but a cheap Cubs cap — and was suddenly gone, precisely ten minutes after entering. Was it the exact timing that bothered Ev? Was it the tightness in his stomach as he watched Gerry gently close the outer door, wiping away an errant fingerprint? Was it the flow of what he should have said that would plague him the rest of the day?

If he were Rachel, he might cry. She had a brother she cried over, a perfectly functional human being with children and a job and a mostly acceptable wife. It was this emotion, this not-crying, that he took with him weekly to the racquetball court with Paddy Limbach. He'd recommended hitting sports for several of his clients in the last few months, having found it helpful for himself. When Paddy had suggested it, Ev could not have imagined anything more unlikely. But he now looked forward to their weekly games, to the unspoken exclusion of women. If Lisel Carson and her dire grief weren't already awaiting him, he might have called Paddy and tried to set up a game. Rachel always thought it was the money that bothered Ev about Gerry, but the money, the thing that brought Gerry time and again to Ev's door, was the very least of it. Ev felt responsible and guilty and angry and despairing — parental, as if Gerry had three instead of the standard two, as if Ev had an extra son — and Gerry seemed both to know and not know it. He came to collect payment on a debt that would never be satisfied.

"The wrong address," Ev said aloud in the middle of his session with Lisel Carson.

"Beg pardon?" she asked. It pleased her to have Ev mutter anything at all during her sessions; he was so quiet she tended to babble.

"Nothing, go ahead, I'm sorry." His old address, the one where Rachel and the boys lived, now swung on Gerry's wrist.

. . .

Rachel drank more now that Ev had gone. She looked forward to it the way magazine articles told her she shouldn't. The first drink relaxed her, made her glowing and somehow optimistic, happily miserable, gung-ho for her glumness. The next three or four dampened her spirits, but they also eased her like a shoehorn toward sleep.

She was prone to reminiscence, and now indulged it methodically, chronologically, as if she were old. She thought about when her boys were young enough to cry in the night, the way she lay in bed with them, cramped and uncomfortable, smoothing one's sweaty hair, rubbing the other's cold feet. How temporary it had been. How condescending she'd felt toward women who approached her to call her lucky, to warn her that she ought not to squander the brief days of her boys' youth. Now it was as if those tiny children had died. She thought about her husband's love, which she had apparently taken for granted. She thought, with genuine amazement, that she had felt too much needed then, as if she were the heart of the house, the busy organ that kept it alive, and of how she had often fled to the bathtub, locking her family on the other side of the door, submerging herself in oily steaming water until all she heard was the faraway clang of the apartment building's plumbing and her own selfish heartbeat. *You, you, you,* it said.

Then, she had felt stuck and frustrated, unable to be autonomous in the world, scattered like buckshot, little parts of her flung all over town, at day care and kindergarten, riding buses and trains with people who couldn't have cared less whose life they touched, short-temperedly, recklessly. Her burdens then had seemed sticky and warmly damp: tears and urine and feverish foreheads. She and Ev had often reached their bed at the end of the day as if it were a foxhole, a place to fall into and take refuge in. It could overwhelm her, once upon a time, such neediness and need.

And now she seemed hardly necessary at all. Zach and Marcus snapped into action every morning as if wound up during the night: they rose before Rachel, fed themselves, pulled on their jackets, took their bus passes and lunch sacks, summoned the elevator, and disappeared down the shaft into the clockwork of their day.

Rachel would rise later, restore herself to reasonable enough shape to attend a consultation or hearing, then return home and stare out her office window. It was a good view for thinking, she'd discovered. Although the rest of the building had had its roof replaced, the patchwork green and brown slate still remained over the elevator shaft, a pitched roof over a box like a cottage in a forest, complete with small, decorative leaded windows. When it rained, water ran over the stones like a stream, a small piece of nature for Rachel to turn her eyes toward: the Virginia creeper sneaking up the drainpipes, an autumn orange flushing its leaves; the water dripping unhurriedly down, down, down. It was a place where elves might be imagined to live, or foundlings, or a warty witch.

Rachel was assessing her life because apparently it had changed, veered around a corner and aimed itself elsewhere. She and Ev had modeled their life on nutrition — for the body, the mind, the soul. The bookshelves were cluttered with books on vegetarianism, nonviolent child-rearing, nonsexist lovemaking, socially conscious consumerism. Two thirds of the daily mail was always dismal left-wing solicitation. Ev's obsessiveness with doing the right thing had taken over their lives like a weed: it couldn't be killed.

Now Rachel felt furtive when she went to the grocery store, purchasing everything legitimately but slinking about like a shoplifter. Ev had left her, and it seemed he took their healthy lifestyle when he went. Gone were the brewer's yeast and organic apples, the wobbly tofu bricks and fat-free cereals; gone were the opaque bottles of viscous carrot drink. Hello, white baguette and boycotted green grapes. Welcome, processed smoked cheese spread, sitting arrogantly on a shelf, defying refrigeration. At home, Zach and Marcus would perch on the other side of the kitchen bar eyeing their mother with something like pity, tainted by suspicion, crowned with simple glee: food they coveted! It was as if they'd gone shopping themselves in a guilty miracle dream. There were even forbidden plastic Baggies — goodbye forever, embarrassing wax-paper–wrapped crumbling whole wheat gritty organic peanut butter and home-canned jam sandwiches! So long, celery sticks! Rachel unloaded what felt like contraband, thinking, *Their father has left them; what possible difference can a single-serving-size ripple potato chip sack make?*

Last she would unsheath three bottles of champagne and a six-pack of orange soda. She not only kept champagne on hand but found herself purchasing saltines and soda to combat hangovers. Was it pathetic? It reminded her of another time in her past, before Ev and the children, when she'd wanted to be thin, dark, and European and poetically undernourished, and had bought food she'd intended merely to rent: eat and then disgorge. This buying of hangover remedies struck her as similar: planning her bad behavior. It was wasteful and indulgent and, she supposed, sick. But she also supposed, when she looked over the stages of her life leading to now — happy childhood, grim college, happy marriage — that it was only momentarily grim. She may have veered down an alley, but at the end was virtue once more, sometime in the future. She would haul her cloth Save-the-World bag out shopping with her, she would purchase little baskets of weightless sprouts once more. In the meantime, she would look forward to having a drink in the evening and ibuprofen and Crush in the morning. Perhaps a sweet Danish or candy bar to go with.

She'd taken to watching television, too, thinking that if she had to have a new, single life, why not adopt a whole new country as well? Sitting in the quiet living room reading, as they used to do as a family, now made Rachel anxious — the turning pages, the militant mantel clock. Zach and Marcus were fascinated and dismayed when she cozied up to the commercial networks; previously they had been allowed to watch only what Marcus called the whale channel, PBS. Rachel was weary of public broadcasting, tired of the British narrators on TV, tired of their stepchildren, the sonorous, self-important radio announcers with their tongue-twisting classical composers. *Bleah,* she thought.

In the late evenings, after her sons had wound down and fallen asleep, when the standup cable comedians were through, when the Chicago street beneath her window was empty of bundled neighbors, Rachel would consider her plight sentimentally, drinking champagne. The bottle's silhouette on the coffee table pleased her. She felt like a has-been beauty from a 1940s movie, tossed and wry. Champagne, contrary to what she'd been led to believe, kept well. You could cork it and have perfectly drinkable wine the next day. Mostly she felt warm sipping by herself in the dark (she'd twisted the thermostat far above Ev's conservative sixty-eight degrees). The windows were beginning to freeze, giving the outside lights a fuzzy aureole-like effect that signaled the onset of winter, and the street sixteen floors down appeared hushed and melancholy, like a village. Outside her study window, the slate roof over the elevator held a light snow in a quilt pattern, the little house in the forest blanketed overnight. She could invest herself in her sadness, she felt so wholly *of* it.

And it wasn't as though Ev were any happier. He was having a crisis, perhaps what would have to be his own idiosyncratic version of the one all men were supposed to pass through in middle life. But he hadn't purchased a hairpiece or a sports car or a rowing machine. As far as she knew, he hadn't fallen in love with some young thing, either male or female. His was a mess of a different color, less personal — *im*personal, as far as Rachel could tell — but still messy. She understood it, though only at dark honest moments she tried to avoid. For those moments, it was as if she were he, so well did she know him. And she worried then that he wouldn't be back, not in any sense, that she had lost him, that he had lost himself.

Her husband required perfection — and that was the good news. From her, from the boys, from himself. It always came back to that single simple premise. He demanded perfection. If he could imagine it, then it was possible. This same philosophy guided his appalling imagination for disaster: any grotesque monstrous act he could envision had undoubtedly been committed, was being committed that very instant. That was the bad news. Certainly the world could bear him out on this supposition; he was corroborated daily.

For herself, Rachel had often thought he was trying to extract something essential from her, something undeveloped or dormant, as if she were a flower he might coerce into bloom. His habit was to test or teach her, as if her soul, like the typical human brain, went ninety-one percent unused.

Her children looked like Ev's parents, Marcus dense and critical like Mr. Cole, Zach big and impervious like Mrs. The personalities that had kept Ev's parents married to each other for forty-three years seemed to sustain the boys' love/hate relationship, too. Marcus would badger and berate; Zach would absorb like a pudgy sponge until he'd had enough, then either cry — fat tears sliding quietly down his cheeks — or casually wallop Marcus across the chest. Rachel had yet to figure her role in their lives; they seemed Cole clones who'd leased her womb for compulsory spawning purposes. Her sons liked her; until they were three years old, they'd thought she was flawless, indispensable. Now, prepubescent and pubescent — such an awful word — and with Ev suddenly AWOL, they'd come to feel a bit protective toward her, giving each other glances. She wanted to slap their faces when they exchanged these worried superior looks. But they didn't *get* her. "You're nice," Zach had tried to explain, "but Dad is fun."

This made Rachel remember the morbid bedtime stories Ev had told the boys about Hot Frank, the wiener dog with an unlighted sparkler for a tail whose life was an epic search for the cook who'd cleaved him, or about the Little Leper, a man whose purpose in the world was literally to scare people to death, by pulling off his own digits and limbs, leaving himself strewn across the countryside.

Fun?

But Rachel had married Evan because he was capable of facing darkness, capable of not being shocked in its presence. He knew humanity could improve itself, but he also knew the depths of its depravation. Rachel appreciated that about him. And his interest in human potential focused so exclusively on her. It was almost parental, not unlike her childhood experience, living in the midst of teachers, people whose inclination was to instruct. Except that her parents had been unnaturally hopeful, optimistic. One Catholic, one Quaker, they'd crafted an odd, seemingly contradictory philosophy of bodily shame and group fellowship. Rachel could explain only by illustration: during her entire childhood, there had always been people living with her family; one or two bedrooms had been occupied by needy friends or students or relatives, a revolving group, their troubles brought to Rachel's parents for resolution. Rachel enjoyed some of them, resented others, occasionally felt neglected, later was proud of her parents' compassion.

At the same time, the house was completely devoid of mirrors. Her parents claimed that mirrors caused vanity, a simple unyielding equation. As a teenager, Rachel had purchased compacts and checked herself in a silver coffee service kept on the dining room buffet. At school she frequently requested bathroom passes so that she could jump up before the sinks and take stock of her flying plaid uniform as quickly as possible in the dingy mirrors, never being sure about anything below her knees. She resented the absence of mirrors. In desperation she'd glued a brand-new cookie sheet to her inner closet door, which presented her with a warbled tinny approximation of herself, like something from the funhouse — though in college it became an anecdote that set her apart from the other women in her dorm at Northwestern. There, under heavy wet skies and suicidal anxiety over grades, a lack of mirrors seemed to give Rachel an edge her classmates envied. They viewed her as someone with a serious destiny. Late at night Rachel might secretly enter the empty fourth-floor bathroom and stand naked before a full-length mirror, touching herself and watching, fascinated with self-pity. It was something she should have been allowed long ago.

When she and Ev met at the university counseling office, Ev had also been interested in her unusual image problems. He was seven years older than she, studying affluent undergraduate women who were depressed. Rachel had been recommended for counseling by her Victorian novels professor, who found her themes on literature "disquieting." Ev, a graduate student at the time, considered her a therapist's dream — bright, forthright, self-effacing. Even then, though, Rachel had felt herself playing a kind of role in which those traits were mandatory. She would sit in his small office and stare out at the enormous squirrels dashing about the campus lawn, relating her life, omitting nothing. "Don't lie to me," Evan had requested, and she didn't.

It was liberating and made her mind race — she wanted to be better than she was, she wanted to behave with integrity, she had high ideals. Ev listened to her, allowed her her elliptical excited style, followed agreeably, and she sensed his pleasure — not judgment but curiosity; not pity but esteem. She fell in love with him. Their sessions ceased — his stubborn ethics would not allow him to date a patient — and became conversations, moving away from his TA office to the cafeteria and student union, their subject matter turning reciprocal, Ev revealing his father's high and insurmountable ambitions for him: he would never be enough. Yet he did not chafe under that ambition, did not complain about it, either.

They were married in the spring of 1977 in a windowless justice of the peace's office. There was no honeymoon; even the word made them scoff. They left the courthouse and took the train down to the city, to Diversey, to Ev's family's duplex. Just an hour earlier, perhaps at precisely the same moment they had been exchanging vows, Ev's father had suffered his first stroke. He was not expected to live more than a few months.

"Let him do what he wants," the doctor told the family. "He gets pleasure from smoking — I can't see any reason to deny him."

It was terrible advice. Ev's father continued to live, on and on, less and less able to do anything except smoke. Ev could still rage over that doctor's flagrantly negligent words. He did not let go of his fury, over this or any other mistake. He held people responsible. He believed in culpability.

Ev. She missed him so thoroughly it was as if he were always just on the other side of the wall, behind a door, disappearing in the mirrors when she entered a room. She could see him that clearly, in his bright T-shirts and black leather jacket, his tidy chinos and round-toed suede shoes. He kept his hands in his pockets, rocked on his heels. He didn't mind staring at people. He was a tense-seeming type, as if he were a man hanging by his feet — his eyes slightly bulged, his face red, the vein in his temple a distinct ripple in his skin, his hair on end. Yet he was right side up.

"You exaggerate," Ev would say, sighing, twisting the tip of his pinky in his ear. His gestures were so constant that Rachel found herself imitating them, twitching while she stood in line at the bank machine, tapping the steering wheel when she drove, flipping from one radio station to another, manic AM, depressive FM. He was not nervous but impatient, worried, highly aware of the waste around him. One of his favorite motifs for conversation was the uselessness of things. At the grocery he would lift a box of Constant Comment teabags and start in. "First, the plastic wrap around the box," he'd say, trailing behind Rachel as she pulled things off the shelves, all the fragile joy of shopping gone. "Then the box, never mind the plastic bag they'll pop this in at the checkout line. Inside are the individually wrapped foil packets, inside that the teabag itself with its paper tag, and finally the tea. About a half a teaspoon. You get home, you have a pile of paper and wrapper and plastic the size of a small bush and a lousy handful of tea. Waste. Unbelievable." This was what Marcus referred to as Ev's Ralph Nader mode.

Rachel smiled, keeping her son in mind as she turned now toward sleep, just a little drunk. She sprawled in the bed. Her husband slept lightly, muttering, curled always tight as a fetus, cold yet producing sweat. His odor Rachel could still manufacture when she lay here by herself; she could smell him despite the fact that she'd laundered the sheets many times by now.

• • •

Five months after Ev moved away to what Rachel had begun thinking of as the Ballpark, the phone rang one afternoon while she napped. Groggy, vaguely hung over, recovering from a sleepless, anxious night before, she listened to Paddy Limbach inquire about Ev's tardiness at the racquetball court.

"You know Ev doesn't live here anymore," she said flatly. Her voice was froggy with exhaustion. Maybe Paddy would find it exotic; that had, after all, been his only appeal for Rachel, that he might flatter her with a cornpone's reverence.

"Well, he wasn't answering his phone. I thought maybe you . . ."

"We separated," Rachel said. The more often she said it, the colder she felt toward the news herself. "I'm not taking Ev's messages. He's got an office and a secretary for that." She frowned; wouldn't Paddy have logically called there in the first place? "Did you try his office?"

"He left already. I figured he was coming to the court, but he's late. I'm really sorry."

Rachel wished he would say "Oh my heck," the way he sometimes did. That was her favorite of his reputed vernacular expressions. According to the boys, he was also known to declare, "Holy catfish!" She yawned, tasting in her breath the dry horror of too much champagne the night before. "Thanks," she told him on the end of the yawn. "I'm surprised Ev didn't cancel your game if he couldn't make it. Actually, I'm surprised he didn't show up. The boys claim he really likes the sport."

Paddy said nothing; Rachel could hear his breathing, as if he were huffing. Then he said, "Well, guess I'll go," as if hoping Rachel would keep him on the line.

"O.K.," she said. *Okey-dokey,* she thought. They hung up.

Rachel looked down at her wrinkled clothes and wondered whether she would bathe today. What was the point of bathing when it was as late as one-thirty? She focused on the wall calendar, relieved to see today's big blank square: no place to go, no one to call. In front of her on the kitchen table were the boys' cereal bowls; the bloated floating Cheerios made her want to fall back in bed.

The phone rang again.

"Rachel?" said Paddy Limbach, as if there were more than one croaky-voiced woman who might pick up the telephone at her apartment. "Rachel?" She couldn't recall having heard her name on his lips before.

"Yes?"

"This is Paddy again."

"Yes, I recognized your voice."

"Well, I was wondering if *you* wanted to play racquetball?"

"Me?" she said, wondering if she should say *I*. "I don't know how," she said. "I have never even *held* a racquetball. Maybe I've never *seen* one."

"It would be blue," he said. "The ball. I can teach you. I've been teaching Ev. It's a good sport."

"Are you feeling sorry for me? Is that why you're asking me?"

"Oh my heck, no," Paddy said. "I just thought since it's nearby, and I've got another hour on the meter here, and I brought all my stuff . . ." His voice faded, as if he were looking down to inventory all the stuff he'd brought. "And it seems like Ev's a no-show . . ." He cleared his throat. "Want to?"

Rachel stood up and then promptly sat back down; she was dizzy, her dehydrated brain shrunk in the casing of her skull like a peach pit. She would have to get her act together or she would become, at the very least, fat and slovenly, and at the worst, an unfit mother. "What should I wear?"

She hung up and promptly drank four glasses of water, swallowing ibuprofen with the last. She put on an approximation of what Paddy had told her: sweatpants and a T-shirt, some paint-splattered tennis shoes. It felt liberating to be costumed as an athlete, something Rachel had never been. On occasion she'd hauled herself on a whirl around Lincoln Park, just to feel her heart pound and her lungs ache. She could *picture* herself being wholesome, but she couldn't quite endure the daily tedium of it.

Paddy's club was a public Y, cavernous and drippy with the inevitable stench of generations of men exerting themselves. She wondered what Ev made of the place — Ev, who had ridiculed competition and teams, male jocularity, jockstraps, sweat.

"Teach me," she said to Paddy, who was nearly unrecognizable in goggles and gear, a bug-eyed exterminator. He led her through a dwarf door into an echo chamber. When the door slammed with a prisonlike, fatalistic boom, the lights flashed on above.

Paddy said, "The basic rule is hit hard and hope. I use the same one for pool."

"Hit hard and hope."

Racquetball, Rachel discovered, was a very forgiving sport. One simply had to smack the ball — it had nowhere to disappear to — with all one's might. It was oddly therapeutic. One could vent a lot of anger here, in this big white box. One could sweat out a lot of alcohol. She watched Paddy crouching in front of her and could imagine Ev there, waiting pessimistically to be smashed from behind by a ball. Of course Ev would fret about this, about being whapped on the head with a well-placed shot. She laughed at the image — Ev's cringing hunched shoulders, his anticipation of disaster. Running and slamming the ball made her happy, and Paddy didn't seem to mind her beginner's ineptitude, her sporadic whoops and curses, her missed swings and erratic charges.

At the end of their third game, as she was trying to send back Paddy's serve into the corner, she hit herself in the face, full force, with her own racquet. Her upper lip puffed instantly, like a balloon.

Paddy was furiously unwinding the loop of racquet rope around his wrist, disentangling himself so that he could help her. "Move your hand," he said, pulling down his goggles and peeling his glove off. "Let me see."

She did as he commanded, feeling the blood run over her mouth and chin, bright and salty on her tongue. He stared at her intently, touching her lip gently with a fingertip, as if it might burst. "Ow," he said.

"Yes." She mopped up the blood on her chin with her borrowed wristband, watching drops fall on the blond wooden floor.

"Are your teeth loose?" He opened his mouth in sympathy, in illustration. Rachel remembered his whiny daughter Melanie now. She also could smell his sweat, the moisture radiating from his chest and neck.

"Oh, it's nothing," she tried to say around her fat lip. She felt herself blushing and wished there were a mirror around so that she could gauge the precise size of her embarrassment.

"Hematoma," Paddy said, poking the blue ball in his shorts pocket to create a big lewd bulge on his hip. Then, without appearing to think it over at all, he tipped forward and kissed Rachel on the mouth, so softly, so tenderly, it was as if a moth had simply flitted by her face.

What an astonishing gesture.

"So that's supposed to make it better?" she asked, trying to cover her alarm. She hadn't been kissed on the mouth by a man other than Ev in sixteen years. Could that be? she wondered desperately, speeding through male faces in her mind to locate one whose lips she'd kissed. Paddy stared hard at her — she could feel his gaze, though she did not meet it, stepped back in order to dilute it. Would he try to make love with her, right here in the YMCA racquetball court number two? Many men, she recalled, were like that, driven and reckless as bulls in the face of passion. She couldn't help looking past Paddy to the observation deck above.

He, too, stepped back and stared with discomfiting severity at her mouth. "It's still swelling."

Rachel ran her tongue over the lip, which felt, beneath her tongue, the size of a . . . well, of a racquetball. "Ick," she said. "I think my fun is over."

She drove home holding ice to her mouth — provided by the boys in the rackety equipment cage, who told her she should take an anti-inflammatory as well and avoid alcohol — though what she felt beneath the cold was not the smack and swelling but Paddy's kiss, that sweet little action. He had pretended nothing had happened, or perhaps he had meant the kiss to be genuinely and exclusively curative. Was it good that he made her think of her dear son Zach, who used to kiss the part in her hair when she complained of migraine?

That night, at the hour when she began pouring herself glasses of wine and when she usually missed Ev most, Rachel sat with her pulsing fat lip and thought of Paddy bending toward her on the racquetball court, touching her mouth with his. There was a twinkling curiosity idling somewhere in her lonesomeness, a bright lure spinning through cloudy water.

Nine

. . . .

MELANIE LIMBACH would not come out of her room when the guests arrived. Evan respected this; he felt like hiding behind a closed door often enough himself.

Her mother banged with her knuckles, protecting her fingernails, which had to be phony and which were painted a flashing bloody red, as if she'd clawed herself with them. Evan could not understand why he disliked Didi so intensely. Perhaps it was simply because he liked her husband and daughter so much. That she wasn't worthy of them seemed obvious; but why bother hating her?

"Paddy," Didi called, "get the screwdriver. I told you we shouldn't have a lock on a child's door."

"No!" came Melanie's desperate little voice from inside the room. "Don't screwdriver my door!"

"I certainly will," her mother promised. "Missy," she added.

What was it about a locked door? Why did it threaten people so? As if the child were dangerous when alone. As if her desire for privacy were an affront. As if she might hatch an incendiary idea in the absence of society. It was empowering, Ev wanted to tell Didi Limbach. It gave Melanie a feeling of control. It illustrated a healthy pleasure in her own solitary company.

He'd had enough, and the evening hadn't even really begun. His agreement to come to dinner had been earned by Paddy's perseverence in extending the invitation, doggedly, without the good intuitive sense of what Evan's persistent turndown might mean. Evan had to admire Paddy's refusal to take a hint. Week after week the request came; week after week Evan declined. Then he just succumbed and said yes, the stipulation being that he would bring the boys.

"Of *course* bring the boys," Paddy replied generously.

Now Zach and Marcus sat on the couch, Zach scratching his head, Marcus scowling at a *Sports Illustrated,* flipping pages in disbelief. The other reading options on the table were an *Old Farmer's Almanac,* a large book of Norman Rockwell prints, a woodworkers' catalogue, a *Family Circle,* and a dictionary-like tome that Evan assumed was the Book of Mormon. He wanted to take that book out of Marcus's reach, so easily could he envision the boy's ridicule of its contents.

"May I?" Evan asked Didi.

She clearly did not want him to succeed where she was failing, but she stepped away from the door. Evan asked Melanie not if she would come out but if he could come in. The latch clicked immediately open.

"I'll be right back," he told Didi, shutting the door in her face.

Melanie said, "You want to build a spaceship?"

"O.K." Evan sat on the floor and wondered what his sons would do with Paddy and Didi. Melanie began tossing animals in his direction, and he began lining them up in a parade.

"This is Noah's spaceship," Melanie said. "With all the animals. God said gather the animals."

"They'll go to outer space this time," Evan said, smiling.

"Sure. He said gather them together."

"To you, he said this?"

"Sure he did." She pointed to her ear. Evan wondered if she had actually heard a voice.

"What did he say?"

"Gather them together in a vessel safe and sound."

Behind her, the door opened and Didi's head poked in, her perky smile pasted on her face. Evan had to keep himself from screaming at her, as if she were the troublesome relative of a favorite client, as if he were in his office. Perhaps he regarded Melanie as a kind of client;

perhaps he anticipated her having problems; perhaps she had them now. He should have locked the door behind him. An oversight.

"Mel?" Didi said sweetly, cloyingly. The little girl whirled, furious.

"Get out!" she screamed. "You get out!" In a flash, she threw herself at the door as if to squash her mother's head like a melon. Evan reluctantly got to his feet to intervene, sure he would have to betray her, ally himself with the adult world of good manners.

Instead, Paddy appeared, pushing the door fully open with a straight arm, holding Didi in the other.

"She's a brat!" Didi said, clutching her ear, where she'd been hurt. Evan wanted to disagree violently; Didi was the brat here, refusing to let the child be alone. Of course, what sort of mother felt comfortable when her five-year-old closed the door of her room with a grown man in there, a virtual stranger, one who probably appeared sinister to her? It was a good thing he hadn't locked the door, he decided.

"Don't hurt Mama," Paddy told Melanie mildly. "She didn't mean to," he told Didi. To Ev, he said, "Women."

"Don't have any myself," Ev said flatly. "Wouldn't know."

"Troublemakers," Paddy said, squeezing Didi, winking at Melanie.

Didi took the opportunity to tell Ev how sorry she was about his separation. Ev asked for aspirin, if they had any.

Later, at the table, there was the awkward moment of prayer. Probably this was where God's voice had originated for Melanie; probably there was a church and some sort of child's service to explain God's order to gather the animals. Didi folded her fingers and bowed her head while the casserole steamed before her, her eyes squeezed shut. Paddy bowed but did not close his eyes, peacefully studying his plate while his wife gave thanks, her voice lilting along without emphasis, as if reciting a phrase in a foreign language, something learned without interpretation. Zach imitated his hosts, tucking his chin as if reprimanded, as if he might fail the prayer test. Marcus continued scowling, waiting impatiently; Ev could hear his foot tapping on the floor. Ev merely let his hands drop to his lap and sighed. He felt sorry for Paddy, for Melanie. He glanced at the little girl seated across from him, who was herself looking around surreptitiously. She caught Ev's eye and smiled conspiratorially at him. He had the strong urge to steal her, to proclaim some sort of eminent domain and adopt her away from her mother. It wasn't that Didi wasn't fit; she just wasn't fit enough.

"Amen," Didi said.

Over the food, she chattered about Paddy's jobs, emphasizing how slow he was at finishing them. Paddy interjected mild objections — he was just trying to do things right, he hated a shoddy piece of work — but mostly listened, nodding. Evan had to admire the man's patience with her. Zach ate so much it was embarrassing, as if his parents hadn't fed him. The food itself concerned Ev briefly — full of fat and chemicals, processed and salty. Although he did appreciate Didi's making him a portion without meat. Melanie insisted on sharing it with him.

"I want to be a virgin, too!" she shouted.

Evan laughed; everyone laughed except Marcus — who noted disdainfully that she no doubt *was* a virgin — and Didi, who blushed and corrected the little girl. "*Vedge-it-tarian*," she said emphatically through her rabbity teeth. "Not *virgin*. Where would she have heard that?" she asked.

But unfortunately, Evan couldn't stop laughing. Tears began forming, his cheeks hurt, his rib cage ached, he couldn't catch his breath. Everyone stared at him, first smiling, then with concern. On he laughed, worrying suddenly about breakdown. Had this been what was coming for so many months now — hysteria? He remembered Rachel's disappointment that he never went helpless with laughter the way she sometimes did; she should see him now, except she'd be worried. Just as worried as his sons, who looked at him strangely, Marcus with disapproval, Zach in simple alarm. He should laugh more, he thought; then it wouldn't build up this way, then it wouldn't surprise everyone. Maybe it was just that fucking simple: he didn't laugh enough. As with crying, it was good to let the dam burst now and then.

Melanie, like a good hostess, joined him in his paroxysm. They laughed until the noise coming from Evan's mouth didn't sound like his own laugh. Afterward, Melanie had hiccups, and Ev had to work hard — uttering the two words that he always used to suppress sappy sentimental impulses, *dog shit, dog shit* — to keep at bay laughter's inevitable culmination: hopeless tears.

. . .

"You think all psychologists are crazy?" Didi asked Paddy as they climbed into bed.

"You talking about the laughing?"

"I thought we'd have to slap him."

"It was odd," Paddy agreed, recalling Ev's red face, the demonic expression his pleasure had caused, as if evil were boiling in his belly.

"At least his wife wasn't here." Didi sighed as she settled like a hen into her soft niche.

"I like Rachel," Paddy said, though he wasn't sure that was true. He was interested in her; she made him uneasy; she was unlike any woman he'd ever been near. Since Ev had left her, she'd become a separate category in his consciousness, no longer simply an appendage of Ev's.

"I was so angry with Mel," Didi went on. "Why does she act so bad around those people?"

The dinner hadn't been as awkward as the one at the Coles' apartment, but it hadn't been pleasant for Paddy. His allegiance to his own life was slipping; he'd caught himself squinting at Didi as if he did not know her. He hadn't considered Melanie's behavior bad.

Months had passed since they'd visited what had been Evan's and Rachel's apartment. The nagging need to repay the invitation had plagued Paddy; he'd been raised by people with a code of manners, reciprocity — doing unto others — being its cornerstone. Finally, they'd agreed on tonight, but as soon as Ev and his sons had entered the house, Paddy had become self-conscious. His home seemed cluttered to him, a barrage of colors and patterns, the smiling mouths of family photos, the coquettish ceramic animals that Didi collected all lined up on the mantel and organ top, and the thousands of flower faces: on posters of famous paintings, on throw pillows, on rugs, in vases, along the tops of the walls. He had never concentrated on his environs until Ev Cole walked in, and in a flash the place felt alien. At the Coles', all the art was original and abstract, international, three-dimensional, each image its own dark shriek on the wall. The photographs were black-and-white, and not of the family but of snake tracks on a desert or of vegetables shaped like naked body parts. And that naked woman table — a piece of furniture you might expect in a museum, in a gallery, but not in a home.

"And *he* makes you feel stupid," Didi repeated, opening her fat romance novel and turning to some midpoint in it. She'd taken to wearing grocery store reading glasses, plastic half-lensed things that made her look like a pretend grandma.

"He doesn't make me feel stupid." Paddy turned his back on Didi. "What I like about Ev is that he's so different from my other friends."

"Night and day," she agreed. "He's a snob, and his wife was a stick. She hardly smiled that whole time at their house, never, even when she made a joke, like we're supposed to laugh but she doesn't have to. I'm glad she didn't come, even though I don't understand why they're separated, they seem so perfect for each other . . ."

She went on, but Paddy stopped listening for a moment, wondering if the Coles were actually perfect for each other, wondering if he and Didi could be described as perfect for each other. What *was* perfect for each other? Opposites were supposed to attract, but he'd married Didi because she liked the same things he did, she understood him, she wanted to go where he went, do what he did.

". . . and their children are rude, I don't know why a parent would let children be so rude. Well, Zach wasn't so bad, but boy howdy, can that child eat!"

"Growing boy," Paddy said.

"Growing tub of lard," she said. "And Marcus is the snottiest little egghead I ever met. He told me the food would have been good if I learned to make pasta al dente. *Al dente.* He even told me what it meant, little big-brained brat. I hated having them over, I hated it."

"What does it mean?"

"What does what mean?"

"Al dente."

"I don't remember — something to do with your teeth." She snapped hers now like a rabbit. For dinner, she'd served manicotti, a dish she'd been serving since she and Paddy had married. Suddenly, tonight, Paddy had been struck by how bland it tasted, how gummy and simple this, her most ambitious recipe, truly was. He'd thought he could detect all the textures that made up the meal, the textures and nothing else, as if the textures were the flavors: pellety hamburger, gluey cheese, ketchupy sauce. Ev had tainted his tastebuds, Paddy thought. "Don't worry," he told Didi. "Now it's their turn to have us over."

"Thank goodness we're square. And I wouldn't go to dinner with either of them on a bet, if the invitation ever comes. I'm going to read — you can put a pillow over your head."

Paddy gave her a friendly peck on the cheek, flashing momentarily on Rachel's fat lip, which he'd also kissed. Yes, Evan had tainted Paddy's tastebuds and also made him feel not exactly sorry for Didi, but superior instead of defensive on her behalf. Paddy covered his head with a thick feather pillow and heard Didi say one more thing. "What?" he asked, lifting the pillow.

"I'd go if I was invited to the new apartment, I guess. I wouldn't mind seeing the bachelor pad."

Paddy grunted, thinking he did not want to take Didi to Ev's new place. He covered his head again and went to sleep in a feathery white noise.

He woke thinking of Rachel Cole. It was two in the morning; Didi had fallen asleep with her book on her chest, the light still burning, her granny glasses still on her nose. He pushed the thick splayed paperback to the floor, removed the glasses, and switched off the lamp. Its base burned his fingertips, which he licked and then blew on. In his dream, Rachel had held him underwater, a game: he'd been swimming through her legs, she'd scissored them shut against his ribs. He would drown if she didn't choose to forgive him. He was afraid of her; he'd kissed her on the racquetball court because he wanted to confront his fear. He was used to making stupid gestures and sometimes generating positive responses from them; in school he'd been the designated imp, the one his classmates looked to for pranks, nearly always benign, covered by his appealing smile, his good manners. He had a talent for knocking people off balance. Sometimes, of course, the responses were exactly what he deserved. Rachel could have slapped him; she could have told Evan, who might have laughed as he had tonight, as if there'd never been anything so outrageously amusing as Paddy's kissing his wife. As it was, she'd turned red, but she'd not minded the kiss — that's what he'd learned from his act. Now, when Paddy dreamed of her coffee table, he confused the dirty silver woman with Rachel herself.

He wanted to sleep with her, he told himself, thrilled and terrified by the truth. She wouldn't have come to the court if she didn't have a soft spot for him, if there weren't some vulnerable place he touched. Or maybe she was accustomed to obliging Ev's friends when they called with their lame ideas. Maybe she was bored. Maybe she'd passed on his kiss to Ev and Ev hadn't even bothered to mention it. Perhaps it was a joke now between them, even though they were separated. Wouldn't a separation involving the cool Coles be so civilized as to include Paddy's juvenile flirtation as a laughable moment, a thing so silly that Evan couldn't even muster a shred of jealousy? Worse, maybe she'd related it and they'd both shrugged: a sweaty kiss on the racquetball court, a gauche instant of absurdity.

To put an end to this line of thought, Paddy rolled toward Didi, who slept solidly, her breath whistling like an innocent child's. He told himself that he should dedicate himself to Didi, that she was the real thing, that they were perfect for each other. When he'd married her, he'd soothed his clamoring heart with the option of divorce: there was an escape clause. But since Melanie's birth he had not thought of himself as a free agent. He'd admired his parents' long faithful marriage, and to be honest, he hadn't yet met anyone he preferred to Didi. She tolerated him, and until he'd met Evan, that had seemed reason enough to love her. He was not someone who made particularly radical life decisions; rather, they were based on comfort, ease, necessity. Didi, like his job, had fit into his family's best interests.

Now he held her from behind and imagined that if he woke her, she might agree to having sex. She didn't like to make love, but she might keep still and allow him to do what he wanted, sighing every now and then, good-natured enough about it. He would have preferred that she enjoyed sex, but it wasn't absolutely necessary. Most often she pushed him away from her when he wrapped his arms around her. "I'm in the middle of this," she would say, waving a spatula or an envelope, hustling from his hug. "I'm too tired," she'd say, if they were already in bed, then fall immediately asleep, as if to prove it. They'd managed to have a conversation or two about the problem, after which they'd wound up in bed. Paddy had won, in other words, but Didi had won, too, since these conversations usually took a good hour or so to wade through, and she usually cried, and Paddy held her in a comforting, asexual sort of way, and then her crying seemed to stimulate some erotic impulse in her, and then they'd be rolling between the sheets.

"Don't those girls in your novels do the deed?" Paddy asked her. "Isn't that what those books are about?"

"Romance," Didi said. "They're very romantic. Not just rutting pigs."

Of course, their sex life had not always been so troubling. Didi had in the past required lovemaking in the way Paddy did, with a single-minded hunger, which had made them seem well suited. Her Mormonism had created a mystique around sex, around nudity, a mystique Paddy had gloried in taking advantage of, in demystifying like a maniac. But Didi had stopped needing sex after Melanie was born. Paddy had waited the six weeks the books talked about, then six more, then a couple more just to make sure, to be a good guy. But the only time she made love anymore was when she had had a little to drink, which made her feel guilty anyway; her logic seemed to be "What the hay?" Otherwise she was not interested, and complained that intercourse hurt her. She blushed as she told Paddy that her obstetrician had been too zealous with the episiotomy, leaving nerve endings exposed. All that had been years ago, five of them — nearly three hundred weeks, Paddy would insist — but Didi was too ashamed to explain the problem further. He knew it was a big problem for her, too, as her family and religion both encouraged having many babies.

Speaking to Ev when he had met him at the racquetball court the preceding week — neither one mentioned Ev's absence the Wednesday before — Paddy had said that sex was the big issue. He had hardly confessed this to himself, but Ev didn't seem surprised to hear it. Ev must hear worse on a daily basis; maybe that was part of Ev's appeal for Paddy, that nothing seemed capable of shocking him. He *expected* the dark and bitter and unpleasant, the perverts and delinquents and unsavories of the world. Other things had wandered into the marriage, Paddy had explained, reporting this as they smacked the racquetball around, having to repeat himself in the noisy echoing room. He and Didi were impatient with each other, he had a recent need to criticize her, there was a sense of tedium and obligation, there were long evenings spent waiting for the hour when they could close up into their private slumbers and dreams. "I'm always checking my watch," he told Ev, who asked if Paddy thought it was the marriage or Didi or he himself who'd changed.

The part Paddy couldn't quite admit was Ev's role. In fact, he might never have considered divorce if Ev hadn't separated from Rachel. Until Ev moved into his new apartment, Paddy had never thought very hard about his marriage. He still believed himself lucky, happily wed, Didi pretty if not particularly carnal. Other men, the ones he worked with, thought she was beautiful, and Paddy had taken pride in that: that beauty was his to hold, his alone.

He'd also never experienced insomnia until he'd met Ev. Of course, meeting Ev had coincided with his father's death, so it was possible that insomnia had been waiting for him regardless; hadn't his father padded around the house at night, checking the locked doors and lighted yard, drinking Ovaltine and reading the almanac? And in Ev's honor, Paddy thought about dying — not as an involuntary subject but as one generated by remembering Ev's claim that he considered his own death on a daily basis. Paddy revved up his imagination, positioning Didi and Melanie graveside, himself disappeared, never to know how it all came out. Despite its now being the middle of the night, he could not muster much genuine fear at the prospect of dying; Ev could make him think of it, but he couldn't make him afraid. The whole thing was too far-fetched.

He rolled from bed and wandered around the house, opening the refrigerator and marveling at the tidy Tupperware, doing the same with the freezer, momentarily shocked by the big Thanksgiving turkey Didi had put there for next week — it resembled a human body part, flesh-colored as it was. He then looked in on Melanie, who was sleeping this week with a birdhouse clutched beneath her arm. Finally he sat on the couch with his bare feet on his own coffee table, thinking of Rachel's. His hand fell on his open pajama fly and he slid it casually along the length of his penis. What made it semierect at night, as if heavier, a larger, lazier instrument than in the daylight hours? This was a question he could have asked Ev but not his other friends, who would make jokes and slug his arm. As usual, he let images of animals flow before him, horses, bulls, their big, eerily unselfconscious readiness to mate, to do what Didi called rutting, the sheer muscular necessity of it, the full-bodied pulsing instinct. He told himself he wasn't thinking of Rachel as he masturbated on the couch, eyes closed, hand busy and busier, his back arched; he told himself it was Didi he imagined, Didi's fair pubic hair and small shy breasts, her painted toenails, her mouth around his penis, her face in his lap. (She made him bathe before she'd even consider taking what she called his thing between her lips.) He told himself he needed to sleep and this would make him sleepy, and Didi would appreciate his taking care of his own needs — wasn't she always after him to do stuff for himself? — and he summoned her image and tried to force it before him. But it was Rachel he saw there, her legs as they scissored around him underwater. He said her name softly, experimentally, telling himself he wanted to make love with her once, just once, once wouldn't hurt anything. He saw her big loose breasts in her black dress . . .

The first thing he saw when he opened his eyes was a red jacket dangling from the dining room doorknob. He started as if caught: ashamed, soggy. An unfamiliar jacket, about the size a teenager might wear. His heart thudded in postcoital animal happiness: he would return it to Zach or Marcus. He would take it to their home.

He wiped his hand on his pajamas, striped ones like his father's, picturing himself as he gave the jacket to Rachel.

· · ·

The next day, Paddy Limbach showed up at Rachel's door with a sweatshirt she'd never seen before. "One of your sons'," he insisted.

She shook her head. She hadn't seen him since their ill-fated racquetball game two weeks ago. He was taller and better looking than she remembered, with his ready smile, his flap of blond hair, and the memory of his kiss made her suddenly frown. She asked him in because he looked clumsy standing in the hall.

"Well, I wonder whose jacket this is?"

Rachel thought he'd bought it just to bring over, just to have a prop. "I can't imagine," she said. She'd been about to go to lunch with Zoë but thought she could offer him coffee, wondering if he drank coffee.

"Maybe Ev's," he went on. His motives escaped her. Surely he didn't think he could seduce her by talking about her husband? "Or maybe it's Didi's?" he suggested, studying the garment anew.

"You want something to drink?" she asked. "Sit down?"

"I wonder whose jacket this is," he said, genuinely fretting. Rachel discovered she had liked it better when he'd believed the coat was one of her sons'. She preferred his innocence.

"Let me ask the boys," she offered, taking the jacket from his hand. "If it's not theirs, they can take it to Ev. If it's not his, he can return it to you. Don't give it another thought." She threw the jacket in her study, out of sight.

Today was Rachel's birthday, November 22, also the anniversary of JFK's assassination. All morning she'd worked hard against feeling sorry for herself. Ev wouldn't call; he didn't believe in celebrating the birthdays of grownups. Over the years, Rachel had succeeded in adapting to his thinking, but now she was lonely. Zoë, who pitied Rachel for her cold-hearted husband, traditionally bought her lunch on this day, but this year was bringing a new boyfriend to the restaurant, a meeting Rachel didn't feel up to. At ten o'clock this evening she would be forty years old. The thought depressed her; middle age would officially arrive. Her sons had remembered her birthday only when she'd turned on the news before school; the mention of JFK had made them both jump. A few minutes later they'd dashed out the door, telling her they'd see her. Their guilt made her feel sorry for herself. She had a whole apothecary's supply of cheap perfume they'd bought for her over the years.

Paddy asked for hot chocolate. Outside, the sky was growing dark; more snow was in the forecast. Rachel's father would have made a joke about the sun and the yardarm, she thought as she decided to open a bottle of champagne. The cork hit the ceiling, the foam churned orgasmically. She clinked cups with Paddy. "It's my birthday," she explained morosely.

He did what could only be described as lighting up. "Hey, happy birthday!" The news seemed to make him ecstatic. Rachel laughed at his excitement. No one, including herself, had had this sort of response to her birthday since she was ten years old; the next year the president had been shot. In her fifth-grade classroom, they'd been planning on singing to her the way they did to everyone on birthdays. In her memory, the song had been about to begin when the news came, everyone's mouth had been open like a baby bird's. There would have been homemade cookies and a small present from Miss Skidmore, a jumprope or a bag of jacks. Instead, Miss Skidmore had wept. She'd had a glass eye, and Rachel remembered attending to the possible difference between a normal eyesocket producing tears and the one with the glass eye doing so. The principal's voice had come solemnly over the staticky intercom and directed everyone to go home. Rachel's mother had accused Rachel of being a selfish girl when she complained of not getting her gift, of the unfairness.

"Don't be so ugly!" her mother had said. Rachel could recall it more clearly than any other part of her childhood.

Paddy said, "What're you going to do?"

"Oh, I'm lunching with a friend and the boys will bring me a gift and tonight we'll order pizza, maybe watch a movie together, maybe not." She shrugged, drinking her champagne. It didn't sound so bad, really. "My friend has a new boyfriend," she said. "I'll get to meet him."

Paddy frowned. "Let me take you to dinner," he said. "I'll just call Didi —"

"Oh, no, that's O.K., don't do that."

"I want to," he said. "It's your birthday, you should have dinner. I'll get Didi to meet us somewhere, you and the boys, a nice place, maybe a Greek place, they can do that flaming cheese for you. That's where Didi took me last year. It was a gas. Oompah."

"Oh," Rachel said. Flaming cheese with Didi. "No, Paddy, really, you're so nice, but the boys will come up with something. I wouldn't want to spoil their surprise."

"You sure?"

"Oh, positive."

Six hours later, after her dismal lunch, at which Zoë and her boyfriend had played footsie with each other and made nothing but sexually suggestive conversation, after the boys had delivered the annual malodorous perfume and waxy chocolate, then headed to their rooms, after Rachel had finished the champagne she'd begun at lunchtime, which had lost a lot of its sparkle, the doorbell rang.

Expecting pizza, Rachel opened it barefoot, with a sack of loose change in her hand. For the second time that day, Paddy stood on her threshold, this time bearing not a red jacket but a red wrapped box, ribbon dangling from it.

• • •

The four of them ate pizza while snow fell outside. Paddy had lied to Didi and was still marveling over the simplicity of doing so. In his lie, it was Ev's birthday. In his lie, he was eating with Marcus and Zach and their father — boys' night out — instead of with their mother. "I don't know how you can do it," Didi had said. "Two nights in a row with that bunch."

He felt like he'd joined a new family, filled the dad slot the way a new actor sometimes did on the soap operas, and was now sitting in his dad chair. He patted the arms of it.

"Do you know how to play bridge?" Marcus asked him, squinting with one eye the way his father did, as if a laser might shoot out.

"I used to," Paddy said. He had played with his mother and her friends, mostly so he could eat the goodies she supplied for her club: little mayonnaisey sandwiches with the crusts snipped off, two-colored cookies in the shape of pinwheels, followed by a minty green, mildly alcoholic drink like a milkshake. Just before dispersing, all the ladies received party favors, baskets filled with sachet or hotel-room soaps. Paddy liked bridge.

"Let's play," Marcus begged his mother. "Let's play after dinner."

Rachel looked at Paddy skeptically, as if doubting his ability.

"I can play," he assured her. "I'd love to." She was beautiful, he thought. Her beauty was not like his wife's — which was right in front of you, the obvious beauty of a cheerleader's perky smile or a doll's groomed perfection — but somehow skittish, elusive, tragic, as if she'd been witness to something unspeakable. The expression on Rachel's face that Didi hated, the little smirk, seemed more shy than smug to Paddy. When she tilted her head to listen to her sons, a long smooth sweep of flesh was created, curving like a ski trail from jawbone to the shadowy cleavage revealed by her workshirt, which was buttoned to hide the rest. How had he underestimated her sexiness the first time he'd met her? Or was he simply drunk?

They'd opened another bottle of champagne to toast her birthday. He'd made her sons sing to her with him, the two of them plodding through the song as if Paddy were punishing them. If he had been their real father, he would have chastised them for their lack of spirit, but as a guest, he simply tried to rise above it.

"What's in that box?" Zach asked, pointing at Paddy's gift.

Marcus gave him the laser glare again.

"That's for your mom, of course, but let's play bridge first, huh?" He didn't want her to unwrap her present until later. He had a feeling the gift was a bit inappropriate. He'd bought it uneasily, making a grander gesture than was called for, just like kissing her had been; charging fifty-some dollars on his credit card at Marshall Field's was something he'd have to explain to Didi, bill-payer, later.

When Rachel looked at him now, across the table, across the two greasy cardboard boxes that had contained dinner, he could swear he saw interest in her eyes, an interest he knew had grown there completely because of grand yet potentially stupid gestures. She was trying to figure him out. She did not take him entirely seriously, he saw that; there was not scorn in her eyes but amusement. *Willing* amusement. She was willing to let him prove himself to be something besides the bungling goof he appeared to be, blue-collar and uneducated.

Paddy wouldn't have contradicted her on that count. Most of the history of the world escaped him, the huge unknown mass of it lurking beyond him like a tidal wave, something likely to overwhelm and submerge him. He'd stayed only a year at college, in Champaign-Urbana, long enough to get a sense of how weighty his ignorance truly was but not long enough to put a particular dent in it. With a new respect for everything he didn't know, he returned home to Normal, to Didi, to his father's farm — the things he *did* know — and then he had gone to his father-in-law's construction company in Chicago, which soon required its own roofing division.

He would come at Rachel with confidence, trusting the only quality in himself that had ever paid off; she would not be able to resist. She had big eyes, big lips, big hands, big breasts, big brains. She was tall and solid and smart, but he could infiltrate if he pretended to feel one hundred percent surer than he actually felt.

・・・

Her sons had been missing bridge, one thing the family used to do together. Dizzily, Rachel cleared the pizza boxes and the champagne bottles and told Zach to find the cards.

Family rules dictated that the boys could not be partners. "You pass information," she complained. "I think you use little signals, you cheaters."

"The Cole Convention," Marcus told her.

Zach, throwing items from the deep buffet drawer, called out, "Then I get Mom for my partner."

Rachel started to ask him to be Paddy's partner instead — Marcus was the most serious player, and he could be sharp and digging with his complaints about technique — but didn't, afraid this was patronizing.

"Refresh me on the rules?" Paddy asked, staring, perplexed, at his fan of cards. Rachel wondered if he was considering how to arrange them — by suit or by value?

Marcus sighed dramatically. Rachel recalled what Paddy's wife reportedly said of Marcus at dinner the night before, acting as if it were a compliment: "He has the vocabulary of a simultaneous translator." Marcus had imitated her, rolling his eyes upward in the campy way of a dumb blonde.

"One spade," Paddy announced, making a digging motion with his free hand, grinning at Rachel. He, too, seemed to be getting drunk. His long legs kept swinging open beneath the table, and his knee had fallen against hers once or twice.

Zach passed. Marcus raised the bid to four spades, adding, for Paddy's information, that that was a cutoff bid. "And game," he tacked on after Rachel had passed and while Paddy sat considering what to do.

"Pass?" he said.

"Doy," said Marcus, scratching his head in annoyance.

"Marcus," Rachel warned.

"And he's *play*ing it," the boy complained. Paddy laughed self-consciously, perhaps drunkenly. Zach led an ace of diamonds and Marcus laid out his hand, snapping five spades down one at a time. "Pretty good support, eh?" Marcus said, pleased.

Rachel could hear Ev in the boy's inflection, though what was gently ironic in her husband came out like arrogance in her son. She felt sorry for him for a second; somebody was going to squelch that tone sometime soon. And she also missed Ev — sharply, angrily. He had bred this personality, but where was he when it needed cultivating?

"*Great* support," Paddy said absently, "just super-duper."

Of course Rachel didn't *mind* that Paddy didn't seem to play bridge. She *wished* he did, but . . . Zach certainly didn't care; after his lead, he'd gone for Cheerios and milk, prepared a bowlful to eat while he threw cards on tricks. But to Marcus the game mattered, and now Marcus's father, who was the superior player, was gone. Paddy was here in his place; Rachel felt his fidgety desire to do well.

"Get the boys off the streets," Marcus chanted in an undertone, leaning over the dummy hand.

Paddy looked at Rachel after she scooped up the first trick. She was waiting for Zach to lead again. Zach glanced over his cereal at the board and then led a club. There was an ace from Marcus's dummy hand, so Paddy pulled it out and laid it on top of Zach's three. Marcus sighed again. "No finesse," he muttered.

Paddy shrugged sheepishly. "That's what all the women say," he said. Rachel tried to chuckle. He tapped the trick closed and set it before him, glancing up at her and grinning again. His eyes, she thought, were quite arresting, blue where Ev's were brown. If he had been standing with the clear blue sky behind him, it might look as if he had two holes in his head. Again Marcus was chanting about the boys on the street.

"Stop it!" Rachel suddenly said, addressing both the game and her own fantasizing. The three males fell silent. A drop of milk slid down Zach's chin.

Paddy tried to lighten the moment, leading with his ace of spades, saying, "What the heck."

"You're on the *board!*" Marcus screamed. In a flash he was out of his chair and down the hall to his bedroom. Since he was dummy, there was no reason for the game to stop except general shock.

Rachel sighed. "Well, he misses his dad."

"Me, too," Zach said, perfectly cheerfully. "But I don't go crying out the door about it."

"No," Rachel confirmed. "No, you don't."

"The 'boys' are the trumps," Zach told Paddy agreeably. "When you get them off the street, it means you try to gather them up."

"Oh-ho," Paddy said. They finished the hand, Paddy going down one. When Zach had had enough to eat, he asked if he could go play with his computer. Rachel excused herself, leaving Paddy at the table shuffling cards.

At Marcus's door she hesitated, listening the way she sometimes had at her husband's study door. When she rapped, Marcus said, "I'm sorry, O.K.?" in an aggrieved voice.

"You all right?"

"Just super-duper."

"What are you doing?"

He sighed loudly. "Reading. A book."

When she closed her eyes, Rachel could feel the gentle spin of her inebriation. It was her birthday, and she didn't want to pursue her son's unhappiness. She hadn't the patience. She was weary of appeasement. "Goodnight, son," she said, laying her hand on the door as she might once have laid it on his back, and then she returned to her guest.

Paddy had moved to the couch in front of the coffee table, the only real furniture in the living room. His gift rested on the open palm of the coffee-table girl, teetering, barely balanced there.

"I need a present," Rachel told Paddy, smiling.

He nodded toward the wrapped box, seeming as eager as she to get rid of the cheery paper and chaotic ribbons. She opened it to discover something purple, velour. A long shirt, heavy and with the odd pliant warmth of an animal in her hands.

"You like it?" Paddy asked.

"Yes," she said, trying to remember the last time she'd worn something velour. Or purple, the shade of which made her think of crayon manufacturers, desperate for more variations. *Eggplant,* they would have named this. *Aubergine.*

"I thought you'd look good in a short dress."

Rachel held the bulky garment up again. Now she saw the gathered waist, the slight flare of the skirt. She turned it around, measuring with her eyes the narrow width of its hips, the clingy aspect of its bodice, the little size 8 tag.

"Try it on," Paddy urged.

Rachel took the dress into her bathroom and shut the door. In the mirror she told herself, "This is ridiculous." She made a dead-fish sort of face, stupid and flabby, her neck and shoulders defeated. "Who does he think I am?" she asked her dour mouth, grateful for her tipsiness.

Though she knew the dress would never fit, Rachel wished it would slide over her like a magic spell, make her beautiful. She wanted Paddy to have that talent. But the purple dress would not go over her hips. The top half was nice, actually, the neckline a daring and successful sweetheart dip, beneath which Rachel's breasts buoyed nicely, but just below her waist the thing wouldn't budge. A lumpy inner tube, it felt alive. Now she had to decide how intimate she felt toward Paddy. Or, more precisely, how intimate she wanted him to think she felt.

Leaving the dress bunched at her waist, she pulled her black pants back on and returned to the living room. "I do busts best," she said heartily.

Paddy stood. "Oh." He winced. "Wrong size?"

"Way small."

"I described you to the saleswoman, and she said this was your size."

"What did you say about me?"

"Well, I don't know." He was close enough to touch her, and did, at the hips, where the trouble was. "There's the second zipper," he said hopefully. "Did you try the second zipper?"

"I wasn't aware of a second one," Rachel said. She felt her heart pumping blood to the surface of her skin. Paddy found the zipper and opened it, the backs of his fingers for a moment next to her flesh, his warm knuckles the texture of brown paper bag. Then he eased the skirt down over her hips and pulled the zipper shut with a satisfied *zzzz*.

"Perfect," he said, relieved. "Take your pants off." He covered his mouth as if she would reprimand him for naughtiness, a gesture Rachel ignored.

She pulled her pants off while he watched. Her legs looked pale and gelatinous to her, like something left too long in cold water. She fled once more to the bathroom, to stand again before the mirror. Her face was splotchy with her sudden desire for Paddy. Perhaps Ev had been gone so long she would fall for any man who seemed to like her. How could she know, when she'd had so little practice? From the drawer beside the sink she pulled black pantyhose. She yanked them on impatiently.

"Rachel?" She heard him at her bedroom door and opened the bathroom door so he wouldn't alert the boys, whose understanding of this scene would be thoroughly certain: another man where their father ought to be.

"You look great," he told her, steadying himself with a bedpost.

"I like it," she admitted, happier than she could explain. She had no idea what might happen next, a condition she'd inhabited without pleasure all fall, but one that suddenly appeared to be edgier and more exciting. Though the dress was snug, it was not unflattering, at least from the front.

Paddy ran his hand over the wooden ball on the bedpost and stared at her. He asked, "How come you don't wear makeup?"

She shrugged. "My mother wouldn't let us look at mirrors when I was young. We had no mirrors in the whole house. She thought mirrors made you vain. Same with makeup. For a while I wore it, in college, but I just quit, I don't remember why." Of course Ev objected to makeup. She quit because Ev found it reprehensible. He had seemed to believe she ought to admire his thinking on this issue, and she supposed she did. "Plus," she confided to Paddy, "I keep thinking teenagers will point and laugh. I was never very good at putting it on. I think you have to learn it young, at your mother's knee, for it to take."

"I'll make you up," Paddy said. His palm rolled over the bedpost. "I used to do makeup for all the plays at my high school. I was good at it."

Rachel raised her eyebrows. "Oh, go ahead," she finally said. "Make me over, I dare you."

In the bathroom, she switched on the panel of lights over the mirror and drew the clothes hamper to the sink to sit on, shaking her hair from her eyes. Paddy stood behind her, blinking in the sudden brightness. She did not want to contemplate their reflections together, him with his sky-blue eyes and corn-yellow hair, his youth and her own agedness. When she had been thirty, she might have looked twenty-five; now that she was forty, she could look thirty-five, but he would still appear to be younger. When people commented on her looks, they most often told Rachel she looked healthy, a word she had decided was simply a euphemism for plain.

She opened a drawer and let Paddy handle the slim, mint-green, pristine containers of pore minimizer and blush and the wine-colored eyeliner, bought long ago during a shopping trip with Zoë, who purchased makeup with insatiable optimism about its transfigurative powers.

He bent over her upturned face, beginning with coverup, spreading it in circles, his lips open until Rachel smiled at him, imitating his slack-mouthed expression. Her chin was aimed at his jeans zipper. Next he brushed highlighter beneath her cheekbones, then lined her eyes, holding the corner of one lid while stroking over it dexterously with the crayon. His hand trembled near her eyes, but he smoothed the snaky line with his thumbtip, creating a smudgy shadow like smoke on each eyelid.

"Open your mouth," he told her, once more opening his. He flicked mascara up and down, over and under the lashes. "I lied," he said softly. "I never did makeup in high school. I just used to watch Didi." His hands were warm and uniformly callused, like leather. He had a physical confidence with her that Rachel both liked and was wary of. He was not good at bridge, but he was good at this, he seemed to be telling her — he was good at touching her.

"I would hate that name, Didi," Rachel said, just to introduce a spouse into the events. "How can she stand it?"

"Her real name's Deirdre. She prefers Didi. Says it's friendlier."

"Oy." She watched him as he worked, moving her features accommodatingly. When he finished tamping her lips with a liver-colored lipstick, she stared at her reflection unselfconsciously. She didn't begin crying, but she began feeling like she ought to. Something pathetic was invading her life, something foolish — this makeup job had just enough of the clown in it to make her see that. There were dots of lipstick on her teeth, circles of cheery red on her cheeks. She was not the kind of woman who would lean onto a friendly man's shoulder and sob. She was just barely the kind of woman who would spontaneously invite a man to dinner and bridge, and because Paddy seemed to understand this, he moved timidly into a position that would appear neither too forward nor too remote, squatting beside the little vanity they'd rigged. "Here's my shoulder," he said into the mirror. He still held the bullety lewd lipstick in the fingers of one hand; in the other, he waved a pink bandanna.

Rachel sighed and lifted her head, tilting her chin to tighten the throat. Her features stood out now that Paddy had emphasized them; her pores had been minimized, as promised by the bottle. How would she ever have predicted this was the way she'd spend her fortieth birthday?

"All vamped up and nowhere to go," she said. "You want another drink?"

They left the bathroom as if suddenly realizing its intimate dimensions (small) and furnishings (toilet and tub and scales, places for naked flesh to rest itself) and returned to the big public living room. Rachel brought out brandy in glasses the boys had made, employing a kit they'd found in the storeroom when Rachel redecorated it.

"I used to buy Didi clothes," Paddy said. "I don't think I ever got her size right either, come to think of it."

"She's a single-digit gal, I have a feeling," Rachel said.

"Beg pardon?"

"I like this dress," Rachel told him. "It was really too kind of you to get it." When he smiled at her, relieved, she saw that his upper lip was bleeding.

"Oh Paddy, I'm so sorry," she said, stopping herself from reaching forward to touch the small cut. "The boys have been recycling jars into drinking glasses. They like to pretend we're so disadvantaged here with no man in the house, surviving by our wits and our Swiss Army knives. What can I do for you?" It would have been possible — so neatly parallel — for her to take her turn at kissing his wounded lip. But she didn't. Though he had given her permission to fall in love with him, she did not yet want to accept the offer. She would have to stare out her window and think it over.

"More brandy," Paddy said, wiping his mouth in a manly manner with the back of his hand, then wiping his hand on his bandanna. "There seems to be blood in this drink."

He wouldn't accept a new tumbler.

"Broken glass has always terrified me," she said, pouring him more of the aromatic liquor, then sitting back on her section of the couch and pulling her legs beneath her. She ran her index finger around the rim of her own glass.

He turned his glass so that he could continue to drink, letting the brandy burn his cut each time he took a sip.

"The boys think our life is falling apart since Ev left. They cope by circling the wagons — isn't that the expression? Pulling everything in tight, taking five-minute showers and clipping coupons." She laughed. "And sometimes I wake up with an empty wineglass beside the bed, and I'm sure I'm turning into an alcoholic — my teeth all furry from forgetting to brush, a half-drunk drink waiting where there ought to be a water glass . . ." Rachel filled her mouth with brandy, let it seep down her throat. "I like to drink."

"I figured that out about you."

"You think I should worry?"

"Nah. How old are you today, anyway?"

She frowned. "Forty. It's dispiriting."

"Forty," Paddy said. "You're older than me."

"You sound surprised. Didn't you know that?"

"Well, no."

Rachel suddenly felt the full bulk of her foolishness: sitting in a tight purple minidress on her fortieth birthday. Flirting with her husband's friend, a man she hadn't even particularly liked until he brought her a gift. Would the future ever offer up sophisticated surprises instead of demeaning ones? At sixty, would she be seducing one of her sons' friends, piercing outrageous body parts, investing money according to zodiac counsel?

Rachel could feel herself slipping into a bitter associative mode that had nothing to do with Paddy, one that would make her miss her husband, who would have known how to pursue a conversation through its peculiar unspoken maze, coming up with a tidbit in five minutes that resulted from following her silently on his own, something that would raise the evening's tone to a more acceptable level. To bring herself back, to rise from the subterranean territory they appeared to be in, she asked, "What are we up to?" She had arrived at a tired bluntness that was not joyfully drunk but simply pre–hung-over.

Paddy scooted over closer on the couch. He put his arm around her, and almost against her will, as if her ear or neck were doing its own thinking, her head lowered itself onto his shoulder. He smelled of some cheap aftershave, a quaint aroma Rachel recalled from her adolescence. "Happy birthday," he said, squeezing her.

She lifted her head, leaving a flesh-toned smear on his white shirt. He'd said "Happy birthday" in such a way that she knew he meant "Goodbye for now." He meant they were going to take things slowly, if at all, which was prudent, and disappointing, and exhilarating.

Ten

· · · · · · · · · · · · ·

LUELLEN PALMER canceled her sessions with Evan before he had a chance to suggest closure. This was like her, he thought: wanting to be in charge, wanting to reject him before he rejected her. He recognized her behavior from his own, the need to preempt, to protect. He reassured himself he'd advised her properly before they parted ways: against having a baby, against one-night stands, against guilt and self-hatred.

But he missed her. He missed the way she cursed, the way she snorted in laughter, the anecdotes she told him, the merciless way she berated her mother and sisters, her colleagues at the photo studio, herself, and especially the men who loved her. Was there any disdain more vicious than that of the self-loather toward her fans?

Instead of filling her weekly time slot, Ev took walks during it. He could have used the money — he was maintaining two homes now — but the urge to escape the office early and get out into the air overruled financial concerns.

His need to walk had grown since leaving his family. Before, he'd taken time over lunch or during a cancellation to walk the streets near his office: under the Loop tracks, down South Michigan, alongside the river, occasionally into a building and up its stairs or elevator. Now he often walked home — over an hour's trip on foot — and sometimes wandered from his new apartment after dinner. The evenings were long and dead, his attention span shrunken. The light bulbs in his apartment bothered him; his neighbors made too much noise and odor. He had no patience for books or music, not even for marijuana, which he'd bought optimistically but found disappointing. It did not cut through his impatience the way it once had; it did not make him able to live happily in a present moment. Life in his apartment should have been as soothing as disappearing into his study had once been; but his family wasn't waiting on the other side of the door, and that made all the difference.

On the other side of *this* door was the world, unbuffered, unmitigated. He began to feel as if this move away from home were senseless, as if he were staying away not because he wanted to but because he was too humiliated to move back. Stubbornness was dishonest, in his opinion. And so was moving home because he found his own company lacking. Hadn't he always insisted that he was someone who enjoyed being alone? Instead, he walked to bars, and he occasionally had more than one drink. Drinking made him guilty; guilt felt like an emotion he wanted to suffer. But then he was walking again, vaguely drunk, improperly guilty.

Only walking allowed him to think straight. Only walking permitted a balance that kept him from sinking. Mindless movement and mindful contemplation: he wondered if his brother had discovered something like this years ago, the need to satisfy a pressing present urge.

He was mugged on a Friday night in December as he walked home from a dull Christmas party. A gun was shoved into his spine so firmly he thought he'd already been shot; the picture of a silencer flashed in his mind despite his never, to his knowledge, having seen one.

"Here we go," said his assailant, snapping the fingers of his free hand. "The wallet and the watch, big guy, Mr. Gay Blade."

In fact, Ev had no wallet, was wearing his only suit, and had stuffed a few dollar bills in his jacket pocket (this for one scotch at a bar; he'd been at a holiday party, but his friends could not know that he was drinking again after so long an abstinence, could not be given yet another aspect of his life to pity; his separation from Rachel was fodder enough). Ev found it difficult to convey his meager holdings to his mugger, as if the encounter were happening in a dream and he were sleepily mute. Eventually the man felt for himself the absence of wallet and watch, one fist ramming into Ev's pockets while the other one held the gun against his ribs, the man cursing Ev while Ev wanted to apologize. He knew he was going to suffer some abuse for not being prepared; he received a hard whack on the side of his head.

Pistol-whipping, the police called it, though that sounded exaggerated to Ev, since there'd been only one strike. However, the skin had been broken and a strange vessel had burst, sending a rhythmic spurt of blood from Ev's cheek, a projectile leak onto his nice wool suit, a pewter gray now dashed with the Tabasco red of emergency. He could not get the bleeding to stop; the police didn't want to leave him by himself, as his utter calm was a reaction they did not understand.

In fact, the gun in his back had not made his life fly before his eyes; he had not experienced a sudden desire to reform. It was with profound patience that he'd suffered his mugging, which he viewed as a kind of ironic cap on an tiresome evening. He'd been walking home from his partner Lydia's, taking a distant detour through Bucktown, the neighborhood of Luellen's bar, Friendly's, the place she went to pick up men. The street had been momentarily empty — cars at an intersection behind him, patrons of a restaurant across the street, Christmas lights over the business fronts as if over a tiny sleeping town — and Ev had been wondering if he was making excuses for searching Luellen out, if he had brought along his dollar bills to buy her a gin instead of himself a scotch. He'd been thinking about her, worrying that her decision to stop her sessions had to do with him. Perhaps he'd committed some subtle fumbling gesture that made her think he thought she was hopeless. But he did not believe he'd been completely honest about his motives; other clients had halted sessions and he'd not sought them out.

He missed her. It was possible he missed her more because he also was missing his wife. And Joni. All the intelligent women were disappearing from his life. He seemed to be driving them away. And at the party, he'd been missing alcohol, and his children, and randy jokes, all the ingredients of a truly festive evening. They were achingly absent at Lydia's apartment, where everyone was tactful and solicitous, where there was no sexual tension and no drunken behavior, where nothing unexpected was going to happen unless Ev himself provided it. The eggnog hadn't even had eggs in it; Lydia was living low-fat, vegetarian, chemical-free — virtues that had once given Ev something to talk with her about and that now, he'd discovered, he was savagely scathing about.

As if abstinence made you blessed. As if denial gave you celestial credit. When Lydia had told him that she'd finally managed to eliminate all animal products from her life, even the ones the animals gave up willingly, Ev had sourly said, "There'll be another star in your heavenly crown."

"Who can we turn you over to?" his cop asked him when he refused to go to the ER. "Who you want to call?"

It was not fair to phone Rachel; he didn't want to endure her pity, either. She'd been angry with his desertion but now seemed strangely sympathetic when he happened to see or speak to her, as if she were making peace with their separation, getting used to the extra space it must afford. He thought of the small gathering of people he'd left at the party: Lydia and her lesbian lover; his other partner, Jean, and her vulturine writer husband; other business associates, all decent enough but with their own grubby reasons for wanting to see Ev further down. He thought of several friends he hadn't spoken with for a few months, who didn't know he and Rachel had separated, married couples who most likely would opt to remain friendly with Rachel rather than Evan. Rachel had more talent for keeping friends; she kept better track of their lives, of their phone numbers, of their habits. Ev could not stand the thought of these husbands leaving their warm beds, leaving their warm wives, arriving smooth and concerned and still warm themselves to care for him. It was the image of the wives, who would rise to phone Rachel, that irked him.

Only Paddy seemed tolerable, only Paddy Limbach, who would leave Didi in her baby-doll nightgown, amble into the police station, mildly fuzzy, wearing his cowboy hat or maybe a fluorescent-orange hunter's cap with earflaps, now that it was cold. Didi wouldn't call Rachel. Paddy wouldn't give advice or make judgments. Ev could see himself sitting with Paddy in a diner afterward, eating greasy hash browns and drinking scorched coffee, surrounded by drunks, the evening weirdly rehabilitated.

But it was Didi who answered the phone, her childish voice alarmed.

"Paddy said he was going out drinking with you," she told Ev.

Ev, annoyed by the dopey lies of typical marriages, could not think of a satisfactory response.

"When did you last see him?" Didi asked. "Were you at a bar together?"

"Listen, Didi, I've been mugged. I'm calling you from the police station. I'm sure Paddy's fine, but he's not my big concern right now."

"Mugged?" she squeaked.

"Yeah, the whole nine yards, my money or my life, that kind of thing."

"Oh, where is Paddy?"

Evan hung up on her. Although Didi was not entirely unlike a few of his clients, he rarely had much contact with people as thoroughly dishonest with themselves as she appeared to be. Her sincere feelings he imagined encased inside her, a vital little nesting doll held in place by bright lacquered versions of herself. He felt sorry for the daughter, Melanie, recalling the way she'd put her hand in his, the way she simply liked him. It was Melanie's trust in him that he latched on to, because he needed to latch on to something. Melanie, and his own sons, those absent, missed party guests. He could hang up on Didi Limbach and he could move away from the double bed he shared with his wife, but the children would still be there. He had forsaken his father, his brother, but he had not left the children. The clarity of this revived Ev.

"You have something for my head?" he asked one of the cops, touching the throbbing blood vessel. A butterfly bandage was located and successfully squelched the messy pulse from his temple. He took a cab to his apartment building and heard his phone ringing as he entered: Dr. Head, who could not sleep until he'd had his nightly chat. Ev had forgotten all about him.

Talking in Bed

In no particular hurry, Ev situated himself at the kitchen table with a cup of water, removed his glasses and tenderly touched his bandage, then lifted the receiver. Dr. Head, unflustered by the improbable amount of time it had taken Ev to answer, asked in his gruff New England voice how Ev's day had been. Ev told him it had been difficult. "I'm sorry to hear that," Dr. Head said, without bothering to ask for details. Then he moved quickly to manholes.

Manholes. Ev let his mind become absorbed by manholes, their comic and civic usefulness, their sudden unpatriotic terrorist potential, enumerated by Dr. Head. Ev sat in the dark, still wearing his ruined suit, waiting for the sky to turn light, listening to Dr. Head, trying to recall where he'd seen a dry cleaner's, anticipating the surprised expression of the person to whom he'd hand his bloody jacket, wondering when the trains would begin to arrive more frequently at the Addison stop. He asked himself why he tolerated Dr. Head, what he himself gained from this nightly exchange. He'd explained to his colleagues and to his wife that he was the only therapist he knew who would permit the man this necessary eccentric treatment, but that couldn't be the only reason. Ev refused to see himself as some sort of crusading martyr.

It was probably that Dr. Head's paranoia topped Evan's, kept his steadily within the realm of the real. If Dr. Head was a genuine paranoid, then Ev wasn't. Out in the world lived all the extremes, and Ev maintained his own equilibrium by calibration. He wasn't as pessimistic as Dr. Head; he wasn't as uncontrolled as his brother. He wasn't as mean as his father had been; he wasn't as smart as Joni had been. He wasn't as innocent as Paddy Limbach, nor was he as kind.

Tonight Dr. Head claimed he had published a volume of poems, some of which would cause him a great deal of trouble if any of his so-called friends ever read them. That was why, he told Ev, he had used a pseudonym. Ev waited to hear what famous poet Dr. Head had selected as himself. He was betting on a Robert: Frost, Bly, Penn Warren. But Dr. Head said, "Dick Stubbs."

"I've never heard of Dick Stubbs," Ev said.

"Well, of course not," Dr. Head growled. "You don't read poetry, do you?"

Ev admitted he didn't, although he thought he probably should read more of it. Hadn't literature, once upon a time, made him feel saved?

"I'll send you a copy," Dr. Head said. "But you have to promise to send it back."

"I'll do that." He imagined a stapled sheaf of typed pages arriving sometime next week with Dr. Head's monthly check, each poem testimony to the world's wickedness.

"What's your book called?" Ev asked.

"*Black Universe*," Dr. Head promptly replied. "It's all about bad seeds like my neighbors, family, et al."

Dr. Head had been suspicious of Ev's new phone number; he thought perhaps his family had gotten hold of Ev and persuaded Ev to talk about him. For a few weeks after Ev's move, Dr. Head had called only when truly desperate, when sleeplessness tormented him. He'd said at one point, "You should go back home," but that was all. He didn't have much interest in Ev's personal life, unlike Ev's other clients. This contrary response provoked a contrary one in Ev: he sometimes wished to tell Dr. Head about himself. Their relationship was so unlikely, and their conversations so thoroughly one-sided.

Eventually, the men wished each other a peaceful sleep and hung up. Ev laid his head and arms on the table and drifted off, a small pool of blood forming beneath his face, his dreams involving the black universe under the city, the one you could fall into if you opened a manhole, the one his brother Gerry inhabited every single day of his life.

. . .

Didi waited up for her husband, who had apparently lied to her. She stared at the telephone as if it were to blame. She resented Evan Cole for waking her, for alerting her to Paddy's deception, and for hanging up on her, as if he knew more than he would bother to say to her.

In Melanie's room the vaporizer whistled quietly away. Mel slept with her mouth open, her face seeming oddly large and unattractive. Much of the girl's prettiness had to do with her huge blue eyes, inherited from her father, which were of course closed now. She had stringy blond hair with a hint of pink in its underside. Her right arm, which had been broken, was still thinner than the left and now lay draped over a fireman's hat she'd insisted on taking to bed with her. Every week she adopted some new object as her favorite, the thing she couldn't sleep without. Her fingernails were black-rimmed, every one of them, and when Didi leaned over to give her a kiss, the smell of soiled clothes made her wrinkle her nose. Didi wondered if her daughter had remembered to use the bathroom before bed.

Didi replayed the evening, which resembled most evenings: the wheedling and clock watching, the mocking laugh track of television, the annoyingly slow and messy snack Melanie insisted on having before bed. For reasons Didi could not explain, it was imperative that Melanie be folded away in bed by eight o'clock. That didn't happen when Paddy was home. When he played with Melanie, it was in that distracted way of his, the way that involved all the blocks and all the plastic figures, all the sets of toys jumbled together in a displeasing chaos of discordant sizes and shapes: the jumbo rocket beside the frail dollhouse furniture, the life-size and lifelike endangered turtle carrying the plastic firefighter — who had no appendages, nothing but a little fireplug figure and a set of black freckles on his smiling face — on his back. These fusings and shufflings distressed Didi. She preferred to have everyone in his place, among his intended kind, within scale. It was as if the toys might all start occupying the same baskets and boxes, all thrown together in a haphazard fashion that might never permit her to sort them out again, to put them right. But Paddy encouraged this kind of democratic hubbub — everything equal, everyone welcome. He did not care where they all went later, for cleanup, and he did not pay attention to the time. Didi found herself circling his and Melanie's play like a sheepdog, herding them toward bed. Although she had chosen against giving Melanie a bath tonight, Didi was now aware of the girl's stickiness. Perhaps she'd forgotten to point her to the potty as well.

Didi hesitated just a few seconds before lifting Mel out of bed and carrying her to the toilet. Her pajamas were footed and had to be unzipped along her leg, a process that made Didi think of boning fish, of her dead father-in-law's skill with the slim knife. "Go. Potty," Didi enunciated, hoping to penetrate the recesses of her daughter's sleepy mind without actually waking her: a command to appeal to the well-trained child. Melanie slept, propped up by Didi on the toilet. Soon there was a trickle, which went on and on; Didi's concern had been justified, she was pleased to note. Melanie's head lolled as Didi shifted, allowing Didi to see the wrinkle of dirt in the folds of the child's neck. Didi wiped away the moist grunge, only to feel more, a tacky, gritty necklace of filth around Mel's throat.

Didi shook her daughter's shoulders. "Wake up," she said to her face, angry suddenly at the child's ability to sleep so soundly, as if she might be taken advantage of later in life. "Wake up and get in the tub," she ordered, already reaching behind her to swing the old metal faucets on full force.

Melanie woke weeping, roused so unfairly in the middle of the night, so harshly, and for something so thoroughly tumultuous. Her mother landed her in the water and scrubbed her throat, her chest, down between her legs, splashing about as if to drown Melanie; the cloth and the hand it covered were fierce over her small chilled body. Some part of her was still asleep, awash in a new kind of nightmare, crying and crying.

Didi did not lather up her daughter's pink hair, decided that that could be tomorrow's project. She carried her wrapped in a towel, still sobbing, back into her bedroom, where she pulled new pajamas over her damp skin and zipped her quickly inside them as if to contain the fleeting perfume of cleanliness. She switched off the light and sat beside Melanie while the child snuffled, wounded by her mother's compulsiveness yet still sleepy, unable to sustain her huff in the face of the warmth and solace of bed, of being stroked on the back.

It was just after Melanie drifted away that Didi heard Paddy come home, closing the front door behind him. On impulse, she slid from Melanie's bed into her closet, a shallow space full of pretty dresses hanging on the bar. She hid, thinking he could have a taste of his own medicine. Let him think she'd left him, abandoned Mel, gone away. She listened as he moved quietly through the living room and dining room and into the kitchen, where the sink tap ran for a moment, then the bathroom, where he peed for a good long while, then spat, then flushed. He would not notice the soggy bathmat or the moist air, the scent of soap. The light switch clicked off; he checked the back door. He opened the refrigerator and moved the condiments around; Didi could hear the clinking, then the soft suction as the door closed. He stumbled leaving the kitchen, catching his foot on the new wooden threshold. In the dark bedroom he was silent — undressing, she supposed. Finally he must have eased into his side of bed, confident of his stealth.

Didi's heart banged the way it had when she had played games with her siblings, full of the anticipation of being found, the thrill of being hidden where people didn't know to look, of being a hider and a seeker, of waiting. Quickly she shucked her nightgown, letting it fall to the closet floor at her feet, breathing in her own sour odor, shivering in excitement.

"Dee?" she heard. He had padded to Mel's room, and she wondered if he would wake their daughter, if Melanie would have to endure another arousal by one of her foolish parents. The light clicked on; she could see the bright stripe beneath the closet door. Mel's dresses hung on either side of her on their plastic hangers. Her ear was against the cool metal bar; a ruffle was at her bare navel.

She stepped from the closet, naked, to see him, naked, leaning over Melanie, about to shake her. He jumped.

"Oh my hell, honey, you scared . . ."

Didi walked through the room without stopping, switching off Mel's light as she left. She returned to her side of their bed and waited for him as if she had beat the seeker to base, her heart still banging away in her chest. He would *have* to come home if she was hidden every night from him in a closet, wearing no clothes. He did not entirely know her, she told herself.

"What's this all about?" he said as he fell in next to her and put his big hands on her hips. She had not lain naked in bed in a long time, although Paddy frequently slept without clothes. He did not smell of liquor. He did not smell of perfume. "I'm sorry I'm late," he said. "I got tangled up in a bid with Jim. Then we went to his house and moved a hot-water tank. I think I hurt my back," he added, looking for sympathy, as if to distract her.

"You said you were going out with Evan," she said. "You said a drink with Evan."

"No, babe, that's tomorrow night."

Now it was Paddy's heart that raced. It was Rachel he'd arranged to meet tomorrow, not Ev. "I can cancel," he said, grateful for an excuse to abandon his plans. He'd been having second thoughts all week. He rolled toward Didi, toward her unusual nakedness. "Wanna fool around?" he murmured in her ear.

She seemed to want him to hold her, but she did not want to make love. If she let him have sex, he told himself, he would break his plans with Rachel. For a while he tried to save his marriage, bumping his erection against her thigh, covering her neck with kisses, but she turned away, and rose eventually to retrieve her nightgown from Mel's room.

When she climbed back into bed, she considered telling him that Evan Cole had gotten mugged. She considered it, but did not tell him. She didn't want to be left alone again. Evan Cole could wait and tell him himself tomorrow.

Eleven

· · · · · · · · · · · · ·

IT WAS CHRISTMAS, Rachel thought later, that was responsible for her affair. It was the fact of the holiday, of gifts and generosity, that made her succumb to infidelity. It was because Paddy liked to
give gifts, and because her birthday fell just a month before Christmas; the combination was deadly. "I find him simple," Ev had said.
"I find him kind."

Rachel and Paddy did not go to bed together until January, at
Paddy's bungalow in Oak Park, on a night when the boys were
staying at Ev's. School had been canceled a few days because of
heavy snows; the wind blew until the streets, deadly serene, shone
with ice and the trees and rain gutters and balconies and playground
equipment were hung with transitory frozen daggers.

In the face of this, Paddy's house was too hot. He had turned up
his heaters — perhaps he'd gone and bought a new one for each
room, big ones for big rooms, little ones for little rooms — in order
to keep Rachel comfortable. She was both touched and frightened by
this gesture. If it was a gesture.

"Where's Didi?" Rachel asked, although she already knew; they
had already discussed Didi's whereabouts this weekend.

"In Normal, visiting my mom and aunt. Melanie . . ." He let his
daughter's name trail off as if he were avoiding the mention of something indiscreet, as if he were being polite, giving only a vague nod to
his certain infidelity. Rachel was tempted to make him be franker, the
way her husband would have. Ev wouldn't tolerate coyness.

Paddy's home reminded Rachel of a mortuary. She had hoped for something surprising, but Paddy and Didi's taste occupied precisely the space she would have anticipated. They went in for studio photographs, she noticed, a whole wall of smiling faces, and then below, bric-a-brac and conventional furniture, arranged in conventional formations, the groupings little girls learned playing dollhouse and tea party and later had ratified by sitcom and soap opera sets. They owned a large electric organ made of faux wood; all of its rhythm and accompaniment levers were flipped flat like a palette of big plastic fingernails. A television sat enshrined in the center of an elaborate wooden structure placed directly in front of and too close to the sofa, to which Paddy had directed her. Rachel felt herself lean away from the dark screen as if it might tip over and crush her. The two speakers were as tall as the coffins of children.

Having devoted all their energies to making sure their meeting was safe, Rachel and Paddy had neglected to devise even a flimsy premise for it. Each was too nervous to eat; neither had considered taking in a film or a play. It was too cold to go for a walk, and besides, the neighbors might notice. They sat on the couch with a plush velveteen cushion between them. Paddy had turned on no music; the television sat ominously, like an uninvited guest, waiting for engagement; the only noise was the murmur of the heaters' fans, humming from every room, flaring on and making the lights dim briefly. Rachel had been busy all day denying what she knew she was going to do: allow Paddy Limbach to put his penis inside her.

Rachel had permitted only a few other men in her life to do the same. There was Evan, of course, and other boyfriends during college, all three of them men she had been in love with. She'd drawn a traditional line, on one side of it every conceivable erotic grope and probe and nuzzle, and on the other irrefutable intercourse. A foolish distinction, she supposed, but related to procreation, to children, to the old-fashioned notion of preserving the consummate act for men with whom she was unquestionably in love. She held on to this outdated idea in spite of her radical politics, in spite of intoxicated arousal. In the center of the cacophony, stimulated by intellectual or alcoholic or carnal overindulgence, Rachel retained a stubborn un-budging sobriety like a pearl.

Now she could feel the plump swell of her diaphragm, inserted an hour earlier. It had been so long since she'd used it, she'd had to fill it with water and examine it over the sink, looking for leaks. She'd flexed it in and out like a toy, testing its suppleness, then applied the goo and clumsily plunged it into place. Many years ago, Ev had learned to do this for her. Because she'd been away from the dia-phragm for a while — she and Ev had relied on rhythm, on with-drawal, on condoms — she had not prepared herself against an at-tack of nostalgia concerning it. Ev had always liked to immerse himself in the dailyness of her woman's business — he bought tam-pons without flinching; he didn't care if she used his razor to shave under her arms — and he'd made a nice foreplayish ritual of insert-ing her diaphragm. Doing it all by herself this evening had almost made Rachel cancel her sleepover with Paddy; she'd had a tearful episode in the bathroom, remembering Ev's dark fingers squeezing the pliable ring of latex, easing it up inside her, then easing himself up the length of her body until his face was beside hers, his sticky fingers between them aiding the subsequent insertion.

Paddy said, "How about a drink?"

"Excellent." Rachel nodded. He hurried to the kitchen as if to rehearse his next, forgotten line.

On the coffee table in front of Rachel lay a tattered *Old Farmer's Almanac*, pages not only well thumbed but marked. She scanned one of these. It concerned itself with little-known facts, like: the military invented the refrigerator during World War II to cool not food but aircraft engines. Sirius is the brightest star. Mars had once had water on its surface. David Rice Atchison was president of the United States for one day. Distilled strawberry juice will tighten loose teeth. Hippocrates treated his patients with vinegar, and if you soak a sugar cube with vinegar and then suck, your hiccups will go away.

It was like "Hints from Heloise" meets Paul Harvey.

"Here you are," Paddy said. "Honey," he added, handing Ra-chel a huge glass the shape of an upturned sombrero. Pink wine sloshed from the side.

"Thank you," Rachel said, wiping the spill into the couch. It was a dreadful sweet wine, and it wasn't particularly cold. "Don't you have any sugar you could put in here?" she would have said to Ev later, if Ev had been here with her, if she had had him to talk to later. Those bathroom tears returned, related directly to the ache just below her cervix from the diaphragm. She tried, in vain, to substitute her friend Zoë as her future audience.

"Cheers," Paddy said miserably, raising his own ridiculous pink drink. Then, "Why are you crying?"

"I'm scared," she said, twin drops sliding from her eyes and through her makeup, applied clumsily in a moment of self-doubt. Now she would have pale streaks through her blusher, she thought. But better that than dark circles from wiping at her mascara. No wonder she'd never gotten the hang of wearing makeup; with it, you had to make minute-by-minute decisions during your crying jags.

"Don't cry," Paddy said. "I hate it when you cry."

"You've never seen me cry before."

"I *will* hate it," he said. "I hate it now." Her crying reminded him of sex with Didi. And that was maybe the last thing he wanted to be reminded of. Crying had been erotic for Didi, and maybe it was for Rachel, too, but it wasn't for him. He liked his partners happy when he went to bed with them. He liked the image of a woman tearing at his shirt with her teeth, smiling. Not sobbing on his shoulder. Like Rachel, Paddy had an ache in his groin, though of course it wasn't from wearing a diaphragm but from thinking all day of going to bed with Ev's wife. Now she was crying, not just sniffling but sobbing, her shoulders shaking, her nose running. Paddy scooted over the cushion between them and put his arms around her. She fell against his chest and breathed deeply. Nothing seemed more certain to Paddy than the obvious fact that she needed to be held, and had been needing it for some time. He was relieved; it was a job he had no anxiety performing.

"It's O.K.," he said into her warm hair. She smelled clean. He liked the idea of her bathing for him, caring what he thought. At her ear, there was no earring to avoid with his mouth, there was just lobe, the downy droplet of flesh he could hold between his lips. She had a nice earlobe with fine hairs at the bottom, larger than Didi's because she was older than Didi, a fact about the human body he'd once read in the almanac.

"Oh," Rachel said. She said it a number of times, very softly. She turned her wide chest toward him, putting one of her breasts right into Paddy's palm, which was the precise size to hold it. He always wondered whether breasts hadn't been designed by God not just to suckle the young but to encourage procreation, the way they swelled beneath the hand, the way they drew the mouth.

Rachel's breasts, he noted, were not as firm as Didi's. They were larger than his wife's but had lost some tensile strength, as in any animal who'd had young. Paddy covered them with his palms, shaping their softness, accepting their pliability. He could love them, he thought.

Rachel had worried all day about the order in which she would drop her clothes. She'd come without a bra, wearing a long buttoned sweater over jeans with the intention of leaving the sweater on like a coverup after removing nearly everything else — shoes, socks, pants, panties. And now, apparently, she was to lose the sweater first, as Paddy moved down the buttons, flicking them open one-handed.

"You're good at that," she told him. "Should that worry me?"

"Uh-uh," he answered. They were murmuring in each other's ears. Their eyes were closed. At some level, Rachel's brain was taking note of the variation, all the differences between this and loving Ev, the familiar versus the unknown. But some other level continued responding while she thought, kept moving closer to Paddy, tugging her body toward his. Her skin wanted his skin; her parts wanted to match up to his, one by one and without exception, the sole of her foot desiring the sole of his.

But two adults couldn't have sex on a couch without inconvenience, and there was no reason not to request a move to the bedroom. "Let's lie down," Rachel suggested, since she was confident Paddy wouldn't come up with the idea himself. Besides, she wanted to watch him walk from here to there with an erection. Erections had always delighted her, and Paddy's jeans — so different from Ev's loose chinos in this moment of excitement — made him move gingerly. He blushed, and Rachel did not have to worry anymore about her own body. Whatever inadequacies she felt compelled to cover most of the time were not going to bother her this evening in Paddy's bed. She vowed to think not of how she looked but of how she felt. And she felt chilled, trembling in fear, in her near nudity.

"It's cold in here," she told Paddy as they walked with their heads bowed into his bedroom.

"Yeah," he said. "I had to turn on all the heaters."

. . .

During their second round of sex, Rachel forgot herself at one point and began to have a conversation, as she would have with her husband. "How do they know, those people in the *Farmer's Almanac*, what the weather is going to be like for the whole year?"

Paddy stopped, lifting away to stare down at her in the semidark. Rachel recalled what they were up to and was embarrassed. And lonely for her husband, who tolerated talking when they made love, who would pause and chat, resume, hesitate again. Ev was uncharacteristically leisurely in bed.

Paddy said, "My dad was a farmer."

"Yes, I know. In Normal."

"Outside Normal."

For no real reason, Rachel said, "What you might call a fur piece from Normal." She was exhausted from weighing her guilt against her pleasure, and sore and physically worn out as well. Sleepy. Happy. Maybe all the other five dwarfs, too. Dark rooms and warm beds made her tired. The almanac on Paddy's coffee table also reported that one's sex drive shut off in the dark; she could believe it.

"You want to just go to sleep?" Paddy asked. He'd remained for a while optimistic about their making love again but now curled around her, sweaty and heavy. This Rachel liked. Ev had not permitted contact in sleep; he cramped himself into his fetal ball as far away from her as possible. His scrunched volume made Rachel aware of her own dimensions, as if she didn't have a right to fill space. An insomniac, he protected his sleep and was surly when wakened in the night.

At Paddy's, when Rachel woke angry with herself and anxious about her sons at three in the morning, Paddy roused himself and told her a story. A story!

"Once there was a woman with a hat," he began. The woman was beautiful — "Of course," Rachel could hear Ev saying, Ev with his automatic tagging of any stereotype. Paddy's character was very vain about her hats. This particular hat was tangerine-colored and shaped like a ship, a great big ship that sat upon her head. She had a temper, the beauty, and one day in a fit of anger she flung her hat from a high window. Down it floated, passing offices and restaurants and stores, the people inside watching it go by, wondering idly where it had come from, making up anecdotes about it while the hat sailed to the avenue, where it whirled in the auto exhaust and smoke before landing in a puddle, from which a friendly dog took it, shook it in his mouth, then carried it home with him, where his owner, a dog-catcher, rinsed out the mud and hung it on the clothesline, from which a brisk wind sent it flying once more, this time over to the shipyard, where it landed on a freighter bound for Shanghai . . . On Paddy went, episodic and steady, the hat story floating in the dark room like the hat itself, Rachel being first amazed, then eventually lulled successfully back to sleep.

In the morning she thought of Zach, who had all his life despised conflict. "Tell me the three pigs story," he had often said to her when he was very little, "except no bad wolf."

"I sensed no rising action in your story," Rachel told Paddy when he woke. "No epiphany, no denouement."

Paddy shrugged. He was the kind of man who did not own up to his nighttime gestures of softness. For breakfast, for example, he served her Grape Nuts and skim milk.

"Ick," she complained.

"It's good for you," he said, motioning with his spoon.

"That's just the problem." They seemed to agree not to mention or even acknowledge that it was Ev who had recommended Grape Nuts to Paddy, Ev who ate them every morning without fail, Ev who extolled their hearty filling nature. Surely Paddy had been a bacon-and-egg man before he met Ev.

. . .

They got in the habit of spending at least part of the night with each other, most often at Rachel's apartment; Paddy appeared at the door on the late Friday afternoons of the boys' weekends with Ev. Quickly sex, too, became a more habitual act. Rachel would begin cooperative and passionate, though not as excited as she'd been the first time. Soon, however, she would become too thoughtful, too guilty, too distracted. In the middle of things she might say, "You know, your wife never liked me."

Paddy, growing accustomed to her style, would stop moving and say, "I don't know about never. You only met her once."

"Still."

"Well, she said you were a snob."

"Really?"

"Yes."

"Do *you* think I'm a snob?" She liked the idea of miffing Paddy's wife.

"No, I think you're a beautiful lady."

Rachel bristled; Paddy's pillow talk, something he'd grown more confident in using, irritated her. He sounded like a cross between a country-western singer and a Las Vegas pimp when he tried it out on her.

"Seepy?" Paddy asked, now tender rather than excited.

"*Sl*," Rachel corrected, enjoying his caresses in spite of his canned dialogue. "I like you," she admitted. "I think you're nice. What are you doing in bed with a snob like me?"

"Trying to get in your pants," he said, slipping a hand under her backside.

"My pants are on the floor," she said flatly. He'd learned his lines from bad movies, maybe bad books. She didn't want him to tell her things he'd read or heard before, especially when they were in bed together, especially then, when it made a great deal of difference that she was not just anyone. She asked him, not for the first time, "Are you *particularly* attracted to me, or did you just feel like sleeping with someone new?"

Paddy stopped moving his hand. Rachel felt the mean urge to ask if he couldn't perform the two things, talk and foreplay, at the same time.

"What do you mean?" he asked.

"I mean, I get this feeling that men sometimes just want to fuck anything, anybody. Sometimes men seem just like automatic weapons, spraying randomly, hitting whoever happens to be standing there. I want to know that you want *me*." Her words sounded suddenly absurd to Rachel. What the hell was she talking about, anyway? Wasn't she in bed with him, hadn't he sought out her, only her?

Paddy lay back on his pillow and crossed his hands chastely over his chest. He was silent for a long while, during which time Rachel reached over to check his penis. It curled, limp and warm, on his testicles.

"I'm sorry," Rachel whispered, closing her hand over his bundle of genitalia and waiting for it to respond. "Please don't be angry. I'm just nervous."

"I don't like that word," Paddy said.

"Which?"

"The F word. I don't like the way it sounds when you say it."

"And how does it sound when I say it? How is it different from when you say it?" Rachel was sitting up now, ready to get out of bed altogether.

"I don't say it," he said simply. "I don't like to hear anyone say it." He scratched his chest, where he still had a tan from last summer, one that ended where his Levi's began. He spent the summer in the sun, crawling around on roofs. He had to be the handsomest man she had ever been intimate with; in fact, his attractiveness played an undeniable role, which was new for Rachel. It had never, in the past, made a particular difference. Once again, Rachel was struck by the ridiculousness of their being together. She was also struck by his apparent code of behavior. He didn't say *fuck*. The word actually upset him. It was like his believing in God, another character trait Rachel had presumed outdated, if not extinct. "You're in the wrong generation," she told him.

"What do you mean?"

"I don't know what I mean." She lay her head on his tanned chest. "Mr. Chivalry," she said. "The gallant guy."

. . .

Another time, Rachel told Paddy about her day, thinking she could charm him in the way she used to charm Evan. "I'm getting so nostalgic and sappy," she said as they lay in her bed, an early winter darkness settling outside the window. "Today I turned on *Sesame Street* just to listen to the theme song. Oh, it was weepy-weepy." She waited for Paddy to hold her, to treasure her female sentimentality, which was so unlike her. This was the way she had flirted with Ev, once upon a time, though he'd become immune to her tender moments as the years passed. He'd quit being moved by them. Beside her, Paddy also seemed untouched. He lay breathing noisily, awake and thoughtful.

She continued, "I never wanted a three-year-old more badly. The boys and I used to watch *Sesame* together every morning after Ev left for the office."

Suddenly Rachel had a scare, an instant's worth of terror: her boys were never going to be young again, her husband was quite possibly never coming back. Well, she knew that, and even now, a second after, the terror seemed manageable. But for that brief instant she had felt the spin of the uncontrollable, the sucking vortex of mortality.

"Paddy?" she said, as if he might have left her, too.

"Uh-huh."

"What are you thinking?" She wanted to hear how enigmatic she was to him; she wanted to hear him fumble for his feelings.

"Well," he said, lifting himself up on one elbow, facing her, "I hope you won't take this the wrong way, but you always seem to want me to feel sorry for you. And I don't want to feel sorry for you.

I mean, I think we're having a good time, besides the sin of it all. Don't you?"

Now it was her turn to fall silent. She cast about for the eager little life vignettes she'd provided him these last few weeks and realized he was correct: she always made herself pitiful. Well. Even Ev, the trained analyst, had not been able to point this out to her. But then, Ev was sometimes oddly ignorant about what Paddy would most likely label the Big Picture. Rachel found herself not hurt by Paddy's observation but in awe of it. It was so astute and smart. And she hadn't thought of him as being smart, that was the real truth, the real thrill — that he might be worthy of her, body *and* soul.

"When I'm alone I imagine you're watching me," she told him then, which was true. She hadn't been able to sustain that game in a long time, not since her last crush, several years earlier, when the boys were ear-infected toddlers and she loved their pediatrician. She'd let him observe her all day long, bathing the boys, tucking them in, telling them clever tales. How she shone as a model mother when Dr. Nixon was around! And of course nothing had happened between her and Dr. Nixon. Soon the boys quit getting sick; then they started going to Ev's GP. But she liked having Paddy's shadow hovering near her. "I pretend you can see me driving along the freeway, singing songs, talking on the phone, whatever. I like to think you'd like me if you could see me."

"I *do* like you." Paddy had been about to tell her he loved her. It would be the first time he would have said it before the woman did; despite his capacity for outrageous gestures, that one he withheld, waiting so as not to be humiliated. But he wasn't sure he *did* love Rachel. Maybe it was age creeping up on him; maybe that thing he used to call love he wanted to name something new, such as affection or friendliness. Well, that was ridiculous, he told himself, he was more than affectionate or friendly in his attitude toward Rachel, but was it love? He knew he would rather be here naked with Rachel Cole than with any other woman he could think of. He knew he thought about her all day, although not in the way she had just described, where he was her audience, but much more about sex, much more about being in bed with her. He postulated to himself that he contemplated sex many more hours of the day than he actually performed it. Perfectly normal thing, he told himself, every man did the same.

Maybe it was having a daughter that made him question calling his feelings for Rachel love. He knew he loved Melanie; she was his gauge. Nobody — not his mother, not his wife, not his mistress — could claim the same sure position in his heart. And given that fact, he told himself he might as well tell Rachel he loved her; certainly he cared what happened to her, he fantasized about her, he wanted to fornicate with her. But if he loved his daughter, he did not love Rachel. It was not the same thing. So he kept this grand gesture to himself, he reserved it guiltily, because it was clear she could use the boost his words would give her.

. . .

It seemed to Rachel she'd been waiting all her married life for an excuse to have an affair. And since Evan had moved away — chosen to leave her — she felt justified. It was flimsy justification, but it would suffice. She drank too much and she slept with a different man.

She had had very little experience in sleeping around. She could count on one hand the men she'd had sex with. On the other hand she could count the boys she might have had sex with, if she had allowed it. And if there were a third hand, she might number the men in her married life she'd wanted to fall in love with.

It was always a matter of falling in love, for Rachel. She had to be in love before she'd have sex, just as Zoë had said of her. Otherwise, what was the point? Her pleasure was a quality of expectation, enhanced by the man's attraction to her, compounded by the forbiddenness of the relationship, enriched by the hours she spent fabricating his personality, until her love was a marvelous creation of her own imagination.

All Paddy Limbach had to do was put his hand on hers. She almost told him she was in love with him after their first night of lovemaking. It was not an entirely happy emotion for Rachel. She still loved Evan, she knew that, but Paddy was new, his problems were fresh to her, his drawbacks still elusive, his simple humanity still in question: maybe he was not a mere mortal like the other men.

"Everybody poops," she'd told her sons when introducing them to the toilet, then tried to talk herself into believing it was true. Some people — men she idolized — seemed incapable of that act. Her problem in love was just that simple, just that absurdly complicated.

Now she spent her days preparing for her evenings, the way she had in high school and college, making a pathetic attempt at improving her thighs by lying in front of the television in the mornings and lifting her legs along with the women on the screen, bathing in the late afternoons, choosing clothes that best hid her flaws, underwear that might distract from the aging portions of her physique. In fact, she bought new underwear, the unhygienic type that gym teachers always claimed would cause itching infections. It was unthinkable for Rachel to appear before Paddy wearing her usual panties, those flesh-toned cotton items — yes, comfortable, yes, functional, but utterly unfun. Fun underwear reminded you of its presence by sneaking between your legs, its elastic biting in ways and places your friendly cotton briefs simply didn't.

For his part, Paddy wore boxers. Rachel couldn't remember seeing a man in boxer shorts before. She liked them. They were modest yet sexy. They looked easier to want to launder than those white briefs with a blue-and-yellow-striped waistband, their stains of uncertain origin. Like neckties, boxers came in colors and patterns, silk and paisley, cartoon pigs, decoy ducks, plaid.

"I love your underwear," she said to Paddy Limbach. "I love the way you leave them in your jeans, all ready for you to hop back in, like a horse waiting for a cowboy."

Rachel did not care what Didi was like. Rachel already knew she was the superior lover, more interesting, more erotic. Her confidence in Didi's inferiority made her indifferent to Paddy's romantic past — surely he'd never known anyone as fascinating as she? But Paddy was curious about Evan, and Rachel didn't mind talking about him. She appraised her husband with complete frankness, not exactly preferring him, but acknowledging his longer claim to her life and affection. She didn't mind noting the differences between him and Paddy; it was like comparing a doughnut to a bagel — same basic shape, but entirely other substance.

One night as they lay in bed, Paddy timidly asked, "Does this happen a lot in your marriage?"

"This what? This sleeping around?" Rachel was flattered: to think, Paddy believed her a veteran! "Of course not."

"Oh."

"And you?" She asked merely to be polite; nothing was clearer to her than Paddy's unpolished infidelity. When the phone had rung earlier he'd bitten his own tongue, nervous to the point of sweating bullets.

"Oh my heck, no." They listened to the elevator motor outside Rachel's apartment. Paddy wanted to know why Rachel would select him over her husband, who was more intelligent, more sophisticated, made more money, and knew better jokes. Was she doing this to get back at Ev? "Listen," he said, "I'm not a pawn, am I?"

"A pawn?" Rachel laughed. She put her dark head on Paddy's shoulder and kissed his chin. She rolled her wide friendly body up against his so that their parts matched. Paddy liked this aspect of her, the fact that she stretched his length, that she seemed capable of utter relaxation beside him. The difference in their weight was maybe twenty pounds. She was unlike little Didi, who always squirmed around during sex worrying about her thighs and stomach, who got distracted by the possibility of becoming fat while Paddy pumped away on top. He used to feel her pinching her own tummy, taking note.

• • •

In February, Paddy invited Rachel to a basketball game. He'd sold his father's farm to one of the assistant coaches at De Paul; somehow this entitled him to tickets. "The boys would love that!" she exclaimed, realizing after he'd gone that they would, in all probability, *not* love it.

The stadium stunned her. Zach sat down beside her and looked around at the mob. He said, "It's like *Where's Waldo?*" Marcus scowled. They knew nothing about basketball. Zach played soccer, but the only sport Marcus had ever played was badminton with his uncle on the apartment building's roof, losing birdies over the side. Out on the floor during timeouts, girls flew akimbo into the air and boys caught them in their arms. While in the air, the smiling girls jerked into boomerang-like positions, then folded into sitting on the descent and, finally, landed cradled in their partners' arms. Every time one flew up, Rachel gasped. How could their mothers watch? she wondered. From living for many years with Ev she had grown graphically imaginative about the disasters lurking everywhere. All she could think when she saw a body sailing up into the stadium air was that if it fell, there would be a broken neck, a crumpled blue-and-white form on the floor.

"How many people are here?" Rachel shouted in Paddy's ear. He was eating popcorn, a handful at a time, and little crumbs were falling over him.

"Fifteen thou," he guessed. "I don't know."

She couldn't recall having sat in the same place with fifteen thousand people before in her life. It made her start thinking about snipers.

A beachball sailed by. People stood and sat, stood and sat, raising their arms and lowering them. "Here comes the wave," Paddy shouted to her, standing and sitting with the rest. It was sort of phenomenal that so many grownups could be persuaded to wear blue sweaters and pretend to be a wave. Rachel tried to think of attending a basketball game as an enriching experience, a mother-son bonding event. She tried to believe she was having fun. It seemed to her that having fun was something she'd outgrown, like reading the comics or going dancing. She'd lost the knack. Or maybe she'd never had it.

Unfortunately, her sons looked as baffled as she felt. Zach chewed a licorice whip and Marcus was reading the pamphlet Paddy had bought for them with the players' names and photographs in it. Up and down the court stomped the teams, great big boys, the basketball sailing from hand to hand, the players' faces hermetic and obsessed. Part of Rachel wanted to escort her sons away from here, hustle them to the car and then back to their condo, hide them from such grotesque displays of aggression. She felt extraordinarily exposed: the proximity of everyone, the noise and action. The other part of her welcomed the normality, the prototypical American fun of it all. The thing about fun, she thought, was that you couldn't concentrate on it. Otherwise you saw how absurd it was. Boys trying to poke a ball in a basket, adults avidly following, up and down, up and down, firing off obscenities, howling at the boobish referees wearing zebra shirts.

But Rachel decided to let it fascinate her. She gave herself permission to study Paddy and his world. She let him take her hand when the game was over and lead her through the crowd to his car.

He knew many things Rachel didn't, but what she came to admire in him was the fact that he owned up to what he didn't know, which was substantial. He had a foggy sense of geography, one inferior to Rachel's sons'. He did not, for example, know where Mount Everest was, nor which countries surrounded France. She'd only discovered this because Marcus had a project due; but it successfully opened the possibility that he knew much, much less.

One of Rachel's most debilitating fears was that people would discover how little prepared she was to understand the world: scientifically, politically, organically. With her brainy son Marcus she feigned feigning ignorance, his assumption being that she did so in order to get him to research his own answers. In social circles where she might have to comment on world events or historical facts, she fell back on idiosyncratic anecdotes she'd picked up from television reports or a recently read magazine article. She listened to the news on public radio every day, but her attention to it was purely temporary: she did not have sufficient background to draw conclusions. And when she asked Marcus to help locate a plug-in for a new reading lamp, he said to her with disdain as he crawled under the sideboard, "Could it be called an *outlet?*" Later, when he sat researching the lifespans of bats, Rachel read a few paragraphs about their feeding habits, their radar and parenting. It was all too much, the world. She could never get an adequate handle on it. Whatever she learned, she seemed to forget: names of painters, philosophies of great thinkers, the temperature at which water boiled, the exchange rate of the British pound, the different types of clouds, the depth of the ocean, the size of the sun, the arrangement of the universe.

Paddy didn't know much of this stuff either, although he read the *Old Farmer's Almanac* religiously. He had a beaming way of smiling at Rachel when she pointed out his ignorance, a smile that successfully let her know she was the only one who thought it was important. Other people, he implied, did not so fervently worry about what they were revealed not to know. He gave her gifts; he certainly would not judge her deficiencies.

And that felt novel. Her husband, she'd believed, found her lacking.

• • •

Rachel knew she had fallen solidly in love — had moved from the temporary, suspended *falling* to the thudding past participle, *had fallen* — when she delighted in hearing her sons say Paddy's name, illicitly and innocently. "Paddy told me . . ." Zach would begin, his side of an argument aided by the simple masculine invocation. And Marcus would answer *"Paddy"* in his scornful, patronizing way. She'd loved to hear them call Ev Papa, to watch them run at him full-tilt when he came home from work.

Paddy, they said now, and her heart bloomed.

Twelve

. . . .

"PADDY SAYS our pipes are lead," Zach reported to his father. Before Evan could reply, Marcus corrected his brother.

"He said the *seams* were lead, not the pipes. Idiot," he added scornfully, a tag intended for either Zach or Paddy, Ev wasn't sure which.

"Marcus." Ev sighed, too tired to get upset. The habit of relentless parenting — stalking, catching, punishing — had fizzled inside him; he wasn't in the mood to rekindle it. The combination of a drink and a long walk had made him successfully exhausted. He'd forgotten the boys would be arriving; they were waiting in the liquor store across the street, sucking lollipops the Chinese proprietor had given them. The lollipops were pink, heart-shaped, a pair of nippled breasts. Evan had purchased cigars just to express his gratitude.

Marcus had eyed the cigar package suspiciously. "You gave up smoking," he told his father.

"I'm being friendly," Ev said. Then, because he thought he was lying and he remembered that he didn't lie to his son, he said, "And I might feel like smoking one later."

Marcus's face made Ev feel villainous.

"If our seams are lead," Zach went on in the apartment kitchen, hours later, "we could be getting brain damage when we have a drink."

Evan sat with them while they did their homework, Zach dreamily, Marcus furtively. Their scritching pencil noise seemed endless; every few minutes, Ev would leave the room to wander around the apartment as if he were looking for something. He was restless and weary at once. When he got back to the kitchen, everything was as he had left it, flat. Time itself was bored with proceeding.

"All Paddy said," said Marcus, "was that we should run the water for a minute before we fill our glasses. That's all. Then the water that's been sitting in the pipes washes away. You always exaggerate, Zach. You're always getting all excited."

"*You're* the one who stayed up all night scared for your brain cells," Zach said amiably. "Not me."

"You don't have enough brain cells to worry about."

Evan wondered why his tolerance for their bickering had lessened instead of grown larger. Wouldn't it have made more sense for him to sort of miss it, to feel nostalgic toward it, to indulge it happily, stocking up for the lonesome moment when they'd gone?

"The plumber said it was unlikely our seams were lead," Marcus told his father, as if he and Ev were the two adults at the table, as if Ev had expressed concern, which, in a former time, he would have.

"Paddy —" Zach began.

"When did you see Paddy?" Ev asked, hoping to distract them.

They looked up at him simultaneously, their expressions the same, that suddenly regretful, "oh, never mind" face.

That came first.

Then there was Paddy himself, oddly sheepish lately, unable to meet Ev's gaze. Zach had reported that Paddy sometimes ate dinner with them, although Paddy had never mentioned it, and Marcus had perfected an imitation of him, a cruel parody of a retarded person, the lolling tongue, the spastic hand gestures. He bulged his jaw and blew hair from his forehead, a move he might have had to study Paddy, maybe for an extended period, in order to acquire.

Paddy and Ev still met for racquetball in the Y, a sweaty warren, a warm haven in the unremitting winter. Ev scrutinized Paddy; Paddy behaved like a man with a guilty conscience and a child with a giddy secret, averting his eyes, demure as if making up for bad behavior, yet gleeful as if in love. It surprised Ev how peacefully he accepted the possibility that Paddy and Rachel were sleeping together. Was he just that incredulous, his ego just that big? Did it mean he had truly left his wife? Or did it mean he couldn't take Paddy seriously as a threat? Or did he enjoy thinking of Rachel as attractive to another man? Perhaps this was how he would have to learn about his feelings, by having them tested, one by one.

His reflexive anger, hidden away from himself, surfaced on the racquetball court. He served into the corner eight points in a row, a shot he'd developed and held in check, now gone wild, merciless. Paddy, overconfident, waited in the corner the ninth time while Ev sent a slow lob in the other direction. The game continued in a childish vein, Paddy hustling to keep up with Ev's trickiness, then resorting to his original advantage of simple brute strength, each forgoing the unspoken restraint they'd previously played with. At first Paddy seemed willing to let Ev win the game, but then he seemed to take stock of the situation and decide, in his boyish way, that he *wouldn't* be losing this third game, never mind whether he'd won the wife.

"Fuck!" Ev shouted when he spun and missed a return. His forehead throbbed; the vein in his temple stood out as if it would burst. Paddy, who'd fallen into the competition easily, recognizing it from high school, from other games with other men, suddenly remembered who he was playing with.

"What's wrong?" he asked, stopping play entirely. The face Ev turned to him — hostile, teeth bared beneath protective prescription glasses, nostrils flaring — startled Paddy and brought him instantly around: he was standing in a locked room with his mistress's husband, who held his racquet like a weapon.

But Ev shook himself. The skin on his upper arms was loose; his white doorknobby knees were decidedly unattractive. Paddy could not help comparing his own muscular arms to Ev's, his own smooth brown back to Ev's skinny flaccid one. He tried to suppress his sense of victory, the surge of pure happiness. Ev might have won two of their three games on the court, but Paddy had Rachel's heart — or if not her heart, her sighs, her teeth at his ears and lips. And having her meant he did not care about racquetball. They finished their game and he lost again, for once not having to pretend to be gracious as a loser. He clapped Ev on the shoulder, feeling for the first time toward him genuine and complete pity.

It was Paddy's smugness, his condescension, that began to convince Ev he was right about an affair. Part of him wanted to shove Paddy onto the floor and beat his mouth until his lips quit looping in a smile around those perfect teeth; another part wanted to quiz Rachel: *now* did she understand the elusive attraction of Paddy Limbach? *Now* could they explore his curious appeal?

In the shower, Paddy and Ev stood silently under two steamy spigots, separated by a partial wall, the tops of their heads and their toes visible to each other. All five of the toes on Paddy's left foot were capped by dented purple nails; he'd dropped a tarbucket on them over the summer, and the injury was slowly pushing out of him. He liked his wounds, the signs of labor. Ev's feet resembled his father's, long and pale, the toes nearly prehensile. He had no deformities that weren't inherited. They were both thinking of Rachel as they soaped their hairy parts: heads, armpits, crotches. They were both considering divorce because of Rachel.

Like their fathers' deaths, this parallel milepost struck them differently. Paddy turned his face to the invigorating spray and grinned, letting the water strike his teeth. He was making a case for leaving Didi, feeding himself a theory that she'd grown as unhappy in their marriage as he: hadn't it been Didi who'd quit enjoying sex? As far as he could tell, Didi spent the day moping around the house, playing church music on her organ, dusting her animal figurines. And as for Melanie, wouldn't the presence of two stepbrothers be good for her, with Marcus teaching her calculus, Zach giving her piggyback rides?

In the next stall, Evan felt the merciless stinging pulse on his scalp and imagined it eating him away incrementally like acid rain ate statuary. He was picturing the future, a frightening absence of image in his consciousness, like the blinding aftereffect of a flashbulb, an explosion of dense mercury behind his closed eyelids. He hated the future, the nothingness of it, the fact that he seemed to be inviting it in, or at least doing little to prevent its arrival.

In another time, the two men would have mentioned their thoughts on divorce; in another time, Ev would have encouraged

Paddy's, and Paddy would have discouraged Ev's. Now their advice to each other would run exactly counter to that. Their advice would reveal their secret knowledge.

"Same time next week?" Paddy asked in the lobby as they retrieved their cards from the file box.

Ev nodded, slipping a toothpick into his mouth. His eyeglasses still held a breath of fog; he could not have clearly seen Paddy, even if he'd wanted to, as they said goodbye.

• • •

Rachel admired Ev's running away, despite his leaving her. She'd always wanted to run away herself — didn't everyone? — but hadn't had the courage: not as an adventurous child or rebellious adolescent, not as a bored adult. But Ev had done it, and she admired him, there was no denying it.

Of course she was also angry. And it went without saying, he'd hurt her feelings. These were the ways she'd found to make her affair justifiable, to make her behavior fitting.

After eight months, she went for the first time to visit Ev in his new apartment, a formerly nice place, now brown top to bottom. The building was just east of Wrigley Field, too close to the Addison el stop. In it lived poor hip young people who played loud music and persisted in leaving the vestibule door ajar, so drunks slept under the mailboxes. Rachel sort of liked the atmosphere, in spite of herself. It reminded her of college, of other romances gone bad: the squeaky floors and Escher-like staircase, the comprehensive industrial paint job — brown, brown, brown, banister, wainscoting, floor.

Inside Ev's apartment hung dirty vinyl shades that snapped open when you gave a little pull; through the dormer window cold light shone from the fluorescent streetlamp. Ev had only to walk next door to fetch taquitos or Schlitz malt liquor — not that Rachel could imagine him ingesting such things, but the proximity of them, the odors in the air of foreign food and diesel exhaust, made his existence appear exotic. Because Rachel had gotten the Saab when he moved away, Ev had no choice but to take the el downtown every morning and probably had established a morning ritual at the station newsstand. In his apartment, Rachel felt the ghostly presence of a long line of single men. She tightened her coat around herself, an alleged ambassador from what was supposed to be the good life, hausfrau come to restore her husband's faith in the same.

His door was ajar that dark Saturday morning in late March; he expected her. Ev had his forehead to the floor when she arrived. "Back exercises," he explained.

"I thought you were praying," Rachel said, though what she'd feared was that he was weeping.

"Well," Ev said in his reflective, philosophical, taking-every-thing-seriously way, "it *is* a kind of prayer. I'm praying my back won't give out." He rolled gently to his side and then all the way over, rocking, grinding his spine against the floor. "Maybe all gestures are, strictly speaking, prayers?"

"So you got a weak back," Rachel said, overriding the philosophizing. "When'd you get that?" As Ev appeared to be considering an answer, she added, "You're supposed to say, 'Oh, about a week back.'" This was a joke she'd learned from Paddy.

Ev grunted, smiling his small tolerant smile, looking at Rachel the way he looked at their sons, pleased with a grudging pride of her silliness. He sat up, wrapping his arms around his legs, still rocking. Though he ate constantly, he was far too thin. In his maroon sweatpants he looked Third World, with the elastic cuffs loose around his ankles. *Skeleton,* Rachel thought. It was hard to remember that it was *he* who'd left *her.*

"Sit," Ev said. Rachel looked around and selecting a file box beneath a paint-speckled wall mirror. Her view was of four windows that looked out on the brick building next door. She'd come to deliver mail, discuss unavoidable household whatnot — condominium bylaw revision, insurance claims, school dues, summer camp registration — but she couldn't believe the papers in her briefcase were in any way critical. Her husband looked like hell.

"Are you sick?" she asked him.

"In what sense?"

Rachel sighed, shaking her head. She turned to her briefcase, to the stack of papers whose lines required his signature.

For his part, Ev studied her for signs of a new sex life. He looked at her critically. She seemed physically relaxed, as if her joints had been lubricated, giving her flex and grace. *Joint oiling,* he thought. *Rachel's joint oiling with Paddy.* One of Paddy's best qualities was his loose limbs, the way he swung them like a marionette when he walked or played racquetball or rested his chin on a fist. Ev pictured those long limber legs and arms around his wife, wondering if it was his incredulity that made the image nearly impossible. He wondered if Paddy would know to pay sufficient attention to Rachel's breasts, which were terrifically erogenous for her. He wondered if he would find the softest stretch of her skin, matching patches inside her thighs. And would they be practicing birth control? Did she worry about disease? Did Rachel have any idea what, say, a dental dam was? His wife seemed a sexual innocent, and Ev found his concern about her possible affair straying toward the custodial.

Rachel leaned forward, and Ev realized she had come without a bra, which made him grieve for his right to touch her.

She said, "You know what, Ev? Statistically speaking, I don't think many couples that have a separation get back together again. I think I read that somewhere."

"That's probably true." He moved his gaze from her chest to her face.

"It makes me sad," she said, and began to cry.

It made her sad in both simple and complicated ways, like weaning her last baby, like watching her grandmother die. Her long marriage to Ev had no single form; its dissolution seemed inevitable and intolerable at the same time. The tenor of her pain kept drifting.

"But we've never been very statistically reliable," Ev said. He scooted toward her on his tailbone, put his hands on her calves, and rubbed the soft muscle.

Rachel let herself cry for a few minutes while he sat patiently on the floor at her feet, rocking sideways, massaging her in a friendly, asexual manner. Then he abruptly moved his thumbs up her legs and rose onto his knees, meeting her mouth with his.

She groaned involuntarily, astonished. He tasted and felt unbearably familiar and right. His hands moved into her hair and she felt herself free-fall, simply relax into his arms as if into the atmosphere from a great height. She loved him best; he knew her better. His tongue roamed her teeth; she reached for the curls at his neck, then slid without thinking off the file box and beneath him, their bodies performing the rites of homecoming as if there had never been any other role to fill.

Ev heard her say, "I love you," her emphasis on *you,* signifying that there was an alternative. His speculation about her infidelity now came to a shuddering close: she was sleeping with Paddy. He had shut his eyes against the moment, unsure why he'd been so instantaneously drawn to her, whether he was making love to her because he loved her or because he was still competing with Paddy, still on the court swinging for a win.

Rachel was crying again, and Ev understood that her reasons for doing so were at least as enigmatic as his in making love. Sex frequently made her cry, from happiness, but she also could feel guilty, or simply overwhelmed. There might be a thousand things the gesture signified. It upset him profoundly to be so ambiguous about his motives, to know himself, or Rachel, so poorly.

Finally, when he stubbornly would not answer her admission of her love, she said, "I also wanted to talk about Marcus. Do you want to talk about Marcus?" She snuffled, wiping her nose with the back of her hand, sitting up awkwardly on the floor.

"O.K." He would not say that he loved her, although he did love her. But he could not tolerate its being evoked merely as a response to the threat of Paddy Limbach. What sort of love was that? "What about Marcus?"

Rachel was pulling her jeans back over her hips, her sweater over her breasts, ignoring the splash of semen he'd left on her stomach, *white mud.* She used to roll onto Ev's side of the bed to leave the damp spot for him to sleep on; he could recall a time when he'd fallen asleep on top of her and they had awakened to find themselves glued together at the navel, the red wrenching-apart.

Ev adjusted his sweatpants, sat cross-legged, his knee touching hers until he very gently moved it away.

"Marcus is hostile." She held up her palm to quell his objection.

"I know you don't trust that word, but he is. I have no idea how he acts around you, but he's being a jerk to me."

Ev said, "To you?"

"Well, to me and to Zach." And to Paddy, she might have added, but why muddy the waters? She looked into Ev's eyes, into the deep knowledge he had of her. Undoubtedly he could see straight into her confused heart, could see the new affection for Paddy sitting beside her dark knotty love for him, a puppy near the teeth of a dingo. She blinked in order to remember her point. "Marcus won't wait for Zach after school — not that he has to do that, of course."

"I'll get Zach."

Rachel nudged her knee into Ev's again to see if he had intentionally moved away from her touch. He moved away again, and she felt like a fool. Her tears threatened to start up once more. "You'll get Zach, that's good, that's a good solution." Rachel sensed herself launching into a tirade, which she did not want to do. It had to do with a rocking rhythm of anger and despair and humiliation in her mind that somehow began to roll off her tongue. *That's good, that's a good solution,* the refrain began, but soon it would naturally be followed with *Just one solution at a time, is that it, I'll just come here for my solutions one at a time, bring them to you like good King Solomon so that you can decide, you can make judgment, you can decree* . . . And so on. Why had he put his hands on her calves? Why had he just fucked her when now he wouldn't touch her? It had been too long since high school, too long since Rachel had been competent at these sorts of games, too long since she'd even recognized her incompetence at them. She had no idea how to play. She had no idea Ev knew how to play. She would fumble, she would fail, she would lose Ev forever.

She stood then, enraged. But where was her right to have rage, anyway? Hadn't all that rage been supposed to translate into sexual desire for her husband's friend? Wasn't that what she'd done with it? Why was it leaking out here? Where was the flaw in her displacement?

Evan was saying, ". . . and then he won't be so angry. He can sleep on the sofa, I'll put him on the train in the morn —"

"What did you say?"

"When?"

"What were you talking about? I lost track."

"I was saying Marcus could come stay with me for a while. Separate the two of you, the three of you."

"The four of us."

Evan stood up, his hand to his lower back. "I don't think that little episode on the floor did anything good for my disk."

Rachel realized that her head hurt. Her husband was giving her a headache. He was too difficult. Maybe it would be best simply to continue with Paddy, who was easy enough. How much simpler it would be to see Paddy if Marcus was gone. Zach slept like a bear. Zach actually liked Paddy.

Rachel's conflicted emotions made her wonder about her own character: was she monstrous? Ev would request the abstract of her, a guarantee of high scruples and constant ethical self-scrutiny: she could be better. It was too much for her, too heady and headachey. Before falling into Ev's arms, she'd considered herself to be kind of happily miserable. Maybe in truth she was one of those people who require drama in their lives. Maybe she needed an occasion to rise to.

Evan said, "Do you think I should move home?"

Taken aback, Rachel paused. "Well, yes, but not because Marcus is being a brat. I don't want you home if you don't want to be there. Obviously," she added, when Ev simply aimed his narrowed gaze at her.

He said, "Let him move here, just for a while, just for a week."

She nodded, already envisioning her own apartment late at night, Zach snoring away, Paddy with his hand over her breast. Paddy's teeth were perfect, she thought, not crooked and stained like Ev's. She looked at the floor, the scrunched throw rug where she and Ev had just made love. It had felt more wonderful than any sex she'd had for a long time. But it was five minutes gone, and after he'd signed the sheaf of papers she'd brought and handed them back to her, Ev didn't touch her when they said goodbye.

When his door shut, it was as if Rachel had imagined the whole unlikely scene. The stairwell was still brown, the vestibule downstairs still exposed to the freezing elements, the liquor store across the street still advertising six-packs for four dollars.

. . .

Marcus had no intention of moving in with his father. His arguments against it were carefully whittled away — he could take his computer, his desk, his collections; the door to his room at home would be locked against Zach and Rachel — until only his naked stubbornness remained, a willful refusal that would not be weakened.

"You're hurting your father's feelings," Rachel heard herself say, but she quickly recovered by adding, "If you stay here, you must shape up. No more yelling at Zach, no more sullenness with me."

He nodded defiantly, and Rachel wished she could gather him into her arms. How hateful adolescence was, how full of isolation. Who could he hug? she wondered. Who would he allow to hold him, to comfort him? He had no physical attachment with any other human, a state of existence Rachel could recall well enough to know that there was nothing she, his mother, could do to help. To try to hug him now would be to force him to push her away.

Later, she wondered at his stubbornness. Did he suspect her of having an affair? Did he know about her and Paddy? Was he staying here merely to police the place? To monitor? To spy? She was tempted to go wake him. Unlike Zach, Marcus slept lightly and woke with a disarming clarity, utterly sentient; she could simply snap on his light and he'd sit up in bed. They could have a frank discussion. He gave all signs of knowing what he wanted and why he wanted it. He was intelligent and sensitive. He thought like a grownup in many situations; he was responsible and careful. The problem was that his childish personality was so well hidden that you thought he might have outgrown it. You might *think* that, but you would be wrong. He was a boy. He missed his father. He blamed his mother. He despised the interloper.

For her part, she was crying so often these days she bought waterproof mascara. The manufacturers seemed to think waterproof mascara was for swimmers, but Rachel knew better: it was for weepers. For years she'd kept makeup in her drawer until it went dry with neglect; now she was culling through a rainbow of colors at the Marshall Field counter, a beautiful young woman with a French accent aiding her. Was the accent assumed? Rachel didn't care; she liked to listen to accents. It was more interesting if it was affected, anyway. The young woman had flawless makeup, obvious yet perfect, like a beautiful mask. What did she look like underneath? An ordinary face, Rachel assumed; as usual, she laid the template of her husband's point of view on the situation. Evan would want to see the girl plain, without her mask. But maybe it was more interesting to see what the girl *wanted* to look like, the nature of her disguise. And perhaps, Rachel thought as the French girl packaged her purchases, people were more interesting in what they desired to be than in what they were naturally.

"Merci," said Rachel, not intending to tease.

But in her cold automobile, waiting for the traffic light to change, she felt foolish. What a ridiculous trip! What an adolescent situation! She'd looked forward all morning to this shopping excursion, as if she had a vital errand. Who was she? Who did she love? Her problem could for hours be comical and meaningless, something to fret over in theory, to turn happily around in her mind like a bright plastic toy, to feel deliciously sexy and flattered about. But on occasion it simply exhausted her. On occasion it seemed to her frivolous and self-destructive, obsessive and wasteful, disappointing and ugly. This was the way Evan would have thought of it, and sometimes his thoughts seemed to Rachel the only true ones, the ones that were her, naturally and thoroughly, underneath everything else. Ev lived in her heart like a kernel of her youthful self; they'd married, young and earnest, intelligent beyond their years about the fittingness of their own match. For sixteen years she'd slept only with him, kissed only him, considered others but always fallen back into his arms, into the sad dark truth that was his grasp of the world.

And now she was miserable again, wedged between other shoppers in their icy cars, cursing the arctic Midwest and its deadly seasons. The setting sun reflected mercilessly from the icy shimmer of every surface. Winter wouldn't go away this year. This was when the pendulum swung into guilt, in the closing hours of the day, when the cold oppressed her and her sons had disappeared into self-sufficiency, when she waited for Paddy to want her, when she waited for the cocktail hour to arrive. It seemed to Rachel she could attach her emotions to a simple clock and watch them play out on her own face all day long: eager morning, melancholy afternoon, resigned evening, and then unknown darkness as P.M. clicked once more into A.M., a time wherein she might be kissing Paddy on her very own marriage bed or she might be all alone.

And so she'd gone to the tropical warmth of the mall, to the unlikely makeup counter and the pseudo-French girl, and bought herself some insoluble mascara. It was a troubled time and she was arming herself.

She wanted to tell somebody about her dilemma, about having two men — did she have two men? — but who? Zoë came to mind, but Zoë was traveling, sending postcards of Turkish baths and gruesome priapic statuary. Finally Rachel had a problem Zoë might fully engage herself in, a juicy bedroom quandary, a story, and, of course, nowhere to tell it.

For about five seconds, Rachel considered going to a therapist. But living with Ev had made her into a psychologist snob: she didn't think anybody could tell her more than she already knew about her feelings. She wanted to talk, but she didn't want advice she would feel obliged to follow. She didn't want to think of this as a serious problem, one to which she had committed money and time. Maybe this was an urge best satisfied by phoning talk radio, discussing her dilemma anonymously. Not that she expected anyone to help her solve it: she just wanted to hear how it sounded, spoken aloud. She wanted someone to say, "Really, two men? And you love them both?"

Yes, she loved them both. They were two sides of Rachel herself, one side hopeful, the other skeptical, one side contented, the other driven by discontent, one side easygoing, the other on edge. And so on. They represented a full range, and Rachel didn't want to deny herself either part. But of course she was going to have to choose. Nobody could live this way, agonizing over the decision. Regardless of who chose her, whether Ev came home or not, she had to choose whom to love.

She read books, looking for someone with a similar problem, but always — without exception — there was an obvious choice to be made. In literature, the spouse was always a secondary character, the product of an arranged marriage, no fun. Society conspired against the lovers, and though the adulterers ought obviously to choose against the spouses, they always ended up miserably guilt-ridden, ostracized, dead — poor Anna Karenina, poor Emma Bovary.

But Rachel loved both men. She wanted to have her cake and she wanted to eat it, too. She was starting to think of them as incomplete without each other. She wanted to fuse them together, their personalities and appearances and the strangely different ways in which they had erotic appeal. She wanted Paddy's body to go with Ev's expressions; she wanted Paddy's playfulness with Ev's irony; Paddy's naiveté with Ev's knowingness; Paddy's shame with Ev's frankness.

At home, she unloaded her cosmetics into the bathroom drawer with the others, the ones Paddy had used to make her up. Leaving the room, she banged her thigh against the counter, and tears sprang to her eyes. She took a roll of toilet paper from the bathroom and lay on her bed, equipped, crying again.

. . .

In the middle of a session with an adolescent kleptomaniac, Evan suddenly could not concentrate. He was thinking of Rachel again, of her long comfortable body, of her whimper when she reached orgasm, of her strong thighs around his hips. He had not officially fantasized about his wife for a number of years, but he now found himself utterly unable to focus on his client's speech. The words had begun coming out like meaningless sounds, a spurt of random notes, confetti.

When he'd finally finished the hour and ushered the boy out, he phoned Rachel.

"You want to fuck, here at my office?"

"Ev?" she said.

His own name stopped his desire cold. Who else would it be? He should have been able to say that to her, but of course he knew who else it could be. He hung up, then buzzed the receptionist to tell her he wouldn't take any calls, not even from his wife.

He wanted her, but for the wrong reasons. She'd said his name, reminding him of the complexity of her sexual life these days, the very complexity that seemed to arouse him, and he'd had to hang up, capping the phone as if capping his desire. He laid his head on his desk, listening to the phone buzz in the outer office, the soothing tones of the receptionist, a temp from the agency who wouldn't ask questions. He stuck out his tongue to taste the unpleasant dry surface of his green blotter. He tried not to, but all he could imagine was Rachel's naked bottom sitting on his desk while he put his face between her legs, then fucked her. He wanted badly to throw himself against her on this desk.

Thirteen

· · · · · · · · · · · · ·

As USUAL, Marcus was having no success at concealing his hurt. He had just been punched in the face, hard, and tears had started up as if his head were full of them, as if he were a walking water balloon, primed for popping.

"White boy, you a fuckin' snail," the boy had said as he pushed Marcus onto the train car. At school, it might have been the baffling opening lines to a friendly exchange; the black students frequently panicked Marcus unnecessarily. They seemed angry when they weren't, he'd figured out; their emotional thermostats were set higher than white people's. But it was a rough shove, and he stumbled over Zach's soccer bag and backpack. Zach always took more than necessary to school; he looked as if he were running away from home every morning — and like a bum by sunset, shirt untucked, belongings leaking from their containers.

"I ain't got the time, whitey," the boy went on, pushing Marcus again.

Staggering over Zach's bag, Marcus fell backward against a post and landed facing the boy from near the floor. The boy casually pulled back his fist and gave Marcus a punch, his knuckles slicing sideways over Marcus's face, as if he wanted to take off the nose. Then he calmly sidled down the crowded aisle and through the doors to the car behind. It was this unnecessary punch that would later infuriate Marcus; after all, he was already effectively out of the way by the time it came. *Gratuitous violence,* he would think, when he was composed.

Zach had not noticed what had happened. It had happened so quickly, in fact, that only the two old women in the old-woman seats beside the door had noticed. They weren't going to mention it, apparently. Marcus purposely trod on one of their feet as he fell into the seat behind them that had just been vacated.

"What happened to your *nose?*" Zach asked, alarmed. Instantly Marcus covered it with his palm. Beneath his fingers he could feel his own pulpy flesh, made unfamiliar by swelling, by humiliation.

"That" — Marcus was unaccustomed to saying something bad about a black — "asshole hit me. Because of all your shit in my way." He kicked Zach's soccer bag. Blaming Zach, of course, felt totally familiar.

"What asshole?"

"Shut up," Marcus said. "Just shut up." He turned his messy face toward the window and watched the buildings go through his reflection. He was furious.

They went north, headed toward their father's apartment. Their weekend visits had grown less interesting to both boys. Zach missed his mother when he was with his father, more than he missed his father when he was with her. His mother kept things normal. She made him feel normal, taken care of. She reminded him to put on clean underwear. She remembered to pick up his Ventolin inhalers, for his asthma, and she remembered to tell him to put one in his pocket when he left the house. She liked to hug him, and she was soft, and she smelled good. She called him "Babe" and "Hon," and "Monkey" if she was especially happy.

His father seemed sometimes to forget the boys were with him; a few weeks ago he'd come home so late they had had to wait at the liquor store for him. Then he'd looked at them, scowling, as if they'd not been invited. As if there had to be an invitation.

"You want to go home?" Zach said suddenly to Marcus. If he'd been punched on the el, that's where he would want to go. "You could go home. I'll tell Dad you aren't feeling well."

Marcus looked into Zach's face. Zach smiled so that he wouldn't grimace; Marcus's nose resembled a yam, discolored and big. The train pulled into the Fullerton station and Marcus jumped up.

"I'm going home," he announced, as if he'd come up with the idea himself.

"Goodbye," Zach said, careful to pull his bags out of his brother's way. He sighed, wishing he had a good reason to go home, too.

· · ·

Marcus ran down the platform steps with his head lowered. His fury at the black boy seemed larger than his body could contain. Here he was, the advocate for equality at his school, the boy who'd phone-canvassed for Mayor Washington's campaign six years ago (at age eight! the youngest one there!) and then wept when the man died. It was utterly unjust, thoroughly unfair, entirely ridiculous and dismaying that Marcus had been struck by a black boy! He could not believe the injustice. Hadn't it been Marcus who had made the gang of neighborhood children insert *tiger* when they said, "Catch a *nigger* by the toe"? Hadn't it been Marcus who had intentionally broken the racial segregation in the chem lab by choosing a black partner?

Without thinking, Marcus ran east, facing the high April wind, heading home. He didn't want to have to discuss his injured face and feelings with his father. He didn't want his father's philosophical, psychological calm. He didn't want to hear how his pain measured against all the other pain in the world, how small his was by comparison. He wanted instead his mother's horror. He would walk into the apartment and thrust his beaten face at her like a rebuke: see. He wanted her sympathy; he wanted her guilt, guilt that she hadn't been there to protect him, hadn't been there to stop the stranger from punching her son.

Fresh hot self-pity filled Marcus's face. Now his nose was sore; now he could feel his top gum throbbing; the nosepiece of his eyeglasses felt newly tight on his swollen bridge, as if he'd bent the wire. The icy wind felt good for once. *Fucking nigger,* he thought experimentally.

In the building's entryway — glorious warmth — he found Paddy Limbach, who stood there like a feeb pulling his work gloves off one finger at a time. Paddy's face went through a few expressions when he saw Marcus: surprise, polite pleasure, then the desired dismay. "Holy catfish! What happened?"

Marcus started up the stairs without answering, unwilling to join Paddy in waiting for the elevator, and besides, plodding up all sixteen floors would leave him winded when he finally reached his mother. He let his blood drop on the carpet. *Holy catfish.* Paddy's presence made him outraged with his father: if his father would move home, that moron wouldn't be coming around.

When Rachel heard somebody at the door, she opened it, expecting Paddy. Instead, her son stood there with a broken nose, heaving his chest mightily, a brown membrane of blood wheezing in and out of one nostril. She gasped, then took him into her arms, the first time she'd held him in maybe years, a thought that saddened her.

"It wasn't fair!" he sobbed.

"No, it wasn't," she soothed, shutting the apartment door behind him and leading him to her bathroom, where she studied him under the bright lights. "Tell me what happened, sugar."

A few minutes later, Paddy stood awkwardly outside the door, wondering if he should go home. His hands ached from working outside in the cold all day, all winter and into spring; he wanted to soak them in hot water and have Didi rub her hand cream on them while he and she watched television. It was a simple enough need, one he could fulfill within twenty minutes if he just turned around and got home. He debated going or staying as he stood in Rachel's quiet hallway. Not many of the other occupants had children, he decided; the place was too still. There was no parking — he'd left his Bronco six blocks away, in a two-hour zone where he'd no doubt receive a twenty-five-dollar ticket — and now her son was here. Today, for the first time, his affair did not attract him as much as his other life. He flexed his fingers, which made his dry knuckles crack; he could almost smell the Pacquin lotion Didi liked to massage in, thinking of the way she warmed it first between her own hands, the wet, vaguely obscene noise. He was just about to turn around and leave, relieved, when he realized that Marcus would have mentioned seeing him downstairs in the vestibule.

He knocked with his sore, bloody knuckles, then wiped away the red stain he had made.

"Need a ride to the emergency room?" he asked Rachel, who did not look all that happy to see him.

"I don't think that's necessary." She led Paddy to the kitchen, where the boy sat with a bag of frozen lima beans on his face. Paddy laughed in spite of himself.

"In my day, we wore steak. How's the other guy look?" he asked, dropping his jacket on the back of a chair.

"What other guy?" Marcus said.

"The one you fought with."

"I didn't fight. I got hit." His voice could be described as fuming.

Paddy took the chair and straddled it, which always made him feel spontaneous and secure at the same time. "You fight back at all?"

"No," Marcus said disdainfully, as if fighting back were only for people who invited broken skulls.

"You ever been in a fight before?"

"Of course not."

Of course not. Paddy nodded. "You mad?"

At this, Marcus's lip began to twitch and his visible eye to narrow. Under his bag of beans, he was seething.

"Sure you're mad," Paddy said. "Guy just sucker-punched you, huh?"

"He was black," Rachel said. She set down an orange soda for Marcus and told him to swallow some aspirin with it.

"So what?" Paddy asked. "Black, white, pink — you punch him back, guy punches you. That's the way it works — boom, boom."

"No, it doesn't." Rachel gave him an impatient, silencing look. Sometimes she got this same look when he tried to sweet-talk her during sex.

"How does it work, then?"

"There are many other options besides 'boom, boom,'" she said vaguely.

Paddy sighed: well, it was her son, she could handle it, discuss options. He would stay for a few minutes, maybe drink a beer, then head home. They weren't going to bed anyway, that much was clear. And his hands were killing him; maybe this was the onset of arthritis. His father had had arthritis.

"If I'd hit him, then his friends would have maybe done something," Marcus said. It was the longest sentence the boy had ever addressed to Paddy.

"True," Paddy said. "But usually guys go one on one, you ever notice that? Usually the friends just step back."

"Really?" Marcus said, peering with his one slitty eye at Paddy.

"Absolutely." Paddy's last fight had been at a bar in Normal ten years ago. He frowned. "Well, maybe not with blacks. I've never hit a black guy. I've had words." Arguing over a bid, over a parking space, over a ding in the paint. Paddy could remember being in the wrong, which he decided not to mention to snotty little Marcus, who thought Paddy was always in the wrong anyway. "The thing about black people," Paddy said, "is that they seem wound tighter than us."

Rachel opened her mouth to disagree — Paddy could see that knee-jerk response — but Marcus said, "You're right!"

Rachel shut her mouth. Then Marcus launched into a long description of the black kids at his school. There were two types: the ones who hung back and made no noise, trying to become white, Marcus proposed, and the noisy ones who hung together, yelling, slapping each other, hooting in halls, jabbing at the air, swaggering, inexplicable. The quiet ones were fearful, the noisy ones unapproachable. He'd tried to be an exemplary citizen, encouraging tolerance, going out of his way to extend friendliness, and where had it gotten him? Punched in the face. The unfairness made him furious.

"I know what you mean," Paddy said. "Makes you mad, doesn't it? That's why you should punch back, just get really dang mad." He held up his hand, because he knew Rachel was going to disagree. She was going to disagree and then they'd have to discuss it later. Discussing it later would be a waste of their private time together, so Paddy tempered his advice, although he still felt Marcus ought to have punched the boy. "Ordinarily," Paddy said, "I would recommend punching back. But with black people, I just don't know. Haven't got experience. It shouldn't be any different, but maybe it is. Maybe you ought to go punch your bed? Or kick your bathtub?"

"Kick the bathtub?" Rachel said. "What sort of advice is that?"

Paddy shrugged, but Marcus was nodding. "Good advice," Marcus said. In his mind, he was back on the train, throwing his fist and foot over and over again into the boy who'd hit him, hoping blood or sweat might splatter the two women who'd witnessed the original punch and done nothing.

Rachel observed her lover and her son candidly. Paddy shrugged when she caught his eye, smiling in his friendly way; Marcus looked thoughtful, less pathetic than before holding his limas. It was as if agreement had been reached about a troubling and persistent problem. Almost palpably, the different disappointments that had bothered each of the three of them lifted; they shifted in their chairs and began looking forward to dinner.

. . .

"He should write his feelings down," Evan said to Zach. "He should explore the contradictory nature of his response. He feels singled out and unfairly attacked. Well, that's exactly how black people feel. That's exactly what prompted his attack."

Zach blinked, wondering what his father would serve him for dinner. Meals here had grown more and more incomprehensible. Instead of shopping at health food stores the way he used to, his father now bought takeout and then complained when the food was unhealthful. Typically he purchased the most wholesome-looking thing on the menu, which frequently was the least flavorful, and then criticized its blandness. It was Zach's experience that all the really good food was not good for you; you'd think his father would have figured this out by now. Down on Clark, they'd find Thai food, Ethiopian, Jamaican. Zach imagined steaming boxes on the table . . .

"But," his father went on concerning Marcus, "he probably did something to provoke getting hit."

"Why?"

"The boy didn't hit *you*, did he?"

"No."

"That's what I mean. That is exactly what I mean. You don't get in fights, you don't show up with a broken nose, you don't go around . . ." Evan stopped. He took off his glasses and rubbed his eyes and forehead and hair roughly, as if trying to scrub out thoughts. He looked sick, in Zach's opinion, like he was coming down with a cold, like he was coming down with whatever Zach's grandfather had had before he died. In Zach's opinion, Ev needed to go home, too, down to their warm apartment in Lincoln Park, to a tableful of food, to Rachel.

"I don't think he did anything to make that boy hit him," Zach said, remembering that it was his own clutter of bags that had started the whole thing. "What are we going to eat for dinner?"

"Why didn't Marcus come with you?" his father asked, his glasses now back on his face, resting on his wrinkles.

Zach shrugged, trying to look innocently perplexed. His father's apartment was cold and loud, lacking all the soft things, like curtains and rugs and pillows. Other people in the building had televisions, but not his father. Other people had food on their shelves and a lot of lights on, but not his father. "Could we go see Gerry?" he suddenly asked. Since his mother and brother were clearly out of the question, he resorted to his uncle, whom he hadn't seen in months. "I'd like to see Gerry," he said, desperate to see somebody besides his father.

So, with some difficulty, Ev located his brother, who was staying not with the first people Ev phoned but with the eighth, a linking chain like a relay race that intrigued as well as irritated him. "What do you mean, 'Who's this?' " he shouted into the receiver. "Who's *this?*" Gerry had sequestered himself like a celebrity, was hidden behind many layers of people, all of whom required proof of Ev's right to know where his own brother was. Finally, it was left that Gerry would telephone within the next half-hour if he wished to be in touch. Ev slammed down the phone and glowered at Zach. Outside, it had grown dark.

"You happy?" he said.

Zach sighed. "I guess," he said bleakly, hoping his uncle would phone soon.

Instead, Gerry showed up at the apartment door forty minutes later. He'd called Rachel to get directions. He stank, but he hugged Zach long and hard.

"How's it hanging, men?"

Evan absorbed his brother's new persona: confident, well dressed. He wore a suit under his coat and muffler, a navy one, and black shoes. He looked theater-bound, and as if he'd been eating a lot lately; his disposition was not strung-out but jolly, as if he'd had two stiff drinks at a rollicking party just before coming up. His face held the high color of gin blossom; his nose was a merry alcoholic berry on his face.

"New digs," he said of Ev's apartment. "Why do you suppose they call it *falling* in love?" he asked his brother and nephew, apropos of nothing, as usual.

Zach laughed. He'd convinced his father not only to find his uncle but to order pizza. Now he busied himself with the pepperoni and cheese — his piece plus the whole surface of his father's, which Ev had scraped off — pouring on crushed red pepper as a way of warming himself up. His uncle was silly, as always, and that cheered him. He couldn't figure out what bothered his parents so gravely about Gerry. You could forget he didn't have a home or a job; he seemed perfectly content, as if he didn't know people considered him incomplete. He always left something behind when he went, a gift of some sort, and tonight he bestowed on Zach both a two-dollar bill and a Susan B. Anthony silver dollar. Zach loved exclusive mementos; Gerry had given him countless unique tokens, including an Oscar Mayer wienie whistle and a first-day cancellation Elvis stamp.

"Who'd you *fall* in love with?" Zach asked.

"Where'd you get the suit?" asked his father.

"Oh, Ev, you always want to spoil things." Gerry sagged like a sad clown onto the futon. To Zach, he said, "I *fell* in love with Yolanda, an improv girl."

"Improv!" Zach said. He licked his greasy fingers and smiled.

"Yes, she improvises. When you meet her, you ask her to show you an assembly line or a country-western singer dry-out retreat." Gerry slid from the folded futon onto the floor, as if still in the process of falling, complaining of the lubricity of the furniture.

"Lubricity." Zach giggled.

His father had brought a kitchen chair into the room and was sitting on it with his legs crossed. Zach's father didn't mind sitting like a girl, with his legs crossed up high and his fingers laced together. Only recently had Zach begun to notice how feminine his father's gestures were, how if he imitated them he got ridiculed by classmates. Sometimes he wanted to tell his father, in case he didn't know. Other times, he suspected his father of *wanting* to be misunderstood, to be thought of as pussy, just to be different from other men. For gestures, Zach had begun looking to Paddy, who liked to pull up chairs and sit astride them like a coach, who flung open the refrigerator and then closed it with his foot.

His uncle Gerry was talking about Yolanda and comedy, but Zach's father had become impatient and stood up. Gerry immediately stopped talking. "What?" he said.

"I've got a headache," Ev said. "I think I'll lie down." He first crushed the pizza box with unnecessary force and then strode off to the bedroom and shut the door.

Gerry said, "He doesn't look so good."

Zach agreed. They smiled at each other. "There's not much to do here, is there?" Gerry said eventually, looking around the empty room.

"No," Zach said.

"I've only been here this once, and I could be wrong, but I think I like your old place better."

"Me, too."

"Maybe Evan will go home soon."

"Maybe."

"You want to go cruise around?" Gerry asked. "I don't have a car or anything, but we can ride the trains for a while if you want."

"O.K.," Zach said, eager to get out of his father's depressing apartment. He couldn't imagine what his father did here all by himself. It was the kind of place where homework became entertainment.

From his bedroom, Ev heard his son and brother laughing. He liked having them there, on the other side of his door. He liked being near them yet not with them. He liked their existence on the other side of the door from his existence. It was a peculiar satisfaction, having guests in another part of the apartment. *Apartment,* Ev thought: apart. Yet together. Then Zach rapped on his door to tell him he and Gerry were going for a train ride.

"Be careful," Ev said, opening the door. He found that he actually *did* have a headache now, as if his power of suggestion were that potent. He handed Zach a ten-dollar bill surreptitiously while Gerry used the toilet. "Don't tell Gerry you've got it unless you run into trouble. You know my number here?"

"Duh, Dad."

Ev crossed the room to open the front door for them. He resisted asking the things that most interested him: where had Gerry's suit come from? Who was this Yolanda person really? "Be careful," he told his brother, noting now the frayed jacket collar, the sheen of thrift store garment, the odor of used belongings. "Be back in a couple of hours, O.K.? And walk him all the way to the door here. He's only ten," he said, indicating Zach.

"Eleven," Zach corrected him.

"Eleven," Ev amended. But he knew Gerry had no full way of processing cautionary information — never had, never would; Ev set down the rules mostly for Zach's benefit. "Have fun," he added as they thumped down the four floors. He wished they would stay, laugh some more where he could hear them.

Later, he would remember his scorn for Gerry's mothball-scented suit, his dress shoes. Later, after Zach returned alone, ambling from the station, Ev would curse Gerry, not yet knowing it was the last time he would see his brother alive.

Fourteen

· · · · · · · · · · · · ·

IN HIS APARTMENT, a nest directly in the city's flow, uncushioned beside elevated trains and busy police station, above liquor store, next to taquito shop, and catty-cornered from newsstand, Evan dreamed of the wilderness. In the hubbub of urban uproar, he dreamed fervently of serene vistas, places he, city cynic, had never visited in his waking life, blinding blue skies, luscious green trees, mountains the color of which he had to concoct out of whole cloth (they were purple, as in the song). In bed he heard and felt the lumbering rumble of traffic and commerce and the strident tone of crime, and even knew, in the way self-conscious people know, that he was lying above the thick city squalor, but he *felt* the sun, unadulterated, resurrecting something dormant, something embryonically hopeful, in himself. In his dream, he felt pleasantly intoxicated, as if high, reveling in the moment rather than experiencing his customary dread of the impending. In his dream, he ignored his anxieties. In his dream, he knew Joni was dead, but he was also holding her hand, nothing more, and they were walking in the overwhelming, luminous, yet fragile landscape where she'd last been. In his dream, he knew he was deluded — his knowledge was the black smoke that floated the illusion, that crept along the periphery of his vision, bubbling up in ominous vapors — but he also knew he could control it, could will a few more moments of abandon, could ride the ghostly crest before crashing once more into Chicago's stark gray morning.

. . .

Paddy dreamed of the Coles' coffee table again, only this time he'd broken it (he'd known all along he would end up breaking it, he could have predicted it from the beginning; it was smart and art, and he wasn't). He'd put his foot through the glass right into the girl's stomach, the way a farm boy could be expected to. Her hand had fallen to the floor and then he'd managed to crush it, too, as he stumbled in the rubble. Rachel was shaking her head, not even angry at Paddy, just so sad to see her table ruined. She certainly wasn't surprised that he'd done it; they both seemed to understand that Paddy couldn't be trusted to walk through a room without knocking over a few things.

He'd fought with Didi before bed, and now he was ruining his mistress's furniture. He was a failed husband, a failed lover. A written test was administered by Evan Cole at the YMCA. Paddy received his back with a D on it, although others who'd also been tested had received A minuses for simple childish drawings. "It's a *written* exam," he protested to Evan, who merely shrugged, disappointed in him.

And then he remembered that he knew Evan's secret, that he could tell Rachel about the suicide woman. No one would expect him to do that. "I'll tell her," Paddy told Ev smugly in the dream. "I'll tell her all about it."

. . .

Rachel dreamed she was watching a movie. She sat between Evan and Paddy. She had her hands in theirs. It was dark, but each of them seemed to be aware of the other's claim to her other hand. They were separated by her. They were seeing the movie differently. To Paddy it was an adventure; to Ev it was an ironic tale of corruption. Rachel became annoyed when she discovered herself thinking about their reactions to the movie rather than formulating her own. Yet she was also entertained by understanding both versions, Ev's and Paddy's. Both were interesting, both were valid, and she was proud of her competence — her superiority — in seeing the situation so objectively. Women mediated, she told herself as the movie washed over her and caused the men to react, each in his own way and each drawing Rachel's complete attention and sympathy and understanding. She squeezed Paddy's hand when the bad guy was in trouble, she squeezed Ev's when a dry line of dialogue emerged, all the while entertaining herself with the superiority of her position, wishing Zoë was there so they could discuss it.

At the end of the film the men argued with each other, but Rachel wandered amiably along, wishing she'd eaten popcorn, great greasy boxes of it, because in dreams, of course, popcorn has no calories, no consequences.

. . .

Marcus dreamed his recurring dream, the one in which Paddy Limbach was tied naked to a cable spool, stretched around it like a tortured man, held in place with barbed wire. Typically, in this dream, the spool would be sent rolling down a rocky hill, off a cliff, and into the ocean. He himself would set the wheel in motion, giving it a mighty shove. Marcus had never loathed anyone the way he loathed Paddy Limbach.

And typically, after Paddy landed in the ocean, Marcus would fall to the ground, horrified, guilty. He'd killed a man, and he would wake frightened, then relieved: just a dream.

This time, however, he didn't push Paddy from the cliff. This time he tried to untie the barbed wire, but it was too late. Away Paddy went, rolling toward death once more. When Marcus woke, he told himself he would have to get to Paddy sooner next time, keep him from ever being near the spool. He was glad not to want to kill somebody.

To Rachel, whom he'd wakened by calling out, he said cheerfully, "I always dream Paddy dies," and Rachel was distressed to think that Paddy's death would affect Marcus so little, that he would want to tell her so cavalierly about it. Why had he called her to his room to report his callousness? Did he really hate Paddy that intensely? Was her son becoming not only cold and dispassionate but proud of it?

But she had a headache from drinking wine and wanted more than anything to get back to bed and her own dreams, so she told Marcus to turn on his light and read for a while, and then returned to sleep herself without giving the issue of his hostility further thought.

· · ·

Melanie Limbach dreamed of the wolf in the woods; the bright cracking shot of lightning became the fall of a tree, her mother's and father's shouting was the voices of all the animals, screeching as they tumbled from or were crushed under tree branches. She was wakened by the wolf himself, who'd managed to creep through the litter and disruption of the falling tree, who'd pursued her even while she'd thought of other things, of the tiny birds flung far from their nests. He crept and pounced, and it was his teeth, so unthinkably near and large, like a roaring drawerful of knives, that forced her awake.

And there was her father, saying her name, *Melanie,* their faces nose to nose, her father's fingers smoothing over Melanie's mouth and eyes.

Their nightmares, Paddy realized in a wild second, were precisely identical: they dreamed of losing each other.

· · ·

Zach dreamed he rode his bike into a grocery store and sacked the shelves, pulling all the food he could into his backpack. He loved the canned beef stew and the frozen tamales and the ice cream candy bars and the sour cream potato chips. Miraculously, everything fit. Nobody stopped him. The aisles were wide enough to navigate easily, and Zach was surprisingly agile on the large bike. He waved to the cashier, he rode through the automatic doors, he rode into the streets dreaming of his booty, the bulk of which rested comfortingly on his back. He would eat and eat and eat.

．．．

Gerry Cole spent the night high on Seconal and morphine. The Seconal made him sleep, the morphine gave him great dreams. In one, he invented a game that involved a chessboard and hardware store goods, nails and screws and bolts and tiny pipes. Moving them required the proper tools, tweezers and hammers and a curling iron and a corkscrew; there were teams, designated by mortal status, the dead versus the living; his father cheated, using a hacksaw instead of a nail file. For a cogent moment Gerry woke, lying on Yolanda's bathroom floor — the bathmat padded, the tile pleasingly cool — and believed himself a pawn in the game. The tool to move him was a clever drug, something poured or shot or blown into him to make him ooze willingly forward. He had to hold on to the sink, he understood. Its smooth pedestal would slide or roll or stump onto the next square, and he with it, if he held on.

III

. . . .

Fifteen

. . . .

SUMMER SWELLED UP once more. The trees burst open along with the windows. All sorts of things leapt free: the song of insects, birds from eggshells, sentimental pink blossoms, the cacophony of neighbors, and a nameless correlating bunch of human urges.

In the newspaper, Evan read about a woman found murdered in Bucktown, Luellen Palmer's neighborhood. He read hungrily, consuming the details that seemed to point to his former client. What perversity made him excited to think it was her? He read without having his fears allayed. For years Luellen had been playing a sexual game of Russian roulette, spinning the nightly round of shells, waiting for somebody to explode in her vicinity. Perhaps there was a statistic to explain the odds; perhaps one in a thousand men was likely to finish sex by beating a woman to death. It seemed utterly plausible to Evan that Luellen had fucked a thousand men in her life; not so many years would have to have passed for that to be the true number.

Apparently nobody had missed this anonymous — pending family notification — woman for a week; neighbors did not know her, coworkers did not mourn her absence. But her cat, a Siamese with the vocal cords to prove it, had run out of food near the end of the week and begun complaining. Ev, who'd brought the newspaper with him to his office, flipped pages on the steno pad in which he'd taken notes during his sessions with Luellen. He did not remember a cat. He thought he'd remember a cat, a liaison with the maternal. Eventually the Siamese had clawed her way through a window screen and onto the fire escape, where she sat on the retractable ladder, howling, until a neighbor across the back pursued an investigation. It was the SPCA, come to rescue the animal, who found the woman-who-might-be-Luellen. Her front door had been left unlocked, her refrigerator had been emptied — as if her murderer had worked up an appetite and taken time to sate it — and her bleeding body had been stoppered with wine bottles at the mouth, rectum, and vagina.

He'd used a lit cigarette on her navel. He did not, it seemed, know his victim.

Evan walked that evening on a mission, with the self-absorbed intensity of a savior. Luellen's bar was called Friendly's; Ev suspected irony in its name, and entered warily, afraid of not finding her, or anything friendly, there. Her phone, he had discovered earlier, had been disconnected; she had quit at the photo studio months ago. Her street address had never been registered in her records, a fact Ev pondered as he walked. He told himself he had good reason to assume it was she who had been killed.

Plus he sensed his culpability. He had let her stop therapy easily, had not insisted on stepping down sessions, had not followed up. Perhaps he took credit when it was not due, but he could assume responsibility just as easily, he told himself. He had failed, yet again, to rescue a life.

But he found her alive, sitting in Friendly's in a short white dress looking quite sophisticated, attractive, at peace despite the throbbing tumult of the place. He'd made her life into a nightmare and her into its victim so completely that he was jolted by how mundane she seemed. Ev slid into a corner and sat there breathing evenly. She was O.K. His relief surprised him; he had not been aware of how seriously he had regarded his fear. A premonition had been successfully dispelled, superstition and self-importance thwarted. Luellen, sitting casually at the bar, had not seen him. He appreciated her living body, the way she shook her ice before she took a drink, the way her head tilted back as she drained the glass. Her bare arms were muscled and tan; she was pretty, here in the benevolent evening light of Friendly's.

Her father had been wrong in naming her unattractive. Calm and pretty, she didn't look like somebody at the mercy of a lethal addiction, her own or anyone else's.

She turned suddenly and spotted him, as if news of his presence had been whispered in her ear. They blinked at each other, then she motioned for him to join her.

"It was like, don't I know him from somewhere?" she said, shouting over the noise. "I used to get that all the time when I lifeguarded. People would see me on the street and go, 'Hey, I didn't recognize you with your clothes on.' I suppose I didn't recognize you without my neuroses on. How are you, Dr. Cole?"

"I'm doing fine, Luellen." He sat beside her, rehearsing whatever excuse he would need to explain his seeking her out.

"You've lost weight," she said. "Or something." She puzzled over his changed appearance, as if Ev had shrunk. Then she shrugged. Maybe it was her.

"Scotch," Ev told the bartender, digging in his pants for his soft dollar bills.

"Those are hard-earned bucks," Luellen said of the limp currency. "You been saving up long for this drink?"

"In a manner of speaking," Ev said. He felt that way about every drink he'd had this year. "How have you been?"

"Unchanged," Luellen said. "Looking for love in all the wrong places. Like that."

"You're not at the photo studio anymore."

"That's right," she said. "What else do you know?"

She was not forthcoming in this atmosphere; Ev did not like her as much as he had at his office, where they had each had a role to fill, where she had been on a running meter, one dictated by his valuable time. Now time stretched ahead of them, a yawning Friday evening. Maybe she was angry with him for letting her disappear so easily. Maybe she wanted proof, like everyone else, that somebody cared. With this hypothesis in mind, he began asking questions, just as he would have during a session: how was she feeling? How were things with her sisters, her mother? Was there something she wanted to talk about?

Even before Luellen laughed at him, Ev could feel the wrongness of his tack, the peculiar way his words sounded when he had to repeat them over bar clatter, when they were punctuated by the real lives of others, laughter and music and small talk and cursing.

"Did you think you were in your office?" she shouted over the jukebox, draining another drink. "Did you think I was still paying to have your precious undivided attention? Did you think this was about moi?"

"I don't know," he said honestly.

"*You* came to *me,*" she told him, using her finger to point. "This is the exact opposite of me coming to you. Welcome to *my* place of employment. You like the decor?"

He shrugged.

"Gloom," she said, leaning close to explain. "Neon, with glass accents, eau de smoke, and desperation." Her drink was gin and tonic, bubbling before her like harmless sparkling water. She sucked on a skinny straw, cheeks going hollow. In the mirror behind the bar, they looked unhappy, both of them. Other people smiled, Ev noted, other people laughed, the music pumped in and they responded, got in the mood. In their cheerless way, he and Luellen were linked: two miserably serious patrons of the planet alcoholic. WELCOME TO FRIENDLY'S, the sign read over the mirror, taunting, cynical.

"Listen," Luellen said, "I'm going to ask you something that you probably knew I wanted to ask you a long time ago. Stop me if you've heard this one, but . . ." She took a breath. "If I wanted to have a baby, would you agree to impregnate me?" She grinned without humor. "How's that for a come-on? 'Knock me up, please.'" She sighed orgasmically; the bartender, aproned, hustling from one end of the bar to the other, took a moment to eavesdrop, to lift his eyebrows.

"I can't see that happening," Ev told her, although he could see it, all too clearly, and all too clearly felt the urge to lead her away into the temporary ecstasy of her request. To drive this urge back where it came from, he asked her if she'd read about the murdered woman.

"Naturally I have. Is that why you're here, checking on me?"

"I came to warn you," he said. "And to say hello."

"Consider me warned," she said. "And hello. And goodbye." She wouldn't relinquish her restlessness; she was angry with Evan, or maybe with the world. Maybe he was simply cramping her style, glowering beside her while potential lovers glided by. Or maybe she had genuinely requested the presence of his sperm. He had offended her by denying the most flattering favor a person could ask of another: come commingle in my gene pool.

"It wouldn't be responsible," Ev said eventually.

"Bullshit," she answered flatly.

He ordered another scotch. One thing in her favor, she didn't mind silence. In that way, she was like Joni, comfortable simply sitting quietly. They sat companionably enough. The more he drank, the tighter and more insular became the pocket he and Luellen inhabited together.

From nowhere, a voice entered, a man's aggressive demand. At first Ev thought he was ordering a drink from the bartender. Then he realized the man was talking to Luellen.

"Lu," he said. "Lu, let's party, Lu."

"Fuck off," she said.

"What's that?" he said.

"Fuck. Off."

Without warning, the guy shoved her. It might not have been intentional; the bar was crowded, and he could have been pushed from behind, sending Luellen like a domino. She fell against Ev. Then the man, short, bearded, relatively mild looking, shoved her again, as if, like a child, he was so happy with the results of his last push he just had to try it again. Ev understood that it fell to him to do something.

"What should I do?" he asked Luellen, who hadn't moved from his thigh and arm. Her white dress felt cool, like ribbed rubber, smooth and riveted.

"Don't do anything," Luellen said, her hair warm against his forearm. "That's your style, isn't it?"

"Not necessarily," he said, hurt that she saw him as passive.

"You could ask him how he's feeling," she said, turning her head so that her mouth was on his arm. Her breath was warm, moist. And then she was suddenly up and swinging at the stranger, who held his hands over his face, defending himself, baffled. She walloped the stranger, but Ev knew it was he, Ev, she wanted to hit.

The bartender reached across to grab one of Luellen's wrists; Ev took the other. Since she was disarmed, the bearded man took the opportunity to strike her fully, with a palm thrust hard into her nose. "Cocktease!" he yelled at her face. "Think you're so fucking good!"

"Fuck you!" she yelled back. "I *don't* think I'm so good, ask him." She indicated Ev, her therapist, but the guy was already on his way to the poolroom, satisfied, sauntering.

Luellen wrenched her arms free and tossed her head. Blood flew. "There's the product of rejection," she said to Ev. "I reject him, and he gives me a bloody nose. You reject me, and what happens? Nothing. Consider yourself lucky."

He had not been a participant in a fight since high school, and then it had been to protect Gerry, who had been accused of being a fag. Gerry hadn't cared. Evan had only slugged the other boy because he was tired of defending Gerry, tired of always having to think about it.

Luellen's nose was bleeding through her fingers, onto her dress. "Leave it to me to wear white the night I break open and bleed," she said wryly. She used little bar napkins to soak up the splashes of red.

Ev realized the extent of her drunkenness by the bartender's expression, by the slow way she processed the sight of her dripping face in the bar mirror. He wished he had a bandanna handy, the way Paddy Limbach always seemed to. He said, "Let me walk you home."

The night was warm. Luellen held a sodden lump of napkins to her nose. She and Ev walked quickly, even though she was very drunk. She had the air of someone who handled being very drunk very well, as if she'd done it countless times and with utter competency. Ev judged his own inebriation, its depths. He, too, could be very drunk (he'd had four scotches on an empty stomach), or he could be very sober (his mind would not let his body off the hook). If he slept with Luellen, it would not be because he was too drunk to do otherwise.

"I wouldn't expect anything out of you except copulation," she said, returning without prologue to their former topic. "Really. You know me well enough to know I wouldn't force some guilt trip on you later. I'm not going to blackmail you or anything. Your family would never know."

"I'm flattered, truly I am," he said. "But the idea doesn't appeal. I don't want children I don't take care of." What a hypocrite, he thought. Where were his sons tonight, for example? What was he doing to be such a grand example of paternal responsibility?

"I mean, the best thing about you is that I can't imagine you'd get involved," she went on. "You don't seem like somebody who'd get attached and difficult about it. You know?" She went on to extol his other virtues — intelligence, healthiness, nice thick curly hair — but Ev contemplated her belief that he was uninvolved, that a child wouldn't compel his interest. It hurt his feelings even as he recognized the truth of it. He preferred to think of himself as someone who could hide the less charitable aspects of his personality.

The walk to her apartment took a bare five minutes. At the building's door, she said, "Please don't just leave me with a bloody nose."

"I'll walk you up," he said, still unsure of whether he would sleep with her. The scotch had shaken his imagination loose: fact and fantasy now joined in a stew. Things that had only resided in fiction for Ev now circulated like probabilities. He remembered suddenly what had once made him give up liquor: not merely its unhealthy hold on his behavior, its demand that he look forward to it, that he count on it to cheer him up, but the more frightening way it rearranged priorities while he wasn't looking. Of course he should accompany Luellen to her apartment, liquor let him lie to himself. Of course nothing would happen, the scotch insisted.

Upstairs, she opened a door into her nightmare. That was the only way Evan could describe it to himself. The room they entered was dark, then suddenly brilliant with what first appeared to be flowers, a busy floral wallpaper. Then, almost instantly, Ev saw the little faces and wide-flung appendages. The walls were covered not by flowered wallpaper but by photographs — magazine models, catalogue bodies, newspaper halftones. Except that everyone was severed: bodies without heads, heads without bodies, familiar people in unfamiliar formation, juxtaposed with guns and knives and penises, everywhere penises, snipped from somewhere and inserted here like sabers, in the eyes, in the mouth, between the legs. The room was chaotic with pain: faces and limbs and genitals and words, pink and yellow and gray and brown and black, soldered thickly together, glued right to the wall with something glossy like shellac, a shining mural of misery, a great greeting card in the style of a massive ransom note.

"My God," he said.

Luellen smiled a satisfied smile at him as she disappeared down the hall. He felt accosted. He felt surrounded, drowning, as if he ought to turn right around and run, run, run. The walls were threatening and specific with the horror they promised. Each was totally covered, up to the ceiling; Luellen would have had to stand on a stepladder, placing tiny figures up high, where no one could make them out clearly. You couldn't focus on the furniture for the howling of the walls. It was intensely layered labor, alarmingly dense with passion. Evan didn't like to consider how much time had been spent cropping these parts, arranging them, and now living with them. He thought about the newspaper account of the stranger's murder, the body stoppered with bottles at all of its tender apertures: anus, vagina, mouth.

"What do you think?" Luellen asked, returning from the bathroom with a fresh wad of tissue at her nose. She did not apologize for the effect such a place would have on the uninitiated, and so Ev felt tested.

"When you bring men here, what do they say?"

"I don't generally turn on the lights," she said. "They don't generally have anything to say about the apartment. And if they *do* say anything, I tell them they have to live with my art. Like it or lump it."

A strung-together series of words ran like a headline beneath a woman skewered by the Sears Tower antennas: I WOULD THROW HIM FROM THE TALLEST BUILDING IN TOWN.

"I ask people how they'd kill somebody," she explained. "This is what they say." EVERY PILL IN THE HOUSE ran around an aspirin bottle with breasts and labia. MY DADDY'S 22 RIFLE, RIGHT HERE accompanied a bathing suit model straddling the barrel of an enormous black-and-white gun; a white dildo was protruding from her mouth.

"Who do they say they'd kill?"

"Themselves, a lot of the time. Ex-husbands, the evil aunt, politicians, talk-radio hosts, their dads. That's who I would have killed, I think, either him or myself."

"Your father?"

"Sure. He was bad, a total fuck. Aren't you supposed to think that's healthy, for me to hate him? Haven't I put my hatred in the right place? I didn't make this stuff up," Luellen told him. "These are direct quotes. I'm just reporting, taking a poll. You'd be surprised how many people want to kill someone."

Ev was surprised, although he didn't think he ought to be. Hadn't he been taking a kind of poll, too, all these years? Listening like a priest as people dumped their secrets, their fury and horror and sickness and guilt, before him? Yet his findings differed; apparently his sampling was of another populace.

"What did you think when you read about the woman in this neighborhood?" he asked Luellen, thinking of the man who'd shoved her at the bar, the one who if asked might say he wanted to kill Luellen, do it with his bare hands, leave her bludgeoned on a barroom floor.

She flipped off the light and lay on the couch, a pillow rolled beneath her neck, her head tipped back to slow her bleeding. She worked at kicking her shoes loose while still holding the tissue to her face. "I thought a few things," she said. "At first, I had a Jack the Ripper response — you know, he's-still-out-there kind of thing. I've been thinking about her a lot, to tell you the truth, Valerie Laven. They said her name on the news tonight, in the bar. As soon as they run her picture in the paper, I'll put it up on the wall." She lay silent for a few moments; Ev wondered if she'd passed out. He stood where she'd left him, the pictures and words mere clutter around him now, lurking like bad dreams, the thankfully hidden subconscious. Then she said, "Dr. Cole, will you stay and talk with me, please? I haven't talked to anybody smart in a long time."

Ev sat on the coffee table beside her. His eyes adjusted to the dark so that faces began appearing once more. To avoid her gruesome collage, he rested his cheeks in his palms, stared at the blank floor through spread legs as if combating faintness.

"Maybe she wanted to die," Luellen said. "Maybe Valerie Laven asked that guy to kill her. The truth is, most people want to kill themselves rather than someone else. That's the consensus, in my limited field research."

Ev turned his head without actually lifting it. He was tired. He could see Luellen's jaw and throat but not her face. "It's a painful way to want to die," he said, leaving the subject open but patently rejecting it as untrue. Luellen may have needed to believe that Valerie Laven had control over her destiny, but Ev needed to believe the opposite. Perhaps because he *had* killed someone; he did not want to hand over the burden of blame. Maybe because he enjoyed hating himself.

Luellen said, "For example, I don't think those bottles were his idea. I think they were hers, and I think the ropes were hers, and I think the stun gun belonged to her, not him, and that's why he left it there, and I think those were her handcuffs. I have handcuffs, so I know they could be her handcuffs." She sighed. "I think I've stopped bleeding," she added, turning on her side, her head still thrown back over the pillow. "I can't taste it in my throat anymore." The wad of tissue plopped on the bare floor by Ev's feet. "Maybe she didn't want to die, exactly, but she wanted to be hurt, that's all I'm saying. You probably think that's projection."

"Probably," Ev agreed.

"And you'd probably be right."

It occurred to him that his sessions at the office might be better run in the dark, under the influence of four scotches, with scary pictures all around. He felt as if he'd finally entered Luellen's mind, here in her dim apartment, beneath the images adorning her walls, the carefully executed windows to her soul, these compositions of brutality. Here he was, looking not at but through the filter of her experience. Finally he'd come into the dark with her. He'd joined her, and he no longer had particular answers, nor a fifty-minute time constraint, nor a little emergency buzzer to hit for help. She was right; *he'd* come to *her.*

"Please stay," Luellen said, as if she'd sensed his impulse to flee.

He would not have sex with her, although the desire was there, like tiredness, like gravity in his limbs. Sex, at this point, did not feel like the most intimate thing he could have with Luellen; they'd already had that. So he did not have to work against temptation, did not have to transcend it; rather, he worked hard to perceive it as a meaningful gesture to forsake.

"Sleep with me," she said.

He eased off the table and onto her couch, reclined to lie beside her, the two of them impossibly close. When she butted her head against his shoulder, he put his arm around her. She settled like a child, squirming, adjusting, poking at his ribs to make herself comfortable. Evan realized that Rachel had often wanted to lie with him like this, to manipulate his arms to feel just right around her, to collapse together in a comforting small space, fulfilling an asexual need simply to be held, and he realized that he had not had the patience for it with her yet now felt no great hurry to leave Luellen. And maybe Paddy Limbach lay at this very moment with Rachel, indulging a similar need. Did this make them even? Ev wondered. Would sleeping with Luellen settle the score?

"Tell me you never thought about us fucking," she said.

"I thought about it," he said, although that wasn't strictly true. He'd entertained the notion, like the rest of her life, only from a great distance, as a narrative for him to behold rather than an actual ongoing existence. He had observed her life as a thing in which he could not possibly make an imprint, and, more arresting, as a thing with no bearing on *his.*

"I was in love with you," Luellen said. "It was starting to break my heart to go see you every Wednesday. I called it Sadnessday.

There's just nobody else who knows me as well as you. Think of that, Dr. Cole. And you didn't seem to be afraid of me. I hate how people seem afraid of me. I don't really try to scare them, but I do. I just do."

Evan understood how that would make him appealing to her; he knew that he himself was drawn to people who weren't intimidated by him. But he was also afraid of her. He hadn't been until he saw her walls; now there was no denying that she had a formidable ingredient in her composition, something that not only acknowledged darkness but traded actively in it. He pursued his fear one step further, then said, "These violent pictures make me afraid. They make me think you find them beautiful. Or true. And I can't stand the idea that you think they're the only true thing, that one hundred percent of this room is made up of killing and pain."

She snuffled. "Shit, I'm bleeding again."

Ev reached for the soggy blood-soaked wad on the floor. When she'd pressed it to her face, she said, "I'm going to sleep now." Her voice was bored, no longer interested in Ev; he had apparently disappointed her, the way earlier his appearance at Friendly's had seemed a letdown to her, as if she'd had a fantasy slayed. "Just hold me, O.K.? You don't have to do one other thing in the world tonight, just lie here with me."

For a long time they lay without moving. Ev's arm, underneath Luellen, fell into a penetrating tingling, then numbness. He paid attention to it as he would to weather, out the window — something that did not involve him. His sleeping arm was another loose extremity in a room full of them, nothing more. At last Luellen slept, her hair on his dead forearm, her bloody tissue in his fingers. Above him her illustrations loomed. Now, if he slept, he might enter her nightmares, her vista becoming the canopy over a tumultuous sleep. Her hell, and the way she woke cheery under its weight in the morning, made Ev more deeply frightened. That day, he began to imagine moving home to his family.

. . .

He needed to see them immediately, ascertain not only their safety but their ordinariness. Valerie Laven had sent him to Luellen; Luellen sent him, if not to Rachel, then to Zach and Marcus, who seemed to sense the desperate nature of his sudden attention to them.

He took them on an uncharacteristic excursion to Melrose Park, to Kiddie Land, where Zach, in the spirit of happy weather, ate and rode everything, and where Marcus grew simply nauseated and needy, like Evan.

"What's *wrong?*" Marcus asked him miserably as they sat on a bench watching Zach doing circles on the Mexican Hat.

"What do you mean?"

"You're mad," Marcus said.

"Not mad, worried. I'm worried about a client," Evan told him. "I'm worried she's in danger." He explained the murder, his concern for Luellen, the pornography on her walls that made her life seem like one long death threat and suicide oath. It was not Ev's habit to lie to his sons. He'd laid the world before them early on; their opposite responses to it seemed confirmation enough that brutal truth alone could not create — in fact, could hardly tint — their individual fates. Zach, the boy now whirling on the sombrero, would accept information of this sort — news from the subterranean, dark sector of life — as material outside his reach. He believed in it only theoretically, like infinity, like mortality, but he was not at its mercy. He might be occasionally moved by it, but he would never be its victim. Marcus, in contrast, fretted, worrying not only that a dark cloud was following overhead but that his very nature would edge into a black realm, that the cloud would slip into his heart, would become part of him, would seize his goodness.

"What kind of pictures?" Marcus asked, of Luellen's walls.

"Naked women, impaled and hurt and horribly tortured."

Marcus was silent for a moment, his large open shoes below his bony ankles a source of pain to his father. He said, "We have a naked woman in our living room."

"That's true." Evan weighed the differences between the coffee table he and Rachel had bought so long ago and the pictures on Luellen's wall. He explained the pornographic aspect of Luellen's pictures, but Marcus interrupted, asking if Ev's client was a nice person.

Evan looked at his son in the garish illumination of the amusement park; the glossy red and yellow shades that flashed over Marcus's eyeglasses reminded Ev of emergency vehicle lights. Marcus's upper lip showed the beginnings of a mustache; perhaps he would soon have to shave. Acne dotted his forehead, scabbed from the boy's predictable picking.

"You're a nice person," Ev told him, answering the question his son really cared about. "You're a good person and you'll be a good man, I don't have any doubts."

Marcus looked sharply away. Zach's Mexican Hat was slowing and falling like a spun coin, soon to lie flat so its woozy riders could disembark.

Ev continued as they stood to wave for Zach, whose eager face searched the crowd, his soft lips open. "My client doesn't think she deserves to be happy. Somebody told her she was rotten so many times that she believes it, even when it isn't true. Does that make sense? She thinks she deserves to be hurt. She's waiting for someone to do it."

Marcus nodded. He wouldn't look at Evan, but he was listening hard, his left eye squinting at Zach, who had found them and was pushing through the crowd, approaching.

"I love you," Evan told Marcus, gripping his son's shoulder. "You boys mean the world to me." Just before he pushed away, Marcus's body felt pliant against Ev, soothed, salved. Then Zach bumped into them and grinned.

"Dizzy," he said, laughing. "Stop giving me the evil eye, Marcus. Can I go again, Dad?"

Sixteen

· · · · · · · · · · · · · ·

IT WAS RACHEL who received the call about Gerry Cole, since her phone number was on his wrist, and it came at the god-awful two A.M. moment when all such calls seem to come. Paddy was spending the night, and they both jerked guiltily awake when the phone began to shrill. Caught! Punished! Each imagined the worst: a death — first of a child, then of a spouse. Rachel could not help breathing a sigh of gratitude to discover that it was her brother-in-law who'd been taken; his death somehow was not punishing enough to be considered her just deserts, not yet the judgment that would be passed on her. She listened to the news while Paddy went to pee, then told him she had to call Ev.

"You want me to go home?" Paddy asked, standing before her naked, scratching his testicles. His hair had bleached to a near white over his summer on the roof; his nose was a dark red like bricks. Below the waist he was sickly pale, and his dark hand by his fair penis appeared not to belong to the same body, as if some other man, some red devil, were scratching him. "What should we do?" he said.

"*You* don't have to do anything. *I* have to call Ev." She dialed, watching Paddy, who sat beside her, his bare thigh touching hers.

"Evan," she said, "there's bad news." She laid her hand on Paddy's leg as if to assure him she still liked him best. Paddy listened to her tell her husband that his brother had died, appreciating the care with which she delivered the news, curious as to why he'd never met this brother. He had always assumed Ev had no siblings, certainly none in Chicago. And he would never have imagined a brother who could die of an overdose of heroin, which was what Rachel was telling Evan, what she'd heard from the police. *Heroin,* Paddy thought, picturing the rubber tie-off belt and the hypodermic needle, black lights and Jimi Hendrix posters, all summoned from his stockpile of cinematic images. And Rachel hadn't seemed alarmed, had seemed to have expected such news eventually, and was even saying so to Evan now. She was using *we* a lot, meaning her and Evan. "We should be glad he died without feeling pain," she said. "It's cold comfort for us, I suppose, but some nonetheless, isn't it?"

They arranged for Rachel to go to Evan's apartment, where the boys were spending the night, and for Evan to go to the hospital morgue to identify his brother's body. Paddy let his sleepy brain idle over the phrase *his brother's body* for a while, curious as to what it could mean to Evan. Paddy had no siblings — his mother's sorrow — and so could only project a half-formed sentimental empathy.

"You can go on back to bed," Rachel said. "You don't have to get dressed."

Paddy realized this was true; there was no reason for him to get up.

While Rachel pulled on clothes, she told him about Gerry. "He hadn't had a job since I think 1984, when he was a nurse in training, or maybe a damned candy striper, at St. Michael's."

"That's where I met Ev," Paddy said, resurrecting the peculiar light of that evening at the nurses' station, resurrecting, too, the time before Rachel, the time when he thought more often of Ev than he did of her.

"That's where I told the cops to take his body," Rachel said. "St. Mike's. Odd coincidence, isn't it? Anyway, he got fired there because he kept stealing drugs. He was a big-time addict and a big-time slouch. He used to write checks on his dad's account, sometimes ours, his friends', forging signatures. Nothing outrageous, just drug money, thirty or forty dollars at a time. Once he lived on our roof for a few months."

"Here?"

Rachel pointed upward while she slipped on her shoes. "Poor Gerry. I haven't seen him in ages — I feel awful. And poor Evan. Jesus Christ, first his dad, now Gerry."

"And Joni," Paddy said without thinking.

Rachel had lifted a brush to her hair but turned away from the dresser mirror to look Paddy full in the face. "Joni?"

Paddy's dream in which he threatened to tell Rachel about Joni had not prepared him for the mortification he now felt. Nor did he have much expertise in spontaneous deception, especially with Rachel. He'd lied successfully to Didi for the last eight months, but his relationship with Rachel was grounded in a kind of forthrightness. Moreover, he had no idea how to explain adequately the role Joni seemed to have played in Evan's life. He feared he could only make her sound more threatening than she'd actually been; he feared he could do nothing but shove his other foot into his mouth while trying to extricate the first.

"A friend," he said lamely. "A friend of Ev's, another shrink, from out West somewhere." Was it Colorado or Arizona? All he could really recall was the image of a rattlesnake in a refrigerator, the woman having to axe the head from the body to make the thing die. That, and the stinking cigar Ev had been smoking when he had talked about her.

Rachel said, "Do you know something you're not telling me? Has Evan been having an affair?"

"No!" Paddy replied — too hastily, Rachel thought. It surprised her how stunned she was, how hurt, at the possibility of Ev's infidelity. But his unfaithfulness would be of a quality different from her own. He would have lied outright to her, where she had yet to lie to him. Plus, to be perfectly honest, she could not imagine a woman better suited to Ev than she herself. She supposed her vanity was just that big: that she could not really imagine him preferring somebody else. Besides, his malaise had seemed on a grander scale; he had been off finding himself, not some other woman. It was not so much jealousy she felt as genuine shock.

She looked at Paddy sitting on her bed. He had gotten as far as holding his Levi's on his lap, undecided about whether to dress or go back to sleep; his bare feet were marked by the tan lines of flip-flops, his hair was unruly as a child's. He was castigating himself and his big mouth; she could practically see the cogs moving. Her husband's complicated life was drawing her back to him; she was going to give Paddy up, she recognized now, feeling the tiny seed of inevitability take root and begin growing.

And then the phone rang once more.

Rachel picked it up. Evan said, "I'm sorry, I'd like some company at the hospital, I just can't go alone." He paused. Rachel imagined the four of them, Ev, herself, their sons, arriving at the morgue in the middle of the night. It was not an altogether unthinkable scenario: a bonding experience, a new rite to kick off their reconstituted family, the solemn chore of identifying the dead body of Uncle Gerry. It was unfortunate that he'd had to die to reunite them, yet perhaps that was the only possible way.

Then Ev said, "I need company, Rachel, so will you please let me speak to Paddy?"

. . .

Ev had identified a body before, an indigent client, a harmless old perverted man whose monthly appearance at his office had accompanied a minor penalty for exposing himself to schoolchildren. And then, ironically enough, he'd died of exposure. Ev had been contacted because his appointment card was the only clue to identification left on the guy. Ev was grateful for the experience; he knew the drill, he knew the morgue would be in the basement. He knew how to find his brother; for once, it would be simple to find Gerry.

His motives for bringing Paddy Limbach along with him he was not at present investigating. He gave himself permission not to think about it for a while. After all, he was the bereaved, the next of kin. He was entitled to irrational behavior.

"Don't apologize or explain," Ev told Paddy before Paddy could do either one. "I sure as hell don't want to hear any apologies or explanations." At least Paddy was sitting in the passenger seat of the Saab. At least Ev didn't have to ride to the morgue with Paddy behind the wheel of his own car.

"O.K.," Paddy agreed. He sat in an appropriately miserable attitude, slumped in his seatbelt as if nothing more than its fabric were holding him upright. He wore a baseball cap with *Limbach Roofing* embroidered on the front. His shirt was wrinkled; Ev pictured it lying on the floor of his own former bedroom, pictured also the green carpet with the tiny Valentine-shaped bloodstain before the bureau. He stopped himself from imagining Rachel buttoning the shirt over Paddy's chest; it was bad enough to remember the morning she'd dripped the blood on the rug, her period early, a surprise. Tonight, she'd stepped into his apartment without saying a word; she just handed him the Saab keys and waved him away, indicating that he should get going, that she would listen for the boys. Ev told her she could lie down on his futon, since Zach and Marcus slept on the bed, but she shook her head. He left her sitting on the box beneath the window, the place where they'd made love not so long ago, her arms wrapped around herself, staring out at the nonview, the brick wall.

And how honest was he being, anyway? He'd wanted to fuck Rachel as soon as he knew she was sleeping with Paddy. What gave him the privilege of feeling so wounded and self-righteous? Ev pulled onto Addison jerkily, heading west, back to St. Mike's, the family hospital.

"I called your house," Ev finally said. "Didi thinks you're camping."

"I know." Paddy simply stared at the passing street. He wished he *were* camping. Everyone else he knew was camping up in Wisconsin. His other life, the one that wasn't difficult, waited in the woods for him. Two years ago he'd been camping with his dad at a lake not far from the one where he should have been tonight. If he had been camping, as arranged, he wouldn't be riding with his mistress's husband to identify the body of his mistress's husband's brother at the morgue. He'd be sitting around a jolly campfire relating the titillating aspects of his affair, he supposed, instead of being embroiled in the nitty-gritty of its consequences. Aside from his father's heart attack, nothing terrible had ever happened while Paddy was camping.

"I'm sorry about your brother," he said quickly, before he put much thought into it. That, after all, should be the evening's primary focus: the dead brother.

"I had already guessed about you and Rachel," Ev told him. "You don't have to pussyfoot around, you don't have to be so fucking guilty and hangdog. I already knew. Snap out of it!" His right hand suddenly jumped away from the steering wheel to slap at Paddy's thigh just above the knee, to give him a sharp flick with the backs of his fingers. The car veered in its perky foreign way, then righted.

Paddy wanted to rub the stinging spot. How he hated that word *fuck,* like a second slap; it never failed to evoke the cruder aspects of sex. What else did he deserve? At least this time Ev didn't have a racquet in his hand.

Paddy had the perverse curiosity of the caught; he wanted to know precisely what had given him away, as if he might rectify it in another lifetime, during his next affair. But the idea of another affair exhausted him. The idea of *this* affair exhausted him. He again wished he were camping, longed for woodsmoke and a flannel-lined sleeping bag, the cold damp mugginess of sunlit tents, the green heat of summer mornings. His associations with camping were solidly linked with his senses, all pleasant associations, things designed to feel or smell or taste or sound or look good. Nothing surrounding him at present — not the car or the city or the dark hour or the situation or Ev, especially not Ev — seemed good to Paddy.

At St. Mike's they were escorted to an elevator by a young security guard who kept one hand locked on his pistol. They rode down without speaking. It was an old elevator named Otis, a metal cage enclosed by windowed doors. They descended through two other floors before landing at the bottom: the gloomy basement, unrenovated, unclean. The first set of doors opened itself; the second set Ev pulled impatiently apart.

"The last dead body I saw was my dad's," Paddy said suddenly.

"Same here," Ev answered. "Here at good old St. Mike's," he said wryly, summoning all of the past two years' irony for Paddy to contemplate.

But Paddy said, "We had an open casket at the funeral. The last time I saw my dad was at Resthaven. Sleeping in his suit, in his coffin. They made him smile, just like when he was alive. I wish you'd met him."

"He wouldn't have liked me," Ev said.

Paddy nodded. This was true. Still, he knew his father would have impressed Ev, and that's what he meant: that *Ev* would have liked *him*. Paddy's father remained, for Paddy, the superior version of himself, the model.

The security guard led them down a hall until they reached a big locked metal door, its handle a huge latch, like something on a Coleman ice chest. There a doctor met them. He was also young, black, with big lobeless ears. He seemed far too youthful to be an M.D. Paddy wondered if this was a sign of his own age, that he thought of other men as too young.

"Did you want the chaplain to meet you with the deceased in the viewing room?" the doctor asked.

"No," Ev snarled.

The young man nodded, unmoved by Ev's choice. He had the security guard unlock the metal door and pull open the suctioned latch.

Paddy thought they were in some sort of anteroom, a chamber preceding the big warehouse for the dead. When neither the guard nor the doctor nor Ev seemed to be going anywhere, he took note of the little room's contents. This, he then concluded, was the morgue, like a walk-in refrigerator, similar to what you might find in the kitchen of a restaurant. A large fan blew cold air from the back; a bright appliance light bulb hung from the ceiling. The temperature was probably just above freezing; along the walls ran metal shelves like those in a refrigerator; on one sat a dishpan with a towel in it. In the middle of the room was a gurney, on top of which lay a shrouded body, that unmistakable prone human shape. No drawers.

"No drawers," Paddy whispered.

"Nope," the guard said. "Everyone thinks there's going to be drawers. That's 'cause of that *Quincy* show. But he was an M.E. Here's our body."

Paddy wished Ev had selected the viewing room instead of the cooler box.

Ev's brother was the only dead person in the morgue tonight, covered with a sheet, zipped in a vaguely translucent bag underneath that. The doctor unzipped the vinyl, and there he was, tinted blue like wax, either by the room's lighting or by death. He wore boxer shorts and a toe tag. Paddy could not see a particular resemblance between the brothers; Ev was so dark and fierce, the brother pudgy and sleepy looking, his fair hair, even in death, boyishly wild.

The doctor turned to Paddy and said, "You can positively ID this man as your brother?"

"No," Paddy said, alarmed, stepping back as if he'd been caught claiming undeserved recognition. He banged into a metal shelf. "Not mine, his."

"Oh." The doctor turned calmly to Ev, his head and its big ears like a radar scanner, and asked the same question. Ev affirmed Gerry's identity.

"That's tough," the guard said, scowling unhappily, hand cocked on the gun at his hip. "I'm sorry, sir."

"He seemed to resemble you," the doctor explained to Paddy, who did not want to resemble the dead man.

Ev now appraised Paddy with this in mind. Could that possibly explain something that had bothered him these last two years — his involuntary affection for Paddy? Could it just be that absurdly transparent and simple, that Paddy reminded him of Gerry?

His brother had a faint guileless grin on his face. Ev had no illusions that his death had been peaceful, as overdoses generally weren't, but it reminded him that Gerry had frequently been accused of foolishness when in fact his natural expression, even at rest, had been amiable, dopey. Ev remembered him slipping down a chair at a party, unable to sit upright, his face turning this bloodless color, his eyes rolling upward. That had been a near overdose; it had been Ev who'd dragged him vertical and forced him to walk, around the block, through the park, along the cold shore of Lake Michigan, with Gerry crying to be let alone, to sit down, to give in to the high, all the time grinning through his misery. You could miss his discomfort if you were only looking at his smile.

Perhaps he had saved Gerry then, twenty-five years ago; perhaps he'd rescued him since; but death had been waiting, not prevented, simply postponed. His brother had been self-destructive, and the inevitable had come to pass. *So high I won't notice I'm dying,* Gerry's self-composed epitaph might have read, on Luellen's wall.

Before they left the cold morgue, Ev reached to the corpse — he heard Paddy faintly hiss, drawing air between his teeth — and placed his hand on Gerry's forehead, which was cool and smooth as a round of cheese, then pushed the hair back instead of permitting it to flop sideways, as it had been, covering one of Gerry's eyes. He repeated this, curious as to whether his brother's forehead felt like his own, like their father's, but the hair remained stubbornly parted, even in death, and the shape of the head was different, as was the texture of his hair: softer, more like their mother's.

"He's the only one tonight?" Paddy asked.

"Well," the guard said, "him and the infant." He indicated the dishpan on the shelf behind Paddy. The bundle of towel inside it now took on sinister proportions.

"Oh," Paddy said, breathing deeply.

"Let's go," Ev said. He brushed past the other three men, eager to be out of the cold room. Paddy wasn't unhappy to leave, either.

That was the end of his old family, Ev thought on the ride back up in the elevator. Now he was the only one left.

In the car, under the familiar green lights, with a familiar white bag of personal effects riding on the back seat, he asked Paddy where he should drop him off. An unexpected moment of déjà vu made Ev's spine feel suddenly weak. It had been summer two years ago when they'd made this same drive. He was not in the habit of being nostalgic, of aching for what had been his. Typically, he was prepared to spurn that sort of useless and dishonest sentimentality.

"Where shall I take you?" he repeated, recovering.

Paddy had left his Bronco at Rachel's place, but that didn't seem a tactful destination. Neither did he want to see Rachel at Ev's place.

Nor could he go home, since Didi believed he was in Wisconsin. "To my office," he said, deciding. It was already four A.M.; he could simply get a start on the day. Not until Ev left him at the front door did Paddy realize that today was Sunday.

Inside, he arranged himself on the waiting room couch, crunched between the armrests, stiflingly hot because Limbach Roofing policy was to turn the thermostat off over the weekends. When he slept, he descended an elevator in his dreams, so hot it seemed he must be destined for hell. At the bottom waited Rachel's family, all four of them alive in the refrigerator; his job was to get her out without disturbing the three sleeping males. And once he'd succeeded, she remembered her baby. "We have to get the baby," she told Paddy. She wouldn't come with him without the baby. "It's dead," he told her. "The baby is dead, I saw earlier." But she wouldn't listen.

Paddy woke on the couch, sweating prolifically, ascertained his true surroundings, situated himself in the real world, then drifted back into an equally horrifying dream.

The last thing Ev had said when he dropped Paddy off was "Thank you for coming with me."

Paddy found his gratitude more tormenting than his anger; *thank you* hit him with the force *fuck you* might have.

. . .

Rachel sat without moving in her husband's apartment. On one hand she could count the number of nights Paddy had actually stayed over; poetic justice had ruled, just as her husband might have predicted. She tried to fix her attention on Gerry's death, but she kept returning to Ev's knowledge of her affair. She concluded that she'd always considered her brother-in-law to be an iffy relation, someone whose continuing vitality should be approached as a random gift; and she also concluded that her husband had always known her better than she wanted to admit. His smoky knowledge made her breathe shallowly, made her feel she'd wasted those months loving Paddy, as if she'd given up a scholarship to the better school.

Ev returned quietly. He locked the door, went to pee in his noisy bathroom, and then came to lie on the floor near her feet, resting his legs on a chair. In the dark, she could see his chest rising and falling. She supposed he considered it her turn to speak, but she had nothing to say, which he also probably knew. They stayed silent for a long while, although the time could not have been calculated with a clock. It was time of a different nature, based on their long relationship, based on grief and obligation. They were having an imperceptible conversation, not saying things to each other but hearing them nonetheless. For a year, Rachel had been exempt from Ev's taxing expectations of her, and she now felt his substance in her body like a forgotten organ, the tumorlike presence of her conscience. It was heavy and joyless, like a documentary film, like a news bulletin from a war zone, like reality.

They stayed up all the rest of the night together, the way they had when he announced he was leaving. They were doing the opposite of arguing, they were having sex without touching, they were talking in bed without customary words or props, they were occupying space that didn't exist, they were surviving together what each would rather not survive alone, they were defining marriage.

Sunday morning happened outside the windows; first birds, then cars, then human voices and the sounds that summoned human attention — churchbells, a police siren.

When the boys wakened to find their mother in the apartment, it was Ev who broke the news.

"Gerry died," he said to them, and they instantly went to Rachel to be held. It was Ev who made tea and brought glasses of milk, working on the periphery, but it was Rachel who cleared her throat and answered their sons' questions.

"What about Yolanda?" Zach cried.

"Who?"

"His girlfriend, Yolanda, the comedian."

"Gerry didn't have a girlfriend," Marcus said. "Gerry didn't even have a house."

"You can have a girlfriend without a house," Zach said. "Somebody should tell Yolanda."

"I'm sure Yolanda will find out," Rachel said. It was hard for her to imagine Gerry with a woman. In the past, there had never been mention of a specific woman; in fact, for many years Rachel had thought of Gerry as a kind of eunuch, without particular sexual disposition.

"What are you doing here?" Marcus asked, stepping back to assess the situation. "Why did you come here?" He was angry to have slept through an evening's events like a smaller child than he was.

"I came to help your father," she said promptly, hoping that Ev would not feel it necessary to explain the night's history fully; he could be such a stickler for the truth.

"Is Dad moving home?" Marcus asked.

"I don't know," Rachel said, sighing. She thought the evening had provided answers and insights, but in fact she had none to share. They dissolved like important but forgotten dreams, like notes written wronghandedly, illegible and misremembered in daylight. She shrugged. "Ask him."

Seventeen

· · · · · · · · · · · · ·

"I KNEW you'd been seeing Paddy," he said wearily to Rachel the day she agreed to let him move home. He'd planned to use *fucking* instead of *seeing* as the sentence's verb, but he just couldn't summon the zest for such candor. His zest had fled, drained out of him like air from a tire. His desire to know people or care for them was sorely absent, and he had to rely on habit. He loved Zach and Marcus the way he loved his vanished mother, wholly, without reservation or rationale. Everyone else was too complicated to love right now, even Rachel, nice as it might feel to be held by her. Evan couldn't stand the thought of talking to her, so he just put himself so close to her that they couldn't do anything but hold each other. And perhaps that had less to do with her than with the fact that, besides his one night with Luellen, he hadn't held anyone for a long while.

Rachel seemed to understand that it was useless to talk. There was nothing anyone could say that would help Evan. Considering this, he wondered if his whole profession didn't operate with a misguided method, this talking and talking and talking, when what was awfully clear to him was the need for silence, and great long lengths of it. Only time would help, and the sooner it began passing, the better. If he could have fallen asleep now and wakened deep into next year, he would gladly have laid back and shut his eyes.

· · ·

Once again the boys had to move their father's furniture, this time without Paddy's Bronco.

"Let's call him," Zach suggested. "Otherwise, we'll never get that futon home. Remember, Marcus? He called it a futron?" Zach giggled.

"I don't want the futon," his father said. "I'm leaving it here."

Zach felt contented with this decision, simply thankful he wouldn't have to lug it down one set of stairs and up into the condo. Besides being a monstrous thing to move, it was an uncomfortable place to sleep. But naturally his brother would not let go of the subject.

"Even if you don't want it," Marcus said, "it's worth money. We could sell it. Let me sell it."

"We're leaving it," his father told him patiently, again and again, in response to whatever possibility Marcus broached for getting the thing back to their apartment.

Finally, Zach figured something out: his father didn't want Paddy to help them. They'd made three trips by then; everything except their father's clothes and miscellaneous books was back home. And the futon, of course. To Marcus, he said, "Dad's mad at Paddy." He laughed at the unexpected rhyme.

Marcus said, "It's wasteful to leave the futon here."

"But he's mad, so it doesn't matter. I wonder why he's mad."

"Because Paddy likes Mom," Marcus told him. "Idiot moron, don't you know anything?"

"He does not," Zach said feebly. "Maroon," he added.

Although Marcus had thought that he wanted his parents to reunite, he found himself dissatisfied once it was happening. And though he had always believed he would someday do something noble and benevolent for his uncle Gerry, he had to admit that he was relieved not to have to think about him anymore. The third thing he felt, forcing himself to be as ruthless and honest as possible in examining his feelings, was that he sort of missed Paddy Limbach, who apparently was not to be mentioned.

Paddy had given him permission to kick the bathtub and to hate a black boy if that black boy deserved it. Marcus believed in due credit. So he could no longer hate Paddy. In fact, he wished he might run into Paddy somehow, ask him about a few other things, girls among them. His mother had questioned him about girls in his classes, transparently trying to make him express interest in one of them. Marcus stubbornly pretended he hadn't noticed girls in his classes. Or if he had, to have paid attention only to their brains, the developmental progress of their senses of humor, their relative talent or stupidity. His father would never mention girls in the knowing, irksome way Paddy Limbach once had. "Got yourself a girlfriend, pal?" he'd said. Pal. At the time, Marcus ignored him. Now he would have liked to hear what Paddy had to say.

Clearly Paddy was in love with Marcus's mother. Clearly he had some thoughts on the subject that weren't about respecting a girl's intellect.

So Marcus would not give up his argument for the futon. He was almost in tears before their father angrily relented and helped the boys roll and shove it down the three flights of dirty steps, then flop it on the roof of the Saab like a big hamburger bun.

"You happy?" he asked, disgusted as he slammed his door.

Nobody was happy.

They started off slowly, Zach's hand out one window holding the mattress, Marcus's out the other. Soon the boys were sitting on their respective doors, both hands gripping the futon, which wanted to slide off. Wind pulled their hair from their faces. Their father drove slowly, but the mattress inched backward as they continued down Clark onto Sheffield. Eventually, even though Marcus would be angry, Zach had to let go — either that or fall out himself. The futon slid from the Saab and thudded solidly on the street; the car behind them screeched to a halt.

"Dad!" Marcus shouted. "Stop, stop, stop!"

But their father wouldn't go back. "Fuck it," he told them. "I didn't want to bring it, I'm not going back for it. Fuck it." And he took a sharp turn down a side street and went right through a pot-hole, as if to punctuate his resolve. The boys looked at each other.

Zach watched out the back window as if their car were involved in a chase scene. His father turned again, then sharply again, then again, until he was back on Clark, headed south. His anger resided in his driving technique, Marcus's frustration came from his narrowed eyes, but Zach felt sort of amused. He imagined all the cars lined up honking at the futon in the road; he wondered if someone would drag it away and sell it, the way Marcus had wanted to, or if someone who actually needed a place to sleep would retrieve it, haul it to an alley the way his uncle Gerry might once have, and fall gratefully into a nap. He wondered if any of the drivers behind them had seen their license plate, and whether police at this very moment were gearing up to come after them.

"I'm carsick," Marcus said sullenly. "All this swerving around is making me sick."

Zach said, "We should have had Paddy help us, with his big Bronco."

They were stopped at a red light, and Evan suddenly leaned over the seatback to slap Zach, who blinked incredulously, believing then what his brother had told him earlier. Paddy liked their mom. Tears came to his eyes.

"Don't hit him!" Marcus screamed, reaching over to slap at his father's seat. "Keep your hands off him, you jerk!" This, too, surprised Zach, almost as much as the slap, because Marcus rarely came to his defense. Usually Marcus was the cause of his crying. And then Marcus looked like he might start crying, too, and the car was moving once more through traffic, although more slowly now, their father sighing behind the wheel.

Zach thought a new, surprising thing, the words so clear it was as if somebody were speaking inside his head: *I don't want him to come home.*

. . .

Paddy remembered what she once had told him, that she imagined him watching her, the audience for her daily life, and now he understood what she meant. Now he knew precisely what she had been talking about.

He tried not to think about Rachel in the way one tried not to think about mortality: it was a solid inevitability around which all other possibilities took shape and from which they derived meaning, the sun in the center of the planets' spinning agenda, something so stunning and luminous one might try to avoid considering it on a daily basis. He launched like a booster into the school year with Melanie and Didi, going shopping for supplies at Kmart, reading over Didi's lesson plans, sitting through shoe and dress fittings. He'd been predominantly unconscious through Melanie's kindergarten experience; he swore to shape up for the first grade, pledging himself to weekly visits to her classroom, an activity he couldn't help imagining Rachel endorsing, loving him for.

He tried not to think about Rachel. He made love with Didi. Because he had not pressured her about sex since January, she was more eager now. It was better sex than they'd had for years. For a few weeks this pleased Paddy, the part of him that felt guilty toward Didi, the part that wanted to be kind to her, to honor the love she clearly still felt for him. In her eyes he could see fear, in her body he could feel it; his lies had threatened her, his absences had forced her to act at fault. In return, he was careful with her; he did not ask her to do any of the things she did not like to be asked to do. But he could not help imagining Rachel as he slipped inside Didi, heightening his moment of climax by putting Rachel where his wife lay beneath him.

He tried not to think about Rachel. He made plans to visit his mother; he'd not seen her since last Christmas, had woefully neglected his duties to her. He made plans to send her to England, where her family had originated, and to Ireland, where his father's family still lived. He purchased a ticket and took off work to drive to Normal, taking Didi and Melanie along, on the long Labor Day weekend. They rode through the heavy haze of the late summer harvesting weather, the hedges thick on the sides of the road, dead insects blurring the windshield. Evening fell and Paddy could not help imagining Rachel in her kitchen, pouring her evening glass of wine, hesitating to switch on lights, wandering into her study, gazing, relaxed, out the window.

He tried not to think about Rachel. He got up early every morning and helped dress Melanie while Didi made breakfast. They ate together, listening to Christian radio ("Have a good and godly day!"); he dropped Melanie at her school, waiting in the line of idling cars until she entered the big double doors — she always turned to wave, happy to see him there watching, her hand lifted as if she were going off to war, never to see him again — and disappeared. He drove to work drinking Coke, listening to country-western music. He switched on the same music at the office and found that all the lyrics applied to him and his life. His poor heart was breaking, his aches were all aching, riding solo in the saddle again. Rachel would have hated it — he could imagine her scorn, the way she would smile at the foolish twanging and wailing — and still he could seriously weep at the applicability of this music to his life.

He tried not to think about Rachel. He was not thinking of her the day he detoured distractedly north, around Hollywood Ave., and got thrown onto an artery that led him, winding past orange cones and jackhammers, hitting every single red light, to Wrigley Field, and from there down Addison until he was directly in front of Ev's old apartment building. Paddy glanced at the brown double door, the scummy glass, its big crack, and there hung the sign, APT FOR RENT, white on red, a phone number Magic Markered beneath. This would be Ev's apartment, the top floor. Paddy swung the Bronco around the next corner, circled back, and parked illegally in a loading zone in front of the liquor store.

The foyer doors were not latched, in fact were breathing in and out with the wind. Paddy stepped in and climbed the steps, which seemed to be leading him to the great unknown. On the fourth floor, Ev's door was open; the air was chalky with the smell of paint. The floor was covered with splattered bedsheets, and a radio played from the kitchen. A fat man and a thin man in white coveralls, black Laurel and black Hardy, stood having coffee over the sink, the fat one shaking milk from his fingers, cursing.

"What?" he demanded of Paddy.

"I . . ." Paddy had no clue what he wanted. The apartment didn't look significantly changed since Ev had moved out, despite the painters' tarps and the ten-gallon tub of industrial white paint. The windows stood open; the wet air of fall blew through.

"I'm the new tenant," Paddy claimed, hoping they didn't know any better than he who the next tenant was.

"Nice place," the thin guy said. The fat man barked. A laugh? A snort?

"You approva our work?" said the thin man. "We doing a good job?"

"Looks fine," Paddy said, turning to go. He didn't like the feeling he got from these guys; he wondered if they were union. If so, he could report them, but for what? Barking?

At the front door a trim brush rested in one of Ev's broken coffee cups, a Pfizer Pharmaceuticals cup with half the handle gone. Paddy had not realized how much he missed Ev until Rachel, too, had departed from his life. It was as if they'd died.

"This was my friend's," he told the painters as he dumped the brush into a dishpan and poured the milky turpentine after it.

"Fuck you, man," one of them called cheerfully as Paddy rushed down the brown steps, his feet sliding on the smooth surface. Why did he hate that word so much? Maybe these guys had painted the building for years; maybe they were responsible for the shiny diarrhea-brown lacquer on the railing and floor. He burst onto the street, memorizing the phone number on the APT FOR RENT sign by various little strategies — his mother's birthdate, the omission of odd numbers. He noticed the liquor store owner's glare before he reached his vehicle and veered that way first to purchase a big jar of olives, a packet of jerky, and a big beer that looked like a can of motor oil, at nine-thirty in the morning.

He told the owner, "I just moved in across the street. In my friend's apartment, did you know him? A psychologist? Looked like Groucho Marx? The eyebrows, glasses?" The owner eventually agreed, nodding nervously; he remembered Ev mostly, Paddy realized, as an attempt to get Paddy out of his store, out of his loading zone.

Paddy phoned from his office; the apartment was vacant, the last tenant's lease didn't run out for another two weeks, Paddy was welcome to wait, there would be new paint, a damage deposit. He wrote a check and addressed the envelope, cutting his lip as he licked the adhesive. When he put his finger to the cut, he thought of Rachel, a hot unbearable flash, her absence something like death, himself like an untethered planet hopelessly at large in the universe. He had to see her again. He told himself he needed only to hold her for a minute, just a little hug, just a quick fix. He told himself he could sleep with her just one more time, that it would be enough to last him, that he could survive if he just had her for a minute. But he needed to see her, he had to see her, he had to put his hand beneath her shirt, had to put his lips to her ear, had to lie with her in bed one more time; he would go crazy if he couldn't watch her walk across her bedroom naked, her rippling buttocks, her lovely skin moving through the room, the whole her.

In most ways, he succeeded in putting mortality out of his mind. He didn't often let inevitable truths and tragedies into his heart. He was distractable; he was optimistic. And though he had worked very hard, had tried diligently and unyieldingly to think of everything in the world except Rachel, there, unfortunately, he had failed.

· · ·

Paddy waited two weeks to try to contact her; she appreciated his tact. Plus she was busy. There was a lot of grief and anger to manage at her house. She had yet to bring up the name Joni, yet to fly that trial balloon and see what fire it drew. Ev had told her about a client, a woman whose sexual addictions led her into mortal danger; Rachel could not understand what made this client different from others, why her squalid situation impinged so dramatically on Ev. In addition, there was his brother's death; he'd run home because he was afraid, exhausted, near the edge of something desperate and dangerous in himself. Rachel had never seen him so whipped, so affectless; his face was slack, as if he were sleeping with his eyes open. The quick emotions that had once characterized him seemed to have disappeared. He approached each day in the methodical, patient way of a drugged person drinking coffee to keep himself awake. Rachel sent him off in the morning like another child, hopeful that the day would spit him back out at the end, that he would return intact.

Paddy phoned to say he missed her.

"I miss you, too," she lied. She didn't have time to miss him, she didn't have sufficient love to include him. He would always be there. There was no urgency in sending him her love; he was stable. At present, her love had to direct itself toward her husband, their bewildered sons.

"I'm moving away from Didi, you know," Paddy told her.

"Oh, no!" Rachel was genuinely distraught to hear this news. Now she was responsible for someone else's misery. Now the affair had larger consequences. "Why are you doing that?"

"Why? Because I don't love her."

"Please don't say that."

"It's true, I don't love her. I can't stand to deceive her anymore. I'm going to tell her everything."

"What do you mean, everything?"

"Us. About us."

"Paddy, I want you just to think of this — what good will it do? There is no us anymore." She didn't want him to use her name. She didn't want to be on Didi Limbach's hit list. She wanted a cleaner exit than she deserved, and she wanted Paddy to endorse it. "Ev needs me," she said. "He's miserable. I'm afraid he's suicidal." This was true, but Rachel's reasons for telling Paddy the truth were dishonest. She wanted Paddy to leave her alone. And besides, there were other kinds of suicide than corporeal.

"See me," Paddy said. "Just one more time, just to say goodbye. We didn't get to say goodbye. It's the least you could do."

It was not the least she could do; she was already doing the least she could do. Rachel closed her eyes. It seemed unfair how her energy was being sapped these days, being taken by people who believed themselves to require it more than she did. The boys needed her to interpret their father's moods, yet she could not fully disclose the sources of his sadness. Ev himself needed company, somebody who knew and understood the extent of his feelings toward his brother. There was no one qualified but Rachel. She was the only one available to fill the job. Same with Paddy, it appeared; nobody else would do. Women's work: being indispensable.

She agreed to meet him, that afternoon, at a hotel. It was decadent and stupid. If Ev found out, the betrayal would be too large to surmount. Rachel turned over all the facts of her commitment and still found herself going through with it, preparing her body, preparing her excuse for being gone this afternoon if anyone asked.

. . .

Paddy reserved a room at the Raphael, an old grand hotel lurking in the shadow of the Hancock building, hidden by the high-rises. He checked in at one and admired the decanters of liquor, the television remote control, the plush hotel bathrobes, two of them hanging behind the bathroom door, and the big wood-framed windows that looked out on Delaware and muffled the noise of traffic. He lay on the bed and felt his heart race, literally put his hand over the fracas. He had been missing Rachel steadily, but now he was afraid of seeing her; he was afraid of having to admit his need for her. What if he couldn't let go? What if she said they'd never meet again and meant it? What if this was the last time? He had to acknowledge that he'd used this goodbye business as a ploy; he knew it wouldn't be enough. He knew he would need her. He would require a dose of her beyond this afternoon.

Furthermore, he'd apparently left his wife and daughter. He'd adopted Rachel's technique and was pretending she was watching him, a witness to his daily nonsense, his selectively summoned spy.

Rachel rang the room and he gave her the floor number. He waited outside the door, appreciating the charming silence of the Raphael at midday. Its fixtures were old, with newer sprinkler attachments; Paddy liked buildings that complied with safety codes. The elevator took forever, but then there she was, Rachel coming around the corner and walking quickly toward him, not seeing him until she was nearly upon him, so busy was she reading room numbers.

"Hi," he said helplessly. She let him hold her. She collapsed into his arms before they even got into the room. Paddy had removed the bedspread and untucked the strictly tucked corners — those parsimonious maids, cinching the sheets, squashing the pillows — had opened the windows and turned out the lamps. The room was to remind them of nature, that was his intention. Nature soothed him; it was his own animal self he wished to indulge. Now they lay on the blank top sheet, their shoes kicked off, their other layers still between them. Paddy was optimistic, since the rest of the bed and room and hotel spread around them like insulation. No one could find them.

Rachel hadn't worn underwear, and in her shrimplike curl she laid her right hand over her left breast for reassurance. Paddy cupped her hand. "I love you," he blurted. "All I do is think about you."

Rachel didn't want to talk. She butted her head into the cave Paddy's chest and neck made. She had created a terrible mess, she told herself, nuzzling her way closer. She had permitted herself to fall in love with Paddy, she had permitted him to fall in love with her; now they'd conceived something between them as ungainly as a pregnancy, as complicated as a child, and they could not just send it away. She sincerely wished it undone. She could not undo it, but she could wish it had never happened; she could wish she had turned Paddy away when he'd come to her apartment door last year. She could have sent him and his birthday gift away.

Hungry for him, Rachel began to kiss his lips, giving him bites, which Paddy welcomed. She rolled against him hard, like a log on a river of logs, and made a grab at his belt buckle. She wanted to quit thinking about Paddy, and that was fine with Paddy. He didn't want to think, either. He wanted to move around in his body, touch Rachel, put himself inside her and reclaim her. He didn't want to consider the future; he certainly didn't want to dwell on the fact that this meeting had been arranged as their official farewell.

. . .

Not far away Ev sat in his office, between clients, realizing that a new season was upon him, one that wouldn't announce itself by his brother's appearance. He could close the bank account he'd kept for Gerry.

What he couldn't do was quit remembering the way Gerry had been dressed that night last April, his suit which had seemed expensive but was old, its nap shining with wear. What had become of it?

The police had found Gerry on Western, not far from the Y where Ev and Paddy had played racquetball. He'd been wearing his shorts and his dog tag, nothing more; his head was resting on an army knapsack full of papers, trash that Ev carried home in the effects bag a few hours later. Ev remembered watching Gerry and Zach stepping into the liquor store across the street before they went up the el steps, Gerry leaving the store with a brown paper bag, Zach trotting companionably beside. Standing at the window, Ev had had the urge to turn the moment into something harmless, had had the impulse to dash down the stairs so the three of them might ride merrily along in the el cars, traversing the North Shore. But he had not been able to join them; whatever distance existed between him and his brother was insurmountable. It made him proud and grateful to have provided a fitting compatriot in his son Zach. He'd sent Zach out to do his job.

Eighteen

· · · · · · · · · · · ·

EV LAY WITHOUT TOUCHING his wife, who lay also conscious of this fact. Paddy seemed to lie between them. She was forcing them to talk about him, as if discussing him would make him less problematic, as if confrontation would defuse his force. Ev knew she'd learned this tactic from him; too bad she didn't know he'd forsaken it.

"Have you noticed how his voice doesn't seem to go with his body?" Rachel said.

Ev said nothing, so Rachel plunged on: "It's a higher-pitched voice than you might expect, since he's tall . . ."

"You mean he has a big dick," Evan said.

Rachel caught herself before she corrected him. Paddy's penis wasn't particularly large, and Ev, in other circumstances, wouldn't have cared one way or the other. He pretended not to care now, but Rachel wasn't going to acquiesce to whatever game he was playing. Moreover, wouldn't Ev have seen Paddy's penis himself, off at the YMCA, disrobing before or after racquetball? And besides, through which maze had he puzzled to arrive at Paddy's penis?

"He's nasal," she continued, taking the high road. "He opens his mouth and is midwestern nasal, that's all."

"To be honest, Rachel, I don't care that you slept with him. I don't really care. I understand everything that went with it, or I basically understand everything. I understand the *idea* of everything, if not the niggling details, but what interests me, what matters to me, is what happens next. O.K., you slept with him. O.K., there was sex, there was romance, there was a crush and a flirtation that went further, there was sexual tension that got played out, consummated, O.K. Fine. But now what? That's the thing I'm interested in. Now. What. Now."

"Now I love you, now," Rachel promptly responded. She'd had her mouth open, waiting for a pause so that she could insert her assurance. "I love you more than anyone, ever." She wanted to reach her hand over to him, to assure him physically, but she held back, waiting for him to signal that such assurance would be welcomed. Since Ev had moved home, they'd been touching each other only in consoling ways, the embrace of people mourning shared losses.

Ev said, "I mean, I can imagine your situation last year perfectly. I leave you for no discernible reason, I ask you to simply wait without any sense of how long that might be, you agree without understanding the terms. Really, you were generous. You were more than compassionate. I wasn't fully honest with you, I didn't confide in you the troubles I was having — to be even more honest, I think they *did* have something to do with us, with me and you, with me toward you, with age, with my father, all of it, all of it had something to do with my feeling that I was going out of my mind. I think I was going out of my mind. I was not myself. I may still be not myself. I may never be myself, or maybe this is myself and the rest was a game, I don't know. In fact, I feel crazy just lying here talking about it, as if I might talk and talk and talk and still get absolutely fucking nowhere."

He sprang out of bed, snatching his glasses from the nightstand, and Rachel watched his dark shape move around the room. His hand swung in the air to locate himself; he bumped into their dresser and said "Fuck." He shut the bathroom door hard but didn't turn on the light. He would have to pee sitting down, Rachel thought, if there was no light. Wasn't that a pathetic gesture for a man, peeing sitting down? Her face went hot with tears. He was still miserable, maybe more miserable than he'd been before. She was directly responsible for his new misery, for not being faithful, for not keeping her life afloat during his brief going-under. She could argue against this perception, but she knew deep down it was the truth: she'd succumbed when she should have held firm. She'd withstood exactly nothing; she was an impressionable, selfish spouse who'd given in to the first man who'd kissed her swollen lip.

The toilet flushed; the tap ran; the medicine cabinet squeaked open and then banged closed. Ev had sleeping pills now, prescribed by a naturopath, big brown pills the color and consistency of pressed dirt, the size of rabbit turds. He took two or three a night, although he tried not to.

He returned to bed in the dark. "Why didn't you turn on the light?" Rachel asked.

"I don't know. I'm up every night and I try not to wake you, so it's just getting to be habit. Kind of a dangerous one, though. Last night I brushed my teeth with cortisone cream."

Rachel laughed, too eagerly, aware of her own eagerness to laugh. When would their marriage be their marriage again? "I'll move it away from the toothpaste." She now rolled toward him, safely within the domestic landscape of the warm double bed, and put her arm over his chest. "I love you," she said. "I love you more than anything. Please don't be sad."

He breathed deeply; Rachel could feel his chest expand beneath her forearm, his breath in her hair as he exhaled. His odor had aged, gotten bitterer, earthier. Or perhaps it had not changed, and she was now accustomed to Paddy's odor, which was younger, perfumed by Old Spice, that American high school institution. Still Ev did not hold her, did not do what must be automatic in most people, return the embrace. Surely it was his reflex, too; surely he was suppressing it, punishing her. And this made her angry and impatient with him. She abruptly let go and scooted back to her side.

"Goodnight," she said, her face toward her clock. The digital numbers read 11:34, a sequence she liked to up-end: *hEll*, the clock said. Digital clocks always seemed to present her with calculated arrangements, as if to entertain her, to make up for the fact that she had to transcribe their message to the face of an old-fashioned clock in order to make meaning of it. Her favorite was 12:51, the lighted green crosshatches so nicely parallel, mirrored that way, looking like hieroglyphs.

It was late. Very late. She was exhausted yet unsleepy. She was tired of her life. In this, she and Evan felt exactly the same.

. . .

For weeks, their arrangement seemed based on survival tactics and nothing more. The cupboards full of sugared cereals and white bread and unrefrigerated peanut butter did not draw Ev's anger or disappointment the way Rachel might have supposed: these were the provisions, he appeared to understand, and that was what he made do with. The boys behaved themselves, Marcus keeping an eye always turned toward his father, waiting for signs, reading him so cautiously that Rachel wanted to knock their two heads together like coconuts.

She and Ev did not make love.

Rachel's feelings about this ran from relief to annoyance, from guilt to self-pity.

Then one evening, after a series of sleepless nights, Rachel drank a bottle of wine by herself. She skipped dinner and fell into bed before the boys, before Dr. Head's nightly call, and had sodden dreams for several hours. They were deliciously sexual, full of strange men and women. She knew she was dreaming, so she just enjoyed the sex, one episode after another, a decadent smorgasbord. Finally her partner was Evan. She felt sated by then, but was happy to see him prepared to turn his sexual attentions toward her again at last. They were deep in their intimacies when she realized that he had no penis, that it had been removed. "What happened?" she asked. "I did it to myself," he told her. Then another man entered the dream room, a naked man who did not really resemble Paddy but who was clearly meant to fill the role. The two men sat beside each other on a chaise longue (this piece of furniture did not exist in their real home, Rachel noted absentmindedly; where had it come from?) across the room from the bed where Rachel lay, naked, waiting for her husband, confused and alarmed by his castration, by his having done it, apparently, for the-person-who-would-be-Paddy.

She woke to find the digital clock reading 3:32, the 2 rolling as she watched to 3. 3:33. Ev lay beside her; the room was cool, the air damp, as if rain had broken outside. He was awake; she could sense his unrelaxed not-moving, the twitch of his toes. She'd been sated in her dreams, but she was not sated now. She moved against Ev, kissing him, rubbing his penis between her palms as if to start a fire, comforted to find it intact. "I want to make love with you," she whispered.

"O.K.," he whispered back. Her relief overwhelmed her; she slid on top of him and reached orgasm so quickly she felt afraid of her need. She sank onto him and his new old smell, reluctant to move.

But then they went to work on his climax. For twenty minutes the clock changed, the wind picked up outside, the two of them turned over, then back, Ev pulling out, then reentering, asking Rachel to lie on her stomach, on her side, then back on her back, her legs scissored around his calves, then wrapped over his hips, then together to increase friction. She was beginning to chafe, to ache, to be impatient, to get her feelings hurt. Her dream returned, this time to corroborate some instinct she had that Ev did not desire her any longer.

"Aren't you attracted to me?" she asked.

He stopped moving, propped on his hands over her face, tired but too frustrated not to try to continue. "I don't know," he said. His cold honesty was unbearable.

Rachel said, "What, you preferred Joni?" and in that instant, as the name emerged from her mouth, Evan came, unable to withdraw before sending semen deep inside her.

They lay afterward without moving, Evan heavy on Rachel's body, profoundly crushing. Incapable of stopping herself, she began to cry. There was an actual hierarchy of dismay for her to feel, pregnancy among the possibilities. She couldn't help crying, and she couldn't help taking solace in the stable presence of Paddy Limbach, reserve backup, benchwarmer. Maybe Ev didn't love her anymore; maybe so much had happened between them that they would never again make love to each other as themselves. But she had Paddy, she told herself. Paddy still loved her. Paddy had moved to the Addison bachelor pad on her behalf. Paddy experienced no difficulty in finding sex with her erotically charged. If she was pregnant, Paddy could be expected to take responsibility for raising another child; she could have sex with him tomorrow, she could claim the child was his . . . For a second, Rachel was appalled at her pragmatic and defensive skill at coping.

"I have to tell you something," Ev said, his voice unexpected despite his stifling physical weight on her. She'd traveled so far into her own despair she'd felt alone.

Rachel said, "O.K."

"Two years ago, when my dad died, I killed him."

"What?" Rachel instantly stopped crying; instantly Ev's weight was as nothing, and her many random thoughts were utterly abandoned.

"I suffocated him. I closed my hand over his mouth, like this." Now Ev leaned away on one arm while using his free hand to cover Rachel's mouth and nose. In the dark, she could not make out his features, just his looming shape. She also could not breathe; the sensation upon her was suddenly dreamlike, as if she had been thrust into black outer space. For a second she felt his strength as she smelled herself on his fingers — his anger, his power, his capacity to behave as he was claiming he had behaved. And she felt his temptation to kill her, just a passing flicker, like a child's perverse impulse to hurt an animal, like the violent downward thrust of the wrist when kneading bread dough, before he took away his hand. It did not particularly scare her, so shocking did she find the whole series of this evening's events. Like space, it was just so breathtaking and vast, blackness without boundary. She felt wise, fascinated by Ev's dark character rather than threatened by it.

"I know his life was miserable, I know he was suffering, I know *we* were suffering, and still, I probably shouldn't have killed him. And the reason I shouldn't have killed him is not that I felt, or feel, guilty, but that I don't feel guilty. That's why. This not feeling guilty has been intolerable. What sort of man could feel that way?" Now he rolled away, sat on the edge of the bed, and palmed his head, back and forth.

Rachel lay staring at the windows. Reflected on them were the city lights, dividing the glass neatly into a tick-tack-toe grid, one that trembled as the curtains moved, as the building settled, a reminder of other lives happening simultaneously with her own. How did they all continue feeling it was worthwhile? Was every life as complicated as hers? She pictured Evan with his large hand over his father's face. And then she thought, *This is a trick.*

His timing, his telling her now, in bed after troubling sex, as opposed to any other time, suddenly made her furious. He was trying to distract her from Joni, whoever that was. He had confessed in order to divert her attention, in order to inspire her sympathy, her awe, perhaps her fear.

"You're too difficult, Ev," Rachel said. "I love you, I guess, but I'm not sure I can live with you — you're just that difficult." She felt too tired and suspicious to manage any kind of conversation. And a part of her felt something new: fear — not of his killing her, which he could do, but of who he was. What her husband seemed capable of had ballooned in the few hours since they'd gone to bed tonight from crass deception to murder. And as an auxiliary irritation, as a bonus annoyance, she still had no idea who Joni was.

• • •

But oddly enough, Evan's confession to Rachel produced precisely the effect confession was reputed to elicit: absolution. In the morning, after an uneasy sleep, he felt curiously nimble. Enthusiasm for his profession had regained some persuasive purchase in his soul.

Rachel, however, felt tender, as if hung over, as if recovering from illness. Her genitals were sore; her head ached from too much thinking; her limbs felt too long for her body, the appendages of a gawky marionette; and her eyes seemed dilated, overtaxed by bursting images. When Ev and the boys left the apartment, she retreated to her tiny study and its calming view. Water trickled gently over the slate, smooth brown and green like the back of a wet frog; the tiny windows of the shaft casing shone black and impenetrable. A plain bird stood on the roof, motionless, brown with a steady yellow gaze. There was her safe cottage in the fairy-tale forest.

. . .

Ev convinced himself on the way to work that geniuses were people whose intellectual powers were inscrutable and whose emotional ones were a mess. He couldn't think of a single genius whose makeup wasn't dependent on those precise conditions. If he were an emotional cripple, which he suspected was the truth, mightn't he still be a kind of intellectual superior, close to cerebral perfection? And should such a theory comfort him?

No matter; it did comfort him. He spent his day like a professional, reading books between clients, following up on difficult issues, making two people cry. "Why do you blame your father?" he asked Rosie Challez coldly, an unempathetic smile on his face. "When will you take responsibility for your decisions?" he demanded of the whining high school principal. And over his nine-fifty break, he opened his mail. In among the journals and book catalogues and junk lay a letter from a P.O. box number here in Chicago. He opened the envelope expecting a query, someone who wanted to become a psychologist, someone who wanted to get free help through the mail instead of paying for it in person.

But no, the note was from Luellen, accompanied by a newspaper photo of Valerie Laven, victim. Luellen's note, like a kidnapper's, was compiled of words snipped from printed matter. *He hasn't got me yet!!* it said; under that, in parentheses, was the single word *Meow,* clipped from a kibble sack. He pondered her note — glued to a paper torn from a stenographer's notebook, precisely the same kind of pad he took client notes on — then quickly composed his own. *Don't let him!!* he wrote, then added *Woof* and tucked it in an envelope. He addressed it and buzzed the office secretary to post it. He thought perhaps he'd engage in another correspondence like the one he'd had with Joni.

It was useful to maintain that shadow presence in his life, the embodied abyss. In his drawer lay Joni's last letter to him; on the shelf below his father's ashes rested his brother's dog tag, *My name is Gerry* on the front, *I belong to Evan Cole* on the back. Here were the dark artifacts of those who'd once balanced him.

But what about the other side of the shadow, the source of light?

Today was racquetball day, but there would be no racquetball. Since Gerry's death, there'd been a tacit understanding that Ev and Paddy would not play ball. In fact, he felt sorry for Paddy. He knew Paddy would be hurt by losing Rachel; he knew he'd flagellate himself, take full blame. If Paddy were his client, Ev would tell him that exposing oneself to the possibility of pain was not a bad thing. One had to open oneself for love. Getting hurt was only sometimes the consequence, not always. Maybe next time it would be better. He knew plenty of people who, after one such hurt, never permitted themselves to be in the position again, never laid themselves open to that sort of punishment. That would be unfortunate, he would tell Paddy Limbach if Paddy were sitting in the client chair. When Paddy felt wrong and foolish and humiliated and angry, Ev would be there to say he wasn't. Was right to love, wise to explore, brave to put himself on the line, and justified in feeling betrayed.

There were people who protected themselves and those who made themselves vulnerable. Ev supposed he himself belonged in the former category, along with his son Marcus, along with Luellen, along with his old friend Joni, along with his father. But all the people who mystified him, who, he grudgingly had to confess, he *admired,* belonged in the latter category: his mother, his brother, his wife, his son Zach, and, of course, Paddy Limbach.

Nineteen

· · · · · · · · · · · ·

ZACH THOUGHT of his uncle Gerry and the night last spring when Gerry had rescued him from a grim evening with his father. The ten dollars his father had given him Zach had handed over to Gerry at the liquor store; his uncle had come up short at the checkout. "Big gulp," Gerry said of his two beers, extra large size. The Chinese proprietor remembered Zach from the time Zach and Marcus had waited for their father in his store; he gave Zach another female lollipop, another pair of pink breasts to suck on while he and Gerry rode the el.

From their seats in the lighted train car, they watched people, Gerry not so secretly drinking from his bagged bottle of beer, making jokes about everyone who got on. He liked to talk to strangers, and although this habit made Zach's brother embarrassed and angry, Zach didn't mind. Usually people responded, laughing along. Only the stuck-up ones refused, passed by as if Gerry hadn't said hello and commented on the weather, which was pretty bad, as usual.

They rode downtown first, swallowed by the tunnel like a screaming snake sucked into the earth, roaring noisily beneath the city, and got off two stops farther south than Zach's parents ever let him go. Up the steps they went, into the dusk, where trash blew, where graffiti covered buildings like camouflage, then across the street and back down, northbound. Underground stops reminded Zach of bathrooms: the white-and-black tile, the echo, the dampness, the odor. As usual, he watched between tracks for rats, although none appeared this evening; summer was coming, they'd resumed roaming the streets above. A band of black musicians were setting up their battered instruments — saxophone, xylophone, drums, and guitar. The vocalist kept singing the same line over and over: "Darling, yoooooooouuu send me." Although Zach and Gerry waited for a good ten minutes, the band never quite got around to joining the singer, nor did the singer ever quite get around to the rest of the words. They went about the setup as if they were on a stage instead of in a train stop. The guitar case they opened for donations was ringed by flashing lights and little electric bells, Christmas tree decorations.

Gerry finished his first beer and delicately set the bottle on an overfull trash can before they boarded a northbound train. Their seats faced backward, so Zach felt as if he were being pulled uptown by his belt loops. They finally returned, bursting onto street level, where the train noise dispersed, where darkness had fallen. Now the wind didn't matter; now it was Friday night. Zach found himself humming the tune he'd just heard. This was the third train he had traveled on that day, and it was by far the jolliest. Work and school had ended; parties had begun.

"You want a hit?" Gerry offered Zach his second bottle, thoughtfully wiping the opening with his palm.

Gerry's beer smelled terrible, in Zach's opinion, and he couldn't imagine he'd ever choose to drink the stuff. The gap between childhood and adulthood troubled him momentarily, that chasm wherein all the unthinkable characteristics apparently attached themselves — and apparently without resistance on the part of the victim. He just didn't get it.

"Does that taste good to you?" he asked his uncle.

"Sure," Gerry said. "But that's not why I drink it."

"Why, then?"

"Because it makes me happy. And I like to be happy."

"Me, too."

"Who doesn't?" Gerry said. "That's what I like about the human race."

In Evanston, where the two of them hopped off on the east side of the track and then immediately back on on the west side, a group of teenagers pushed aboard with them. They wore evening clothes — boys in tuxedos, girls in velvet dresses — and they brought a cloud of perfume on board with them. "Prom," Gerry said ominously as he and Zach sat in their plastic bucket seats.

He waved to the prom kids and they tittered in response, the boys making snide remarks to each other that Gerry and Zach couldn't hear. "The thing is," Gerry went on, finishing an earlier thought, "that most people don't get happy on a daily basis, which is very, very unfortunate. You sure you don't want a hit?" He put the sack in Zach's hand. "You know, it was your dad who took me drinking first. He and I used to ride the trains drinking beer. I can remember sitting with a couple of six-packs at the Howard Street platform for hours one night, laughing. Back when he drank. Back when we drank with each other. Back when a six-pack apiece was plenty for us."

Zach liked the image of his father and Gerry sitting on a train platform together. He realized he liked the idea of his father happy, because Ev didn't ordinarily seem very happy at all. "I'll try it," he told Gerry now. He wanted to tell Marcus later that he'd gotten drunk with his uncle, that their father had once done the same, to propose that perhaps that the two of them, Zach and Marcus, might later in life also drink together in or around trains, maintaining a family tradition. But Gerry's beer, warm from being held between his legs, tasted ghastly, sour and fizzy, like carbonated vinegar. With difficulty, Zach swallowed a mouthful, positive he would never be able to talk Marcus into it.

"You know what I love?" his uncle asked him.

"What?" Zach handed the bottle back, fighting the urge to spit.

"I love it when somebody just walks along belting out a song. That happens sometimes. I rode behind a guy on the escalator the other day just wailing opera — perfectly normal guy, singing his heart out."

Much as he enjoyed Gerry, Zach still hoped he wouldn't burst into song on the el. Around his own brain circled the single line he'd heard downtown — *Darling, yooooouuuu send me, honest you do.*

Talking in Bed

The train was hot, although the evening outside was windy and cold. Inside the car, the Friday night festive feel had increased, the prom group had grown livelier. Their sweet perfume wafted forward. "We're slumming," they called out. "Going to the top of the cock!" They screamed with laughter, contagious, outrageous.

"What's that?" Zach asked his uncle. "What's the top of the cock?"

"Hancock building," Gerry said. "I go there, too, sometimes, look at the lights. Doesn't cost a thing to look. You've been there, right?"

"Oh sure." Zach summoned the knee-quaking elevator ride up, his popping ears and the feel of floating. When his uncle gave him the bottle, he took another mouthful of beer. It wasn't as bad as the first; perhaps each swallow would be less difficult to manage, until he was successfully silly, like Gerry.

"Look there," Gerry said, grabbing Zach's thigh, his hand on the window glass. "See that sign? That's Yolanda, my girl." The platform flashed by; the bench ad was for a show, somebody in costume.

"That was a man," Zach said, giggling.

His uncle joined him. "That'd be something to get your dad riled up about, me with a man. He *thinks* he could handle it, but we know better, don't we?" They laughed together for a moment. "No, not the person, just the club. Yolanda warms up the club with her troupe."

"Troupe," Zach said. It was his turn with the bottle, so he took a big glug and swallowed a burp afterward. Already he could feel a slackening, the relaxation of his face muscles, contentment swimming into his system as in the moment before sleep.

Gerry said, "There are two different ways to spell *troupe,* but I think they're both about groups."

"Boy Scouts," said Zach. "Monkeys."

"Troop of drunks," Gerry said, meaning the prom kids. They clung to each other and rocked from side to side, their gestures broad, their volume loud. "And her," his uncle went on, "what do you think her name is?" The girl he meant was a thick-haired blonde wearing a lot of makeup. Her friends were skinny and dark, but she was large and pale.

"Jennifer," Zach said promptly.

"And what do you think it'd be like to kiss Jennifer?"

Everything was making Jennifer laugh so hard she had to bend forward. Her dress was tiny, green velvet, and she was stuffed into it like a bundle of cozy, clean pillows.

"I don't know," Zach said. She leaned over her boyfriend again to laugh, exposing her big soft breasts.

"I think it'd be sublime," his uncle said beside him, tipping the bottle to drink, then handing it to Zach. "Absolutely sublime."

Sublime sounded like something vaguely sewer-related to Zach, which reminded him of the taste of this beer. But he drank as much as he could manage before the Addison stop, convinced that his light-headed joy was the beginning of drunkenness, and then left his uncle on the train, waving. Gerry let Zach go off alone because he didn't want to have to buy another ticket; Zach understood.

His uncle's word accompanied him home to his father's apart-ment, floating along in his blood like the sour beer, like the song lyric: *sublime, sublime, sublime.*

"What does *sublime* mean?" he asked his mother after Gerry had died. She was trimming his hair; he wore a towel, and his neck itched.

"Heavenly," his mother said, snipping above his ear. She thought of her afternoon with Paddy at the Raphael, their last en-counter. "Grand."

"Oh," her son said, and suddenly bowed his head, which made her cut him, a little nick at his temple.

• • •

Rachel told her friend Zoë about her affair after it appeared to be over.

"You *what?*" Zoë cried. She could not believe Rachel had slept with another man.

Rachel decided to tell her other shocking things. "Ev knows all about it," she said. "It was with his friend Paddy. I could be pregnant." This last part was not true, but could have been true, which was almost as good. Rachel had had unprotected sex, had tempted fate.

"The *roofer?*" Zoë said. "That dope?"

They wandered around the botanical garden, their pace slow, their faces damp. "Not a dope," Rachel said, less excited to discuss Paddy now. Now she remembered how she'd characterized him in the past; for a second she held both views, her old one and her new one, enjoying the contrast. "He's sweet," she said lamely, missing him suddenly. He would enjoy mispronouncing all the flora names.

"Who's the father?" Zoë asked.

"I'm not sure I'm pregnant."

"Who would be the father?"

"I'm pretty sure I'm not pregnant, but it would be Evan."

"If it was the roofer, then you'd have a real problem," Zoë said. Zoë had had four abortions in her life, two of them of pregnancies with unclear paternity; Rachel hadn't had any abortions and always knew who'd caused what. This was the first time in their friendship that Rachel's life appeared the more muddled and preposterous, but after the initial thrill of shocking her friend, Rachel found she didn't enjoy the attention very much. Zoë made it seem both sordid and trivial instead of sad and crucial, and she wouldn't let it go. They finished with the garden and then ate lunch, discussing Paddy the whole afternoon. By the time Rachel got home, she had nearly forgotten what Paddy was really like. The person Zoë had constructed was different, reduced by speculation, enhanced by romanticism, a kind of lewd little boy, the sort of man Zoë herself frequently brought home.

Her affair had been better when it was secret, Rachel concluded. Her love had been purer when she had held it only in her own heart.

• • •

At the mall, Didi Limbach found the You're a Star! studio. Inside on glass tables sat plates of cookies and pickles, Dixie cups of Coke — the same fare one received after donating blood. The receptionist, who was notably unattractive, asked if Didi had an appointment.

Didi admitted she did. The receptionist sent her to wardrobe, where two young men tried to help her pick out clothing.

Paddy had moved away, leaving Didi stunned; she'd heard on Christian radio that women were doing it more than men these days, abandoning their kids and spouses six times as often as men. It was supposed to be her leaving. Adding insult to injury, Paddy had told her that he was having an affair with Rachel Cole. "No, you're not," Didi said. The idea was ludicrous; Rachel Cole was a snot, for one thing, and older than Paddy, for another. "She's older than you," Didi cried. "How could you be having an affair with her?"

He did not elaborate on how, just said that he couldn't live with Didi anymore. Only after he packed up and left did he reveal that his affair was actually over.

"You idiot!" Didi wailed. "Those two have messed up your life! And you let them do it, you let them make you a big fat fool." *Let him suffer* was her thought then. Then, she'd wanted to disassociate herself from something so humiliating as her husband's being duped by Evan and Rachel Cole. But after a few weeks she realized it was she who was suffering, she and Melanie, who asked daily when her dad was coming back.

"How about this?" one of the You're a Star! assistants asked her now, holding what looked like a torn wedding veil. He danced it in his hands, teasing her. Once rearranged, it was merely a white bathing suit, high cut, with lace where there should have been material.

"Just this?" Didi asked, fingering the garment skeptically, noting a smear of pink foundation on what was probably the shoulder. The other young man pointed to a picture on the dressing room wall: a young woman with enormous breasts lay on a beach in precisely this outfit. Her knee was raised, her blond hair spilled over her shoulder, her white teeth shone like the sun. Surely Paddy would have found her alluring. She bore no resemblance whatsoever to Rachel Cole.

"It's you, girlfriend," said the first young man.

"Definitely," said the other.

They left the room the way nurses did at the doctor's office, promising to return when she'd changed clothes. Didi undressed quickly, as if they might pop back in unexpectedly. Her face felt hot; her actions felt furtive. Also like the doctor's office was the fear that something unpleasant would be revealed by the examination to come. The costume looked awful, sagging at her chest, stretched tight at her hips. Her skin was pale, her thighs dotted with some little bumps that had come with adolescence and never gone away. She sucked in her tummy and turned before the mirror as if she simply hadn't found the right angle yet. The young men rapped at her door and then entered.

Didi grabbed her own dress to hold over herself. But they behaved professionally, clearing a seat for her to have makeup applied, yanking bottles of hairspray and mousse from the shelf, getting down to the business of her beauty.

"This doesn't fit," she said timidly.

"We'll pad it up a bit, then you'll be great." Two bladder-shaped balloons were produced, each with the weight and heft of breast matter, like Baggies filled with oil. She was directed to insert them below her own small warm breasts, where they filled the costume helpfully. Like shoulder pads, they gave balance. She liked the effect. In the swivel seat, she was made up and her hair teased. The more the men touched her, the less shy she felt. Her body became an objective subject for all three of them; they argued its assets and liabilities as if they were three cooks discussing a cake. The men pretended they couldn't believe she'd had a baby. They — Todd and Scott — both told her she had wonderful skin. What did she do to keep her skin so beautiful?

They covered Didi with a white smock, as if she were a piece of art, and walked her across the hall to the studio. There, too, food was sitting out, this time deviled eggs and more cookies, more Cokes in Dixie cups. The air smelled of onion; the photographer, a fat woman, was eating a submarine sandwich.

"Gorgeous!" she yelled through her full mouth. "Oh, give me a blue background, it's got to be blue." Todd pulled down a screen like the sky; the floor was covered with a white cloth speckled with glitter. Didi was to lie on a lawn chair, as if at the beach.

"This doesn't seem very realistic," she said to Scott as he fussed with her hair.

"Understatement of the century," he responded under his breath.

"Leave that to us," said Todd. "You're going to be so pleased." He arranged her sideways on the chair, then stood behind her and pulled her bathing suit tight, tying the rear straps back with a shoelace. Didi's breasts, pushed from below, pulled from behind, plumped over the top of the suit.

"Warm Caribbean breeze," the fat woman called, and Todd hurried away to switch on a fan.

After all, Didi told herself as the fat woman took pictures, Paddy had always claimed to love her body. She'd made a mistake to turn away when he wanted to have sex. He'd started an affair because she wasn't being a good wife.

"You wax your bikini line, don't you?" the fat photographer asked. "I can always tell."

The pictures were ready a week later, contained in a professional-looking folder, each one with a little embossed You're a Star! in the corner, a five-pointed star containing the words. Scott had taken Polaroids at the time, so Didi knew more or less what to expect. But still the photos frightened her. She'd returned to the studio to pick them up, and sat in the lounge area eating cookies, flipping through the images cautiously, staring entranced and terrified. Her legs had been lengthened, her rash of bumps erased, her skin given a nice tan glow instead of its current pasty tone. Her teeth sparkled like the model's in the dressing room. Instead of a glittering dropcloth, white sand now rose in dunes around her lounge chair, and the blue backdrop was the clear sky, with a few clouds floating above, riding the same wind that lifted her hair from her neck.

As if she could be a lingerie model. Or, more accurately, as if she could look like one that simply. She began her campaign to regain Paddy's affection that afternoon, by putting one of the five-by-seven pictures in an envelope and addressing it to Limbach Roofing. Let his coworkers see what he'd given up, what waited at home for him like Victoria's Secret. Let everyone know what a fool he'd become.

She had no other audience, so Didi showed Melanie the pictures of herself. "What do you think?"

"You look pretty," Melanie said. "Like a rabbit princess." She studied the picture, then asked to keep a copy for herself. "I can see your lumps," Melanie said slyly, meaning Didi's breasts.

. . .

The pictures arrived at Limbach Roofing the same day that Paddy purchased *Anna Karenina* from the seedy used-book store across the street. The bookstore had been invisible to him until he realized he was in the market for books. *This* book he'd seen at Rachel's, resting among many others on her shelves; he chose it for its weight, for its page count, for its foreboding black cover, and for its familiarity. Lying on Rachel's bed, he'd run his eyes over the spine a hundred times, mentally tripping as he tried to pronounce *Karenina* — either Karen Ina or Kara Nina. He wanted to know what Rachel read. Now that he couldn't see her or touch her, his attachment to her was becoming more scholarly. If he read what she read, he might think what she thought, feel what she felt, know what she knew. It was the intimacy he would have to settle for. It was as if his education had formally begun, and this was its first text, the pages of which felt warm to him, as if recently turned by other hands.

But already he was having trouble; the book's first assertion, its very first line, he did not believe. For instance, prior to knowing the Coles, his family had been happy, and he thought Rachel's family was now restored to happiness, but those two happinesses, those happy families, were not alike. Maybe this antagonism he felt toward Tolstoy was more correctly called an antagonism toward Rachel.

Sometimes he called her house and listened to her voice as she said hello. He knew she knew it was him.

Sometimes he visited a fantasy in which he and Rachel and Melanie and Zach drove away in the Bronco, the man, the woman, the boy, and the girl, perfect dolls in their proper seats, heading toward their new, better life out West, where a beautiful high-ceilinged farmhouse waited for them, painted traditional white, roofed with red asbestos shingles, surrounded by majestic cottonwood trees whose silver leaves twinkled in the breeze like coins, a stream washing serenely by, calm domesticated animals waiting patiently to be of use on the green, green grass. Melanie had a farm set that looked spookily like Paddy's fantasy, except that hers included two white-haired grandparent dolls as well as the nuclear four, and although her plastic playhouse offered up far too few bedrooms for its inhabitants, Paddy's dream home would accommodate them all.

His fantasy often fell apart when he tried to bring his father into it. Apparently his imagination couldn't bear up under the strain of resurrecting the dead; nor could it do much with the extraneous living: Ev, Didi, Marcus.

The photographs of Didi made Paddy feel like crying. The desperation they revealed, and the misunderstanding she had of the nature of their separation, made Paddy wholly sorry for her. He had pushed aside the happy family bit and started to read about Oblonsky when the mail came; without thinking about it, he laid Didi's picture in the thick book to keep his place, her legs peeking out the side of the yellowed paperback, her hair out the top. He didn't want to read anymore — a previous reader had underlined passages, sentences that must have been significant but that Paddy could not understand as more meaningful than any other part, which distracted him and seemed to highlight his ignorance — and he didn't want to look at his wife in unrecognizable underwear. Those legs — how had he missed Didi's legs?

He sat paralyzed in his little low-ceilinged, fluorescent-lighted office, the phone, slick with someone's hair oil, ringing, the attached machine taking messages from contractors who called to update him on his business, their monotonous voices, like Paddy's life, unbearable: halting and dull and endless.

Twenty

· · · · · · · · · · · · ·

In their bed they lie both awake, ostensibly because they are holding hands, a position they've never, to either's memory, fallen asleep in. Paddy Limbach still lingers between them, less distinct, dissipating. His offstage role in their lives intrigues them both, although neither will ever see him again.

There will be Rachel's birthday gift, this November 22, a beautiful golden puppy left anonymously, whimpering and leaking at her doorstep, an exuberant young blond animal wearing a red bandanna around its fleshy neck, sent as Paddy's surrogate into her life, a fellow for Zach and Rachel to love like a baby, without reservation, for Marcus and Evan to observe with skeptical affection, to love secondhand.

And ten years later, when Paddy and his wife have been divorced for longer than they were married, their sixteen-year-old daughter Melanie will take an overdose of Valium and end up at the St. Michael's emergency room for the second time in her life. Paddy will weep beside her bed. It will be Evan Cole he thinks of then, and the Shedd Aquarium of years past — the way she followed Ev, the way her yellow hair glowed green before the murky tanks of water, the way the small plaster cast on her arm stood for the worst thing that had happened to her yet. It is her father she'll want at the hospital — adamantly not her mother — but Paddy will wonder if it wouldn't be more honest to admit it's Ev she has really sought. It was he who defended her and it is he Paddy will emulate when he talks with her. Paddy will find himself pretending Ev can see him, Ev and Rachel both, witnesses and patrons. With his daughter, from the time she was four years old, from the Shedd Aquarium on, Paddy has tried to think how Ev would handle her various crises and quandaries. As the years pass, he will more and more often squelch the voice in his head that rants about the money involved (the ambulance, the hospital, the therapy that will come), the voice that is his father's, the one that calls episodes like these "stunts," the voice that responds to terror only with anger. When Melanie pleads with him not to tell her mother what she's done — her clawing fingers, her wild, panicked eyes, her appearance and behavior, which Paddy desperately tries to link to something recognizable from his history with animals, and can't — he will go to the pay phone beside the complimentary scorched coffee — as if anyone in an emergency room needed further stimulation — and be convinced it is time to call Ev.

But for now, the Coles lie together in bed.

Rachel thinks of her sons, their uncertain lives ahead of them, their characters so firmly set from the moment they were born — placid Zach, discontented Marcus, each with the possibility of joy built in, a dependency on the peculiar tricks of their fates, a desire to be loved, some inclination toward kindness, pleasure. She tries not to think too much of Paddy, who, she is sure, will be her only affair. How do people manage more than one? The conundrum that frequently occupies her finds a way to apply here: is she like other people, or is she different? Even though she is forty years old, she has no idea how to answer, and she expects she never will. She wants to be like everyone, and she wants to be different from everyone. Against her wishes, she imagines Paddy, and a renegade thrill loops in her torso, an electric eel in the bathtub of her quiet home. That he is also thinking of her, and that she knows it without question, as if a taut string were linking their chests, makes it seem as if they are still lovers. It is possible to love two men, she understands, but they have to be good men, and each has to love her exclusively. It is utterly unfair, and utterly wrong, but that is her thinking: she can keep them both. But only in her heart. In the land of the living, in the true and literal house, she has chosen her husband. And now, although she takes enormous solace in the existence of Paddy — a presence in the world like happiness, known, yet always elsewhere — she holds her husband's hand.

That Ev is a good man she accepts as a matter of faith, as she does the correctness of her gesture in having chosen him over the other.

Ev is thinking about his father. He does not run his hand over his forehead and through his hair because Rachel is clutching it as if she were falling from their bed, so instead he is treated to a memory. In it, he is still young enough to lie on the floor before the radio, his feet on the couch, young enough to be unselfconscious as the wind from a fan blows on his thighs through the open holes his shorts make, an oscillating breeze over his sensitive skin, his antsy penis. Horsehair sofa beneath his calves, cool slick floor beneath his head. A Chicago summer night, the dim lighting of childhood, the slender spyglass of memory. From the floor, he looks up at them, his family — brother, mother, father — from their knees to their laps, where their hands are at work, Gerry slipping a knife beneath the paper label of a ribbed tin can, his mother embroidering, stabbing a needle into the tight surface of a white oval, his father holding a book, and he feels contented. It is hot, but the heat does not bother him, although it seems to be sitting on his chest, pressing him pleasantly to the floor. The hour of his and Gerry's bedtime has passed long ago, but no one is noting it; they are consciously not noting it, as if the heat has also stalled the clock. Everyone, the young Evan thinks, is aware that they reside in a pocket of peace, a moment outside the ordinary friction of their life as a group — that the fragility of this happiness, this ease in which they can love each other, demands their complicit silence, their conspiratorial care, their studious attention to not moving from their places. Anxiety has taken a rest, floated away, carrying with it fury and sorrow and pettiness. Only the radio speaks. Only the hands shift, bearing knife, needle, book. Only the fan seems to breathe.

"Goodnight, babe," Ev's father said to his wife when she went to bed. "Babe," he said. Evan blinks beside his own wife, fingers fluttering in her palm. In the two years since his father's death, he has not heard this voice so clearly. Not the voice after the strokes, resolutely not the one that gradually became mechanical and monotonous over the years, turning unrecognizable, anonymously robotic and just as impersonally driven, but his father's true voice. "Goodnight, babe," he said, simply, unfailingly, night after night, mild as milk.

Ev tightens his hold on Rachel's familiar hand, which is large and dry and soft, and which has been held by a better man. He knows Paddy is a preferable person, that humanity would benefit by being populated more fully with his ilk. He assimilates this fact and vows to treat it as a fact, indisputable, humbling. As for his own character, his true nature, he supposes he is cynical and selfish, a nagging reminder of the dirty urges that run concurrently with the decent — not evil, but its occasional conduit. Once he arrogantly, ungraciously assumed the luxury of leaving his life, of walking away from the merciful claim of his family, and now he knows he must not make that mistake again. The world is crowded with people, and yet the ones that are, and were, important to him have been falling unjustly, disproportionately away. To death he has lost his mother, his father, Joni, Gerry; to other forces he has lost Paddy, and he has almost lost his wife. He needs Rachel, he needs his boys. They need him, he believes. The land around them all is both benign and brutal, and Evan its most useful mediator.

Maybe.

If he were still in the habit of taking his emotional temperature, he might note that he is, if not happy, then not unhappy. Akin to being not guilty instead of innocent. Not unhappy. "Happy" is something Ev might expect to be the name of a pet. (In fact, in November, they will name their new dog Happy.)

The phone rings: dutiful Dr. Head, who mistrusted Ev's move home as thoroughly as he did the move away, and who is punishing him by ringing late at night. Rachel squeezes her husband's hand before letting it go. She admires his concern for his irascible client;

she believes Dr. Head represents one version of a helpful sort of father figure to Ev, the man he will never let himself become.

"Back in a minute," Ev tells Rachel, knowing that by the time he returns to bed she'll be asleep, her body warm and solid, her self off in its own abundantly mysterious, secret life. In the dark, Ev needs no lights, no clothing, no glasses, as he crosses his home to take the call.

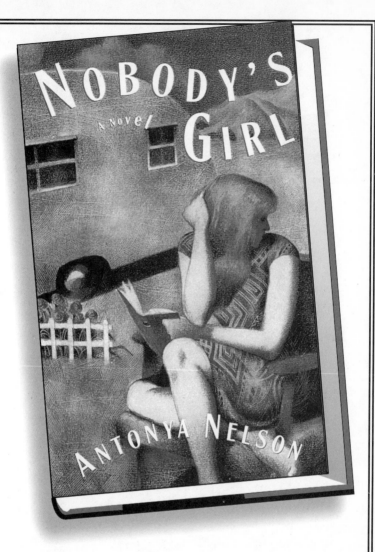

A buoyant and evocative new novel about the
mysteries of life in a small New Mexico town.

COMING FROM SCRIBNER IN FEBRUARY 1998.

0-684-83932-6 • $22.00

SCRIBNER
A Division of Simon & Schuster